Place of Fear

PLACE of FEAR

A Novel

by

Ken Pelham

Marjorie,
Thanks so much
for getting me in
touch with BZD4 !

— Ken

ISBN 978-0-9895950-1-8

For Amy and Jennifer

Acknowledgments

Many thanks to my in-house beta readers and intrepid travel companions, daughters Amy and Jenny, and my wife, Laura. Special thanks to my hardworking editor, Marsha Butler, for her laser focus, quick wit, and quicker redlines. Thanks also are in order for the anonymous judges and reviewers of the Royal Palm Literary Awards, whose critiques helped make the book better.

The good folks we met in Belize and Guatemala deserve special thanks also for getting us into and out of some tight spots. I've never met nicer, more helpful people on the road.

And thanks at last to readers, who make it all so much fun.

Chapter 1

Darkness wrapped the prisoner like a funeral shroud.

Up until now, his only amusement had been in contemplating the details of his own death. The hell with that. He'd even given up anticipating the vengeance he would take on his jailers. Appealing though that thought was, it'd seemed pointless. Now, though, he might get to throttle the bastards after all. At the very least, he'd cooked up a possibility of escape.

He examined the little finger of his left hand. He felt it, stretched it, bent it this way and that. Hell of a finger, it was. It had served him well, but it would have to go. A small price to pay for freedom.

If he bit down hard enough in just the right spot, using only his incisors, he could get most of the way through the bone. He'd have to tear the remainder off. With luck, he might not bleed to death. In the filth of his cell, infection crept into even the tiniest scratch.

His finger or his life. Easy decision when you looked at it that way.

The revelation that death loomed had struck like a fist. Not many get the luxury of knowing the exact minute. Even death row inmates had to be told when their gig was up, but he'd deduced it on his own. *Damned brilliant!* He didn't have much, but he still had a brain like Einstein's. Maybe better, after all that had happened. Einstein had *limits*.

What a whopping cosmic joke! He knew the exact minute. The hints, the secrets, the myths, all pointed to it, yet he couldn't tell when that minute would arrive. Captivity without light,

1

without the passing of the sun, robs you of time. Minutes, hours, days no longer exist. That time becomes an abstraction when you can't measure it, now *that* was a revelation. Might make a hell of an essay someday.

Yet he still had some small measure of time. He measured it by cycles of eating, sleeping, and shitting, and the sporadic visits of his jailers. He could only guess when the end would come, but he knew it would be soon.

Messages in a bottle were a popular, stupid myth. Chance in a million, almost as impossible as the nightmare he'd fallen into. But that was what he was reduced to. Hell, there was lots of symbolism in a finger.

The base of the finger, the sweet spot, where proximal phalange connected to metacarpal—he'd sever it right there. His knowledge of anatomy came in handy, a benefit of his profession. Of course, his profession had gotten him into this fine mess, so that kind of canceled out the benefit.

He placed his little finger into his mouth and positioned his teeth at the correct joint. He paused to consider just how awkward biting your finger off could be. These skills, they just don't teach them any longer.

The Communion drug had not quite worn off, so the pain might not be debilitating. He could have performed the operation immediately after last Communion, but that would have been a disaster; he would have been bark-at-the-moon crazy in its delicious grip.

Man up, he told himself. Count three, and do it.

One…

He bit down with all his might, felt the crunch and tear in his teeth. The proximal phalange separated from the metacarpal.

Dem bones, dem bones gonna walk around…

Pain seared his finger, a white-hot flame of agony. Clouds gathered and swirled through his brain, urging his body to shut down, to end the stupidity, to end the pain. To preserve life.

Still he bit down. The last bit of flesh resisted, tendons tough as leather. He pulled back with his teeth. The finger would not yield. He bit down harder, and yanked his head back, tearing through the last bit of tendon and muscle, his finger at last severed.

He spat it out, and felt warm blood spill down his hand. He licked the wound and swallowed his blood, unwilling to waste any in his weakened state. He clamped his good hand over it to stanch the flow.

His message-in-a-bottle lay bloody and ready on the cell floor.

He leaned his back against the wall and slid to the floor to wait, praying that the next visit would not be from his usual jailers, but the other one—the sneaky one. The bastard better come soon, or he'd bleed to death.

Better than a visit from the goons would be a visit from the girl. What was her name? Did she have a name? When she first came to him, he hadn't really cared. Now he realized he did. That impressed him a little.

He figured his odds of death had dropped to ninety-five percent. Not exactly good Vegas odds, but sure as hell better than a hundred percent. Death no longer loomed as inevitable. He could not, in good conscience, let it happen without a struggle, because he'd become the most important man in the world.

Hell, why the modesty? He'd become more than a man.

He'd become a god.

Don't flatter yourself, Doctor Jekyll. A nine-fingered pansy meekly awaiting execution is a sorry excuse for a god.

The prisoner marshaled his thoughts, tried to concentrate. That was the funny thing; even as his mind had expanded in this stinking black hole and cast aside limits, part of it had grown weaker. He had felt reason slip like sand through his fingers.

Maybe godhood demanded insanity.

Chapter 2

Carson Grant stood on the battered dock of Snake Eye Springs and shoved his dive gear into his duffel bag, his gaze fixed on the golf shirt at the other end of the dock, the one blabbing and worrying over the paramedics.

Fender Caldwell avoided Grant's stare. He was at least smart enough to stay the hell away.

The body retrieval had gone without a hitch. Almost. Grant's secret demon, claustrophobia, had reared its leering head in the cave, as usual.

His dive buddy, Diane Butters, touched his arm. "Let it go, Carson. Caldwell's got danger signs posted on both caves. Cave divers know the risk. It's not his fault."

"Like hell. He keeps the east spring open for the daredevil money, but it's the most dangerous cave dive in Florida. Five deaths in six years in the east eye, and there's never been a death in the west eye."

"Let it go."

The paramedics zipped up the body bag. The victim's girlfriend, wailing uncontrollably, fought to free herself from the grasp of a deputy. The paramedics placed the body in an ambulance, and climbed in after him. The ambulance eased away, the crowd parting to let it pass.

Caldwell glanced at Grant, a sick look on his face.

Grant headed toward him, his fists clenched. "Happy, you son of a bitch? He was just a kid."

Caldwell turned and spoke to a deputy, pointing. The deputy

glared at Grant and shook his head.

In the edge of his vision, Grant glimpsed a tall man, all angles and limbs, slip out of a parked car and step quickly forward. He seized Grant by the arm. Grant pulled free and spun on him.

"Carson," the man said, "forget that idiot. We need to talk."

"Gene Tennyson. I'll be damned. Man, your timing stinks."

* * *

The coffee finished brewing and Grant poured two steaming cups. It was midday in June and hotter than the sun, but the chill of the dive had seeped into his bones. Grant cradled the cup in both hands, relishing the warmth.

Tennyson took a sip and grimaced. "You strip paint with this?" Another sip, another grimace. He pushed the cup away. "I caught you at a bad time, Carson. That was gut-wrenching back there at the spring. What happened?"

"The kid went into the killer cave, the east one. Got separated from his girlfriend, panicked, and blinded himself by kicking up a cloud of silt. He drowned."

"You weren't really going to punch out the owner, were you?"

"You bet. You kept me out of jail today."

"I doubt it. That cop was going to look the other way."

Grant blew on his coffee and took a sip. "I thought you were in Mexico."

"I flew in to Jacksonville yesterday, stopped off in Gainesville, then came straight here. I'm flying back tonight."

"What do you want, Gene?"

Tennyson rubbed his chin. "I need you for a Mayan dig. Without delay."

"Because archaeology is such urgent business. Let me ask another way. What the hell do you want?"

"You know Maya culture better than anyone in the world. Other than Robert Lindsay."

Odd phrasing, Grant thought. Gene seemed to be having a difficult time letting go. "We all miss him, Gene."

Tennyson nodded, almost imperceptibly. "We do. Trust me though, you're ideal for this expedition."

"Look. My career is finished. I'm poison. If you want to

compromise your little dig, by all means, sign me up. The university torpedoed me for a reason."

"I have some things to show you." Tennyson opened a specimen case, revealing a crusted, reddish-brown object nestled in molded foam. He eased the object from the foam, causing flakes of rust to shed and fall. "I *never* handle this, nor do I let anyone else." He handed it to Grant. "That's how much I value your involvement."

Grant held it delicately, hefted it up to the light. A flattened metal object as long as his forearm, caked in rust. Heavy, maybe twenty pounds. One end formed a heavy knob, the other flared into a blade seven inches wide. Geometric patterns peeked through the rust.

"An iron axe head. Nice find. Where from?"

"Chichén Itzá. We inherited Lindsay's dig just outside the park. The tomb belonged to a nobleman, most likely a king. Buried some spectacular pieces with him. Copper, turquoise, gold necklaces, jade, silver. You'll be reading about it in *National Geographic*. I found this at the close of last summer's dig. I couldn't believe it. I was pissed my site had been contaminated with junk. But it kept nagging at me. The shape, the look of it. Out of all that wealth, this rusty piece of iron lay by his side."

Carson rubbed the axe gently. Iron could mean only one thing—it was *not* Mayan. "If it's not a contaminant, then it's Spanish, stolen from or given to the Maya. So it dates to when, 1530 or thereabouts?"

"We got some excellent carbon-14 dates, thirty in all. They average out at 998 AD."

Grant lowered it and looked at him. "Is this a joke? I'm kind of not in the mood."

"No joke. Five centuries before Columbus, I'll bet my career on it. It'll dump the whole goddamn apple cart of history." Tennyson rubbed the rusting blade with a thumb. "Grant, this is your chance. You were *right*."

Grant felt the skin on the back of his neck prickle. "I've been down this road before." He handed the axe head back to Tennyson. "*Geographic* won't print this shit. They have standards."

"They don't know about it. I need to build my case first."

"You found this yourself?"

Tennyson hesitated, glancing at the axe head.

"Didn't think so. Who found it?"

"Stansfield."

"Cripes, Gene!"

"Frank Stansfield may not win Miss Congeniality, but he's a good scientist."

"We'll debate that later. What's he think?"

"He's licking his chops."

"You're too smart to fall into the same trap I did. What's this really about, Gene?"

Tennyson sighed. "Listen, the Chichén dig is just to whet your appetite. Our real goal is in Guatemala." Tennyson opened a smaller case. Couched in molded foam was a gray piece of metal. He handed it reverently to Grant. "Exhibit two."

Grant turned it over several times, studying it, feeling the markings. A silver coin, thickly tarnished. He shook his head. "This is from Guatemala?"

"El Petén, specifically. I bought it from a dealer. Ernesto Hidalgo."

"The mayor? No one's slit Ernie's throat yet?"

"He's a cautious little man. So am I. I asked to see his supplier. It was a little Maya boy."

"The little hustler cast it himself?"

Tennyson shook his head. "Too perfect. Besides, what souvenir peddler would be stupid enough to try and pass this off as Mayan? Or Spanish? Look at these markings. Runes, Carson. It's friggin' Norse! Corroborating evidence. The kid said he found it in a *cenote*, a sinkhole. A haunted one, no less."

Grant handed the coin back and shook his head. "Two artifacts, found two hundred miles apart, most likely fakes. Take my advice, keep this to yourself and don't kill your career."

Tennyson looked at him closely. "Okay. Reason number three, the real reason you're coming with us."

"Goodness! Pins and needles, here."

"It's Lindsay."

Grant leaned in. "You've heard something about Robert? They found his body?"

"There is no body, Carson. Somewhere in the goddamn jungle, Robert is *alive*."

Silence hung in the air.

Tennyson nodded. "This isn't a dig. It's a rescue."

Chapter 3

Grant stared at him, his thoughts racing. "Alive? How? Where is he?"

"Hell if I know. He's still missing. But I have reason to believe he's alive."

"Quit screwing around. Is he alive or not?"

"You tell me." Tennyson withdrew a third case, a steel-gray cylinder no more than seven inches long, and handed it to Grant. "It's a refrigerated thermos. You have no idea how tricky it was to smuggle this in. TSA would hang me by my balls."

Grant slipped the hasps and opened the box. Inside were two things; a small, slender bundle a few inches long, wrapped in a dirty scrap of cloth and bound up with a bit of twine, and a worn photo print.

"These were left on Hidalgo's doorstep three days ago. Be my guest."

Grant picked up the photo print and smoothed it out. "Nikki," he said.

"Exactly. But only half the photo. You remember the shot; Robert and his wife at the Grand Canyon. After Nikki died, he carried this everywhere."

Grant set the print aside. He picked up the bundle, set it on the table, untied the string, and spread out the cloth, exposing a severed human finger. "Jesus! Are you insane?"

The finger was filthy and gray, with black dirt underneath the yellow, split nail. The severed end was ragged, the cut blackish red, granulated, like raw steak left exposed. A faint odor of rot hung about it.

Tennyson pointed. "The photo's got a note on the back."

Grant turned over the print. The note was written in English, in a shaky hand: *GRINGO TRADE NO POLICE SUN ON HIGH MIDDLE YEAR WELL SPIRIT*

"A ransom note?"

Tennyson nodded.

"What's 'well spirit' mean?"

"The *cenote* where the boy found the coin is called the Well of Spirits."

Grant took a deep breath and picked up the finger. He turned it over, studying it.

Tennyson tapped his foot, a nervous beat. "Robert had an incredible dig going in Chichén Itzá, but he sprinted off to Guatemala alone. Why? He never worked alone. Tell you why he left; he *thought* there might be something in your theory after all, but he wasn't about to broadcast it. He saw what happened to you."

"Saw it? He engineered it."

"He had no choice. Get over it. This is bigger than that."

"Easy advice from a bystander. You sure managed to keep *your* name clear."

Tennyson's eyes flashed, and a hard quick silence passed between them. "You're going to hear me out, Carson, damn you. Robert found evidence to support your theory." Tennyson picked up the coin. "Hidalgo bought this from the Maya boy last year and contacted Lindsay. Lindsay has no poker face; Hidalgo smelled a payday and refused to sell. Lindsay learned the source from the boy, and struck off alone into the rainforest to find the *cenote*. He disappeared, presumed dead. Until now."

He picked up the photo. "Robert carried this with him every waking hour. But this half only shows Nikki. Why? Because only those close to him would have known her, and his kidnappers didn't want to release *his* image. They want to deal only with those close to him, people motivated to save him. Hidalgo wasn't picked at random. He has a connection to Robert, and, therefore, to Robert's friends and relatives."

"'Friends,'" Grant muttered. He reread the note. "'Sun on high, middle year...' The solstice?"

"Exactly! June 22. The summer solstice. Lindsay disappeared last August, two months *after* the last summer solstice. So this doesn't signify a date already past. It's the coming solstice. Hidalgo guessed that the gringo was Lindsay because he's the only one to go missing lately. He panicked and called me. I met him and then caught the next flight out. When I got back to Florida, I went straight to Gainesville and did some hustling. I pilfered the fingerprints in Lindsay's employment file and took them to the medical examiner's office. An old friend matched the prints on this finger to Lindsay's. It's *his* left little finger, and he was *alive* when it was severed, not more than two weeks ago, tops."

Grant thought back. Lindsay had disappeared in El Petén a year ago and had not been seen since. No trace, just swallowed by the jungle. A massive dragnet yielded no trace of him. Grant felt a chill creep up his spine. He wanted to tell Gene the whole thing was preposterous. But it *wasn't*.

By and large, Central American looters were illiterate, even in Spanish. The rare one who spoke and wrote English expressed himself in a stumbling hand like this note. And "sun on high," in midyear, was as good a depiction of the summer solstice as a poet could muster.

"June 22," Grant said. "Eleven days from now."

Tennyson nodded. "Robert's alive. I can feel it. Put aside the bad stuff and remember him as the friend he once was. I've cashed in some bonds and drained my bank account. I'm going to buy his life back, and I'm leaving tonight—with or without you."

Chapter 4

Ten Days to Solstice

Elisa Anderssen stepped out of the warm shade of the visitors' center into the blast furnace of the Yucatán midday. "Mad dogs and Englishmen," she murmured, and retreated into the shade. She had been in Chichén Itzá for two weeks and had not yet become acclimated. The Americans had warned her, but that was silly; she was from Norway. Nothing could have prepared her for this. This heat had form and mass.

A listless herd of tourists plodded past toward an open bus, kicking up drifts of dust that hung in the air and clung to sweaty bodies. Mexican guards leaned against ruins, enjoying the spectacle, preventing vandalism and wastes of shade.

An arriving tour bus rolled to a stop, its air brakes sighing. The door hissed open and a fresh, eager group filed out, cameras at the ready. Tennyson came out, accompanied by a scowling man she recognized from news stories. She waved, and they made their way over to her.

"Elisa," Tennyson said, "I'd like you to meet Carson Grant."

"Dr. Grant, I've heard so much about you."

"Lies, all of it. Dr. Anderssen, I presume?"

"That's me."

Grant started to say something, paused.

"Is there something on your mind, Dr. Grant?"

"I needed your support—or at least your goddamn opinion—three years ago."

12

"Your evidence was not terribly convincing."

"Yet here you are chasing a more preposterous version of it."

"Dr. Tennyson has evidence that can't be ignored."

Tennyson cut in. "Can't we sort this out later?"

"Fine," Grant said, nodding carefully. "Wrong foot. Dr. Anderssen, please accept my apology."

She hesitated. Grant was one of *those* men, she thought. Very well. She had held her own against worse. "Apology accepted," she said stiffly. She held his gaze a moment longer. Perhaps bringing him in had been a mistake after all.

* * *

Linda Stein fidgeted, watching porters unload luggage from the bus's side bays. Sweat beaded on her face the moment she set foot on the dusty sidewalk, so sudden and intense was the heat. Or maybe it was travel anxiety. Her luggage always seemed to end up in an airport on the opposite side of the world, so why should this trip turn out any differently? With each bag unloaded that wasn't hers, her anxiety grew. How much stuff could those little bays hold? They had to be almost empty. She began to wonder why she'd come here at all. This place was fifty degrees hotter than Boston, and a thousand miles different. Archaeology didn't seem quite so romantic when the tropical climate licked you in the face like a dog.

Her burgundy tow-along appeared. She pumped her fist, swooped in, and hauled it to the safety and relative cool of the pavilion. She turned at last to view Chichén Itzá.

The city lay before her, gleaming white in the sun, alive with the glow. Fantastic stone structures dotted the landscape, dominated at the center by a towering pyramid.

She forgot all about luggage.

This was why she came here.

After a moment, she switched on her phone and scrolled through saved files, tapping the folder labeled "Chichén Team." The bios and photos opened and she glanced about at the tourists swarming all about, trying to match faces to photos.

Bingo. She recognized a lanky, tanned gringo off to one side of the pavilion as Gene Tennyson. He talked and gestured into his cell phone, while a vaguely familiar man and a woman stood idly by.

She approached them, her suitcase clicking over the tiles. The trio didn't seem to notice her. *Par for the course*, she thought.

"Excuse me," she said, quietly. No response. She could feel her face reddening. "Excuse me," she repeated, louder this time.

They turned. Tennyson tucked his phone into his shirt pocket.

"I'm Linda Stein," she said, extending her hand to Tennyson.

"Ah, Linda. So happy to meet you." He motioned to his companions. "Linda is joining our dig, a first-timer." He introduced his companions.

She understood now why they looked familiar. They were once both giants in their field. One of them still was. "It's such an honor," she gushed, feeling like a schoolgirl. "I had no idea you were here."

"It's a surprise to me too," Grant said.

She looked at him for a moment, and glanced at Tennyson.

"He's quite the joker," Tennyson said. "And a sudden, lucky addition. Dr. Anderssen has been with us for two weeks."

Grant turned to Tennyson, his face darkening. He opened his mouth to say something, stopped, and continued. "They don't know, do they? Holy damn."

Anderssen looked at Tennyson. "What is it we should know?"

"Later," Tennyson said. "Soon. When we're all together."

"I'm not partial to secrets, doctor."

Tennyson nodded and glanced away. "Our site is just north of Chichén. The others are waiting." He flashed his identity tag to an attendant and, without a word, started off toward the center of the city.

"I guess that discussion has been tabled," Grant said.

They followed Tennyson to the base of the Castillo. The pyramid towered above them, coarse and white, glowing in the light of midday. "This is Chichén's heart," Tennyson said, turning to Linda. "The pyramid of Kukulcán. The Castillo."

"Europeans apply European names to everything," Grant said. "Present company excepted, Elisa. Man, I've missed this job."

"It's stunning," Linda said. For all the aggravation and dust stirred up by the sight-seeing hordes, Chichén was spectacular, a

Paris of the Yucatán. Majestic temples of limestone towered above the city. Gods and monsters, mysterious and beautiful, glowered from every wall and space.

"A newbie, huh?" Grant asked.

She nodded, peering at the summit of the Castillo, shielding her eyes from the sun. "I thought the Maya were in decline when Chichén was built. It doesn't look that way."

"Yeah, the city-states had collapsed all over Yucatán and El Petén by the late tenth century. Chichén was a backwater, bypassed by the overall collapse. Invading Toltecs from the North overran it."

Tennyson pointed out the chiseled dragonheads at the base of the pyramid. "This was Kukulcán's town. The Feathered Serpent, mightiest of gods. He's everywhere, but this pyramid was his crown jewel."

Tennyson led them past the base of the Castillo and followed a boulevard north that ended at a broad, round, sinkhole, green with stagnant water. "The Well of Sacrifice," Tennyson said.

They continued along a faint path through scrubland, and entered a clearing with an airstrip. They crossed the runway to a high, chain-link fence. "Leaving the park now," Tennyson said. A narrow, padlocked gate blocked the path. Tennyson fished a ring of keys from his pocket, and opened the gate, locking it behind them. They left the scrubland and entered a *milpa* of corn, beans, and squash. After another half-mile, the path ended at a second fence, this one enclosing about an acre in a rough circle. "This little site," Tennyson said, sweeping his hand, "will soon be the most important in the Western Hemisphere. This area's been searched for decades without success. Lindsay bagged it in one day with ground-penetrating radar."

Two soldiers sitting under a small tent next to the gate, shooing flies, got to their feet and opened the gate. In the center of the enclosure, four Maya laborers toiled with shovels and picks in a broad trench eight feet deep that exposed a rough limestone block wall. A large canvas pavilion tent stood to one side of the enclosure, with three sleeping tents nearby. Two men sat in directors' chairs in the shade of the pavilion, each nursing a bottle of water. Linda recognized them from her notes, twenty-something wunderkind Frank Stansfield, and a grad student, Bill

15

Watts. Her confidence suffered another drive-by shooting; these two guys were more than ten years her younger, but light-years ahead of her on experience.

Watts looked up, grinned, and hopped to his feet. Stansfield glanced their way, frowned, looked back at his notes, shook his head slightly.

Grant extended his hand to Watts. "Long time."

Watts hesitated, his grin fading, before he took Grant's hand.

Frank Stansfield closed his notebook slowly. He glanced at Linda without apparent interest, and nodded indifferently to Grant. "Been away for a while, Grant?"

"I've been busy."

"You may want to do some catching up. Three years away from the field is like missing a generation of study."

"Twenty years of experience will cover any lapses. Call me when you get there, Junior."

Tennyson put his arm around Linda's shoulders. "Everyone, I'd like to you meet Linda Stein, our new colleague."

Stansfield grunted. "You were supposed to be here yesterday."

"Yes, doctor. Sorry."

"Don't be late again."

"No sir."

"Did Gene put you in charge, Frank?" Grant asked.

Stansfield glared, his face reddening. He sprang from his seat and loomed over Grant.

Grant didn't budge, amusement glittering in his eyes.

"There are such things as protocols."

"Sit down, Frank," Tennyson said.

Stansfield opened his mouth to speak, but returned to his seat. "What are you doing here, anyway? The real world spit you back out already? And you, Gene, where the hell have you been? It's your dig and you up and leave with no explanation."

"Gene," Grant said. "It's time you told them. Do it quick, before I throttle this kid."

Tennyson looked from Stansfield to Grant, worry in his eyes. He nodded, and motioned the group to be seated. "It's about Robert." He opened a metal case, revealing a couched silver coin and a small wrapped object. He gently pried each from its foam. "I have something to tell you."

16

Linda listened to Tennyson's story unfold. She tried to hide her excitement, but her foot had a mind of its own and tapped out a quickening beat.

Chapter 5

Tennyson finished the story, and looked down at his hands. Grant studied the others, gauging their reactions.

Stansfield grunted. "You kept this all to yourself? Damn you."

"I had to be sure. There was no point in dropping this in everyone's lap on the weak possibility of it actually being true."

Stansfield jerked his thumb at Grant. "Yet you went straight to *him*."

"In spite of all that's gone down, Carson's my friend—and Robert's. I need him for this."

"Plus, I'm just smarter than you, Stans."

"Carson, stop, damn it! I couldn't do this alone."

"What the hell, 'alone?'" Watts said. "You thought I wouldn't help?"

"Negotiating with kidnappers is not like haggling over a straw hat in a flea market. These guys play for keeps. Grant's dealt with looters before and he has skills that, you might say, go beyond archaeology. Without him, I wouldn't even consider it. I'd turn it over to the Guatemalan police and they'd screw up the whole thing." He paused. "Now there's a *chance* of success. But it won't work with just the two of us. I need the appearance of a legitimate expedition. Guatemalan law demands we hire a Guatemalan for a dig, and I'm asking you and Frank to join us. So we'll have five men, one being a local. Strength in numbers."

"Count me in," Watts said.

Stansfield scowled. "I don't like the sound of it. Robert's being alive sounds iffy."

"Hell, Frank," Grant said. "He was alive a few days ago. That much is fact. And his captors want to talk."

"Based on a semi-literate note? Sounds like a nice way to lure more hostages in."

"There's no point in taking hostages other than money. Kidnappers don't just keep taking hostages forever without cashing them in. They're smart capitalists; they've made an investment, they've watched it ripen, and now they want to profit."

Tennyson sighed. "Look, Frank. Robert was alone and an easy target. Everyone assumed he was murdered. But they kept him alive. They may even have put him to work as slave labor, or better yet, used him to judge the different artifacts they looted. They've dried up the hole and can cash him in now."

"What's to keep them from taking all of us?"

"Risk versus payout. They had to cover their tracks and move around until the search was abandoned. It's hard enough with one prisoner. They know they can't pull it off with five. The manhunt for all of us would be incomparably bigger than it was for Robert."

Watts said, "Don't be such a pussy, Frank. You're a mountain of a man. One look at you and these guys will shit their pants. When you return as a hero, the networks will be falling all over you. This is the chance to punch your ticket for life."

Stansfield looked at him for a moment. "At least there'll be a little science to do while we're there."

Grant noticed Linda edging shyly forward. "I'm going with you," she said.

Tennyson shook his head vigorously. "No. We keep this small. To be honest and a bit sexist, women will only get the looters' minds off money and onto other possibilities. I'm not about to put you in that kind of danger."

"Thanks for your chivalry, but I'm still going. You need me."

Stansfield snorted. "We do?"

"Let me ask you something. Why am I here? A suburban Boston housewife, chucking it all to pursue her fantasy of becoming an archaeologist?"

"Good question. Lindsay offered you a job out of pity. Gene made good on it."

"But why *me*? Lindsay had applications from more qualified folks."

"Come on. You know why. You bought your way in." Stansfield looked at Tennyson, his eyes arched. "Right, Gene?"

Tennyson squirmed. "It's not really relevant."

"*Right*, Gene?"

"Yeah, there was an endowment for the dig."

"A large one," Linda said. "The kind you don't turn down. It's all true. I bought my way in."

"Much appreciated. You're still not coming with us."

"Did I mention my old money family? It's also big money. Really big, and I have access to it. You've scraped together a little, but what will you say when the looters say they need ten times that much? They've had time to do some homework and may know they've got a real prize. Whatever the amount, I can have it within hours. *If* I'm on the team. And that's why I'm going."

Tennyson opened his mouth to speak.

"I can also cut off your funding within a few hours, but let's not go there."

"Shit!" Stansfield said. "You're blackmailing us."

Grant chuckled. "Guess she's going with us."

"I'm going, too," Elisa said. She was studying the silver coin under a magnifying glass, turning it this way and that.

Stansfield sighed. "Okay, what's your angle? Were you Lindsay's secret lover?"

Anger flashed in her eyes. "I've been here two weeks now, as a skeptic. The axe head was intriguing. This coin, though, is the icing on the cake. There are no ruins at the *cenote*, so the looters have ignored it, but they'll get to it eventually. We need to make the site ours, with a sizable expedition. If we do that, then move on, they will assume that we found nothing of value. If we *do* find something, we'll have to leave quickly, empty-handed, and return with a sanctioned expedition. You *need* me to verify anything Norse, because the truth of this trip will eventually leak out, and my corroboration will be the only thing that gets you back into the country."

She looked at each of them. "So. Did the cats get your tongues?"

* * *

A gray tarp shaded the work trench, peaked and sloped to shed water into a small ditch and protect the new excavation from erosion. The ends of the trench sloped down eight feet from the natural grade, narrow at the ends, widening in the center. Along one side of the trench rose a vertical wall of dressed limestone masonry blocks, painted a gorgeous red. The image of a grimacing serpent, painted a brilliant teal, adorned panels along the wall. Linda caressed the ancient stonework, unable to resist.

"It being buried, the structure's original colors are still intact for the most part," Tennyson said. "The tomb was built in an excavation, and apparently buried after the interment."

Near the center of the wall, massive collapsed limestone beams and lintels had been exposed. A narrow opening had been cleared through the rubble, and steel struts had been screwed into place to prevent further collapse.

"Now, kids, the great tomb," Tennyson said. He stooped and edged through the opening.

Grant bowed slightly and waved Linda in. She ducked, bumped her head painfully, ducked lower, and squeezed inside.

LED lights, strung from tripod mounts, lit the room in a pure white light. A skeleton lay on a low stone platform, its disjointed bones adorned with a tangle of pendants, bracelets, rings, and necklaces of dazzling color, some red with cinnabar, some fashioned with hematite, gold, silver, and jade. Desiccated brown and black tissue that had once been flesh and organs encrusted the bones. The skull, its lower jaw separated, lay staring into emptiness. The burial mask, a construction of jade and silver discs strung with cord, with eyes of milky opal, had slipped from the face of the skull and lay to one side. A pair of obsidian knives, inlaid with jewels, rested alongside the corpse. Strings of teeth—jaguar, crocodile, monkey—draped the feet of the skeleton.

Clay pots—some whole, some shattered—lay about, their rotted contents of nuts and grains spilled upon the floor. On the cracked plaster walls, a mural in reds, blacks, greens, and blues depicted a ruler brandishing tools or weapons. The same tools and weapons lined the floor at the base of the walls.

Linda swallowed hard, the power of her decision to flee her

comfortable life striking her. "Look on my works, Ye Mighty, and despair," she murmured.

"We've deciphered the glyphs on the broken stelae outside the tomb," Tennyson said. "Say hello to Jaguar 2, laid to rest following much deceit and warring. The glyphs date his death in Maya long count calendar to 998 AD, matching the carbon dates we've collected."

He pointed to charred wood piled around the edges of the tomb. "A fire was set before the tomb was sealed. Once the tomb is sealed, no one gets in, and there wouldn't have been enough oxygen available to incinerate this much wood."

Grant turned to Tennyson. "Where'd you find the axe head?"

Linda glanced at Stansfield. Everyone knew he'd found the blade, including Grant. Stansfield remained silent, glowering, and shot her a challenging look.

Tennyson pointed to Jaguar 2's side. "Displayed in prominence, alongside an obsidian knife. The axe handle has rotted into dust."

"And this mural?" Linda asked. "What's it say?"

Tennyson adjusted his glasses. "Lord Jaguar 2 here is shown... well... ruling. Striking a pose, gesturing with one hand—a sign of leadership and wisdom—wielding a knife in the other. The glyphs proclaim his greatness, with certain exaggeration. No other tomb in Chichén is like this. Ritual burns, segregation; these were no accidents. Jaguar 2 was indeed segregated, perhaps by choice, perhaps not. A Norse axe head was buried with him. It could have been traded from tribe to tribe from as far away as Nova Scotia, a gift from a Viking explorer, or a spoil of war taken from that Viking explorer."

"No, this guy *was* that Viking," Grant said. He placed his index finger on the skull's face. "Jaguar 2 has none of the craniofacial markers of American Indians. See? The narrow nasal aperture, with a long, straight spine and sharp sill. The incisors. Very Caucasian. Hell, just the sheer size of this guy. The Maya are short. This guy was, what, six-and-a-half feet tall?"

Linda felt useless. Grant observed and analyzed like Sherlock Holmes. She glanced at the others. World-class scholars, every one of them. She was a runaway socialite. What the hell had she been thinking? She'd be lucky if they let her run copies and make coffee.

Elisa leaned closer, her blue eyes shining. "Norsemen were fearless but not stupid. They stuck to the coastlines when they could, yet crossed open sea to discover Iceland, then Greenland, then Nova Scotia. As Dr. Grant theorized, if they followed the coast south long enough, they would eventually end up in Florida, and then the Gulf of Mexico. This burial makes sense. Good iron was valuable to the Norse, passed on from generation to generation. Only a man of great importance would be buried with his iron. Pre-Columbian Americans had copper, silver, and gold, but no iron. The axe head was most definitely an import."

Elisa regarded the skeleton for a moment. "He was a warrior. His axe was a battle axe and, judging by the scars, endured many battles. Spectroanalysis found organic matter imbedded in the blade."

"Organic matter?" Grant asked.

"Human blood and hair."

Chapter 6

A charcoal sky burst and poured rain down on Lago Petén Itzá, causing the lake's surface to dance, the raindrops slanting hard and fast in the late afternoon. A man and a little boy snugged their jackets tighter and bailed their little wooden boat with tin cans.

After a few minutes, the rain slackened, and ended as quickly as it had begun. The boy looked up eagerly.

The man smiled. "You fish, Chiam," he said in K'iché Mayan. "I'll bail."

Chiam clapped and cast the line once again into the water. A fish struck, a flash of silver. The boy jerked the rod and set the hook, angling the fish toward the boat, his rod bent double. He grimaced, working the fish nearer. The rod pinned against his chest, he clutched the line with one hand, stumbled, righted himself, and hauled the thrashing fish into the boat.

"It is the biggest fish ever!"

"A rather cute one," the man said, grinning. "I've caught bigger."

To the east, another rainfall smeared the sky, flickering with lightning and drifting toward them. "Leave a few fish for another day, Chiam," the man said. He took up the oars and leaned into them, pulling the boat toward the lights winking on in San Andres, on the north shore of the lake. The boy baited his hook again and trailed the line out behind the boat, watching the cork intently.

They landed and dragged the boat onto the gravel beach at the end of a street of huddled buildings as the rain began again. They took refuge under a thatched hut and lit a pair of candles. The man drew an oiled cloth from his sack, and unwrapped a knife. He stroked the blade against a whetstone, tested it against a calloused thumb, and began to clean the fish. The boy scaled and rinsed them. The man bucketed the fish and covered them with a clean cloth. He climbed into a rusty American pickup, switched on the ignition, coaxed the engine to life with a cough, backed to the beach, and hoisted the dripping boat onto the truck bed.

They set off into the gathering twilight. The truck bounced along twelve pitted, muddy kilometers to Chultun and rattled to a stop at a small house on the edge of the village. The boy scampered from the truck.

"Riga," the man called. "We are home."

A woman appeared in the doorway. The boy tried to dodge past her, but she caught and squeezed him. The man kissed her lightly on the forehead. "Look," he said, uncovering the bucket. "Chiam is almost as good a fisherman as I am."

Riga took the fish.

"Wait," the man said. "I will take two to the day keeper."

Riga selected the two largest, wrapped them in paper, and handed them back.

The man walked through the dark village to a thatched hut and knocked. After a moment, the door opened and an old man appeared. "Ah, Pacal, it is good to see you."

"I've brought fish," Pacal said. "Chiam caught them. Have you had fish lately?"

The day keeper ushered Pacal inside. "You did not come to discuss fishing."

Pacal shook his head. "Riga is worse. I worry about the boy too. Can you tell me what you know?"

"We shall see." The old man took a seat on the floor and Pacal followed.

A sleeping mat and blankets lay against the far wall. A kitchen, of sorts, occupied the near wall, pots and pans of various sizes, jars of foods. A cooking fire blazed warmly in the center of the room, enclosed by a rusted steel ring and grill.

The old man took one of the fish and rubbed spices onto it, spread the glowing coals evenly, and lay it across the grill. "We shall share one tonight, eh?"

The fish sizzled and dripped and the aroma filled the hut. The old man fetched a bottle of whiskey and two tin cups and toasted the bad weather. "What is it you would know?"

"I fear Riga will never be well. Chiam is just a boy, but it weighs upon him also."

"There is more than you are saying."

Pacal hesitated. "Balam, my father, I feel that something is happening. I do not know why."

"You know why, yet you fear it." He shook his head. "Eat first. Then talk." Balam removed the fish from the grill and divided the fillet in half. They ate in silence, and drank the whiskey. Balam withdrew something from a jar, placed it in his mouth, and chewed. "Chicle," he said.

Pacal knew it was not chicle.

Balam folded his legs underneath him and chewed, gazing at the glowing embers of the cooking fire. Minutes passed. At last, he blinked, his eyes glistening, and looked up. "Outsiders are coming. Americans, I believe, seeking riches and fame, as outsiders always have in El Petén. Trouble for your family."

"They wish us harm?"

Balam shrugged. "Harm unwished is harm nonetheless."

"What should I do?"

"A man's family is his guidepost. Do what you must." Balam rocked slowly side to side. He took a pouch of tobacco from his shirt pocket, rolled a cigarette, and lit it. "Northerners rest when they have what belongs to others." He stretched. "I thank you for the fish and your company, but I am old and tired and I wish to go to bed."

Pacal opened his mouth to speak, but the day keeper waved his hand, silencing him. He was through, and that was that.

* * *

Riga Itzep put Chiam to bed with a kiss and stroked his hair until he slept. Pacal lay in his own bed. She lit a candle and began mending buttons on a shirt of Pacal's. When at last she heard the deep sighing of his sleep, she put her mending aside and sat on the floor. She drew her knees up under her chin and embraced them and began slowly rocking. Memories returned, as they did every night. Memories malicious and cruel, memories of men and gunfire. It was late but she did not want to sleep.

Sleep would bring dreams more awful than the memories.

Tears gathered and slid down her cheeks, and she shook with sobs.

Chapter 7

The Yucatán twilight came swiftly, the cooling air lifting spirits on the terrace of the hotel restaurant. "Order anything and everything," Tennyson said. "Starting tomorrow, the expedition is on traditional dig expenses"

"He means 'cheap,'" Watts said.

Linda turned to Tennyson. "Anything?"

"Anything."

Linda ordered lobster thermidor with a tray of appetizers and an expensive Chablis.

Elisa turned to Grant. "I'm dying in this heat. Do you know how Dr. Tennyson lured me to this misery?"

"I've wondered."

"He emailed this." She opened her laptop and clicked on an image file.

Grant set his fork down and stared. "Good lord."

The photo image was of a gold coin.

Grant looked at Tennyson. "You're *recruiting* with this shit?"

"You still don't get it, do you, Carson? Listen: you were *right*."

"I had heard about your academic uproar, Dr. Grant. Who hasn't? Frankly, the notion of Norse runes on a coin from Florida was preposterous so I ignored the story."

"Thanks so much."

"But then I received this." She clicked on the image and zoomed in. "These markings are undoubtedly northern runes, but any *Lord of the Rings* geek with a laptop could concoct believable runes. The average hacker wouldn't get much past that.

"These runes are clearly Norse, clearly Icelandic. The message is simple: 'Eric Rex.' Eric was Eric Bloodaxe, an unpleasant sort who controlled York in Britain about 950 AD. Like any good politician, he valued public relations, and having his name stamped on money meant, 'I'm better than you.' Now take a closer look. What else is there?"

She zoomed in, near the edge of the coin, revealing faint markings. "There are markings underneath, much older than the Norse runes." She manipulated the image; red lines outlined the fainter markings. "Project the lines of the remaining markings into the obliterated portion, and we get reconstructed letters. Latin letters. This was originally a Roman coin, Hadrian's reign, around AD 130, probably paid as Danegeld—protection money—by the Brits.

"Norse minters stamped coins with hammer blows. This stamp obliterated the earlier Roman stamp, except along this one edge."

"Coins are easily hoaxed," Grant said.

"Hoaxing a coin to this level of complexity boggles the mind. No. This is real."

She clicked open another image. "Now, Gene's Guatemalan coin."

The piece was a gleaming silver coin. Just as in Grant's coin, Norse runes obscured a worn, older Latin script.

"The stamps are identical," Elisa said. "Right down to flaws in the script. These two coins, found a thousand miles apart, were struck with the same stamp."

Elisa allowed the silence. "Of course, the two of you could be in on some colossal hoax, but frankly, you couldn't pull it off. Therefore, I'm convinced. The Norse reached Florida *and* Yucatán."

"Thanks again, I think," Grant said.

"It's clear why Lindsay became obsessed," Tennyson said. "It's revolutionary, Vikings among the Maya."

"Don't cream your pants just yet," Grant said. "The racial traits of the skeleton will be disputed as an aberration."

"DNA analysis, maybe?" Linda suggested.

"The bones are too old for a worthwhile test. That's just the way it is, an uphill battle, way short on evidence. But I've been

29

thinking about Jaguar 2. That tomb belonged to a powerful man, a king at least."

Stansfield rapped his knuckles on the table. "At least? What else is there? An emperor, maybe?"

"A god."

The waiter approached, and the party fell guiltily silent. He offered a bottle of wine. Grant said, "Vodka, *por favor.*"

The waiter frowned and skulked away.

Grant continued. "Jaguar 2 may have been blond or red-haired. He was a giant, broad-shouldered and barrel-chested, six-and-a-half-feet tall. Flat-out alien to the Maya."

"My size," Stansfield said. "Does that make me a god?"

"It might have. Consider the time. You nailed down a date of 998 AD yourself, Frank."

Stansfield paused and drummed on the table for a moment. He looked up, his eyes widening. "Kukulcán?"

Grant nodded, leaned back. "Chichén Itzá *is* Kukulcán. Maya classical civilization reached its zenith long before Chichén Itzá became the hotspot. The city-states were at each other's throats, and collapsing left and right. Up north, in Tula, in Central Mexico, the Toltecs were also in chaos, until Toziltpin seized power and ruled as the god Quetzalcoatl, the Feathered Serpent. Quetzalcoatl was a gentle ruler, and put an end to the ancient practice of human sacrifice. This screwed the high priests and really pissed them off. They are said to have summoned the evil god Texcatlipoca—the Smoking Mirror, god of sorcerers and warriors—and sent him against Quetzalcoatl. Quetzalcoatl and his followers were driven out around 987 AD, leaving by sea on a raft of serpents. That same year, Quetzalcoatl arrived in Yucatán and entered Chichén Itzá. The city was overthrown by this new god and his Toltec army.

"Quetzalcoatl became Kukulcán to the Maya. Just as in Tula, he was revered and loved. Look around; monuments to him are everywhere. The Castillo pyramid's staircase is bordered by feathered dragons. On the spring equinox, the shadow of the staircase brings the dragons to life; as the sun climbs, the shadows look like serpents slithering down the pyramid."

"Jaguar 2 was Kukulcán?" Watts asked.

"No. Kukulcán's image is everywhere *except* in Jaguar 2's

tomb. He was a powerful figure, but *not* Kukulcán."

Elisa shook her head. "That doesn't explain why his tomb was segregated from the city."

Tennyson spread a map of Chichén on the table. "Note the orientation. Directly on axis with the Castillo, eight degrees east of north, in line with the Well of Sacrifice." He spread a map of the Western Hemisphere on the table, pinned a string on Chichén Itzá, and stretched out the other end. "North, eight degrees east. The axis runs thousands of miles, straight through Greenland. Jaguar 2's tomb points the way home from the heart of Chichén Itzá. He was homesick. Look at the Maya here in the restaurant. Dark complexions. Dark hair, smooth faces. Quetzalcoatl was light-skinned and bearded, with hair the color of the sun." Tennyson drained the last of his beer and leaned forward. "And worshipped as a god in Central America, half a millennium before Columbus."

Elisa studied the map. "Then where did Kukulcán go?"

Chapter 8

Grant lay awake in his hotel room, listening to the whisper of the ceiling fan. The past had come snarling back. He got out of bed, fumbled around and switched on the light, and squinted against the sudden brightness. He found the bottle of Dinsmoor and a plastic cup that didn't smell too bad, poured a shot, and knocked it back. He moved out onto the balcony and stared out at the sparkling night sky, and let the memories pour in.

He had once been as close to celebrity as an archaeologist could get. He'd been excavating a miraculously untouched Timucuan mound south of St. Augustine, on an old philanthropist's scrubland. The philanthropist died and her heirs settled like buzzards. The mound was nothing extraordinary, yet there was a sense of urgency in that it'd never been studied, and the heirs planned to bulldoze it for condominiums. The city commissioners salivated: Native American dirt piles didn't pay property taxes, but condo owners did. The heirs' contributions to the election campaigns of all the commissioners had bought them a Tallahassee rubber-stamped allowance for a windshield study of the site. Grant had filed for extensions, but the judge, also a grateful recipient of campaign funds, decided the site was of little significance. Grant asked him if it was okay to build apartments on his grandmother's grave. The judge was not amused, but the news media were. *Newsweek* ran a story labeling him the "archaeologist for a new century."

Fame had a downside.

While some colleagues applauded him, others resented his

touchy-feely methods. They would just as soon dig up bones and let the courts handle it if someone got pissed about it.

The deck was stacked against him when he made his big discovery.

The clock ticking, Grant rushed through layers of material, laying bare the earth beneath the site grid. Late one afternoon, he found the piece that would ruin his life.

He uncovered the skeleton of a tall Timucua warrior of high rank, judging from the articles buried with him. That was a stroke of luck; pothunters had looted nearby mounds years before, removing whole sets of remains for display in garages and dens. A number of bone tools—fishhooks, needles, combs—had been uncovered and catalogued. He was working shoulder to shoulder with Billy Osprey, a Seminole administrator who attached himself to the project. Over time, Osprey became an excellent field archaeologist and friend.

Osprey stopped digging and motioned to Grant. He held up a small object that glinted in the summer sun, and gently brushed it.

"Billy, you know better than that," Grant said. "Don't just pluck objects out. Archaeology is context."

"Can't help myself when I get excited."

Grant took the object, turned it over. "Where'd you find this?"

Osprey pointed to the indentation in the shell matrix.

"Holy shit. You sure?"

"Course I'm sure."

"It's European."

"Yep. But this mound's pre-Columbian."

"That's right."

"Holy shit."

"This site dates to 1000 AD, give or take. This is impossible."

The piece was a *European gold coin*—alien to pre-Columbian America.

Grant had already scheduled a presentation in three weeks at a Smithsonian conference in Washington. A run-of-the-mill paper, it discussed techniques he'd invented for mapping sites with technologies from other sciences. He was a digital guru, eager to share his methods. He scrapped that presentation and devoted every waking minute to the coin, and when he took the podium at the Smithsonian, he described passionately his discovery of a gold Viking coin in a Pre-Columbian Indian mound in Florida.

One by one, eminent scientists stood up and throttled him. They all began with "you have no credible evidence" and went downhill from there. By the end of his hour and a half, Grant's reputation had morphed from visionary into that of a shoddy archaeologist who had sacrificed scholarship to ego, at best, and, at worst, an outright fraud. Robert Lindsay slipped out of the room before it was over.

The university pulled the plug on his employment, but not before the media got wind of it. They had a field day. Vikings in Florida! Grant was lumped with UFO abductees and Bigfoot hunters. He declined countless interview requests and took an unlisted phone number.

His career crashed—a ruin of what had once been.

He could have fought through that. He knew how he'd screwed up. Never, never go public with even the most mundane of theories and proposals until you're sure what you have. What he had was a single coin, plucked from the matrix of a burial mound. The context was unbelievable, and he'd known that the moment he'd found it.

But he *hadn't* found it. Billy Osprey had.

He reexamined everything about the dig, everything about that day, that moment, when Osprey had shown him the coin.

Grant had not actually seen Osprey remove the coin. He didn't even know Billy that well. They'd gotten along okay, but the guy had a penchant for making waves in the press in order to achieve his ends. Osprey liked attention. Maybe his goals weren't as altruistic as he'd let on.

Grant went to Osprey's house six weeks after the Smithsonian debacle.

"Billy, I need to know. Is the coin real or isn't it?"

"What do you think?"

"I think not."

"And what else?"

"What else? My career is over because of a coin you happened to produce when no one was looking."

"You were *with* me, Carson."

"With you. Not watching you."

"Careful where you take this."

"Careful? Why? I'm out of the field I've given my life to."

"Look. I saw something way out of place and got excited. I'm not a professional. I'm new at this and I screwed up. You think I don't know it? Carson, you're not the only man that got hurt. Tribal admin fired me. They don't like shit any more than white academia does. I've got no income but I've got alimony and child support hanging over my head. At least you got a whopping paid severance from college. I've got nothing but bills. All I've got, I hope, is forgiveness."

"I'll defend what's left of my name."

"What you saying, Carson?"

"Get a lawyer, Billy." Grant slammed the door behind him.

Osprey hung himself that night with an electrical cord ripped from a lamp. He left no note.

Grant moved to Snake Eye Springs, left his phone off the hook for a month, and took a job as a diving instructor. Success was judged on simpler terms. People learned to dive or they didn't. Bodies were retrieved or they weren't.

And each night he wondered how his life had gone so wrong.

Chapter 9

Nine Days to Solstice

Elisa sank into the hot vinyl front seat of one of two ancient taxis Tennyson had hired at Goldson International, outside of Belize City. The sagging door rattled shut with a rusty protest, and she considered holding it in place. The driver settled in, twisted up the volume on his radio, stretched and adjusted his bulk, checked his mirror, scratched his balls, and hit the accelerator. Hot wind blew into her face from the open windows. Elisa stiffened and shot a glance at Linda and Watts, their faces ashen, in the back seat. She dug her nails into the ruptured armrest, and felt about unsuccessfully for a seat belt. The taxi hurtled along, stopping abruptly on occasion to creep over speed bumps the size of crocodiles. "Sleeping policeman," the driver said with a chuckle, as he cleared each and floored the gas again.

Hitting the outskirts of the city, Elisa wondered that the driver had not left carnage in his dusty wake; yet pedestrians seemed oblivious to the junk heap that flew past within inches of obliterating them.

The taxi shuddered to a halt in front of a hotel of cracked gray plaster, on the bank of the brown Belize River. In the distance, a line of brown water merged with the glittering blue of the Gulf of Mexico. The driver sprang from his seat, gingerly lifted their bags from the trunk, and eased them onto an almost imaginary sidewalk.

Tennyson tipped both cabbies and led his small group into the hotel.

Elisa sank onto the creaking old bed, her knees still shaking.

* * *

Grant and Tennyson made their way down a broken-window street of warehouses along the river. They found the storefront they sought—*Wild Belize Adventures*—adorned by a painted scene of parrots, jaguars, and sharks. They pushed the glass door open, a little bell tinkling against it, and entered a pastel yellow lobby. A tan, middle-aged woman gave a tight smile, ushered them to a leather couch, whispered into the phone, and went back to filing.

A hard, angular man emerged from a back office, grinned broadly. Gray flecked his thick black hair and moustache, and he was impeccably dressed in a tailored suit. His handshake was firm and confident, comfortable with authority. "Hector Santiago, at your service. I received your e-mail and am so pleased you sought me out. I trust you have heard good things?" He stepped aside and waved them into his office.

"You come with the highest recommendation," Tennyson said.

"Excellent. From whom, might I ask?"

Grant glanced at Tennyson. Gene was not an accomplished liar but, in a pinch, he could pull it off. *Wild Belize Adventures* sounded as good as any of the others. The only advantage this one offered, if you could believe the ads, was gear of specific types, ready on short notice, with an unorthodox delivery system.

Tennyson's hesitation was brief but clumsy. "Señor Fuentez, in Chichén Itzá. As you know, we have Guatemalan permits for wilderness trekking and camping in El Petén for two weeks."

Santiago smiled warmly. "Fuentez. Of course." He clicked the mouse on his computer several times. "I greatly appreciate your business, but if I may be so forward, summer is not the best time for trekking in El Petén. The rains come hard and fast and the *bajos*—the swamps—flood. Impassable. Mosquitoes and malaria. Tough sledding, as you say in America."

"Bugs and mud, hell, they're part of the adventure, and anyway we're packing industrial-strength DEET. An extreme rainforest experience. Our outfitting request is somewhat unusual. We can't drive the gear in and we can't carry it in."

"You have not gone backcountry in El Petén before?"

"No."

"The forest is not a kind place."

"Exactly what we want to hear. Extreme backcountry."

Santiago chuckled. "Americans. You pay good money for your hardships, it is true. Ah well. Your hardships furnish my apartment with flat-screen televisions much too large, no?"

"Too large and with high-def 3D."

"I shall enjoy it immensely. Might I recommend a guide? I shall be consumed with worry if you do not have one familiar with the backcountry."

"We'll hire a Maya guide in Flores."

"An Indian." He regarded them for a moment. "Guatemalan Indians are not the most reliable for this type of excursion. History has made them a bit... suspicious."

"We avoid politics. Knowledge of the forest is our only requirement."

"Very well. I'll list a few other guides, to be safe." Santiago scribbled on a paper and handed them the note. "These gentlemen can be reached in Flores."

"*Gracias.*"

Santiago tapped a cigarette out of a pack, lit it, inhaled, and blew a wreath of smoke into the air. "Your equipment list is interesting. Dive gear? You are planning to explore the famous coral reefs of the jungle?"

Grant laughed. "We find any flooded *cenotes* or caves, we're going to have some fantastic diving."

Santiago tapped his cigarette lightly into an ashtray. "Fun indeed. Please, call the guides I recommend. An American disappeared in that region just last year. What if one of you is hurt? The bite of a fer-de-lance is fatal."

"Medicine and snake boots. Add it to the list."

"I shall just have to think about my new television," Santiago said. He slid a paper across the desk. "Rental fees, shipping, plus a small security against the return of the equipment, as discussed."

Tennyson fished in his wallet and counted out a thousand dollars, Belizean, and slid it across the desk to Santiago.

Santiago slipped the money into a desk drawer, uncounted. He swiveled toward a small refrigerator, withdrew three bottles of beer. "A little tradition of mine. We must christen your adventure properly."

"Wouldn't want to screw with tradition," Grant said.

* * *

Santiago slapped shut his laptop, crushed out his cigarette and lit another. His office was quiet and dim, the way he enjoyed it most in the evening. He leaned back in his chair, his fingers laced together behind his head. He rocked slowly, watching the smoke drift to the ceiling.

The Americans were fucking with him.

An hour of internet searches provided him with a wealth of information on these "adventure tourists."

He thought that he had recognized a couple of their names and he was right. Why would archaeologists feel the need to sneak in and out of Guatemala, without legitimate dig permits? They could be jailed for a long time for such a stunt, and certainly would not be denied the permits.

They were after something of great value—too valuable to relinquish to the Guatemalan government. There could be no other reason.

What's more, they were colleagues and friends of the American that had vanished.

He crushed out his cigarette, stabbing the ashtray with it. Those sons of bitches. They were using Belize as a back door to sneak into Guatemala and loot her. *His* Guatemala, though he had fled it years before and could not return.

Not legally.

He picked up the phone and dialed.

Chapter 10

Eight Days to Solstice

Elisa watched the green hills and farms roll past the next morning as the party sped along the crumbling Western Highway from Belize City in a taxi van to the Guatemalan border. They disembarked, paid their Belizean driver. They nodded and smiled through line after line of suspicious immigrations officials and armed guards, hounded each step by currency changers with thick wads of *quetzales*. At last, they were waved through and found their waiting Guatemalan driver, Eduardo, and headed west again.

Eduardo negotiated miles of dust-clouded, teeth-rattling washboard road, patrolled by soldiers on the lookout for drug armies. They reached Santa Elena, crossed a short bridge, and entered the narrow, curving streets of Flores. A sudden urban frenzy seemed to possess Eduardo, and he careened the van around tight turns, squealing tires, bumping over curbs, until he skidded to a stop in front of Hotel del Sol.

Elisa glanced at Linda. They released a collective breath, grabbed their bags, and hurried out as soon as the beaming Eduardo slid the van door open.

The little yellow and blue hotel had an Old World charm, and more importantly, a deck and bar overlooking the lake. Grant sipped a beer and relished the ceiling fan and dazzling lavender sunset, his feet propped up on the railing. Linda and Elisa emerged from a nearby restaurant. He slapped some *quetzales* on the table and hurried down the steps toward them.

"Sneaking out of the convent?" he asked.

"We didn't want to take the chance of dining with Frank at the hotel. Tomorrow we'll be stuck with him. Not tonight."

Grant looked about. "Luck is with you. The coast is clear."

Dark gathered and the air cooled, and people spilled from the houses and hotels.

They strolled through the darkened town and ended up on the shore of Lago Petén Itzá. A full moon cast silver upon the town and diamonds upon the lake. Bats fluttered overhead, winging after mosquitoes that were beginning to swarm.

"Lovely town," Linda said. "Like a dream."

"It hasn't changed much in three hundred years," Grant said. "Still has that colonial feel." He pointed to a jutting peninsula on the north shore of the cove. "See that little rise? That's all that's left of Tayasal, the last Maya capital to fall to the conquistadors. It took the Spaniards until 1697 to take it."

Grant pointed beyond Tayasal to the eastern horizon, where a red glow hugged the landscape. "That's the glow of progress. Slash and burn agriculture. The forests are falling in the south of El Petén. Once they're gone, this gorgeous lake will silt up with mud."

"And where we're headed?" Linda asked.

"Fortunately, it's surrounded by *bajos*. About as remote as you can get in the Americas, outside the Amazon. The Petén's protected, but enforcement is strapped for money and manpower."

"You don't sound hopeful."

"That's my nature, always the life of the party. The forest will be lost within fifty years. People with vision know that it's more valuable as a wilderness and archaeological heritage than an infertile farmland, but either way, people are pouring in."

They were silent for a time. Elisa turned to Grant. "You have reservations about my findings, don't you?"

Grant gave her a long look. "This is a rescue, Elisa. That's all it is."

"You still doubt the Norse connection?"

"I'm focusing on getting Lindsay—and ourselves—out of this alive. But hey, knock yourself out."

"But it's your chance for vindication."

"Or further humiliation."

"Gene seems excited," Linda said.

Grant picked up a pebble and tossed it into the lake, causing a splash of silver light. "He's talking rescue but he's got that look you get when you think you've found King Tut's tomb. It caught him when you started in on those coins. I know that look. Caught it once myself."

"It could be revolutionary. If we can—"

"Bullshit. This is Gene's chance for glory and he doesn't want word to get out. This is going to get dicey, even if we concentrate every thought on getting Lindsay and ourselves out alive, but Gene's got that look. He wants to keep it all under the radar because he doesn't want the Guatemalans to steal *his* dream. But damn it, it's their heritage, not his. We're bound by law to hire locals for any expedition, and rightly so. Gene doesn't want a local blabbing so he's sending for the boy who found the coin. I guess he plans to pay the kid with trinkets and baseball cards."

"Something else is bothering you."

"I need to work. This is therapy."

Another silence. It hung between them, heavy and humid.

Linda fidgeted. "Do you still think about Billy Osprey? That wasn't your fault."

Grant shot her a quick hard glance. "You know about Osprey?"

She shrugged.

"You're very clever for a runaway bride. One article and you psychoanalyze me."

"I didn't mean it that way."

"No one ever does." Grant turned and moved away. "This has been peachy. I'm heading back to my room."

Chapter 11

Seven Days to Solstice

In the early morning, Eduardo drove them around the east end of the lake, and north to the tiny village of Hacienda Benitez, an unpaved half-mile off the Tikal road. He deposited them in the muddy front yard of Ernesto Hidalgo, the self-appointed mayor. The sun was high and hot already, and Eduardo collected his fee and sped off in a cloud of dust. Silence enveloped them in the small jungle clearing. The door to Hidalgo's overdone Spanish Colonial home hung ajar. Tennyson knocked on the doorframe, waited, knocked again, louder. "Mayor Hidalgo! Hello?"

Grant glanced about. This was rich. He poked Tennyson in the ribs. "You let him know we were coming, right?"

"Of course," Tennyson snapped.

"We're *alone*?" Linda asked. "Out here?"

"Guatemalan punctuality is not the same as back home," Watts said.

"Time is time. And we've lost our ride." She opened her phone, grimaced, and waved it in the air, trying to snag a signal.

Grant took off his hat and sat under a tree. "He'll be here. Sit in the shade and don't blow a gasket."

An hour later, a blue and dust sedan pulled up. Hidalgo got out, stretched his back with an audible series of pops. "My fine gringo friends," he cried, beaming and clapping his hands. "It is so good to see you!" A young Maya boy of nine or ten, and a woman of maybe thirty sat in the backseat, watching in silence. The mayor wagged a finger at them, and hissed something sharply. He turned and smiled.

"I have fetched the boy, Chiam," he said. "Nice boy. And his mother." He gave a little snort.

"Are our cars ready?" Stansfield asked.

"The best in Guatemala, my friend. Come."

He showed them around the side of the house to the back, and led them to a large wooden building. He twirled the dial of a combination lock, clicked it open, slid the heavy chain off the doors, and swung them open. Inside were boxes and crates piled high, and tables of auto parts, broken furniture, books, and piles of tarp-covered objects.

A pair of old Land Rovers awaited them. "My beauties," Hidalgo said. He climbed in behind the wheel of the nearest, switched on the ignition. The engine purred and he eased it out of the shed. "My well-muscled beauties." He got out, popped the hood, and stepped back with a flourish.

"British vehicles," Stansfield said. "Oh boy. If we break down, the nearest spare parts are going to be in Guatemala City. *If* they even have them."

"These don't break," Hidalgo said. "They are British."

Tennyson glanced at Watts. "Bill?"

Watts nodded and leaned over the engine. His fingers flew over this and that, prodding, tugging, testing. "Looks all good to me."

"Fine." Tennyson withdrew his wallet, hesitated. "Cash, Mayor?"

"If you insist. In *quetzales, por favor.* No large bills."

"It must be hard to make change up here in these hills."

"Yes, that is the reason."

Tennyson hesitated with the cash. "And our gear?"

Hidalgo adopted a wounded look as he opened the back hatches of the vehicles. He hefted a pair of red plastic gasoline tanks. "See? Both tanks full, with ten full cans in each car. Plenty of petrol." He pried the lids off a pair of large plastic tubs. Inside, neatly arranged, was assorted camp and trail gear. Tennyson consulted a list and checked off the gear.

"And the weapons?"

Hidalgo pulled a tarp from the nearest table, revealing a rifle and two revolvers.

"I asked for seven. One for each of us."

"I am not an arms merchant. You have here a fine hunting rifle, a .308 bolt action; and two .38 revolvers. I have also packed five machetes and two hunting knives in your gear. You will be well armed."

"You know we're dealing with looters, right?"

"To the contrary, you are dealing with kidnappers."

"That makes me feel better."

"Listen, my friend. I have dealt with both. They are not the same. Kidnapping is a lucrative business, and frequently involves the police. Exchanges are made without violence. But this exchange *must* go off without police, who would want this to remain nonviolent and out of the news, as they have more pressing issues with Mexican drug lords coming in from the west."

"I hope you're right."

"Me too. Because if the Mexicans are involved, you and I are dead already and no amount of weaponry will change that. I realize you have not always considered me the most... reliable of associates. Nevertheless, I consider you my friends. Dr. Lindsay's finger was sent as a message. Listen: during the Maya unrest of recent decades, there was an officer fond of cutting off the fingers of captives. That man vanished after the wars, but many people believe he's still alive. He may be who you are dealing with. If so, you are dealing with a monster."

"Thanks, sunshine." Tennyson handed a roll of currency to the mayor. "I'd like to talk to the boy now."

Hidalgo shushed him with a finger while he counted the bills. His eyes lit up as he tucked the money into a shirt pocket. "This way, please."

He led them to a thatched-roof shelter in a corner of the yard. The boy and his mother remained in the car. He motioned to them. The boy hurried over, the woman approached with reluctance.

Even at a distance, Grant could see that the woman was stunningly beautiful, with classic Maya features: jet-black hair, high, strong cheek bones, oval face. Her dark eyes—intent, penetrating, suspicious—studied each of them.

Tennyson knelt by the boy, and held out his hand. The boy stared at him. Tennyson glanced at Hidalgo. "Pure-blooded Maya. Which dialect? Yucatec?"

Hidalgo shrugged. "K'iché. Or gibberish. There isn't much difference."

"I am pleased to meet you," Tennyson said in K'iché. "I am Dr. Tennyson. I'm a scientist." He took the boy's hand and shook it gently.

The boy's mother stepped forward, pulled the boy's hand away, and backed him up a step. Wariness lined her face. The boy looked at her.

"May I speak to your son?" Tennyson asked.

The woman made no reply.

"She is mute," Hidalgo said. "An idiot."

"Shut up," Grant said. He turned to the woman. "The boy's name is Chiam?"

The woman looked at him, and gave the slightest nod.

Hidalgo shrugged.

Tennyson unlatched the case and revealed the silver coin. "You found this?"

Recognition crept into Chiam's face. He shook his head.

"You sold Señor Hidalgo this coin for thirty *quetzales* just last summer. Surely you remember?"

Chiam shook his head.

"Thirty, Mayor?" Grant asked. "Really? You cheap bastard."

Hidalgo grinned sheepishly.

"Chiam, we need your help," Tennyson continued. "Do you remember the American who asked about this coin?"

The boy nodded.

"That man was my good friend, Dr. Lindsay. He disappeared into the forest after you met him and we thought he was dead, but now we believe he's still alive and we need help finding him. We think he searched for the *cenote* where you found the coin. Can you find it again?"

Chiam shrugged.

"Can you show me on a map?"

"I do not know maps," the boy said softly, in K'iché.

"Can your mother find the place?"

Chiam glanced at his mother. The woman watched them with searching eyes. She nodded.

Tennyson turned to Hidalgo. "What is her name?"

"Riga Itzep."

"Riga, I wish no harm to either of you. I wish to employ you both for a few days."

Her gaze remained fixed upon him.

"I will pay ten thousand *quetzales* for a week's work."

Hidalgo whistled. The sum was a decent year's wages for most Guatemalans.

A scowl shadowed Riga's face.

"She wants more," Stansfield said. "What a surprise."

"Perhaps I can accompany your expedition," Hidalgo said.

Grant shook his head sympathetically. "You have a town to run, Mayor. I would hate myself for depriving Hacienda Benitez of leadership."

The mayor looked crestfallen.

"Grant is a joker, Mayor Hidalgo," Tennyson said. "You are much more valuable here than with us, but ten thousand *quetzales* await you also if you maintain our cover and keep inquisitive officials distracted until we return and have left the country."

Hidalgo swallowed hard. "I should be able to do that. Si. But you waste your time with the woman. She is ignorant. *Muy loco.*"

Riga glared at the mayor.

"Asshole," Linda said.

Tennyson shot her an angry glance.

"Riga doesn't trust us one bit. Look at her. She's not here to make money off the gringos. She's looking out for her son." She turned to Riga. "Let me talk to her."

"Fine. Go ahead."

"*Habla Espanol?*" Linda asked.

The woman nodded slightly.

"You are a good mother," Linda told her in Spanish. Linda unzipped a pocket on her overnight bag, withdrew a photograph, and held it up. "This is my son, Stevie. Isn't he handsome? Like your son, very handsome."

No answer.

"Where is Chiam's father?"

No answer.

"When my son was eight, I was driving him to soccer practice. We ran late and I ran through an intersection. A shriek of tires, and a truck smashed through the passenger's side. I relive that split-second over and over again. Stevie's death was my fault and I miss him every day. Every day I wish I could take his place. I understand your fear. You will not place Chiam in danger. Ever."

Riga's glare softened.

"Linda," Tennyson said, "I don't think…"

The roar of an engine being gunned interrupted as a battered pickup raced around the corner and scratched to a halt in the loose gravel, sluicing up a cloud of dust. A Mayan man climbed out and slammed the door. "What are you doing to my family?" he demanded in K'iché.

Chiam rushed to the man's side, grinning, and hugged him. The man looked him over, whispering. He turned his attention to Tennyson, and then to Grant, his eyes burning. "What are you doing to my family?"

"We wish to employ them," Tennyson said. "You are the boy's father?"

"Are you in charge?"

"Yes."

"Keep your money and leave us be."

"It is a lot of money, Pacal," Hidalgo said.

"We do not want it."

"We can help you," Tennyson said.

"You are not here to help us."

"Ten thousand *quetzales*," Stansfield said. "Bet we have your attention now."

Grant winced. "Christ, Frank."

"Do not insult me, gringo," Pacal said. "I am a policeman. I was warned of you."

Grant looked at Hidalgo, eyebrows raised.

"Pacal is tribal police," Hidalgo said. "Not a real policeman. He has an active imagination but I assure you he is ignorant of you."

"Hire the mayor," Pacal said. "He will be happy to take your money."

Linda touched him lightly on the arm. "Your wife and son will be looked after."

He swept her hand away, glowering. "She is not my wife and he is not my son." He turned toward Chiam and Riga. "Come, we must go now."

Chiam looked at his mother and took a hesitant step toward Pacal's truck. Riga turned to Pacal. She shook her head, and stepped behind Linda.

"Riga, get in the truck," Pacal said.

She remained still. Chiam slipped behind her and buried his face in the fabric of her dress.

"Get in the truck!"

Riga gently pried the boy apart from her and nudged him toward the truck. He went to the truck, dragging his feet, and climbed in. She faced Pacal and shook her head.

"Money talks," Hidalgo said. "Eh, Pacal?"

"Shut up." Pacal faced Tennyson and edged closer. "Very well. Let me educate you." Pacal was stocky and muscular, younger than Tennyson, but the older man held his ground.

"I know this forest," Pacal said, sweeping his arm toward the horizon. "You are ignorant of it. I will find you when I want to. My sister will not be harmed. Do you understand?"

"Yes."

"You will bring my sister back to this place in one week."

"Understood."

"Know this. I am a Maya policeman in the village of Chultun. I answer only to Maya elders and I protect only Maya. I will not protect you. I know the place you are going. It is to be avoided."

"Why is that?"

"It is haunted."

Stansfield chuckled.

Pacal looked at him. "I am not so smart as you, gringo. Or perhaps I am. That place is remote and few have ever seen it. Those who know it stay away." Pacal's voice dropped, the anger in his eyes fading, replaced by resignation. "Evil dwells there. Riga knows this. She is going only to protect her child from involvement with you and the ghosts of El Petén."

Grant studied the man's eyes. The Maya were not especially superstitious, but were dead serious about certain beliefs, among them the holdovers from pre-Colonial religions. They seldom joked or lied about those beliefs. This man, Pacal, believed what he was saying.

"We need her to guide us to the *cenote*," Tennyson said. "Chiam found this coin there."

"Chiam has never been there."

"You may want to ask him about that."

"I shall." He turned and went to his truck, leaned into the passenger's side, and withdrew an oily blue bundle. He uncovered the cloth to reveal a pistol and two boxes of bullets. "The jungle is dangerous and you are taking my sister into harm's way. This is a Glock 22. You *will* take these." He handed them to Grant.

Tennyson and Grant exchanged a look. Grant accepted the pistol and bullets. "I shall return these soon."

Pacal looked to Linda, then to Riga. Riga turned away.

* * *

Pacal skidded his truck to a stop outside his house in Chultun. He ordered Chiam inside, then stalked across the village to Balam's hut and pounded on the door.

Balam answered, rubbing sleep from his eyes.

"You took Chiam to the Well of Spirits," Pacal said.

"Come inside, Pacal," the old man said. "We must talk."

The day keeper hung a kettle of water over the fire. He faced Pacal, and motioned him to take a seat. "A year ago, when Chiam went with me into the forest for a week to learn the trade, we came near the Well. It was time to refill our canteens. I told him of the power and danger of the Well. I had him hold back while I peered over the rim into the water before I let him approach. We filled our canteens and Chiam pleaded with me to let him swim. I lowered a rope to the water and let him swim for a time. I have never taken him back."

"He found a coin and sold it to that idiot Hidalgo. Somehow the American that disappeared last year is involved and now more are here seeking the Well of Spirits."

"They are no different than looters."

"Riga made up her mind to go with them before I arrived. She is willful and I could not stop her. I saved Chiam. He shall stay untangled in this."

"Riga must be allowed to go if she wants, Pacal. She has much to overcome."

"Tell me about the Well of Spirits."

Balam leaned back and considered this. "It is beyond the world of men. That is all you need to know."

"You test me, old man. I played the superstitious Indian for the Americans, but I don't believe your ghost stories. If the Well of Spirits is evil, it is the evil of men. My sister is with the Americans. How can I protect her if I am unaware of the nature of the evil?"

"Evil takes many forms, but Riga will be protected. I will protect her."

"You! Spells won't save her from hatred and lust."

"I am a day keeper. I know the past and bend the future. Trust me to bend it now."

Pacal stood and went to the door. "You warned me that outsiders were coming and that they brought trouble for my family. Now they are here and they take my sister to a place you say is evil. Against my judgment, I gave the Americans a gun with which they may kill me." Pacal shook his head. "I know the powers you possess, Balam. You would astound the world yet you remain among our people. I honor you for it, but you ask too much when you ask me to stand by silently. Yet I shall heed your request. For the moment." Pacal shoved open the door and stepped out into the bright hot day.

* * *

Pacal finished his patrol through Chultun and wiped the sweat from his eyes. All was quiet and there was plenty of time to drop in on the nearby villages, to keep everyone on their toes. It was good to avoid routine in his inspections, preventing mischief from thriving on a schedule.

He was policeman by default, ordained by the province elders, elders with no real powers of their own. The job carried no training, no salary, no staff, and no equipment, other than two aging pistols, and he'd just given one to total strangers. He had to support his family, and did so by doing odd jobs: carpentry, masonry, fishing, whatever afforded him the flexibility to get out and patrol his seven villages northwest of Flores.

A policeman, indeed. It was laughable.

The Department of the Petén had a real police force, but it was overwhelmed trying to deal with the armies of the drug traffickers and poachers. If Maya robbed or killed Maya, the police would look into it, write a report, and be done with it. It had gotten so bad that his village and others had stitched together their own unauthorized police force.

He jiggled the key in the ignition of his old pickup, coaxed a start out of the engine, and rumbled down the limestone track to Chacrió.

What did Riga want with the Americans? The money was more than he'd earn in months, but there was more to it than that, something in the sad darkness of her heart.

There had been a time, years ago, when Riga was brilliant as the sun. She had been a little girl then. Now she was a shadow of that girl. Civil war had done that to her.

The war, and Pacal.

Chapter 12

Manuel Cabrillo took a long drink of water, wiped the sweat off his face with his sleeve, and studied his chainsaw. He tugged gently at the chain. A bit loose, but well oiled. He placed the saw on a greasy blanket, tightened the chain with a wrench, and tested it again. It had been start-and-stop all day with the damned chainsaw. Cutting rock, even soft rock like limestone, had played hell with it.

Manuel looked about. It was just like José and Garcia to find excuses to leave him to cut stone alone in the jungle. Lazy bastards.

The sun was dying in the west, angling scant light through to the forest floor. It would be dark soon, but he would slice off one more carving before quitting. Ten minutes should do it.

He lit a cigarette and perched it in the corner of his mouth. He gave the saw cord a hard yank. The saw sputtered, coughed white smoke, and whined to life. He squinted through cigarette smoke, studying the gray limestone stela before him, making sure of the proper cuts.

He touched the whirring saw to the stela. The chain bit into the limestone, and sparks and flying grains of stone stung his forearms. The saw screeched as it sank into the cut, spraying him with a cloud of white dust.

The chiseled stone depicted a knife-wielding warrior brandishing the severed head of an enemy. Someone had carved the stone with care, so Manuel would take equal care in dismantling it. The careless work of amateurs disgusted him. Of course, craftsmanship had benefits. The better the condition, the higher the price it would fetch.

A second stela lay in five segments on the ground nearby. He hated dividing it like that—the cuts were difficult to mask with grout when reassembled—but getting caught with a carved block of limestone guaranteed prison time. His love of art had practical limits.

The fallen stela was adorned with the same warrior as on the stela he was cutting, but on the fallen stela, the warrior bestowed food and drink upon grateful subjects. Combined, the stelae offered a simple set of teachings: *follow me and I'll care for you. Cross me and I'll cut your goddamned head off.*

Manuel withdrew the saw and switched it off. The blade whirred to a stop, and he placed it on the blanket. He gripped the stela and wrenched it. The last bit of limestone in the cut cracked and he rocked the piece free. He pushed the top of the stela off the lower piece and it fell with a thud into the soft earth. The ancient stone warrior lay there, glaring defiantly up at him.

He wiped his brow, admiring his work. Ten minutes? He'd finished in eight. No cutter could match that.

The fallen stelae would remain where they fell until José and Garcia returned. No use in killing himself trying to move them alone. The stone warrior had survived centuries alone in the jungle, surveying a lost kingdom. It could manage a couple of days lying in the mud.

Manuel took a drink of water and studied the tree-covered mound that had lured them here. The mound had remained unknown to all but a few old *chicleros* until the boss bought the information of the site's location. The oblong mound was the size of a city bus. Exposed blocks, rich in detail, peeked from underneath the tangled roots of mahogany trees. Whether it was a house or temple, he knew the mound would be laden with treasure. Stelae did not honor unimportant men.

He glanced about at the encircling trees. He listened intently, shook his head. He did not much care for being alone in the forest.

He and his compadres had dug a trench alongside the mound. He hopped across the trench and peered into it. Bits of treasure peeked from the loose earth in the wall of the trench. Pottery, mostly, but even that would fetch good money. The figurines and jewelry awaiting them within the mound would fetch far more.

Night was coming on, and he stoked the smoldering campfire, coaxing it into a roar, and relaxed his aching muscles. He poured a cup of tequila and gulped it down. The flame waned; he spread the coals, and skewered a piece of howler monkey meat. Soon the meat was sizzling and dripping into the coals. He sliced off a piece and ate it ravenously with tortillas and another cup of tequila. He eased back and put up his feet.

The eyes of the fallen stone figure kept up their endless, angry stare.

Manuel admired the artistry. Chiseled stone eyes that could give you nightmares were certainly the product of great skill, though it seemed that Mayan pieces were seldom of a happy nature.

And there were the local legends that spoke of this part of El Petén being haunted.

Manuel chuckled. Silly bedtime stories, told to scare children.

Nevertheless, he covered the stela with a blanket.

His arms and legs felt like weights, and ached, but the tequila took the edge off that. He folded a blanket against his duffle bag and stretched out against it. The flames flickered and danced, hypnotic in their rhythms. His eyes eased shut and he nodded off.

A brittle snap woke him. He looked about in the darkness, listening. After a moment, he closed his eyes again, only to hear another soft sound, the rustling of underbrush nearby.

He looked in its direction. At least he thought it was the direction. He wasn't quite sure.

It would be his amigos, returning from their jaunt to Santa Elena. "José?" he called.

Another rustling, closer in the darkness.

Manuel picked up more wood, tossed it onto the fire, and fanned it. "José, do not make sport of me," he called out. "Come, I have meat on the fire. You must be hungry."

He scanned the darkness. It could be an animal. An ocelot, possibly. More likely, a jaguar. That thought worried him. The big cats hunted in the night, biting through the necks of prey, sometimes including grown men. He tugged his collar up. The fire was growing, expanding the range of his vision. Good. He tossed another piece of wood onto it.

He hoped it was an ocelot. But ocelots do not stalk men.

He felt his hip pocket for his revolver. Not there. He glanced about. Surely, he had it near, as always. He looked back at his tent. That's where it was. "José, my brother, show yourself," he said, striding to the tent. "I am not in the mood for games."

He threw open the flap of the tent and fell to his knees, feeling through the blankets and his few belongings. At last, underneath his bedroll he felt the reassuring hardness of the revolver. He thumbed open the cylinder. All six chambers were empty.

He listened for a moment. Had he heard it again? He thought that he had. The sound seemed magnified, or was his mind playing tricks? He patted his pockets again. Where were the damned bullets? He felt underneath the bedroll, cursing himself. He never worked without his weapon more than two steps from his grasp, loaded and ready to use. Rainforest ambushes were commonplace, especially with so many poor people creeping into its remote areas to scratch out a living. Why had he been such a fool this time when he actually might need his gun?

What about the faded blue rucksack leaning against Jose's tent? His brother always kept ammunition there. He eased the tent flap open and peered out. The clearing was empty. He craned his neck to get a look at José's tent and the rucksack. Still there. He took a deep breath, swung open the flap, and stepped out.

The campsite was quiet, but something seemed different, out of place. He looked about, trying to determine what was amiss.

The blanket that had covered the fallen stone idol was gone. The eyes of the statue glared at him, its mouth grimacing with hatred.

Another sound, nearer, just beyond the firelight. Guttural, deep, throaty, like the cough of a jaguar, but a jaguar had not uncovered the idol. Manuel swallowed hard, ran to the rucksack, dumped its contents onto the ground. He ripped open a small cardboard box, spilling bullets. Snatching up a handful, he flicked open the revolver cylinder and shoved the bullets into the chambers with shaking hands. He filled each chamber, slapped the cylinder back into place, and spun with the revolver loaded, cocked, and aimed. The gun trembled in his hand.

Nothing.

The sound came again, this time from behind José's tent. He spun and glimpsed movement, a shadow. He fired two shots, lighting the forest with flashes. The echo of the gunshots hung in the air. The sounds of the forest, the humming and chirping of insects, hushed, silenced by the gun blast.

The echo died. Silence hung over the forest.

Four bullets left. He drew a breath and steadied himself.

The stone idol's eyes mocked him. He aimed at the grinning, hateful carving and fired. One eye shattered into a spray of pulverized limestone, leaving a fractured pit in its place. He fired a second shot and the other eye exploded.

Now the eyeless figure bore the face of death, mocking him from empty sockets.

What a fool he was. He'd wasted two shots on a piece of stone, and now he had but two bullets in the chamber. Several more lay on the ground at his feet, where he'd spilled them in his haste. With one hand he scooped them up, holding his revolver ready in the other.

A footfall in the darkness to his right. He whirled to meet it. Another behind him, one to his left.

The pistol trembled in his hand. He cracked open the cylinder and fumbled the first bullet, dropped it, grabbed it, took a deep breath. The way his hand shook, he doubted he could reload swiftly and efficiently. His mind screamed: *Do it now!*

Steadying himself, he chambered four bullets, giving him a fully loaded weapon. He slapped the cylinder back in place and glanced about. The mound, steep and tree-covered, offered a defensible spot. He ran to it and scrambled up the side, slipping in the mud, and reached the top. He positioned himself with his back to the largest tree.

A bellow, neither human nor animal, erupted from the jungle opposite José's tent. Another and another joined in. The din sent a shiver through him. He fired once in the direction of the first bellow, hoping to silence it.

Movement flashed to his left. Manuel wheeled and fired. A grunt followed, then the sound of something heavy falling to the ground. Hope leapt inside him. He would kill these things or drive them away. He would survive this night.

A shrill cry pealed from the other side of the clearing. He spun to face it, fired once; he had four bullets left in the gun. He would keep one bullet in the revolver at all times to shoot while reloading.

A sudden movement caught his eye. A huge figure raced toward him in silence. He swung his pistol about but his attacker struck his hand aside and bowled him over. A powerful hand closed around his throat. Something metallic, *sharp*, glinted in the dying firelight.

He caught a glimpse of the stone warrior, and the warrior's threat raced through his mind.

Cross me and I'll cut your goddamned head off.

Chapter 13

The Land Rover jolted over a fallen tree slick with slime, bottomed out atop it, skidded across, and landed with a *whump* on the opposite side. Elisa banged into the door, bruising her shoulder.

"Rough road, huh?" Tennyson asked, glancing over from behind the wheel.

She looked at him. "What road?"

They'd toured Tikal in the morning, as much for maintaining the appearance of tourists as for letting Elisa and Linda see the magnificent city for the first time. Tikal dazzled, its white pyramids jutting like dragon's teeth above the steaming forest.

After Tikal, the road north to the ruins of Uaxactun punished them for two hours. After Uaxactun, it became less a road than a trail for seventeen miles, then worse still, an unmarked track.

They pounded jarringly past the forest, close all around, unbroken, a riot of lush, rampant growth, rot, and decay, filled with shadow, beautiful in a frightful, oppressive way.

The wheels spun, slinging mud and vegetation. At times, the vehicles fishtailed across slick ground, careening into trees, incurring more dents and dings. Mayor Hidalgo would be looking for reparations.

The route dipped into a muddy, pooled slough stretching across their path, some forty meters wide. Grant, driving the lead vehicle, slid to a stop and climbed onto the hood to survey the way ahead, pointing and arguing with Stansfield. At length, they started forward again, veering right. After a minute, Grant's vehicle slogged through to the other side of the wetland.

Tennyson muttered and slammed the gear into low. The vehicle crept forward, following Grant's track, staying clear of the ruts they'd cut. Midpoint, the wheels slipped and spun. Tennyson cut hard left and gunned the engine. The vehicle lurched free of the mud and careened forward, whined, and plowed to a stop five meters from the slough's edge.

"Crap," Tennyson said, pounding on the wheel. "You drive." He shoved the door open, slid out, slogged to the front of the truck, unreeled a steel cable from the winch, dragged it past Grant's vehicle, and looped it around a tree. He gathered fallen wood with Grant and Watts, and lay it across the path, jamming some underneath the tires. He returned to the truck and flipped a switch. The winch motor whined, drawing the cable taut. The vehicle groaned and lurched forward.

"Punch it," he called to Elisa. The tires bit into the wood, and the Rover inched across.

The vehicles crawled for another hour in thickening growth, until the lead truck stopped at another flooded slough.

Grant climbed out. "End of the line for the trucks. This *bajo* is eleven miles across. We hoof it from here. Hope you've been taking your malaria pills."

Tennyson unzipped a bag and withdrew a small device. "Global positioning time." He switched on the GPS and climbed onto the roof of his truck, moving around and waving it in the air. "Ha! Got a reading." He climbed down, held up a compass and oriented it to north, and consulted his maps. "Unless we find openings in the canopy from here on, we go the old-fashioned way, compass reckoning and by the seats of our pants. The *cenote* is a straight line nineteen miles from here." He pointed. "That way."

They unloaded their gear and cinched into backpacks by early afternoon. "We should make the other side before dark," Tennyson said. "We camp there."

"You're the boss," Grant said. He took the lead with the machete and slashed a wide arc ahead. Three steps in, he was in black coffee water to his waist, and the group plunged into the dense tangle of the *bajo*.

A hundred yards in, Elisa stopped, gasping for breath. The

mud and water had fought her every step, sucking at her legs. The forest had lost its exotic beauty. Now it was heat and mud and bugs and reaching, grasping limbs and vines. She had drenched herself with DEET, but sweat poured from her, branches tugged and scratched and drew blood, and every bug in El Petén answered the dinner bell. She swatted and brushed at them to no avail.

Grant paused and shook sweat from his eyes. He came over and gently restrained her wrist. "The secret, Elisa, is not to fight them. You're wiping the repellant off. What we're wearing may stink but it'll stop a bull elephant." He released her hand. "Relax. They won't bite. You're just convinced that they will."

She stood like a statue, fighting the urge to swat at the bugs. Miraculously few lit, and those that did took off immediately. She let out a slow, deep breath. "Thank you. Very Zen approach to bug-fighting, isn't it?"

"Become one with the forest, grasshopper. We'll make a jungle queen of you yet."

"That will take more than bug spray."

Stansfield raised his hands, an exasperated look on his face. "Hey, Grant, you going to play footsy or cut the goddamned trail?"

"Frank, don't be afraid to take a turn at the front."

Stansfield pretended to adjust some straps on his pack.

"Back to the salt mines," Grant said, resuming the lead position and slashing ahead.

Elisa's face was flushed, hot, and red.

Linda leaned close. "You're blushing," she murmured. "Kind of cute, isn't he?"

"Who?"

Linda laughed. "Have it your way."

* * *

Riga Itzep struggled out of the muck with a last lunge, swung her pack to the ground, and sat heavily beside it, panting. She took a long drink from her water bottle and lay back.

The others lay sprawled about, exhausted and muddy.

After a rest, the Americans pitched tents and made camp in

the brief tropical twilight. Riga helped collect wood and clear an area of brush, and Grant soon had a fire blazing. The one named Watts prepared the meal. American food she'd eaten in Ciudad de Guatemala was all but inedible, but the aroma of this, something called jambalaya, put her stomach into a fit of growls.

Tennyson brought her a plate of food and sat near.

She took the plate and eased away.

Chapter 14

Six Days to Solstice

Linda awoke slowly the next morning, a thrumming sound beating around her. Someone shaking the wall of her tent.

"Linda," Tennyson said, damn him. "Up and at 'em."

She stretched and sat up. Her back ached. Her feet ached. Her *hair* ached. The night had brought a creepy, close feeling. Wilderness trekkers called it "seeing the elephant," the realization that one is far from civilization, at the mercy of the great unknown. Primeval, gut-level fear. Linda thought she would toss and turn all night, yet this morning she felt as rested as she had in years.

Watts had pancakes ready by the time she had her sleeping bag and tent rolled, and dished out generous portions with syrup, saying he wanted everyone good and carbed. She wondered how a pancake could taste so good. How he carried such good and copious food in his backpack was a mystery, but one she didn't want to jinx.

* * *

Tennyson signaled a stop in the middle afternoon and raised his GPS, squinting. He shook his head and walked about, trying to pick up a triangulated signal through the dense canopy. At length, he gave up.

"Terrific," Stansfield said. "Your bargain basement equipment is failing. Like we're not already in over our heads."

"Shut it, Frank," Tennyson said. "Hi-tech always has limits in the wilderness. You knew that when you signed up."

With Grant again leading the way with a machete, the team resumed the hike, mercifully free of swampy ground, but full of the same ticks and clinging, scratching plants.

At last, they broke into a small clearing where a giant mahogany had toppled, taking with it a few smaller trees, leaving an open sky. Sunlight poured in. Tennyson held his GPS aloft, captured a signal, and shoved it toward Stansfield. He loudly announced their coordinates.

"That's inspiring," Stansfield said. "But you may want to hold your voice down a bit." He pointed to the open sky in the southwest. "Someone else is here. Maybe a half-mile away."

A distant wisp of smoke rose above the forest.

Tennyson frowned. "Probably a *chiclero's* camp."

"What is a *chiclero?*" Elisa asked.

"A gum collector. He usually travels alone, harvesting sap, the *chicle*, from sapodilla trees. *Chicle* used to go into chewing gum in the United States. That market's dead, but *chicleros* still ply their trade. The few left know the forest like the backs of their hands."

"Pipe down," Grant said. "Maybe it's a *chiclero*, but I doubt it. I'll check it out." He slipped the rifle off his shoulder, opened the chamber, slid a round in, and bolted it shut.

"I'll come with you," Elisa said.

Grant turned to her, hesitant.

"Don't say what you're thinking," she said. "It's inadvisable."

"Fine. Gene, give her your pistol, and keep the other one loaded and ready. Rest of you, watch my signal and stay a hundred yards back. No talking, not one damned word. If you hear a commotion, *then* raise as big a racket as you can. Sound like an army that's really pissed."

Elisa started in the direction of the smoke, swinging her machete and slashing through a vine.

"Uh-uh," Grant said. "Absolute silence. No swinging of machetes. We're spies now."

"Then why take them?"

"For protection." Grant opened his pack, withdrew the revolver, and loaded it. "Don't worry, Gene says it's just a harmless old *chiclero.*"

Elisa felt a tightening in her stomach. The adventure suddenly became less enticing.

They eased ahead. Grant took the lead, and Elisa watched his movements. He slipped through the brush gently, easing it aside, leaning this way and that to avoid contact. Almost soundless. She copied his movements and found that she could be remarkably stealthy.

Grant paused and looked back. Elisa followed his gaze. The others were barely visible. He waved them ahead, turned, and continued.

After half an hour, he motioned Elisa to stop. "Let's get dirty," he whispered.

What was he thinking? She couldn't get any filthier, but he dropped onto his stomach, scooped a gob of mud, and smeared it across his face, motioning her to do the same. She sighed, and smeared her face brown.

Grant belly crawled to a fallen tree. He took a small pair of binoculars from his hip pocket and peered ahead. "There's a clearing fifty yards up," he whispered. "And it's what I was afraid of."

Her pulse quickened. "What?"

"A looters' camp."

He studied the site for several minutes, eased forward, paused, and moved again. He motioned for her to stay behind.

Ten minutes later, he returned, walking upright. "It's clear." He motioned the others forward. When they'd caught up, he said, "Don't make any loud noises. It's a looters' site, fresh one too, but something's wrong. It's been abandoned. I've never seen a site left like this."

Grant led them to the site, halting at the edge. To one side was a head-high mound. A few trees had been cleared from the site. Two fallen limestone stelae lay on the forest floor. Three small, cheap tents stood on the opposite edge of the clearing. The remains of a fire smoldered in the center, curling a wisp of smoke into the air. Segments of tree trunks set on end surrounded it, presumably as seats. A trench, a yard wide and two deep, ran the length of the mound.

"Post-Classic pieces," Tennyson said, pointing to the fallen stelae. He faced the mound. "Beautiful workmanship. Someone important is buried here."

Grant went from tent to tent, and peered inside. "Nothing much left. No artifacts, nothing. Gene, we need to leave immediately."

"Not so fast," Stansfield said. "We're ahead of schedule. You want to rush off and leave a site like this? A bird in the hand, you know."

"Are you blind? The looters haven't been gone more than a day or two. They've barely scratched the surface. We don't want to be here when they return." He looked around. "And that's not what worries me most."

"What else, Carson?" Elisa asked.

He glanced at her. "There's no one here."

"I thought that was a good thing."

"Some of them might have left for provisions, but you never leave a site unguarded. You keep at least one man here. Where is he?"

"He's right," Tennyson said. "Looters don't abandon gear. Look, there's the chainsaw out in the open. Hazard a guess, Carson?"

Grant shrugged. "Beats me. Maybe a rival crew drove them off and idiotically abandoned it themselves. Maybe the guard went to take a leak in the forest and got lost. There are a lot of possibilities, but all end with either this bunch or an equally dangerous bunch returning, and returning soon."

Tennyson stooped at the base of the mound, and poked it with a finger. He scaled it and traversed its length, pausing near a large tree growing from the peak. "Take a look," he called. He stooped over and held up a revolver.

Grant and Watts climbed the mound to join him. Linda followed. The pistol was of cheap make, but well kept.

"That's a looter's weapon," Grant said. "At least it's not a drug cartel weapon. They pack firepower far superior to this."

Tennyson popped open the gun's cylinder. "Four rounds left, two chambers empty." He sniffed the weapon. "Fired recently."

Linda dropped to one knee and brushed her hand through the decayed leaf litter. "We've got blood," she said. She looked about. "Also on the tree trunk. See the way the blood is spread? Those aren't 'drip-drip' bloodstains. Extreme violence caused it to spray like that."

"You're a detective now?" Stansfield asked.

"My uncle is."

Elisa studied the blood-spattered ground, the dark, clotted, stains nearly invisible in the browns and blacks of the rotting vegetation that carpeted the forest floor. Linda's keen eye impressed her; she may have missed her calling when she went into archaeology.

Grant slid down the mound and approached the fallen stelae. "Fresh chainsaw cuts. Expert workmanship for a thief."

"Look at the face of this warrior," Linda said. "See the fracture pattern? His eyes have been shot out. Fragments and dust are still on the ground."

"The looter stood to make a big profit from these two stelae alone. Why shoot the eyes out of a piece that'll go for thousands of dollars? A claim-jumper wouldn't vandalize them either."

"Why then…?"

"Lunacy. Panic. Maybe both."

The filtered light dimmed, the air cooled. A faint breeze rustled the canopy, and a distant rumble of thunder sounded. Tennyson studied the sky for a moment. "Thunderstorm coming. All right then. We'll document the site as best we can. I want us out in ten minutes. The storm will cover us. Carson, are you all right with that?"

"Right as rain."

"Bill, stay on the mound with this pistol and watch north and east," Tennyson said. "Carson, you take south and west. Okay, people, this will be the fastest archaeological survey ever. Sketch pads and cameras, asses and elbows. Note everything, touch nothing. Leave no trace you were here. Let's get to work."

Linda enlisted Riga, and together they dragged a tape measure lengthwise and crosswise across the clearing, and sketched a roughly scaled map. Riga's eyes shone with excitement.

Elisa snapped digital shots from every angle, with close-ups of the fallen stelae. The eyeless face in the stone seemed to mock them, and dread boiled deep within her. She shook the feeling. It was silly; she was a scientist, not a superstitious twit. Nevertheless, the power of the carving was real. She could imagine the figure before the eyes were destroyed. No wonder they had been shot out.

Satisfied with her photos, she glanced at her watch. Seven minutes left. She withdrew a twined sheaf from her pack, and pulled from it a large sheet of translucent paper, a roll of tape, and a stick of charcoal pencil. She taped the paper to the face of the stela and rubbed the pencil over the paper. The image jumped to life in the rubbing in richer detail than any photograph. She quickly finished the face, torso, and legs, and moved on to the glyphs, then began a new rubbing on the second stela.

Grant nodded to her. "Good idea. This is the last time scientists will see these stelae. They'll be carted off to market by this time tomorrow."

Grant glanced at his watch and held it up for Tennyson's benefit.

Tennyson nodded, looking up at the darkening sky. "That's it. Everyone load up. Get your rain gear on unless you want to be even more miserable. Each minute we stay could be the minute we all die, and I don't want to be remembered as the leader of the lost expedition."

Thunder boomed. The first fat drops of rain fell, splashing into the foliage. Within another minute, the expedition slipped into the forest. Grant cut a sapling from the forest and swept the small clearing, erasing footprints. Just like mopping a floor. Never rely on a too brief shower to hide your tracks.

He paused and scanned the site. No sign of their passing as far as he could tell. The fallen idols lay silent and still. The eyeless faces seemed to watch their every move. He looked at the mound and the small, rusty stains spattered there.

Violent death was always a risk in remote wilderness. It had occurred in this small clearing, but something more hung over this desecrated site, something evil and far more worrying than the threat of discovery by cutthroats miles from civilization.

The rain opened up with full, sudden force and beat down in buckets. The team became invisible and soundless in the rainstorm, and he could hear only the wash of hard rain and the cracking of thunder. The wall of sound enveloped him, dampening the life and movement of the forest. He raised his face to the downpour and let it wash away the grime. It was cool and cleansing, but the roar of it lent this abandoned outpost an air of unreality. Unreality and dread.

Something was wrong with this place.

Horribly wrong.

Chapter 15

Pacal Itzep looked at Maria Escobar's face, frowned, and delicately touched the purple swelling that ran from her swollen eye down to her chin. She winced and pulled away.

Pacal glanced at her husband, Tomas, leaning against the doorway, his thick body silhouetted against the light outside, a bottle of beer dangling in his hand, a ghost of a smirk on his face. He shrugged and drained the rest of his beer.

Pacal sighed. "Are you sure you do not want to report this?"

She glanced at her husband, withdrew a step, and nodded. "I fell. It was an accident."

"I see." He turned to go, and stopped. "Actually, I would speak with Tomas. Alone, for just a moment. Tomas, if you will?"

Pacal led him around the back of the house. "Women, eh?"

Tomas grunted. "I have things to do. Get on with it."

"Believe me, I know women. They can be difficult, no?" Pacal removed his belt and holster and placed it on the ground. "The thing is, you will never lay a hand on Maria in anger again. Do you understand?"

"Get out of here, Itzep. Come back when you become a real policeman."

"You are a big man. Much bigger than me. That is why I have removed my gun. I want to make this a fair fight."

Tomas smirked. "I could kill you in less than a minute."

"I will advise your wife to leave you after I have beaten you senseless."

"You'll call the real police after I have beaten you. I'll not be baited."

"Perhaps I shall call upon her after she leaves."

The smirk faded.

"Maria is very pretty. Perhaps I will fuck her."

Tomas lunged, swinging wildly. Pacal ducked and planted a fist in his stomach, a hard right to the side of his head. "Did you know I boxed professionally for three years?"

Tomas wheeled and rushed him. Pacal backed nimbly, firing three quick jabs into Tomas's face. Tomas slowed, dazed. "I was good too," Pacal continued. "My signature was a devastating right cross. Like this." His fist smashed into Tomas's jaw, and he felt the jawbone dislocate. The man tottered, a blank look in his eyes, and crashed to the ground.

Tomas lifted himself on his arms, shook his head, saw Pacal's cocked fists, and sank back to the ground.

"You will not lay a hand in anger upon her again. If you do, I will be back to administer another beating and I will not stop until you are dead. Do you understand?"

Tomas nodded dully.

"She may or may not leave you. A poor woman rarely can leave marriage. But she is now under my protection."

Pacal turned and left.

A thunderstorm gathered in the east. Pacal leaned into the accelerator, hoping to avoid this mudslide of a road in a downpour. Four-wheel drive or no, he could be stuck for hours if that happened. Enough police work for one day. His right hand was swelling from that fool's concrete block of a head, and his knuckles ached. He looked forward to getting home and seeing Chiam and having a stiff drink.

The police radio he'd purloined from the station in Santa Elena buzzed with news about a liquor store robbery. Nothing of interest to Pacal. He dialed the radio up and down the seldom-used bandwidths, listening to the scratches and pops, as he had compulsively done since the Americans dragged his sister off to the woods.

He paused. A voice, in Spanish with a bad accent, came over the air, punctuated by crackles of static from the lightning.

It was the American, Tennyson. "Mayor, are you there? Pick

up, *por favor.*"

Pacal twisted the volume higher and leaned in.

"Mayor, are you there?" Tennyson repeated the message twice.

After a moment, a stronger signal replied. "*Sí*, I read you." Pacal recognized the voice of Ernesto Hidalgo.

"Mayor, we—"

"The fewer names, the better."

"Right. Listen, we have discovered a looter's camp in the forest," Tennyson said. "Northeast of Uaxactun." He read off the coordinates.

"Looters, that is bad," replied Hidalgo. "You have seen them?"

"No, the camp is abandoned, but it won't be empty long. They were in the middle of looting an undocumented site. There has been a crime, we think, probably a murder."

"Very bad. Very bad indeed. You should leave that place and return. Immediately."

"No, we are continuing our journey."

Hidalgo paused. "It must be reported."

"Agreed. We are required to report this and I wanted to make sure someone trustworthy has the coordinates, to prevent further looting. But don't call this in just yet. We need the time we discussed."

"You are being foolish. Did you find a body?"

"No, but there's blood."

"A result of cleaning fresh game, no doubt. If there is no body, there is no murder. We leave it at that and discuss it no further. I will see you soon. I hope."

The conversation ended with a static hiss.

Pacal pulled over, switched off the engine, and drummed on the steering wheel.

The Americans were moving in the direction they'd planned, but taking unnecessary risks. Rooting about in a looters' camp? Were they insane? They could die of stupidity and he would not care, but placing Riga in danger was inexcusable.

And they had lied.

They were not on a pleasure hike. He'd known that from the start. He had done his homework. They were archaeologists.

They were on a covert expedition to scout some site they'd rather not let the Guatemalan government know about. There was more than that, though. Something important enough for them to risk jail and, more likely, death.

They did not know El Petén, the thousands of square miles of wilderness, rife with danger. The government couldn't keep an eye on it. What few resources it had had been thrown into the fight against the drug lords in the west.

He would keep his radio on at all times with the volume a bit louder.

Looters. A blood-stained camp.

He turned his truck around and headed toward Santa Elena. He needed to buy bullets.

* * *

José Cabrillo awoke with a start, roused by the pounding on the door of his Santa Elena hotel room. He sat bolt upright, spilling his skinny whore from the bed. She cursed him savagely. He gave her a quick, apologetic nod, and approached the door.

"What is it?" he demanded.

"The colonel is on the phone." It was the innkeeper's voice.

"I will call him back in twenty minutes."

"Do you think that wise? The colonel wishes to speak with you *now*."

Cabrillo grimaced. "I'll be down in two minutes."

He pushed a wad of *quetzales* into the whore's hand and told her to get back into bed. He pulled on his trousers and shirt and headed downstairs barefoot. The innkeeper handed him the phone. Cabrillo covered the mouthpiece with his palm, and stared the innkeeper away.

"What do you want?" Cabrillo said into the phone.

"God damn you, Cabrillo," Hector Santiago shouted. "What are you doing in Santa Elena?"

"Provisioning."

"You are drinking and whoring! Do you have any idea what is going on?"

"We have a rich site. We will make more money from it than from any we have found."

"The Americans have also found it and radioed their fool, Hidalgo."

Cabrillo chuckled. "Do not worry. Hidalgo has obviously forwarded the location to you, and you will make some calls and delay investigation for months. Even years, no? I will drive the Americans from the site."

"They have left on their own."

"That makes no sense. That is a valuable site, the tomb of a nobleman."

"Why then did you leave it unguarded?"

"We left it secured. My brother is there, armed."

"The Americans found the site abandoned!"

Cabrillo hesitated. "Then my brother heard their approach and hid in the jungle."

"They found blood on the ground. Manuel is dead. You have left a fortune in the jungle to be stolen by Americans, and you left your idiot brother to die. You have cost me a great deal of money with your whoring, Cabrillo. I should come to El Petén and slit your throat myself."

Cabrillo's skin prickled. "If someone has killed Manuel, he shall regret it."

"*You* shall regret it if my site is lost. I do not waste money and effort on fools who cannot deliver on the work I bring them. Where is Garcia?"

"Also in Santa Elena."

"Find him. How long will it take you to reach the site?"

"It is deep in the forest, difficult to reach. I will be there in two days."

"Then I had better have good news in two days." The phone went dead.

Cabrillo replaced the phone and went up to the room. His whore had fallen asleep again. He grabbed her by the arm and dragged her from the bed. "Out, *puta*! You have been paid more than you deserve. Did you expect breakfast and a wedding too?" He shoved her screaming and kicking out the door, clad only in the bed sheet. He tossed her clothes after her and locked the door.

He opened his bag and withdrew the radio. It hummed and crackled when he switched it on. "Manuel, are you there?" He waited, turned up the volume. He fiddled with the knobs. He repeated the call a half-dozen times, and received only a radio hiss in reply. A sick feeling grew in his stomach.

Manuel dead. Could it be?

He sat on the bed for many minutes, staring at the floor. He unscrewed the cap off his bottle of tequila, took a drink, and smashed the bottle against the wall.

Chapter 16

Linda plodded along, staring at the ground, when Grant called a halt. She glanced up, too late, and blundered into Frank Stansfield. Stansfield muttered something, but she was too tired to care. Any stop was a good stop.

Grant wiped his face and conferred briefly with Tennyson. Tennyson turned and announced, "Ladies and gentlemen, the Well of Spirits."

Linda shrugged off her backpack and sank to the ground, the muscles in her shoulders and the small of her back mercifully unshackled. Her feet were hamburger.

She took a drink of warm water. Boston was another planet now, and she fantasized about sitting on a bench in Beacon Hill, nursing a six-dollar cup of coffee, watching civilization hurry past.

Tennyson looked at her expectantly, beaming, fishing for a show of emotion. She'd pass on that, unless fatigue counted as emotion. She sighed, rose to her feet, and trudged over to the *cenote*, wondering how big a thrill a malarial piss hole in this steaming jungle could be.

Quite a thrill, she realized.

The mouth of the *cenote* formed a circle, sixty feet across with sheer limestone walls, draped with foliage like the hanging gardens of Babylon. The water sparkled in the dappled sunlight, a brilliant diamond, ten feet below. A sandy bottom, like pearl beneath blue glass, lay thirty feet lower, as clear as if it were mere inches away.

"It's beautiful," she murmured.

Grant leaned over the rim. "Water this clear, it's got to be a flowing spring. There's no surface outlet. My guess, it's a sink on an underground river. Gene, don't you have a call to make?"

Tennyson nodded. He flicked a switch on his radio pack. "We're ready."

After a moment came Hidalgo's voice. "Ah, I am pleased. I worry for my friends, you know."

"Mayor, we have found our site. Get your pencil."

"Amigo, it is already in hand."

Tennyson looked at his GPS finder and read out the coordinates, backwards as they had agreed.

"Excellent! My colleagues in Santa Elena will make delivery within two hours."

"Find us four decent, hot pizzas, ship them, and there's an extra five-hundred *quetzales*."

"I believe that can be arranged."

* * *

The prisoner lay unmoving, remembering the first time they'd given him the drug, shortly after his incarceration…

He drew a slow breath. The air stank of rot and filth. Bile rose in his throat. He rolled to the side and vomited and closed his eyes.

He brushed a hard, round object that tipped and rolled. He knew it instantly, the roundness, the blunt teeth, the empty eye sockets. He choked off a cry, kicked the skull away, and sat back. To hell with exploration.

Silence and darkness weighed on his senses like a heavy black cloak. What a clever punishment solitary confinement was. Alone in the dark, the primal fear. No wonder it was a preferred method of torture the world over.

He rocked on his haunches. Twisting, random thoughts squirmed through his brain, malignant thoughts. He fought them, fearing his mind would slip over the edge.

Time passed without meaning.

He lay in filth, not wanting to move. That drink they'd given him, that shit was the worst thing he'd ever tasted, and his gut burned. He spat on the floor and wiped his tongue across his arm. That helped a bit and he sat up to think.

Turning his head, he cocked an ear, listening to a faint scuttling across

77

the floor. He peered hard in that direction, then cursed himself. Trying to see in pitch darkness was a waste of time.

A roach scurried away.

He blinked—did he imagine it? Even growing accustomed to the darkness, there was not enough light to see by. Yet there was the faint shadow of the roach crawling away.

And he heard it.

He looked about. He could make out details that had escaped him before. The coarse stone masonry, some inscribed with glyphs. The low ceiling, just inches higher than he stood. The muck and dirt that covered the floor. And the bones of the long-dead.

He sniffed the air. Odors he had been oblivious to, the smells of ages, assailed his nostrils. His senses grew, a spiral of awareness. Trapped in a lightless, soundless hole, he was aware of the world for the first time in his life. He breathed deeply and fully.

Slick with sweat, he felt underneath his jaw for a pulse and found it racing furiously. His heart thudded in his chest and he knew he was running a fever.

Power surged through him. He pounded a fist against his chest. Was this what men missed? Were men ever truly alive? He felt like a wild beast, alive for the first time.

Alive, caged.

Caged!

He hurled himself against the door, staggered back, only dimly aware of incurring a gash on his shoulder. Blood trickled from the wound, and the smell of it filled him. He sprang again at the door, pummeled it with his fists. He felt no pain. Blood streamed into his eyes as he raked his nails across his forehead, the intermingling sensations and smells heightening his rage.

Time passed as if in a dream. Still, he flailed at the door, clawed at it, threw his weight against it. His hands became raw and bloodied and swollen. Two of his fingers protruded at crazy angles from the others, and a fingernail hung, bleeding, by a scrap of flesh.

At last, he collapsed, drained, and slid to the floor where he lay panting, his eyes darting, focusing and unfocusing, on nothing and everything.

His thoughts grew less jumbled as his breathing slowed. He recalled the experience vividly, though he could scarcely believe it was him he remembered. He must have entered some sort of trance. He wasn't sure. He'd once blown a little coke with some students and knew the rush, but this was like that a hundred times over. This was Jekyll and Hyde, the real deal.

The pain in his mangled, trembling hands awakened, causing his broken fingers to throb with a dull, deep ache.

Thinking back on his strange, heightened state of rage and awareness, he hungered for it once more.

Was this what gods felt?

* * *

Grant held a small LED lamp against the trunk of a mahogany, set a nail, and hammered it in place. He wiggled the lamp, making sure it was snug against the tree, and flipped a tiny switch. A quintet of tiny lights blinked on. He switched it off again and tripped a second switch, setting the radio signal. He snapped a leafy twig from the tree, and stapled it to the trunk next to the lamp, partially hiding it.

That was the last of thirty alarms, arrayed in a circle about the camp, with a radius of a hundred feet. Equipped with motion detectors, the lamps would strobe on when someone passed within twenty feet of them and would signal an audio alarm in the camp. It wasn't much, but it should warn them if someone approached. He hoped.

This completed the outer of two concentric circles from the camp. The inner circle was a zone with a sixty-foot radius, centered on the Well of Spirits, hand-cleared of brush with machetes. The tents had been pitched in a line five yards from the *cenote*.

Grant studied the layout, feeling less than confident in what they'd gotten into.

* * *

Two hours to the minute, the distant beating of a helicopter caught Linda's attention. The sound grew to a roar and a sudden rush of wind blew down, whipping the branches of the trees. The aircraft hovered low overhead, blue and white, just visible through the canopy. Tennyson waved frantically. Linda watched, appalled at the obvious failure of planning. There was no way to deliver the equipment without putting both helicopter crew and expedition in mortal danger. Tennyson, renowned as a fiend for logistics, had underestimated El Petén. No landing zone, no breaks in the canopy, no gear. This had disaster written all over it.

He shouted into the radio in Spanish, and the helicopter eased directly over the *cenote*. A netted bundle appeared in the open bay of the chopper and descended on a cable lowered through the canopy in the center of the clearing with scant clearance between the tangle of branches.

I'll be damned, Linda thought. It might actually work.

Tennyson seemed to read her mind, and grinned. "Piece of cake."

"You're going to set the gear down in the water?"

"Just watch."

The gear stopped at eye level. Tennyson uncoiled a rope, handed one end to Grant, and walked around the *cenote* carrying the other, looping it back upon itself and encircling the cable from the helicopter. Watts stood nearby, radioing details to the pilot. They swung the bundle toward them and settled it lightly on the ground.

"Damn it, Gene," Stansfield said. "We wallowed in mud for two days to get here. If the airdrop was so easy, why didn't we just drop down with the gear?"

"You know why. An airdrop is high-profile and we can't have that. The pilot doesn't know us, and I want to keep it that way. He doesn't even know what we look like and how many of us there are. We can't let information slip."

Four more bundles followed and, an hour later, a full-on expeditionary camp was set up, high and low-tech equipment everywhere. A large tent housed the communications and GPS equipment, laptops, and racks of sample bottles, chemicals, digging equipment. Another became Grant's dive shop, where he stowed his scuba gear. He duct-taped a handwritten *keep the hell out* note to it.

By nightfall, camp was complete.

* * *

Frank Stansfield dragged his camp chair a few feet beyond the firelight. Grant had taken a seat closer than he cared for. Grant glanced at him and shrugged.

Grant acted like he owned the expedition and Tennyson didn't have the balls to set him straight. No surprise; it had always been like that, from the day Stansfield had interviewed for the staff opening. He'd just finished his grad work and would have gotten the hell out, maybe to New Mexico, but there wasn't much open in archaeology at the time—at any time, really—so he applied when the dean's retirement caused a reshuffling and an opening. And there sat Grant, muscling in on the interview, asking irrelevant, social questions, the touchy-feely bullshit he'd built his name on, while Lindsay smiled and grinned like an idiot.

They'd offered him the job the following week. So why did they wait? There were only four applicants and Stansfield towered heads and shoulders, talent-wise, over all of them. That was Grant's doing. Grant had treated him ever since as a rookie, not a colleague. Stansfield had published, had solid peer review of his work, and was the equal or better of anyone in the department.

Grant sat in a camp chair, the rifle cradled in his arms, silently staring into the forest. His colleagues sat around the fire, chatting, nursing cold beers.

Each had serious limitations. Tennyson hadn't had an original thought his whole life, and Watts toiled along as a gear-head. Grant had bungled a site, made himself a laughing-stock, and had run like a scared rabbit hoping it would all go away.

This crew was supposed to be a collection of leading lights. Ha! Stansfield knew better. Same old story, don't let the newcomer all the way in. Just give him a peek, just enough to make him want it.

The newbies weren't getting this shit. Anderssen was apparently one of the two or three top scholars of Norse archaeology, but she'd done nothing to show it. She deserved a little credit, but there was more to it than that, and it wasn't subtle. She had the looks. A cliché, the Scandinavian beauty. Tennyson and Grant slobbered over her, and Watts would, too, but women weren't really his thing. Cripes, let her do something of value before you coronate her.

What really gnawed at him was Linda Stein. What was she, some rich divorcee from New England who thought the hip thing to do would be to remake her dull life? What a joke. She had zero experience, yet Grant and Tennyson valued her opinions more than his.

He wished he'd stayed in Florida, or better yet, gone to Albuquerque for the summer to make connections. UNM had funding and was gearing up for two years of mapping in Petroglyph National Monument. Robert Lindsay hadn't really earned this kind of loyalty from him, and he wondered what he'd been thinking when he agreed to come on the search. More and more, this trip looked doomed to failure.

He sipped his coffee. The others joked around, ignoring him, giddy at their arrival at the Well of Spirits, when all they'd accomplished was setting up camp. A quick survey of an acre or two surrounding the sinkhole turned up no artifacts of any kind. Usually you'd find something—a worked stone, a potsherd, something—giving away a Maya site if one had ever existed.

His gaze settled upon Riga. She sat well back from the circle, staring into the fire, rocking. She had not said a word since joining them. Probably mute, like that idiot Hidalgo claimed. Probably more than that. She was missing a few marbles.

Tennyson had made a show over bringing her along as a guide. What a joke. Not once did he ask her the direction, even though she seemed at home in the woods. She was just insurance against the Guatemalan antiquities laws, and had the added benefit of being mute, and presumably wouldn't talk about what she saw. Grant had actually snapped at Tennyson for that, claiming it unwise to endanger her life for such a weak reason. You had to give the guy a little credit for that, but Stansfield doubted his sincerity. He was just trying to score points with the women.

Anderssen walked over to Riga and knelt beside her. She smiled and placed her hand upon the woman's shoulder, speaking softly and motioning toward the group. Riga shook her head. Anderssen said something more, patted her on the shoulder, and returned to her chair.

Stansfield smirked. What a weak attempt at drafting her to join the clique. White social worker guilt. The girl would have none of it.

He appraised her more carefully. Riga was classic Maya— exotic, mysterious. Better still, she had a figure of curves and firmness that should not go unnoticed.

Or wasted.

She might make this miserable expedition tolerable.

He carried his chair over and set it next to hers, nearly touching. She glanced up, her black eyes glittering in the firelight.

He'd underestimated her. She might be an imbecile, but a stunningly gorgeous one. He took a seat and offered her coffee. She looked away.

"You're alone here," he said. His K'iché stank, but it would carry a conversation. "I understand. Do not worry. I will keep you safe."

She glanced at him again, the firelight reflected in those gorgeous dark eyes. He'd gotten a response. Good. He wouldn't push it. Arthur Miller didn't nail Marilyn Monroe on the first date.

He looked at the others. They were getting louder, guffawing over stupid jokes, knocking back drink after drink.

Except Tennyson. Tennyson stared at him.

Stansfield raised his cup, grinned, and winked.

Tennyson's face darkened.

Oh, screw you, Stansfield thought.

Chapter 17

Five Days to Solstice

Grant tugged the sleeves of his wetsuit, adjusted his regulator, snugged his mask tight, and stepped off the rope ladder into the *cenote*. The morning was heating up, and the water embraced him with a welcome chill.

The water glimmered like clear glass to the bottom thirty feet below. Riga's son must be a heck of a swimmer to have reached the bottom, plucked treasure, and returned to the surface. That would be a feat worthy of any good adult swimmer, much less a kid. A feat almost too worthy. Chiam probably made up the whole story.

He blew into his BCD, floating himself comfortably on the surface, and pulled his fins on. Tennyson lowered himself off the ladder and into the water and eased alongside. Grant gave him an okay and they headed to the bottom.

Dark, deep shelves of rock jutted from the wall of the *cenote*, lined with black growth and swaying, clinging grasses. Small silver fish, curious and unafraid, darted about. Hidden somewhere in those dark crevices and projections, artesian pressures moved the water through limestone caves.

Coarse sand covered the bottom. Grant eased his fingers into the sand and sank his hands up to his wrist. The digging promised to be nice and easy.

He motioned Tennyson to be still, and removed a tiny plastic vial from his BCD pocket, popped off the cap, and squeezed red dye out. The cloud formed in the water, hung there, and drifted toward the southeast wall. The dye disappeared into the wall, marking the point at which the water flowed out from the sink. They moved closer, and Grant switched on his flashlight, illuminating a crevice, six feet wide and a foot high.

He returned to the surface. The others had gathered about the rim, watching expectantly. "Well?" asked Stansfield.

"It's gorgeous."

"Spare us the travelogue. Did you see any artifacts?"

"Nope. There's water movement and a thick bottom of sand. Heavy objects would have settled and been covered." Grant stretched his arms and shook them. "Brr! Cold down here. Bracing. How's it up there, Dr. Anderssen? A tad on the warm side?"

Elisa flipped him a middle finger.

Watts lowered a net holding two cameras into the pool. Grant corralled them, gave one last, luxuriant stretch for his sweating audience, and returned to the bottom.

He snapped a series of overlapping digital shots for a full 360-degree composite stitch at several levels, using Tennyson in a couple of shots for scale. He returned to the net and withdrew the second camera, a laser scanner. He anchored it on a tripod in the sand in the center of the *cenote* and opened a small keypad and tapped in instructions. Green digits blinked onto an LED screen.

Grant followed Tennyson to the ladder and climbed out of the pool behind him.

"Digital survey is up and running," he said. "We should have images in an hour." He slid out of his tank and shook his mask and regulator free of water. "Beautiful spring here. I think I'll build some condos on it."

* * *

Watts wiped his laptop screen with his sleeve. "Glare is the enemy of genius," he grumbled. "Gene, you've got a big ass. Manufacture some shade for me."

Tennyson laughed, and shifted to block the sun.

"Better. We're getting a point cloud image from the laser. A full three-sixty, top to bottom." Watts tapped on the keyboard. "And here it comes."

Red points, thousands of them, assembled on the screen. "Now we color the points for depth and angle." He tapped on the keyboard and the points divided into luminous reds, greens, and yellows, in three-dimensional relief.

They were seeing the interior of the *cenote* now. Watts gave it a slow, panoramic turn. Deeply shelved walls leapt out in precise, clear relief, the nearer surfaces yellow, graduating to reds and dark greens in the deeper recesses.

"Take us into this one," Grant said, pointing. The image zoomed close, revealing a cave that seemed to have no end. "There's your underground river."

"Rivers have places to go," Tennyson said. "Bill, the satellites, if you will."

Watts pulled up the infrared aerial and zoomed into a frame with the *cenote* at its center.

"The outflow is in the southeast wall," Grant said. "Pan southeast."

Watts clicked and dragged the frame southeast. A faint, dark line snaked across the lower right of the screen, clear against the bright pinks and reds of the foliage.

"That's it," Grant said. "The river surfaces four miles southeast and forms a tributary of Rio Azul."

"All right," Tennyson said. "We've got five days of science before we deal for Robert's life. Remember, observation only, digital photos only. No written reports and no objects are to be brought up. We don't want to give the looters one damned thing to steal from us."

Tennyson and Grant returned to the bottom. They fanned the bottom, whisking the top layers aside. After fifteen minutes, Grant tapped Tennyson on the shoulder, unclipped a wire mesh scoop from his vest, and worked it into the sand eight inches deep. He pulled it slowly back to the surface, working it side-to-side, sifting. It came up empty. The third try revealed a red potsherd as the sand slipped through the mesh. He photographed it, measured it, and set it back on the bottom, brushing a light layer of sand onto it. Tennyson gave him an okay, and began digging with his own sieve.

Within a half-hour, six more artifacts—three potsherds, a bone fishhook, a spear point, and a small jade bead—were uncovered, photographed, and replaced. Tennyson checked his pressure gauge, signaled that he had 500 psi remaining, and pointed his thumb toward the surface.

* * *

Watts copied the photos onto a tiny stick drive and deleted them from the cameras. Looters would likely as not rob them of the cameras, but the stick could be hidden anywhere. Watts plugged it into his laptop and opened the file.

"The *cenote* is loaded," Grant said. "This was a busy place at one time."

Stansfield pointed at the image of the jade bead. "Classical Maya, circa 10th century. Even has a tiny glyph inscribed on it. Exquisite craftsmanship."

"It's a hell of a piece," Grant said. "But there's something about this place—an unexplored *cenote* in the heart of Maya country. *Cenotes*, even minor ones, are almost always littered with artifacts and bones. The site surrounding the sinkhole should also be rich in artifacts. Yet we've found nothing outside the sink, not even a fragment."

"Looters?" Elisa asked.

Grant shook his head. "You saw that looters' camp. Looters leave scars. Trenches, pits, cuts, fireplaces. There's no sign of that. This site was cleaned of objects intentionally."

"Why?"

"Someone didn't want attention drawn to it."

Chapter 18

Ah Puuc, the owl god, moved swiftly and soundlessly through absolute darkness, hands outstretched, his fingers tracing a path along the corridor wall, guided by memory, touch more valuable than eyesight. He stopped often to listen. The corridor sloped downward, and its dank, slippery surface felt good against his bare feet.

Ahead, a faint rectangle of light outlined the doorway he sought. He eased close and peered in. A massive man sat with his back to him, motionless in the light of a single oil lamp.

Ah Puuc considered turning and leaving, but the bat god was expecting him. He drew a deep breath and entered the chamber.

Zotz did not turn, but remained still. A brazier of coals burned aromatically, and a spilled goblet lay near his open palm. His eyelids fluttered and his lips formed silent words. Finally, the great figure shivered and roused, and turned slowly to face Ah Puuc.

"They are still with us," Zotz said in a low, distant voice, like wind through the caverns.

"Yes."

"That cannot be allowed."

"Can't it?"

Zotz shifted his massive frame, pulled back the hood that obscured his face, and shook his long, black hair loose. "Do not try me. Who leads them?"

"There appear to be two leaders. The death of their comrade did not turn them back."

"The slain one was not with this new band of thieves. They indeed are enemies, all after the same plunder. The slain one's friends will return to pursue this further."

"Perhaps they will kill each other."

"Perhaps. But if not..."

"What concerns you?"

"With the dreaming eye, I've seen a woman that can harm us. She is more lethal than the men."

"There are three women."

"Two do not concern me. Just the one."

"You would kill her?"

"When the time comes."

Ah Puuc fell into an uncomfortable silence. Zotz's luminous green eyes fixed on him, evaluating, burrowing into his soul.

"There is talk," Ah Puuc said finally. "Disturbing talk."

Zotz continued to watch him, his eyes implacable.

Ah Puuc felt his resolve weaken, but felt he had not yet been too forward. He would continue. For the moment. "Some feel that we have lost our way."

Zotz's eyes narrowed into slits.

The room seemed to fade, leaving only Ah Puuc and two malevolent slits of green.

"And you, Ah Puuc? Do you subscribe to sedition?"

Ah Puuc hesitated, transfixed. *Speak, fool,* he told himself. A misstep will be your last. He began to speak, and the words again faltered.

With terrifying speed, Zotz sprang into Ah Puuc, bowling him to the floor. Zotz's hands circled his throat and closed tightly, and drew his face close. Hot, foul breath washed over him. Zotz growled in his ear. "And *you*, Ah Puuc?"

Ah Puuc struggled to speak through the tightening grip on his throat. He shook his head, helpless in the powerful grip. The fingers tightened. Ah Puuc clutched Zotz's wrists, struggling to pry them free, but the grip only tightened. Zotz could crush his neck easily.

"You resist. That is disloyal, and disloyalty is treason. Would you die a traitor?"

Ah Puuc shook his head.

"Then trust in me and do not resist."

Ah Puuc ceased struggling. His vision blurred and darkened. He moved his lips to speak, but no sound escaped.

"What did you say?" Zotz asked. "You must speak louder."

Ah Puuc mouthed soundless words again.

"Are you loyal?"

The grip slackened, and Ah Puuc gulped air. "Yes," he gasped. "My lot is with you."

Zotz's eyes held his, while hands like talons gripped his throat. He could not look away from those eyes.

"That is good," Zotz said. He lifted Ah Puuc by the neck and hurled him across the room. Ah Puuc slammed into the opposite wall and sank to the floor, clutching his throat, gasping for breath.

Zotz returned to his seat and sat with his back to Ah Puuc. "Get out of here."

Ah Puuc staggered to his feet. Hatred welled up inside, but fear pushed it down. Hatred would get him killed. Fear would keep him alive, perhaps long enough to see his plan through.

Chapter 19

Riga sat apart at dinner again that night, watching the Americans laugh and joke. She studied each carefully. They seemed to accept her, but that was all. They looked through her, thinking her an idiot. Perhaps for good reason; thus far, she had done nothing of any value. They found the site without her help, studied it without her help, and all she could do was stay out of their way. Why then bring her along? Because the law required a Guatemalan on the expedition. She'd discovered that much.

She was being used, just as she'd always been used.

Pacal had warned her.

She missed Chiam. She had not been apart from him in his life and had sworn that she never would be. Yet here she was in the forest with cold, uncaring strangers. He would be asleep in bed this very moment, and she should be stroking his hair. A sob welled in her throat and she wiped away a tear, hiding it from the others.

She caught Tennyson looking at her. He quickly looked away. Why? She was pretty. She knew that. Men had always desired her. Tennyson desired her but lacked the will to reveal it.

Stansfield was also looking at her. He smiled, crossed the camp, and sat beside her.

He might find her contemptible, but he at least masked it, and sometimes that was all one could hope for.

He spoke, softly and reassuringly, in K'iché. "I should like to sit with you, Riga."

She stared into the fire.

"You are better company than my colleagues. You have a depth they lack. They care little for you, and I think you know it. But I care. I'll take care of you on this trip. Do you understand?"

She glanced at him. He was young, too young, but his eyes seemed sincere.

"You are afraid," he continued. "You don't need to be. Not of me anyway." He motioned to the others with a sweep of his hand. "Although you would be wise to avoid them."

His hand lightly touched her arm. She remained still. He glanced at the others, then back to her. "You are a beautiful woman. I will sit with you and keep you company."

She gave the slightest of nods, and stared into the fire.

Stansfield caressed her arm. "When the others have gone to sleep," he whispered, "I shall be awake, and my tent open."

Tennyson watched, his face creased in a frown. This time he did not look away.

Stansfield removed his hand from her arm. "Tennyson disapproves. He despises the Maya. I must go now to avoid fighting within the party. Remember, Riga Itzep, my tent is open tonight."

Stansfield again touched her arm. His hand brushed against her breast. "Tonight," he whispered.

Riga stared into the fire.

Was it true? Did they hate her? She felt alone, but that was the normal feeling of life. She had always been apart, even among her own people.

No, not always. She had once been happy, as a child.

Unhappiness had been born of evil times.

The memories lurked just below her thoughts, and the nightmares returned when things were still and quiet. She avoided quiet for that reason. Activity was sanity.

Now, just as last night, just as every night, the horror flooded over her again. There was no escape, except perhaps someday in death.

She remembered gunfire in the night. She remembered Father, going to investigate. Father, beaten and dragged from the village by men. Mother, crying, urging her to run, to hide, her not knowing what to do or where to run. The flashes of light and sound.

The dead, everywhere.

The gaunt man, the officer, grinning, pointing his revolver at mother, approaching.

Mother, screaming and screaming and screaming.

Mother, dragged into the street, thrown to the ground.

Her mother.

The men holding her.

The gaunt man, taking Riga.

The men, laughing.

The men.

She shook her head clear of the images and looked at the others in the firelight. They retired to their tents, one by one. Tennyson glanced at her and went to his own tent. He hesitated, then entered. Only Carson Grant remained by the fire, keeping watch.

She went inside her own tent and lay down. She lay awake, listening.

At last she rose, looked out at the quiet camp, unzipped the tent fly, and padded across to Stansfield's tent. She paused, reached out to touch the fly. It was open and she went inside. He was sitting up, bare-chested, smiling. He held his hand out for her.

Afterward, she lay quietly beside him. His lovemaking had been rushed and greedy, and now he lay breathing heavily. The closeness had been good. She needed closeness. He lay silent, then said, "You'd better go now. Tennyson runs an expedition like a goddamn kindergarten."

She returned to her tent and lay with her back to the opening. The jungle was alive with the hushed sounds of the night.

She closed her eyes and the nightmares returned.

She began to cry.

The men.

Chapter 20

Four Days to Solstice

Grant checked the pressure gauge. They'd get a good fifty, sixty minutes diving in. Where the hell was Tennyson?

Fins and mask dropped to the ground next to him.

Elisa, in swimsuit and T-shirt, lugged dive gear to the rim. "You didn't expect to keep the fun to yourself, did you?"

"That's Gene's stuff."

"I talked him into letting me take the morning dive. It's a horrible fit, all of it, but I can make it work."

"Don't spring surprises on an expedition, Dr. Anderssen. It's impolite."

"I've dived fjords by the midnight sun in the Arctic Circle. A little dip in a clear spring in Central America is not to worry over."

"Are you a certified cave diver?"

"It's a *cenote*, not a cave."

"Then you're staying behind."

"You can teach me."

"Not in five minutes. The science part of this expedition's on a short-assed fuse and I'm not wasting time teaching you to cave dive."

"You're hostile to a woman diving?"

"Stop it. You're not trained for caves and I'm not in the mood for body retrieval. I need to buddy up, and guess what, you're not it. Simple as that."

Elisa's face darkened. "I've okayed it with Gene."

"But not with me." Grant slipped into the water. He wasn't going to give her the chance to extend the debate.

Tennyson approached. "The idea didn't take, I presume?"

"Get into your gear, Gene." He pulled his mask down, squeezed it against his face, and took the mouthpiece in.

Tennyson said, "Wait for me, damn it."

But Grant had already dipped under. Gene could catch the hell up.

He waited at the mouth of the cavern, sizing it up. It opened into a narrow crevice, tight, but passable. Grant had anchored a line to a tree at the rim and now linked it to a spool of thin cable at his waist and released a catch, allowing the line to play out. Tennyson pulled up alongside. Grant glared at him, but signaled with an okay, switched on his headlight, and wriggled into the opening.

Ten yards in, the cave twisted downward to the left. The current was negotiable, handholds plentiful, and he pulled himself along. He stopped to check for side caverns—the slayer of divers—every few feet.

The slot opened into a room ten feet high, twenty wide, and fifty long. The current eased. Sand and silt carpeted the bottom. The walls and ceiling were barren, white stone, unlike the blacks and greens of the *cenote* walls. Their exhaled air bubbled in trains to the ceiling, collecting there in shivering pools of quicksilver.

Tennyson came alongside. Grant unhooked the camera, snapped a series of shots. He unclipped a plastic slate and grease pencil from his belt, and sketched the room. Tennyson swam the perimeter, dragging a tape measure, signaling the numbers.

Absolute darkness had reigned in this cavern until pierced by the beam of their lamps, and the effect was one of purity and solitude. Grant noted the utilitarian character of his sketch. Simple lines and notes. Factual, economical, and inarticulate. He wished he possessed for one moment the eye and hand of an artist.

He continued upstream another fifty feet, and the cave angled upward. At ninety, he paused and checked on Tennyson, who gave him an okay. Grant made a quick calculation. If the upward trend of the cave continued, it could only mean one thing.

A hundred feet later, his hunch confirmed, he broke surface in an air-filled cavern. He pushed his mask up and removed his mouthpiece. The cool, clean air felt good in his lungs.

The room was thirty feet across and fifteen high. White stalactites hung from the ceiling, their shadows dancing in the light. Water dripped, *plinking* softly into the pool. The far end of the room disappeared in blackness.

Tennyson surfaced and pulled up his mask. "Wow. This is a hell of a room."

"Air's fresh, too. Must be surface vents somewhere." He swam toward the opposite end. The bottom inclined and the water grew shallower until he stood knee deep. He snapped a series of photos. "There's no end and it widens ahead of us. I hereby dub it Lord Tennyson Hall. Let's go toast your exploits with beer."

They pulled their masks back on, took in their mouthpieces, ducked under, and let the current carry them back into the submerged caves. In the last room, a familiar shape and color caught Grant's attention, something half-buried in the silt.

It was a human skull.

* * *

"He or she didn't swim upstream from the Well of Spirits," Grant said, tapping the skull's photo on the laptop monitor. "That's impossible without dive gear. This skull was swept downstream. Alive or dead, he or she entered this river somewhere else."

"Could be a diver that got trapped," Stansfield said.

"There's no diving gear to be found, either in the cave or the sinkhole. A scuba tank would be a cinch to spot."

"And the skull is ancient," Tennyson said. "The coloration is typical of bone immersed in spring water for centuries." He turned to Elisa. "You're being quiet."

"I'm sure Dr. Grant knows what he's talking about."

Grant glanced at her. *Great, back to Dr. Grant again.* He handed his sketchpad to Watts. "Bill, this sketch is rough but the dimensions are good. Plug them into your graphic of the *cenote*."

"You got it." Watts pulled up the 3D image and zoomed in on the inlet they'd entered. He typed in the coordinates and dimensions and each point appeared in succession from the *cenote*. At the last one, he said, "Now we fill in gaps." He typed in another command and a wireframe model of the cavern appeared.

"The direction tends northwest," Tennyson said. "Bill, drag some aerials that direction. Look for another *cenote* or a surface river. That skull had to enter somewhere."

Watts turned to a second laptop and paged through the aerials of the region, clicking and dragging. After scrolling some twenty miles, Grant interrupted. "That's not working. What else you got? Infrareds?"

"Yeah, and some space-radars." Watts opened a series of files and found an image of orange, red, green, and blue. "You can see a pinprick of blue right here. That's our *cenote*. Cool, huh? Infrared couldn't care less that tree canopy hides it. It marks the *cenote* by the heat differential between water and foliage." Watts dragged images through twenty miles worth of terrain. "Sorry, not finding anything."

"Stop looking for water," Stansfield said. "Look for a cave or a hole in the ground. Refine your temperature gradient."

Grant hated it, but that idea made sense. "How fine a point can you put on these images?"

"I've got it to a tenth of a degree."

"Can you go smaller?"

"Hell yeah, this is NASA's latest stuff." He toggled open a menu, found a gradient chart. "I'll be damned. It's good to a hundredth of a degree." He selected the smallest temperature differential.

The detail of the image snapped into photographic precision. "Wow," Watts mumbled. He dragged the infrareds, starting again at the *cenote*. At six miles northwest, he paused and zoomed in. There, nestled in the fluorescent greens and oranges, a faint yellow square appeared.

"A ruin," Tennyson said. "Big one too. A foundation or something buried under the canopy. We can make it in three hours."

"This is a rescue," Grant said. "Not an exploration. We can't go splitting up."

"The solstice is still four days out. We can check this out tomorrow and be back in the early afternoon."

"No. Hell, no. Those guys could be anywhere in this jungle. They could be at that ruin and digging it up even now."

"I'm going, like it or not."

Grant stared at him. "Fine. Bill, get the sat phone up."

"Okay, but we'll need a bit of luck. Tree canopy, you know." He opened a leather satchel, withdrew a small phone and a pad the size of a book. He plugged a cable into the phone, connected it to the pad, and unfolded two wings of the pad. He moved it to the edge of the *cenote* and fiddled with the panels. "See if there's any reception here."

A moment later, they had a signal. Grant snatched the phone from him and punched in a long number.

"Ginnie Pavlic, Kennedy Space Center, please."

A voice came over the speaker. "Dr. Pavlic, RS lab."

"Ginnie, it's me, Grant. Listen, I need that favor. You remember what we talked about?"

There was a pause. "The less said, the better. Just give me the points."

He recited the coordinates. The sound of rapid typing came over the speaker.

"I'm not on speaker phone, am I?"

"Course not."

"Funny, it has that speaker phone sound." A few more keyboard taps. "Okay, done. The transmission will start in a few seconds. Grant? Bring Lindsay back, okay?"

"Thanks a million, sweetheart."

Watts tapped in a command. An aerial photo filled the screen.

"This shot is the closest thing there is to a real-time image of that ruin." Grant said. "Zoom in and search the area."

Watts set the cursor and expanded the image. "Unbelievable resolution. Like it was shot from two hundred feet, not two hundred miles."

"Well, technically, this is not quite declassified yet. And, yeah, you could do fifty years in the federal pen for stealing these. So stop diddling; it can't be copied, and we get only thirty seconds of photo and thirty of infrared, and then a NASA encryption scrambles it. Take a good close look."

"There's nothing there."

"Good! No looters, no camp, no nothing. Here comes the infrared."

The image blinked into green, blue, and orange.

"Still nothing. If someone was even sleeping under a bush, we'd see a heat signature. Pull back to the larger area."

Watts toggled the image, revealing several square miles.

"See? No one within miles. Here comes the second site, the looters' camp we found southwest of here."

The photo image showed a pristine site.

"The camp is gone," Grant said.

"They've pulled up stakes and left. Show us the larger region, up to and including this *cenote*. If they're headed our way, we'll see them."

Watts expanded the image region.

"Clean! They've split and gone," Tennyson said. "There's no danger in any direction, and we've got four days until the rendezvous. We can do this."

Grant shook his head. "Gene, you're getting way off-task here."

"So be it. I'm taking a look tomorrow, by myself if need be."

"I'll go with you," Stansfield said.

Tennyson looked at him, surprise written on his face. "Frank, I appreciate that. Glad someone's still got balls." He looked at Grant. "What did you get into science for? To *not* discover things?"

"Shut up," Grant said. "I'll go. Frank will come with me. Neither of you has the bushwhacking experience to get there and back quickly. We have one more dive in the morning, Frank, so be ready immediately after." He turned away. "But damn both of you for putting us in more danger than we're already in."

* * *

Grant sat up, the rifle cradled across his lap, and stirred the smoldering coals with a stick. He watched as the tip briefly caught and burned. He looked at his watch—11 p.m. He was the last one still up, and had two more hours on watch. Quiet hung over the camp. He poured whiskey into a paper cup and withdrew a Tampa cigar from his breast pocket. Lighting it with the burning stick, he tossed the stick back into the fire, and puffed the cigar to life.

He listened to the forest as the whiskey warmed him, and settled deeper into his camp chair.

This expedition was screwed.

Tensions festered, and he was as guilty as anyone. Some were to be expected; expeditions were damned uncomfortable and always managed to stoke egos and resentments.

Stansfield was a jerk, as usual. The kid had not grown up during Grant's hiatus. He had, in fact, become more aggressive and self-absorbed, if that was possible. He got his little barbs in at Grant. Fine. He'd always done that. The thing was though that Stansfield was now working Gene.

But that wouldn't work, because Stansfield was up to something with Riga.

The fly on Riga's tent flapped open and she emerged. She looked at him for a moment, then crossed the camp and entered Stansfield's tent. A rustle caught Grant's ear and he turned to see Tennyson's tent door zippering shut.

Grant puffed his cigar. It really was none of his business. He was not the morals guardian.

But this had gone beyond a mere harmless dalliance. Riga hid something from them, a deep pain maybe. She'd not spoken a word since joining, but that was by choice, Grant thought, rather than inability. She chose silence, and whatever was haunting her, that little shit Stansfield used it to get laid.

Grant threw the last of his whiskey into the coals, kicking ash and smoke into the air with a hiss. He doused the remainder with water and sand, and settled deeper into his camp chair.

He turned to study the dark jungle. Something seemed wrong. Maybe the mystery of raw nature wore on him, but the forest felt sinister tonight.

His skin prickled as though the forest was watching. He scanned the quiet darkness, alert for movement and sound, palmed open the bolt on his rifle, making sure he had a round chambered and ready, and slapped the bolt shut again.

The night forest enveloped him, silent and still.

He shook his head and stretched his legs, feeling his trick knee pop. It would be a long time until Bill relieved his watch, and he needed to push back the dread that had crept into his bones. There was nothing stirring out there, nothing afoot.

Nothing watching them.

Chapter 21

José Cabrillo tapped his cigarette, dislodging a trickle of ash, and glanced at the clock on the wall of the Santa Elena hotel. Nearly midnight, and Colonel Santiago was an hour late, a measure calculated to make him squirm.

At last, the door swung open and Hector Santiago strode in, a crumpled paper bag in one hand. Cabrillo greeted him, but Santiago raised an objecting hand and went to the lobby desk. He scribbled a note and spoke softly. The clerk motioned to a door at the end of the lobby. Santiago headed for it, and Cabrillo followed.

The room was spare, a small round table and wooden chairs the only furnishings. Santiago shut the door behind him, dragged a chair noisily from the table, and took a seat. He motioned Cabrillo to sit. He placed the paper bag upon the table, and withdrew a bottle of whiskey and two shot glasses. "It will not do, José," he said, "that one of my men, my best cutter, is dead."

"Colonel, I do not believe the gringos killed Manuel."

"You have seen him?"

"I have not."

"You have heard from him?"

"No."

Santiago pushed a shot glass across the table to Cabrillo, and unscrewed the cap off the whiskey. He filled his own glass, ignored Cabrillo's. "How is it you have decided he lives?"

"That is not what I said. He has been kidnapped or killed, but not by the Americans."

"You exasperate me, Cabrillo." Santiago's voice fell to a growl. "Perhaps he went drinking and whoring. Like you."

Cabrillo squirmed. "Manuel is a better man than I."

"At last we agree. Convince me he is not dead."

"Colonel Santiago, Manuel was a cautious man. He would never leave a site unattended. Nor would he be surprised by noisy gringos blundering through the forest."

"There are but a handful of explanations for Manuel's disappearance. He was killed by rivals, by thieves, by the Mexicans, by the police, by the gringos, or by you. Trust me; looters, thieves, and police, often indistinguishable, are well aware of my projects and stay far away. That leaves the Americans, the Mexicans, and you. I shall excuse you as a suspect. Do you object?"

Cabrillo slowly shook his head.

"Of the remainder, I fear only the Mexican drug gangs. Listen to me. Manuel was alone. Why did you leave? You presume to change my rules?"

The Colonel lit a cigarette, pinched the match out. He took a candle from his pocket and held the wick to his cigarette, and puffed. The wick lit and he melted a few drops of wax onto the table and pressed the candle into it. For a minute, he sat and smoked in silence, the faint red glow of his cigarette reflecting in his eyes as he regarded Cabrillo. He leaned back in his chair, took a long drag from his cigarette, and blew a cloud of smoke that hung about his head like a halo. He got up, went to the window, pulled the blinds shut, and switched off the lights, his silhouette outlined dark against the wall. "Cabrillo," he finally said, "These are trying times. I need your allegiance. Your loyalty."

"You have it, Colonel."

"Loyalty is proved by obedience."

"Si."

"Are you an obedient man, my friend?"

"Si."

Santiago reached down to his calf, pulled up his pants leg, and withdrew a great hunting knife. It glinted in the candlelight. "I am, of course, forbidden to be here in Guatemala, my homeland. Although I live in exile, I remain a patriot. I have done many times what Guatemala asked of me, often without being asked.

Do you know my reputation, Cabrillo?"

"You are a man of influence in the trade, Colonel."

Santiago chuckled. "No, no. Before I left Guatemala. During the last unrest. The Maya problem."

"You were a great patriot, Colonel."

"The time required men of consequence. Guatemala could not afford weak men. Alas, now it has many. Some favor appeasing the Indians. So be it. I did my part and I washed my hands of it. All that remains is ensuring that I take my reward in exile in any way possible. Are you weak, Cabrillo?"

Cabrillo shook his head.

"Place your left hand upon the table with your fingers outstretched."

Santiago's eyes grew cold, like a snake's, and glittered in the flickering light.

"You hesitate, Cabrillo. You must learn to trust."

Cabrillo felt blood rush from his face and sweat beading on his forehead. Fear welled up inside, making it difficult to speak. "Colonel..."

"Your hand, if you please."

Cabrillo glanced at the door nearby. He would knock the table onto Santiago and bolt from the room, alert the police that Santiago was in Guatemala. He would be done with Santiago for good.

No. Santiago had earned his frightful reputation. Cabrillo had seen it with his own eyes. The man was thirty years his senior, but quick and powerful as a jaguar, his slightness of frame belying his power.

Still, perhaps he could overpower him.

No.

Looters everywhere whispered that Santiago belonged to a brotherhood forged during the wars. He would possess every scrap of information that existed about Cabrillo. He would find Cabrillo's mother and father and sisters. And if Santiago were killed, his brothers-in-arms would react swiftly and surely. They guarded their pasts with extreme prejudice. That was the key to their survival.

There was no way out.

Cabrillo placed his trembling hand on the table.

"There, that is good, is it not?" Santiago asked. "Trust and loyalty are such fine qualities in a man." Santiago placed the knife two hand lengths away from Cabrillo's outstretched fingers and laced his own fingers together an equal distance from the knife.

Cabrillo looked at the knife, so agonizingly close to his hand.

"You tremble, José. Are you nervous? You have nothing to be nervous about."

"I am anxious to get back to my work in the jungle."

"Ah, a conscientious worker. Dedication is also a fine quality." Santiago tapped his fingers on the table softly, slowly, in rhythm, three slow taps followed by four rapid taps, repeated again and again. Cabrillo knew that beat.

Tap, tap, tap, tap-tap-tap-tap.

The slow, halting beat of a tango.

"Now then," Santiago said. "Why did you leave?"

Tap, tap, tap, tap-tap-tap-tap.

Cabrillo opened his mouth to speak, stopped. Any reason for leaving the site would be a crime. "We needed provisions, Colonel."

"Provisions."

"The camp was running low."

Santiago's hand shot out, snatched up the knife, and stabbed the tabletop between the outstretched fourth and fifth fingers of Cabrillo's hand. Cabrillo winced and his heart leapt, but his hand remained in place. He blinked, surprised to see his fingers still attached.

"My camps are well provisioned. Perhaps you would like to rephrase. Why did you leave?"

Cabrillo swallowed, his eyes fixed upon the knife. "Garcia was afraid."

"Afraid?" Santiago looked puzzled. "Afraid of what?"

Cabrillo looked from Santiago's eyes to the knife and back to Santiago. "Garcia is superstitious, filled with silly thoughts. The Indians say that region is haunted."

Santiago snorted. "You fled because of *Indian* ghost stories?"

"It was more than the stories. The place felt wrong, as if someone or something watched us. In the night, there were stealthy noises about."

"Of course there were noises, you fool. It is the forest. It is alive. You have spent many nights in the forest, yet only now you grow afraid, like a rabbit."

"Something unnatural lives in that forest."

"And you, Cabrillo," Santiago continued. "Are you also scared by silly stories?"

Cabrillo wanted to lie. If ever there was a good time to lie, this would be it.

"Yes. I was very afraid."

"You were afraid, yet you left your brother alone."

"Manuel did not fear the forest, but I am ashamed of my cowardice."

Santiago wrenched the knife free from the table and hefted it. "That is good and I shall not cut your finger off."

Cabrillo expelled a breath of relief. *"Gracias."*

"You shall cut your own finger off."

His blood ran cold.

"Come now," Santiago said gently. "You shall retain ninety percent of your fingers. That is not so bad. Many I have known have willingly cut their own fingers off, including many women. Even a few Indian whores. Are you less than a whore? It is very odd to see someone cut off a finger. Have you ever seen such a thing? It is painful, to be sure, but the pain passes in time. Pain can overwhelm if one lets it, but it can be controlled. One hears such a great fuss over pain. What good does fuss do? It does not make the pain any less. All it does is annoy others."

Santiago slid the knife slowly across the table. "Of course, one might refuse to cut one's finger off. One might try to take the knife and kill the person suggesting such a thing. One might, but I would not recommend it. There are worse things to lose than one's finger, no? One could go through life as somewhat less than a man, no?"

Cabrillo trembled, transfixed by the knife. It grew in his mind, filling his vision. His hand remained in place on the table, palm down, fingers outstretched.

"I like you, José," Santiago said. "You may keep most of your finger. Lose only that portion from the last knuckle. Here's a hint; if you split the knuckle joint, you might avoid bone. Of course, that requires care and skillful knife work. Some prefer to chop the finger off with a single hard stroke rather than working through the flesh slowly. It is a matter of taste."

Cabrillo picked up the knife. The sheer weight of the weapon frightened him.

Santiago watched closely. "I suppose you could turn that knife upon me."

He considered this. He could do it. In the blink of an eye, he could be at Santiago's throat. Santiago would beg for mercy.

"Give it a try," Santiago said.

Cabrillo swallowed. He placed the glinting knife against the last knuckle of his little finger. The weight of the blade alone cut into his skin, drawing a thin line of red. He withdrew the knife and examined the cut. A drop of blood welled from it and splattered on the table.

Santiago's eyes glinted with amusement.

"Colonel," Cabrillo said, "might I be permitted a glass of whiskey?"

"Of course. Afterwards."

Cabrillo gritted his teeth. *I will do this thing, and one excellent day I will kill you in your sleep.* He placed the great knife against the bleeding knuckle again, closed his eyes, held his breath, and bore down with all his strength.

The knife cut through to the table, and pain exploded in his finger. Cabrillo dropped the knife and rocked back in his chair. He crashed to the floor, cradling his bleeding hand against his chest, his mind clouding.

He grew dimly aware of Santiago chuckling.

"Outstanding, José," Santiago said. "You have proved your loyalty."

I will kill you in your sleep.

Pain washed over him like a wave. Darkness gathered in swarming black flecks and he struggled to maintain consciousness. Slipping out of his thoughts would bring welcome relief, but he could not show weakness in Santiago's eyes. Anything but weakness.

Santiago poured a shot glass of whiskey. He sniffed it and held the glass to the light. "Excellent color." He drank it down in a single gulp. He poured another shot and pushed it across the table to Cabrillo. "I am a man of my word. Drink to courage, José, and be proud." He took a roll of gauze from his breast pocket and tossed it upon the table. "Bandage that well. We go into the forest in the morning. We can't risk infection."

He turned and left the room, taking the bottle with him.

Cabrillo clutched the shot of whiskey and gulped it down. He unfolded his hand and looked at his slaughtered finger. Blood spattered to the floor. He snatched up the gauze, tore off a long strip, and wrapped it tightly around the finger. The bandage quickly stained red, and he raised the bleeding hand above his head.

The severed tip of his finger lay the table. He picked it up gingerly and wrapped it in gauze also. Perhaps a doctor could reattach it.

No. He could not show weakness. He threw the fingertip against the wall.

He had but one thought now to sustain him.

I will kill you in your sleep.

Chapter 22

Three Days to Solstice

Pacal scraped the skillet clean and set it aside. He and Chiam had enjoyed a fine meal of fish and now he stretched out, full and satisfied.

The boy sat by the kerosene lantern in the corner, reading his favorite book of dinosaurs, his lips moving. He loved dinosaurs. It was not a primer for children, but a book for adults. Pacal marveled at the boy's intelligence. At ten, Chiam consumed the harder books, and it was becoming difficult to find books that challenged him.

The boy flipped pages ahead to a picture of a dinosaur clinging to the back of another, its teeth sunk into the neck of its victim, while two more circled, looking for an opening. "I love allosaurs," Chiam said, grinning. "Not as big as tyrannosaurs, but faster. These are attacking an apatosaur."

"Read to me."

The boy nodded and began. "'Allosaurs were the top North American predator of the Jurassic age. They are believed to...'"

"No. Not in Spanish, in K'iché."

The boy looked at him. "But it is written in Spanish."

"I know."

Chiam nodded and scanned the page. He began again, in Mayan.

Pacal laced his fingers together behind his head, listening. The language would survive another generation if he had anything to do with it.

After a few paragraphs, Chiam jumped ahead a few chapters, to a page titled, "K-T Extinction: End of the Dinosaurs." An illustration of a fireball smashing into the earth told the story. "This is how they died, uncle. A meteorite killed them all."

"This meteorite, did you know it fell near here?"

"Really?" asked the boy, wide-eyed.

"Yes. On the edge of Yucatán, five hundred kilometers from our little village. Scientists found and mapped the crater. Chicxulub, they call it."

"How do they know it was the one?"

"They have determined the age of the crater. The rocks were shattered sixty-five million years ago, when the dinosaurs died."

"Uncle, that is wonderful! It is not in my book."

Pacal opened the front cover and found the copyright date. "Your book is too old. We must find you newer books. Come now, it's time for bed."

"Will you read with me again tomorrow?"

"Yes, tomorrow."

He tucked Chiam in, patted his head, and returned to the other room. He thumbed through the book of dinosaurs. Perhaps he could sell fish to tourists to pay for newer books. He set the book aside and closed his eyes, needing the quiet to think.

The Americans had blundered into a looters' camp. Now, today, he'd heard that looters had slipped out of Santa Elena, accompanied by a mysterious man with a wicked past, headed for their abandoned camp, where a murder may have been committed. That leech, Hidalgo, warned Pacal to stay out of it. He would stay out of it—for now—but because his sister had requested it, not because of Hidalgo.

Trouble brewed. He would patrol deeper into the forest tomorrow. Near to where Riga had gone with the Americans.

He picked up the book on dinosaurs and flipped through it, his eyes glassy with weariness. He should make ready for bed but was in no hurry to fall asleep. His nights had grown restless of late, disturbed by dreams of deep, dark places and ghosts not quite seen.

Chapter 23

Stansfield refused to hurry, picking his path carefully, wondering what had possessed him to volunteer for this nonsensical side trip. He'd stepped on a fer-de-lance an hour before and nearly pissed his pants jumping off the startled snake. The encounter still shook him; a snake bite like that would sink him in deep shit by now. Grant, on the other hand, bulled ahead, thrashing with his machete, bushwhacking with abandon, his teeth clenched. Hadn't spoken two words since they'd left.

At last, Grant stopped and looked about, frowning.

Stansfield came alongside, wiped his face. "What?"

Grant twisted his GPS finder this way and that. "We should be right on top of the ruin."

Stansfield looked around. He stabbed his machete into the dirt, gulped down a long drink of water, and kicked at the ground, scattering bits of decayed vegetation. "Nothing here."

"Something's here. Satellites don't lie." Grant withdrew a short metal rod the size of a pen from his pocket and telescoped it into a thin shaft four feet long. He plunged the rod into the soft, yielding ground to its full depth, withdrew it, moved a couple of feet, and plunged it again. He repeated this twice more and finally met resistance. "Got it," he said.

He probed in four directions from that point, and the outline of a wall five feet thick, three feet underground, began to emerge. With each strike of the wall, he marked a point with fluorescent orange spray paint. "Get some photos, Frank. And start an excavation right here." He kicked the orange mark with his foot.

"I'm going to mark the perimeter of this thing."

"Taking the easy job, eh?"

Grant ignored him and moved off, probing the ground and marking with spray paint.

Stansfield yanked open his pack and withdrew his camera. Grant was going to play mind games now, was he?

He snapped a panoramic series of shots, and returned to the spot Grant had indicated. He sighed and began to dig.

He struck stone at three feet and worked toward the outer edge, then excavated two feet deeper. He climbed out of the hole and followed the stone with the probe. An artifice protruded perpendicularly underground from the edge. He measured it, and proceeded along the line Grant had marked, finding a similar buried structure protruding from the line some thirty feet away. He probed further, finding the buried stonework to be continuous.

Within the hour, Grant had marked a gigantic square on the forest floor, three-hundred-sixteen feet to a side.

Stansfield marked structures along the square and stepped back to study the layout, reconstructing the components in his mind. The puzzle took shape, and the intellectual challenge drove his misery away. He rejoined Grant, who had excavated five shallow pits at random within the square.

"There was a staircase on this side," Stansfield said, "and the outer slope of what's left of the wall is steep, sixty-five degrees. Obviously, there was a pyramid."

Grant nodded. "The top layer of earth within the square is natural. Below, it was backfilled with soil and a lot of rubble thrown in. Standard Mayan construction. Let's shoot some corner GPS and see if Bill can work his magic."

Twenty minutes later, Grant raised Watts on the radio and uplinked a satellite, connecting his laptop. "Bill, we've got our site. Round up the team."

A minute later, Watts responded. "Fire away, Carson."

"Get ready to receive data. I want a wire-frame from it." Grant recited the GPS coordinates of the corners. The data downloaded and Watts reconstructed the horizontal layout and projected the sloping walls in three dimensions..

"We've got a floor plan and a good measurement of wall

angles. Steep son of a bitch. A good-sized terrace stood here at one time. It'd be nice to know the height."

"Hold on a sec," Watts said. "I'm opening the aerial infrared. See your location? The higher ground, indicated by lighter greens? On your screen to the west, maybe three hundred feet, is a shallow depression, roughly rectangular. Looks artificial. I suspect that's your borrow pit that supplied the fill for the terrace. We can calculate the volume of the pit, and from that the volume of the building. Find it and call back."

Grant looked at Stansfield, a small, thin smile on his face.

Stansfield groaned.

They beat through the brush to the depression, a soggy pit overgrown with trees. Stansfield probed the bottom with a stick. "Two feet deep."

"Ah, were it that easy. There's ten centuries of muck. We have to find the original bottom."

"Oh Christ."

"Think of it as a spa day." Grant unslung a camp shovel, sloshed into the muck, and began digging, whistling "New York, New York." Stansfield grumbled, snatched up the other shovel, and waded into the mud. He hated Sinatra.

Each shovel of mud brought an equal amount oozing into the hole. Stansfield's misery returned full bore. He could not imagine a human being filthier than he already was.

After a half-hour, Grant stopped digging. "Got it. We've reached undisturbed soil." He lowered a tape measure. "A hair over five feet."

They returned to the square and raised camp again. "Good call, Bill," Grant said. "It's artificial all right."

"Thought so," Watts said. "I'm doing the math. Five feet deep, twenty-one hundred feet long by eleven hundred wide. Okay, that's eleven and a half million cubic feet of dirt someone moved."

"If there was a small pyramid here," Grant said, "its construction would follow the standard Maya technique of compacted earth encased in limestone masonry. I'm guessing a flat-topped pyramid, thirty or forty feet high, probably built to keep an eye on *bajo* farming and engineering. Bill, project the volume within an imaginary pyramid with sides at sixty-five degrees."

The wire frame pyramid reappeared on the screen. A moment later, a series of dots began to fill the wire frame from the bottom up with a scale superimposed—each five feet indicated by a bar across the image.

"Okay," Watts said. "I've put a flat top on the peak of the fill, since pyramids were generally topped with terraces for temples. Looking good here. Ten feet. Fifteen. Twenty. Hey, you may be right, Grant. This sucker may top out near forty. Thirty-five. Forty. Fifty…"

"Look at this thing grow," Tennyson said. "Sixty feet. Seventy."

They fell silent. Stansfield shot a glance at Grant, who had a puzzled expression on his face. They had underestimated—vastly underestimated—the size of the vanished structure.

"We're at a hundred feet," Grant said. "What's Temple IV in Tikal, two hundred feet tall?"

"Two twelve," Tennyson said.

They watched the fill click to one twenty, one forty, one sixty.

"This can't be right," Grant said. "We've made a mistake."

"No," Stansfield said. "No mistake. You examined the soil matrix yourself. The material in the base of the terrace is identical to that in the pit. The earth from that pit isn't stockpiled anywhere, and it's the only fill source around."

The pyramid grew to one eighty, two hundred…

"Impossible," Tennyson said.

"Gene," Elisa said, "what's the tallest pre-Columbian structure in the Americas?"

"The Pyramid of the Sun in Teotihuacan near Mexico City. Two hundred thirty feet high."

The pyramid grew. Two twenty, two forty, two sixty. It stopped at two hundred and eighty-six feet.

Stansfield stared at the screen in disbelief.

"Throw in a Tikal-style temple on the upper terrace and this thing would have been over three-hundred feet tall," Grant said. "It would have been the highest pyramid ever built in this hemisphere. One of the highest in the world."

"No," Tennyson said. "The fill dirt must have been used elsewhere, in other structures."

"Gene, the satellite images don't show anything else in the area," Watts said. "Did you find more?"

"Just the buried wall."

"Excuse me." Stansfield recognized Linda's voice. He rolled his eyes. The woman annoyed him even when she was miles away.

"Yes, Linda?" Tennyson asked.

"Pyramids don't just disappear, do they?"

"Apparently this building was dismantled. Completely."

"But the stonework is unaccounted for," Grant said. "There should be an incredible number of dressed stone blocks somewhere."

"Buildings all over the world are built of recycled stonework," Tennyson said. "The Spaniards built cathedrals from blocks plundered from Meso-American temples, tearing down one set of buildings and gods to install another. The blocks of this structure had to be carted off to be used elsewhere, but on a different scale altogether. It defies logic."

"Unless the builders didn't want it found," Linda said.

"Oh please," Stansfield muttered. Linda was casting about again, trying to impress, a climber of the worst sort.

Still, she made some sense, in her ill-educated way.

Pyramids *didn't* just disappear.

* * *

Santiago tore his headphones off and slung them away. He paced about the small camp. He had to move. He thought best when moving, his nervous energy fueling his brain.

The damned gringos thought they were so smart. They thought they could get away with this thievery.

They were wrong.

Cabrillo sat apart, scraping the last of a plate of *chili rellenos*, stealing glances his way, cradling his bandaged, blood-stained hand in his lap. Garcia had drunk himself to sleep, an empty bottle of tequila by his side. His head bobbed and rolled against his chest, and he snored softly.

The Americans had lied from the start, and now the lies grew clearer. They were on the trail of the gringo that had disappeared, not out of concern, but out of greed. Lindsay had obviously found something of value, and had most likely died at the hands of looters.

If Lindsay had been killed by looters, they were rivals. There were no other kind, and so precautions would be in order. They would have a stake in this affair, but once they learned who they were dealing with, they would most likely slip out of the region as quietly as possible.

So. The Americans thought Vikings stumbled into Guatemala a thousand years ago. The idea was too fantastic to be true, but it was clear they were serious.

Damn them. They were cleverer than he'd suspected. They'd hired a local guide, as required. Some crazy, mute *puta*. The perfect guide, one that could not tell anyone of their expedition, and would not be believed if she could.

The Norwegian, Dr. Anderssen. She had never been involved with Mayan archaeology in any capacity. Now it all made sense. The woman had studied Norse history and archaeology at great length. She was the key to the whole idea.

And now they had found the remains of what they thought to be a vanished pyramid, taller than the giants of Tikal! Who knew what treasures the place held? Treasures that would make Santiago rich beyond belief. His mind swam with the thoughts of what was being uncovered. Although Guatemala still abounded with undiscovered, unprotected ruins, they grew scarcer, and the profits smaller. The damned Indians themselves had picked over the choicest sites. Now he had stumbled onto a bonanza, protected from fearful, ignorant Indians by superstitions.

The Americans killed his best cutter and would pay if for no other reason than that. They had lied and screwed his operation. No one had ever gotten away with that, and he would be damned if gringos would be the first.

He turned to Cabrillo. "The Americans are trying to rape Guatemala. Think what you will of me, but know this: I am Belizean by residence only. I am Guatemalan and a patriot. It is true they came here for archaeology, yet they intend to rob our homeland."

"It is valuable then, Colonel?"

"They have discovered two great sites. You have heard of the

Well of Spirits?"

Cabrillo nodded. "The haunted well."

"'Haunted.' Americans may be stupid and greedy but they are not superstitious like you. Regardless, it is the other site that is important. They are not outfitted to plunder it on this excursion, but will return under yet another ruse and pick it clean. We will not allow this." Santiago unholstered his revolver, and rubbed it with oilcloth.

Cabrillo squirmed, his eyes on the gun. "Gringos have powerful friends. Their friends know where they are. If something happens, soldiers will descend upon the place."

"By the time their friends realize they are missing we will have earned our share, and will be basking in the sun on Ambergris Caye." Santiago aimed the gun at Cabrillo and squeezed the trigger. The hammer fell with a loud click. "Guns perform so poorly in this steamy jungle, don't you agree? I will be quite glad to quit this place."

Chapter 24

Linda, dozing in the light of the campfire, jolted awake. She sat up, stretched, willed herself to wakefulness. It was her first duty on watch—she'd insisted on a stint—and she'd dozed. How reliable of her.

She peered into the woods, listening, wondering why she'd awoken.

The campfire crackled and whispered. A spark popped.

She thumbed open the cylinder release of her revolver and counted bullets. The gun looked ancient, like a long-barreled cowboy weapon. As if she would know. She eased the cylinder shut with a click. She settled back again, grateful she hadn't shot anyone.

Something rustled in the darkness of the nearby forest.

She should be accustomed to this by now. Rainforest nights were deathly quiet in comparison to Boston nights, but that was just the problem. It would take a gunshot or a siren to jar her awake back home, but mere whispers did the trick here. They signaled movement. The jungle was alive, teeming. Jaguars would be about, prowling. The big cats had killed and eaten grown men on occasion.

Man-eating jaguars. Nice. No chance of sleep now.

Grant slumped in his chair opposite the fire, sound asleep, snoring softly, reassuringly. Not quite enough to set her at ease. The others had gone to bed. He preferred to stay with the watch, a visible, armed backup.

What would be more comforting than Indiana Jones sound

asleep would be Indiana Jones wide awake. She coughed, gently.

Grant slept on.

"Grant," she said.

No response.

"Hey, Grant!"

He stirred and rubbed his eyes. "What?"

"I didn't say anything."

"Hm. Okay."

Linda glanced about. "I'm hearing things in the woods. Maybe those sounds woke you."

Grant sat up. "What kind of sounds?" He picked up his rifle.

"Something moving."

They sat in silence for long moments, listening. At last, Grant said, "The alarms haven't tripped. That's a good sign. Anything big would have set them off." He looked at his watch. "Why don't you get some sleep? You've only got ten minutes to go. I'll cover for you."

"I think I will. Thanks." Linda rose. "Take this." She awkwardly handed him the revolver and headed to her tent.

Grant stretched and watched her go. Nothing new. A dark rainforest was alien to her. Of course she'd be spooked.

A twig snapped somewhere in the forest.

Startled, he glanced about.

Shit. Now she had him doing it.

He listened intently, studying the dark for movement. None came. Stillness and quiet lay all about. He relaxed and settled back into his chair.

Another sound came, barely audible, like a carefully placed footstep in yielding grass. Stealthy.

Near.

He slowly lifted the rifle to chest level, slipped the safety, and tucked the revolver into his belt. The sound, again. The distinct impression of size. Not the random rustling of small creatures.

He ran through the nocturnal animals that fit the bill. The forest swarmed with creatures, but few of size would venture close to a camp. A jaguar, maybe. He hoped it was. That would be preferred over what was more likely.

Another sound came from the opposite side of the camp.

A jaguar wouldn't have moved that swiftly around them, and

jaguars were solitary hunters. There were at least two of whatever made the sounds, and that ruled out jaguars.

He caught a furtive movement in the darkness, forty yards away, just outside the perimeter of light alarms, a vague silhouette. That made three, then.

Another sound, and then another.

Beasts far more deadly than jaguars were about.

Chapter 25

The camp slumbered, helpless.

Grant stood and stretched, watching the forest from the corner of his eye. To yell out could coax an attack sooner than necessary.

He eased toward Tennyson's tent and tapped on the wall. "Gene," he whispered. "We have company. Get your gun and extra ammo. Keep quiet and get up slowly."

Tennyson appeared, sleep still lining his eyes. He glanced about as he emerged. In his right hand he held the second revolver, in his left, a machete. "Who's out there?"

"At least three, probably five. Camp's asleep, and we're surrounded."

"We have two revolvers, a Glock pistol, a rifle, machetes for each of us, some knives, a flare gun. Against an unknown number of undoubtedly heavily armed criminals. Any ideas?"

"Four options," Grant said. "First, we wait for an attack and we fight."

"Looters have guns. They can shoot from cover of darkness. We can't wait."

"Agreed. Second option, don't wait, start shooting."

"Except we can't even see them. Same outcome. Wouldn't stand a chance."

"Agreed. Third, surrender and hope for the best."

"I'm not giving up my weapons to cutthroats."

"Me neither. Fourth, reason with them and fight if it comes to that."

"They've crept up on us in the dark, violating our agreed-upon meeting. They're not here for a roundtable on etiquette. But maybe it's not even the group we came to deal with. I think that's our best shot."

"Our only shot. And if they come in shooting, their tactic of surrounding us doesn't make much sense. They'd be shooting in the direction of their own people. Be ready but don't do anything threatening." Grant eased toward Elisa's tent and rattled the fly. "We've got trouble."

"I heard. There really is something out there?"

"Someone. We're going to speak softly and carry a big stick." He held out the revolver. "Here's a big stick. Take it and grab a machete."

She looked at the revolver. "I don't think…"

"Take the damned gun! We don't have time to build a consensus."

Tennyson roused Linda and Watts. Riga emerged from Stansfield's tent, followed by Stansfield. Tennyson looked at Riga, and handed Stansfield the flare gun and shells. "Think you can handle this, Casanova?"

Stansfield snatched the gun from him and chambered a shell.

Grant passed out machetes and explained the predicament. "Form a semi-circle, backs to the *cenote*, no one within four yards of the next, except you, Bill. You get on the radio and get an SOS out as quickly and quietly as you can. They're spread out east of the well. Linda, take the Glock and watch the west, just in case. Everyone, keep your weapons lowered—for the moment."

They fanned out. Watts slipped into his tent. A low wash of static could be heard, indicating he'd switched on. His voice was soft, urgent: "*Attencion*, Santa Elena. This is Bill Watts, with an American team fifty kilometers northeast of Tikal. This is an emergency. We are in urgent need of assistance. I repeat, this is an emergency…"

Grant called out, in Spanish, "You out there! You have come upon us in the night. Respond if you mean no harm."

They waited. Only the hush of the forest could be heard. Grant called out again. Again, no response. He called out in Yucatec, again only silence in reply. "So much for negotiation."

Something moved in the shadows, setting off an LED alarm,

causing it to flash like lightning, and tripping the audio alarm inside the camp. Shrill electronic bursts pealed with ear-splitting sharpness.

A dull thud came from the woods and the strobing of light ceased. "They've smashed the lamp," Grant said. The audio alarm pealed unabated.

For many seconds, nothing changed.

A hoarse bellow erupted, joined in chorus by another, and another, and then by an unknown number. Human voices— barely—laced with the guttural resonance of beasts. Grant fought the urge to raise his rifle to his shoulder. He'd never heard anything like it, had no idea a human being could produce such a sound.

His companions stared into the shadows, transfixed.

The bellowing grew louder, mesmerizing. Grant shook himself to clear his thoughts. Forget negotiation; talk in the face of such venom now seemed suicidal. He snapped the rifle stock into his shoulder, ready to fire. "Weapons up!"

Another light strobed in the forest, and another, and three more, white lights flashing among the trunks, scored by the shrill, growing shriek of the audio alarm.

"Grant!" It was Watts, emerging from the tent. "To your right!"

A huge man strode into view, illuminated by the flashes like a flickering black and white movie.

If it were possible to match a human being to that bestial roar, this would have been the one. The man stood six and a half feet tall, his neck and shoulders broad and thick, his torso barrel-like, his legs like tree trunks. His face was Mayan, oval, with a long, hawkish nose and straight, black hair, his eyes round and black.

His skin was shockingly pale, white, like paper, smeared with dirt and sweat and blood. White, like paper, like a ghost...

The ghosts of El Petén...

The pelt of a jaguar draped over his shoulders, the animal's head forming a hood. He carried a gigantic axe with a broad flat blade that tapered at one tip into a wicked point, and he swung it viciously from side to side.

His eyes, glittering and malevolent in the firelight, locked on Grant's.

123

Blood streamed from a dozen cuts on the man's arms and hands and face. The giant pounded his chest and raked his nails across his cheek, drawing parallel lines of blood. His roar rose to an animal shriek.

"He's berserk," Elisa murmured.

Two more pale giants emerged, one draped in a black animal skin, the other in a reddish brown skin, both wielding axes, their voices rising and merging with the shriek of the first.

Grant raised his rifle and leveled it at the first. "Come no closer!" he shouted in Yucatec.

The giant threw his head back and made a whooping call eerily like that of a howler monkey. From the distance came a din of answering howlers. The man began shaking, and ran toward Grant, swinging his axe high above his head.

Grant squeezed the trigger.

The gunshot echoed through the forest. A tiny mark appeared in the man's chest. He stopped, glanced at the wound, shook himself, and charged again.

"God Almighty," Grant said. He pulled the bolt on his rifle, ejecting the empty casing, slid it back into place, and fired again. The man staggered, regained his balance, and lurched forward again, eyes glaring wildly.

Grant bolted in another round and fired point blank into the giant's face.

The man's jaw exploded, blood and bone and flesh spraying from his shattered face. He jerked, fell into Grant, smearing him with blood, and crashed to the ground.

Other giants rushed in.

Tennyson steadied his revolver with both hands, squeezed off two shots. Red bloomed in the stomach and chest of the closest giant. He clutched at his wounds and blood spilled from between his fingers.

Grant drew aim and fired across the clearing, striking the one in black. Four shots so far. His magazine held five. The giant stumbled, regained his feet, and rushed forward again.

A fourth emerged from the forest and strode toward Grant, swinging an axe and grinning maniacally.

Grant backed and stumbled into the aluminum dining table, and leapt over it, positioning it between himself and the new attacker. He fired, hitting the giant in the abdomen. Blood spun like a twirled rope from the wound. The man stumbled, righted, and arose again.

His magazine exhausted, Grant fumbled in his pocket for another, slapped it into the rifle, and bolted in another round.

The man raised his axe and rushed ahead, swinging.

Grant dodged, the axe whistling through the air inches from his face, and jammed the barrel of his rifle into the man's chest. The gun roared and a red mist sprayed from his back. The attacker fell back, grunted, and lunged again. Grant scrambled away.

Two wild men, one soaked in blood, backed Tennyson and Watts toward the pool. Five more appeared. Tennyson fired at the nearest, striking him in the shoulder.

The man sprang between Watts and the pool, isolating him, and swung and split Watts' hand from fingers to wrist, sending the revolver flying. Watts backed away, eyes wide, staring at the bloody wreck of his hand.

Grant aimed at the giant; he had time enough only to get off one shot, one chance to save Bill, and had to make it count. He squeezed off the shot and the bullet split the giant's knee with a spray of blood. Grant's own assailant lunged, slamming into the table, driving him back. Grant managed to bolt another round in. The giant swung. In the same instant, Grant arced his rifle around and fired, hitting him in the shoulder. The axe struck the rifle, inches from Grant's face, sending a shock through his arms. The rifle shattered, pieces of it flying.

Grant struck the giant in the face with what was left of the rifle and darted away. The giant staggered to one side and stumbled into Bill Watts, who had been backed closer to them.

"Bill!" Elisa cried. "Run!"

Watts backed away, his destroyed hand pressed against his chest, swinging his machete wildly with the other. The giant lunged and Watts struck him, slicing open his forearm. The giant swung overhand and his axe sank into Watts's shoulder, cleaving through muscle and bone to his chest. Watts's mouth gaped and his lips moved. A hiss of air escaped him. The giant wrenched the axe free with a slurping, tearing sound. Watts slumped, and the giant swung again, severing his head and sending it spinning.

Elisa screamed, and blasted away at Watts's murderer, five shots missing and the sixth and last bullet caving in the side of his skull.

Another giant rushed Grant, lunging and swinging. Grant thrust the table up as a shield. The axe blade struck, fracturing the metal of the tabletop. A shock wave jolted Grant's arms, and the attacker rained blows upon the table, driving him back. He planted his feet, trying to slow the onslaught, but the unrelenting ferocity of his attacker forced him back again.

Tennyson retreated, firing. Two men pressed him, shrugging off his gunshots, backing him toward the *cenote.*

More wild men emerged from the forest.

Grant's mind raced. In less than a minute they would all be dead. This fight was already lost and there was no way out.

Except one.

The scuba gear lay sealed in duffels by the rim of the *cenote.*

"Elisa, get behind me. Couple the tanks to the regulators and shove them into the water. "Flares and lights, too. I'll cover you until everyone's in."

Elisa looked at him. "What…"

"I can't hold this monster. We have to dive into the cave. Move!"

She dashed to the dive gear, tore open the duffels, withdrew the tanks and regulators, and feverishly began attaching them.

"Everyone into the Well!" Grant shouted.

Tennyson stumbled to one knee, trying to reload. The wounded attacker lunged and arced his axe high above his head for the killing blow.

Riga darted in and slashed the back of his knee with a machete, slicing muscle and tendon, and leapt away. Blood poured from the wound. The giant looked at it dully, and took another step toward Tennyson. The leg buckled and he collapsed.

The second attacker wheeled on her. Tennyson smashed the chair into his back, staggering him. The giant regained his footing, wheeled, and kicked him in the chest with a sharp crack, knocking him aside. Tennyson clamped an arm against his side, wincing, and scrambled toward the sinkhole.

Grant tripped and fell backward, still shielding himself with the table. Another blow, and the table disintegrated. Grant slung it into the face of the giant.

The giant raised his axe for the kill.

Light exploded and the man's face was ablaze in a hissing white fire. He screamed and swatted at the flame engulfing his face.

Frank Stansfield pulled Grant aside, the flare gun clutched in trembling hands.

The wild man lurched about, clawing at his eyes, and teetered on the rim of the *cenote*. Grant threw himself into him, and toppled him into the pool with a splash.

Two wild men came between Linda and the Well, sealing her off.

Grant grabbed a camp chair and slammed it into the attacker nearest her, and backed away, drawing the giant with him.

Stansfield rushed to her side. The flare gun popped, and sparks burst against the midsection of the second giant. Stansfield shoved Linda away as the axe whistled toward her. The axe struck, spraying blood from her head, and she fell backward into the tent. It collapsed and engulfed her. She lay motionless.

"Linda!" Stansfield shouted. He ran to her and placed a hand on her arm.

The wild man swatted the sparking flare away with a howl of rage and lumbered toward him.

"Run, Frank!" Grant shouted.

The wild man's axe sank into Stansfield's side. He was lifted bodily off the ground, suspended on the axe head. The wild man shook the axe and Stansfield fell free and hit the ground. Another axe blow fell and he lay still, severed nearly in half.

Riga took a step toward Linda.

Tennyson, clutching his side, gripped her arm and pulled her toward the *cenote*. "You can't help her."

The attackers charged.

"Jump!" Grant cried. He sidestepped and raced to the pool.

Elisa lit a flare and tossed it into the pool. It sank, shimmering and lighting the water with white glow. She shoved the tanks into the water and jumped in.

Riga and Tennyson leapt in simultaneously. Grant followed, struck the water, plunged under, and kicked his way back to the surface.

The wild man that had fallen in floated several feet below the surface, unmoving. Grant shoved the corpse toward the wall.

The other wild men gathered at the rim, pacing, bellowing, their frustration boiling into uncontrolled rage.

"They're not coming after us," Elisa said.

"Not yet anyway," Grant said.

"I've got two tanks ready on the bottom."

"Two tanks for four of us. No jackets and weights, so we won't be buoyant. We'll have to fight like hell to get from the bottom to the cave." He looked at Tennyson. "Gene, you okay?"

Tennyson shook his head, wincing. "Son of a bitch broke my ribs."

"I'll buddy with you. Elisa, you take Riga." He explained to Riga how to take the mouthpiece and breathe and return it to Elisa. She nodded fearfully.

"Let's get moving." he said.

They all drew breaths together and dived below the surface.

The flare Elisa had dropped lit the water with dancing white light.

When they reached the bottom, Grant hooked an arm around one tank, took a breath from the regulator, and passed it to Tennyson. Tennyson drew a breath and signaled okay. Grant switched on a flashlight, and handed it to Tennyson.

Holding Riga's hand, Elisa shared the mouthpiece with her. They made their way to the cave and pulled inside. Grant pulled Tennyson along after them.

A splash. A wild man had jumped in, and clawed his way toward them. Even in the night water, by the light of the flare, Grant could see madness and fury in his eyes. The force of his entry propelled him toward them. He seized Grant's ankle in a viselike grip, and powerful fingers squeezed into his flesh, long fingernails lacerating his skin. Grant kicked him in the face, and kept kicking. The man released and Grant yanked Tennyson away. He glanced back as they entered the cave.

The wild man was struggling, dragging himself into the cave, his hands reaching, clawing. Air bubbles streamed from his open mouth. Grant could hear him through the water, still bellowing.

The wild man was drowning. And still trying to kill them.

Chapter 26

A crackle from the police radio stirred Pacal from sleep. He rubbed his eyes, glanced at his watch. It was past midnight. He sat upright and leaned close to the radio, hearing only the hiss of background noise. What had awakened him? He shook the sleep from his mind and tried to concentrate.

White noise never woke him, nor did the pops and crackles of static. He had trained himself to ignore irrelevant chatter and background. He'd heard something more than noise.

He had heard a man's voice, shaky, lined with terror.

The gringo had spoken in Spanish, but with an accent. An American accent.

Thunder boomed in the distance. A late rainstorm drifted across El Petén, daggers of lightning punctuating the radio with static.

The message had drifted in and disappeared like a phantom. Why did the gringo call in the middle of the night? Perhaps he'd switched to another band. Pacal dialed up and down the bandwidths. He picked up idle talk from the police in Santa Elena, a debate concerning which whores were most compliant with police orders.

He switched back to the original bandwidth, certain he'd picked up only a snatch of the message amid the static. He tried to focus on the instant he'd awakened.

The words returned to him. *Northeast of Tikal...urgent assistance.*

Pacal felt a sick feeling in the pit of his stomach. It was as he had feared. The Americans underestimated the forest. They had taken his sister and disappeared into the wilderness. Now they were radioing a desperate plea for help. A plea cut short.

Pacal slid out of bed and threw on some clothes. He shook Chiam awake, took him to his neighbors, and convinced them to look after the boy for a couple of days.

He hurried to Balam's. The old man answered and ushered him inside. Pacal told him of the fragmented message. "Tell me the way to the Well of Spirits. I am bringing Riga home. Tonight."

The day keeper raised his hand, hushing Pacal. The old man lit a pipe and puffed slowly. He leaned forward. "You know the stories of the Well, Pacal. What do you think of them?"

"They are bedtime stories for scaring children."

Balam sighed. "You are the smartest man I have ever known, yet you hear only what you wish." He gestured toward the corner. "Fetch my walking stick. We are going into the forest."

Chapter 27

Blackness melted to gray. Ringing filled Linda's ears, and her head throbbed with pain. Ringing gave way to roaring, bellowing. Animal sounds. The sound of wild men.

She remembered.

Crazed men rushing them from the forest. A scramble to escape, an explosion of light. Screaming.

Bill Watts...

An axe flashing toward her.

Nothingness.

She touched her scalp and her hand came away wet. Blood trickled into her eyes, stinging. She blinked and wiped them. The axe had grazed her skull and knocked her senseless. A half-inch closer and she would have been dead. Half an inch to death. The explosive burst of a flare had saved her life.

The flare. Where had that come from? Something was missing...

The tent lay in a heap all about her. She gently lifted the flap and peered out. The wild men paced the rim of the Well of Spirits, their backs to her, their shadows ominous against the forest.

All about lay dead men. A body lay just feet away from her in a wide smear of blood, split nearly in two.

Frank Stansfield.

Terror and remembrance flooded her. Frank had rushed to her aid, fired the flare shot that saved her life, and now he lay dead. He hated her, yet he died to save her.

Bile rose in her throat, an overwhelming urge to vomit. She swallowed it back, knowing if she didn't she would be found and slaughtered.

The wild men had forgotten her or left her for dead. One noise or movement and she would be found.

She studied the bodies. Watts was there; she remembered his horrific death. Where were the others?

Grant had been shouting, urging everyone into the pool to escape into the cave. Elisa, scrambling to outfit the tanks. They had gear and they'd mapped an air-filled cavern, and now the wild men were pacing the pool rim, searching, frustrated, and enraged. The scuba gear was missing.

Could they have escaped? Was it possible?

Had they *abandoned* her?

They *had* to. She tried to picture what they witnessed. Watts, slaughtered. Stansfield, slaughtered. Her own blood now drenched her. It was a scalp wound, not deep, but a profuse bleeder as all scalp wounds are, and she'd been knocked out and motionless. Any rational person would have believed her dead.

They *did* escape into the pool. If they'd fled into the forest they'd have been quickly caught. They *did* escape. They would wait for the wild men to leave and return to the Well.

Her heart sank at her own prospects. Even if she could dash to the pool without being slaughtered, she could never get through the cavern without a tank. It was only a matter of time, maybe seconds, before they turned their attention to her.

She counted five at the pool. Maybe that was all, maybe not. Whatever the case, she had to make her break.

She took a deep breath and inched out from under the tent. Once clear, she crouched and slipped behind the next tent. Dizziness swept in. She gritted her teeth, let it pass. So far, so good. The strobing lights would actually help her, throwing wild shadows about, masking her movement. All clear. She readied herself for her break.

But what would be the sense of disappearing into wilderness blindly? She'd die there as surely as if she stayed.

Tennyson had set aside most supplies in the open, but had placed a boxful inside his tent, adhering to the philosophy that it was best not to place all the eggs in one basket. She slipped behind the next tent, listened, and hurried to his tent.

The interior was dark. She fumbled about and found the crate. Dry foods and bottled water filled it. She felt for and found a knapsack, stuffed it with bottles of water and tins of food, and headed for the door.

To go where? She would be hopelessly lost. The compasses and maps were in Grant's tent, and that was the closest to the Well of Spirits.

She could do nothing about that. She'd have to guess at direction and keep moving.

The wild men still paced, slower now. They were losing interest in the Well of Spirits and would be turning back to the camp at any moment.

She took a deep breath, slipped outside, and crept into the vast black midnight of El Petén.

The forest closed around her, but for the first time since she'd entered El Petén, its vastness comforted her.

She padded quietly away, though it seemed each footstep crashed noisily in the brush. A sudden howl of fury broke behind her, and the sound of fabric ripping and equipment being smashed.

She bolted ahead, stumbling, the pain in her head ratcheting up with each step.

She could hear them coming.

Hands outstretched, she felt her way through the inky darkness as best she could, straining to hear, trying to get a feel for their movement. Unbelievably, her trail had been picked up in this tangle at night, and her pursuers were closing the gap.

A drop of blood splashed onto her neck from the wound on her head. She touched the droplet. A sudden, chilling thought took her.

They smelled her blood.

It seemed impossible, but the thought ballooned into certainty. Panic gripped her. She plunged ahead, heedless of the thick, scratching growth, and rummaged frantically through the knapsack. She found a hand towel and held it to her scalp, stanching the blood. She tore a bloody scrap off, dropped it to the ground, and changed direction.

The sound of the wild men receded and she let out a pent-up

breath.

She pressed on and the sound of pursuit disappeared. At last she slowed and allowed herself to breathe deeply and slowly.

Her thoughts reeled with the memory of the attack, and a flood of images overwhelmed her. Friends, cut down just feet from her, horribly, brutally. Swift, violent death, far beyond anything she had seen in movies, beyond imagining. Bill, cleaved from shoulder to stomach with a single stroke, his lungs and heart ripped from his body and spilled to the ground. Frank, sliced almost in half. She broke out in a cold sweat. Her stomach heaved and she fell to her knees and vomited.

She retched until her stomach emptied, the spasms continuing even then. She wiped her mouth and closed her eyes. She had been carried through on sheer terror and adrenaline. Now that the immediate danger had passed, horror crushed her, and she began to shake and sob.

Struggling to her feet, she forced herself to think clearly. The murderers would be doubling back in her direction even now. If they picked up her trail again she could stay ahead of them for only so long. She took a drink of water and started off again.

The forest crowded in, a black, directionless maze. She tried to maintain her direction, though she had no real idea where that would lead. Her original course slewed away from camp, roughly southeast. Okay. She set her jaw and determined she'd keep the same way. Circling blind would be fatal.

The forest hummed, and though the sounds were alien to her Boston sensibilities, she'd grown used to being serenaded to sleep the last few nights. Now the sounds whispered threats, coming from all directions.

Dizziness. She'd lost a lot of blood, and her legs grew shaky. She wanted to curl up and sleep, but pushed on, stumbling deeper into El Petén.

A boom of thunder close by, and a breeze stirring the trees. Gathering thunderclouds, rendering the jungle even blacker. She slowed, feeling her way.

Rain began to fall, and she wanted to both curse it and praise it. The downpour would erase her trail, but the drenching cold made her shiver—her misery complete.

Far behind, a howl both animal and human arose, haunting

and angry. But for the rain, all other night sounds hushed. The howl hung and faded. She hoped to never hear it again.

Hours later, exhausted and shaking, she nestled against the trunk of a giant tree and held her arms tight about her body. The rain had slackened, and she could rest for a moment.

For just a moment...

Chapter 28

Two Days to Solstice

Elisa sat upon a rock shelf in absolute darkness, far beneath the earth, soaked, shivering, her legs tucked under her for warmth, her head on her knees.

She could hear Grant moving about a few feet away.

"Cover your eyes," he said. She did so and heard a pop, as the brilliant lavender of a flare illuminated the cave. "A little light, a little heat."

She scooted closer and the flame began to chase the cold from her limbs.

Riga and Tennyson huddled nearby. Tennyson shook, his breathing rapid and clipped.

The dive through the cave had been an insane idea, but the greater insanity would have been to remain on the surface. Grant had passed her a lamp and taken the lead, one arm encircling Tennyson's chest, the other holding a flare and pulling them along the safety line. Riga had proved to be a strong swimmer and negotiated the dive well. Seeing Tennyson now, Elisa wondered how he'd survived it.

She understood now why Grant had kept her out of the caves. They twisted and turned, narrowed and widened, riddled with holes, crevices, and vents, each a lethal trap.

Each few feet she had had to trade off the mouthpiece with Riga. She had half-expected Riga to panic and drown them both, but she'd stayed calm, suicidal though it must have seemed to her. Giving up the mouthpiece in a flooded cavern defied instinct, and Elisa marveled at Riga's strength in the face of it all.

Grant slid close to Tennyson. "Let's take a look, Gene."

He gently lifted Tennyson's shirt. His right side was swollen and bruised, and lacerated with a six-inch cut. Grant gingerly touched the wound. Tennyson flinched.

"We'll get you good as new," Grant said. He removed his own shirt, tore a strip, and wound it around Tennyson's chest. He leaned Tennyson back against the wall and sat close to him. "Better?"

Tennyson nodded, his eyes shut tight.

The flare sputtered and died. Grant lit another.

The attack played out in Elisa's mind. She shut her eyes, hoping to will the horror away, but the vision only grew. She shuddered.

Grant looked at her. "How are you doing?"

"What do you think? Our friends were slaughtered right before our eyes!"

"You don't have a monopoly on pain, Elisa. My stomach is in knots." His eyes glistened. "I'm trying to think what to do next, and I need your help."

Riga, her face lined with worry, slid closer to Elisa.

"It's all right, Riga," Grant said in K'iché. "Stay with Gene and keep him warm."

Riga nodded and returned to Tennyson's side, encircling him with her arms and legs.

Grant put his arm around Elisa and cradled her head against his shoulder.

Elisa sobbed. "They're dead. Linda, Bill, Frank. They'd be alive if we hadn't come here. We wanted to save Robert but we only lost more friends."

"They knew the risks. It's not your fault, anyway. It's mine."

"Bill was so young, and Linda wanted nothing more than to fit in. And Frank..."

Grant shushed her and rocked her head slowly. She could no longer hold back the tears and wept until she had nothing left but emptiness and sorrow. She lay her head upon Grant's lap, allowing him to stroke her hair, and gave in to sleep.

* * *

She awoke from a dream about Oslo in winter. The darkness enveloped her, the hard stone beneath disoriented her, before memory and reality swept back in.

Grant stirred, stretched. Her head still rested in his lap. Warm, yellow light flickered, illuminating Grant's face, and shadows danced on the walls and ceiling.

"You built a fire," she said. "How...?"

"Driftwood." He handed a stick to her. "Lodged here and there. We can't keep burning flares."

"It feels wonderful."

"Better than that. Driftwood means there's an opening to the surface, upstream."

She turned to him. "Won't it burn up our oxygen?"

"No. The smoke swirls up and out through the ceiling. The air is moving. Another good sign."

Tennyson lay breathing fitfully. Riga slept next to him, her arm around him.

"How is Gene?"

Grant shook his head. "He's bordering on shock. He lost some blood, and I think he's bleeding internally. He's one tough son of a bitch but he needs a doctor, and soon."

Elisa shuddered and her throat tightened as the slaughter of her companions forced its way again into her mind's eye. She focused on the feeble, guttering flame. Fire was magic, reaffirming, protecting. A hundred thousand years ago, humans huddled in similar cold, dark caves, and knew this. Fire is life.

"I'm sorry, Carson," she finally said.

"For what?"

"All the trouble I've been."

Grant was silent for a moment. "Elisa, you came with us knowing there were risks. You did it for Robert. You didn't know him that well, so I figure you also did it for us. You're strong and we're lucky to have you here. I should be apologizing to you for this nightmare."

"Those men—you shot them and they just kept coming." Elisa continued.

"I'm having a hard time believing that myself."

"You hit them squarely, point blank. They felt no pain, only rage. How can one fight that?"

"A cult of some kind?"

Elisa poked at the fire with a bit of driftwood. "Remember what I said? I said they were berserk."

"Understatement of the year."

"You don't understand. Those men are berserkers."

He looked at her. "Like the Norse myth?"

"Not myth. Berserkers were quite real. 'Berserk' is not an English word, you know. It's old Norse, from 'bear sark', which literally means 'bear shirt.' All Viking warriors were feared, but a select few, the elite, became berserkers. They were the most powerful and fearless of all, but that in itself was not enough. What stood out about our attackers?"

"They were flippin' psychotic."

"In a trance, perhaps?"

Grant nodded. "Almost possessed."

"They *were* possessed. Death did not worry berserkers. They wanted only to deal death to enemies. They readied for battle by consuming some sort of drug, ratcheting their fury and courage to an inhuman plane. To go even higher, they cut themselves, bit themselves, bit their shields, bellowed and roared like wild animals. They dressed in the skins of wolves or bears. They wore the bear sark, the bear shirt. To be berserk was to be half-human, half-animal. That's what we saw. Berserkers, draped in the skins of predators, blood streaming from self-inflicted wounds."

"Vikings? In twenty-first-century Guatemala? They're nothing of the sort. The faces, the black hair, those are classic Maya."

"But their skin? They were white."

"Beyond Caucasian white. The color of paper. Albino, almost."

"How do you account for that?"

"I don't," Grant said. "Make-up? War paint?"

"The ghosts of El Petén, perhaps?"

"Very effective look for them." Grant nodded reluctantly. "They're huge sons of bitches too. The smallest stood at least six-three, and the largest well over six and a half feet tall. You just don't see Maya that size. A Maya man would be lucky to stand five and a half feet tall."

139

"You don't see any slice of *any* society as big as that, outside of American football players. Scandinavians are large. Viking warriors were especially big, and berserkers were selected from the largest of them."

"My career got derailed for thinking like this."

"So I've heard."

"My specialty, my passion, is native Florida cultures. Particularly the Timucuan. Familiar with them?"

"A bit. Through your work."

"The Timucuan dominated pre-Columbian Florida along the northeastern coast. Fierce warriors. And though some scholars dispute it, Spanish explorers, who were rather short and swarthy, described Timucuan men as giants." He paused. "You know how I got in trouble. I found a Viking coin in a Timucuan burial mound."

"You think they intermingled with Norse berserkers?"

Grant shrugged. "This can't be right."

"Carson, they attacked with the Viking weapon of choice, the battle axe. With iron blades. Who in the world uses iron battle axes?"

"Good point. The ancient Maya used war clubs and spears mostly. No axes."

"The attack came relentless and furious. That was the berserker way, and the axe was ideal for it. Men with swords and shields had no chance against berserkers with axes. Simple physics. An axe concentrates its mass in the axe head, unlike a sword, which has evenly distributed mass. That concentrated mass delivers blows like cannon shots. A powerful warrior could swing and slash nonstop, the blows coming so fast the defender can't help but fall back, each blow on a shield sending a shock through the arm of the defender. The defender's arm is numbed, drained of strength, helpless. Berserker and axe; the most perfect marriage of warrior, weapon, and tactics in history; the berserker going all out, without regard for pain or life, raining blows like cannon shots until his victim succumbs."

"I admit. My arms were putty after a handful of blows and I was seconds from collapse. But berserkers? Drug-addled thugs playing dress-up, maybe. I don't know."

After a moment, Grant said, "We have two things we can do.

Return to the *cenote* and hope it's clear, or move upstream and pray we find a way out."

"Neither sounds promising."

"Neither are." He examined the pressure gauges on the air tanks. "We've got plenty of air to get back to the *cenote*."

"Can Gene make the dive again?"

Grant glanced at Tennyson. He hesitated, but she could read his eyes. "Gene needs rest, no matter which direction we take. But I can't sit still. I'm going for a little swim."

* * *

Grant checked his watch. Five a.m. He held the tank close, took in the mouthpiece, slipped into the cool water, shining his lamp all about. He worked his way along, the current pulling him with it. Nearing the *cenote*, he switched off the lamp.

He surveyed the pool, found it too dark to see. Good. He removed the mouthpiece and turned it vent-down, shutting off the stream of bubbles. He wedged the tank into a crevice, pulled himself into the Well, and drifted toward the surface.

He collided with the corpse of a drowned berserker and eased it aside in disgust.

He swam to the wall, seeking the cover of shadowy overhangs, and broke the surface with the slightest ripple.

Three berserkers paced the rim. One looked in Grant's direction, shouting. Another wheeled toward him and hurled something. A stone the size of a football smacked into the limestone inches from Grant's head. Grant slipped beneath the surface, and returned to the vent. He could hear more objects striking the water's surface.

He retrieved his tank and drew a breath, switched on his light, and turned and scanned the *cenote* floor. He spotted a dark object in the sand. The drowned berserker's axe. He picked it up, surprised by the weight of it, and returned to the cave.

He reached the air-filled cavern, hoisted the axe onto the rocky shelf, and pulled himself up. The fire glowed warmly, a little weaker now.

Elisa looked at him hopefully. He shook his head. "Still there. Still pacing the rim, still hunting us. Still crazy as hell."

"Norse berserkers stayed in trance for hours. Sometimes days. They are tireless."

He pushed the axe toward the light. "One of our drowned friends dropped this."

Elisa held the axe close to the firelight, and drew her breath in sharply. "Without a doubt, a Viking battle axe. The finest I've ever seen." She traced a finger along the head. "See this long, curved cutting edge? That's not for chopping wood, but for flesh and bone. And how the bottom edge of the blade tapers into a wicked hook? That's called a bearded axe. The berserker hooks his enemy on the back swing and rips out entrails if the blow finds its mark." She lowered the blade. "Carson, these things can't exist. You don't have to say it, but we likely will die here. That can't happen. We *must* survive. We have too much to tell to die in this hole."

* * *

Wakefulness eased into Linda's mind, and the world slowly ordered itself. Daylight filtered through the canopy to the forest floor. She twisted about and took stock. She lay curled amid the buttressed roots of a towering ceiba. Pain ricocheted through her skull. Her arms and legs were scratched and filthy, her bare feet caked in dried mud. Bare feet. She had fled camp in shorts and T-shirt, and both were stiff with grime and blood.

She touched the wound in her scalp, and winced. Insects buzzed greedily about it and she shooed them away. Some bugs would love nothing more than to feed on her blood and lay eggs in the wound. The bleeding had mercifully stopped, and the cold that had crept into her bones in the rain had disappeared.

She found a bottle of water in her sack and took a long drink. She tore open a chocolate bar and wolfed it down. Feeling better, she looked about.

What the hell now?

Keep going. Staying in one place, she would get caught or starve to death.

But which way?

She studied the sky. What little she could see was gray, the soggy remnants of the thunderstorm. Even her footprints had washed away.

She dug in her pack and withdrew everything from the main compartment. Four bottles of water, a bag of trail mix, two packets of noodles, five more chocolate bars. She searched the five smaller compartments.

The maniacs would be tracking her and she had to move as far and fast as she could. Just pick a direction and go, she decided. She shrugged and began walking.

Her mind buzzed with doubt. The tents had been more or less aligned on an east-west axis, their doorways facing north. She had escaped by fleeing to the rear of the tents, southward. She'd changed directions twice during her flight, once about forty-five degrees to her right, west, and again at about another thirty degrees to her right. If that were the case, she'd been moving southwest.

Dumb luck sure beat no luck. Her only plan when she'd fled in terror was escape, and leaving a confusing set of tracks. This direction would bring her close to Uaxactun, the nearest peopled settlement.

The direction she'd chosen just moments ago headed straight back to the Well of Spirits.

* * *

Ah Puuc moved slowly about the Well of Spirits, stooping often to inspect the forest floor. His berserkers watched in sullen silence, awaiting his verdict.

All the marvelous belongings of the outsiders had been removed. Not a trace remained, not a footprint, not even a crushed blade of grass.

Ah Puuc ordered three of his men to guard the Well, and waved off the rest, watching as they melted into the forest. He knelt, scouring the ground one last time for sign. He plucked a strand of grass, sniffed it, and blew it out of his palm.

Outsiders had come once again, and once again had met with senseless, violent death.

The berserkers had slain as they always had. They were not to be faulted.

It had to end.

But for that to come, he must first survive.

Mistakes were never acceptable, yet he'd made a colossal one. He would make certain that Zotz remained ignorant of it.

Seven outsiders, and two corpses to show for it. Four had disappeared into the water and surely had drowned. Would that satisfy Zotz? They would eventually wash out into the Well and he'd have his proof.

Yet an outsider had escaped. *He* had seen to it.

She had been left for dead and had slipped away. They had lost her track in the night storm. At least that was what the berserkers believed. The woman stumbled away, hurt and bleeding, a foreigner, out of her element. The notion that she could escape the berserkers was preposterous.

Ah Puuc had held back from the attack, unwilling to participate in the slaughter. He had seen her slip away. He could have caught her easily himself. When the berserkers discovered her escape, he sidetracked their pursuit, spreading her blood and scent in the wrong direction.

Now she was certainly lost. The forest would swallow her whole and her death would come slowly and painfully. But she had at least a tiny chance of survival.

He turned to follow his men, paused, and turned back for another look.

He knew the stories of the outsiders. The few berserkers allowed to journey freely to the outside world, the jaguar spirits, told of the ability to send voices and drawings through the air across great distances, of buildings taller than pyramids, of machines that sped men over the earth and through the sky.

People with such things would have other things too. Things that could track them down and exact a terrible revenge upon the order.

Ruin would come to them all, unless he could prevent Zotz from bringing it to that. Yet Zotz would likely kill him long before he could.

Zotz. Ah Puuc thought of the man with growing anger. Zotz had knowledge of the outside world, but guarded it jealously, sharing it as suited his needs. Zotz knew the things outsiders could do, but his were tales of fear, and he regaled his people with warnings of the ever nearer outsiders. He spoke of weapons that could kill thousands in the blink of an eye with a terrible fire. He lied, of course; such things were impossible. But managing truths and untruths gave him power.

Ah Puuc cursed his own weakness. He had allowed power to slip from his grasp. *He* was the rightful ruler. What was Zotz, but a lesser god? Ah Puuc's line had ruled since time immemorial, as true gods.

Zotz held power by claiming distant, growing enemies. Ah Puuc had witnessed it happening, had let it happen, and had been thrown aside for an imaginary threat, reduced to a mere lieutenant carrying out Zotz's commands.

Warriors *embrace* war, he told himself.

He turned, disgusted and ashamed, and hurried after his men, leaving behind a small, clear spring in the forest that appeared to have never been touched by human hands.

Chapter 29

The night storm left in its wake a steaming jungle as the sun climbed, flooding El Petén with mist. Pacal, with Balam grumbling at his side, coaxed his truck far into the forest, crisscrossing game trails, and stopped at last at the great *bajo* the Americans would have had to cross. He maneuvered the vehicle into dense brush and camouflaged it with even more cut brush. It was never a good idea to leave a vehicle unattended in these parts, remote though they were. Looters loved free equipment as much as unknown ruins.

He saddled himself with as much water and provisions as he could carry. Balam chuckled, and carried nothing more than the clothes he wore. "Pacal, you are a baby."

"A police officer," Pacal corrected.

"I disappear into the forest for weeks and emerge weighing more than when I entered. I'll find food and water and keep us both well fed."

"That's inspiring, but I go nowhere without my next two meals accounted for."

Pacal dialed his radio up and down the bandwidths. The police bantered idly on a couple of channels but the Americans remained silent. He'd radioed for help in mounting a search, but apparently a sudden, overwhelming amount of urgent police work took priority. Anyway, the gringos wished to be left alone, it was explained. Gringos were like that.

Few ventured into this remote part of the forest. Those who did were cutthroats or *chicleros* who lived off the forest and knew

146

its ways. Others stayed away, superstitious as they were. Pacal stayed away for practical reasons; if no one else ventured here, neither did he.

In the last decade, seventeen persons entered this region and vanished. The forest devoured them. Five were Americans, young backpackers, foolish or idealistic or both. Their grief-stricken families had organized expensive and futile search parties.

A thousand things could kill a man in this forest, some armed with fang and claw, some too small to see. Some walked on two legs. None required superstition.

Malevolent spirits walked the forest, the gullible said. The official explanation differed; El Petén spread out vast and dark, and people vanished all the time.

"No sign of the Americans here," Pacal said. "They could have set off across the *bajo* for twenty kilometers in either direction. Even if we knew where they started, the rains would have obliterated their tracks."

"You worry too much. Come. I know the way."

Pacal checked his compass. Balam chuckled again, and they set off across the wet, mucky *bajo*, sinking to their knees. The summer rains had been falling hard and the waters gathered.

Pacal took the lead, hacking with his machete. Balam seldom spoke, and then only to nag Pacal to change course now and then, or to swing his machete just so, and not so much like a little girl. Pacal stewed, reluctant to engage in chatter, deciding it best to let Balam navigate the forest undistracted.

Balam paced himself, frustrating Pacal. Fear for his sister pushed him, and he slashed relentlessly with his machete, switching hands often. He'd warned Riga. Bad things were bound to happen and they had. Almost certainly they had encountered looters, and such encounters never ended well. Looters frowned upon exposure, and El Petén was riddled with countless unmarked graves of those who had stumbled upon them.

Americans liked to lie. He'd learned that as a boy on the streets of Guatemala City, watching them barter for Riga's services. Tennyson had reaffirmed it the moment he'd opened his mouth, an idiot laying the foundation for disaster.

And what of the tall American, the one that had inspected Riga like a plate of food at Hidalgo's compound? Even his own

147

companions detested him. There would be jealousies and frictions on their expedition. Riga would respond to his overtures, accepting him if pursued, and he would certainly pursue her once they were beyond the critical eyes of conservative Maya society. Riga was a beautiful, intelligent woman, yet regarded as an idiot. Men saw in her a mute whore— the best kind—and women saw in her a threat. She was neither.

The day wore on and light angled through the canopy. They should be near the opposite side of the *bajo*. Pacal hated the thought of night falling while they still slogged through the swamp, but there could be no stopping until they had traversed it. "Is this the only route to the Well of Spirits?"

"Every point in the world has infinite routes leading to it."

"That's most helpful."

"This is not the only route; it is the shortest."

The brief twilight gathered and El Petén became black, and still no end came to the *bajo*. Pacal shined a flashlight on his compass. They must have strayed—surely they should have crossed by now—but the old man showed only certainty of the direction.

At last, the muck bottom rose in elevation. Pacal climbed out of the mire and fell heavily to the ground. He shined a light on his watch. Midnight.

"A fine place to camp," Balam panted, matter-of-factly. He drew a flask from his pocket—he carried provisions after all— and took a long drink of whiskey. The old man stretched out on the ground, and within seconds his head drooped and he began to snore.

Pacal slumped against a tree. Calm eased through his limbs, and his eyelids grew heavy.

He had an odd, fitful dream about men more animal than man, and a mysterious, golden figure, a serpent with shining feathered wings that beat the air like a hurricane, a serpent that rose above the forest like an apparition.

* * *

Pacal awoke, stiff but rejuvenated. Balam sat nearby, smoking, and motioned toward a palm leaf upon which were spread nuts and fruit. Pacal had overslept and he cursed himself. Dried, stinking mud plastered him to his waist and he bore a great number of scratches and insect bites. He peeled off his clothes, rinsed them in the coffee-colored water of the *bajo*, checking himself for leeches and ticks, and removing many of each.

He waved off Balam's pitiful breakfast, opened his pack, and contributed tortillas and jerked beef. The old man's eyes twinkled at the taste of the jerky, but Pacal got no further thanks. No matter. That was enough.

They set out again, heading northeast.

In mid-afternoon, Balam came to a sudden halt, raising a finger to his lips.

A sound came through the brush ahead, an irregular cadence of human footsteps.

Pacal drew his pistol and checked the chamber, as he and Balam knelt behind a mahogany trunk. The footsteps drew near. A single individual, blundering noisily through the brush.

"Gringos do not go abroad alone and on foot in this jungle," Balam whispered.

"Only crazy old *chicleros* are foolish enough for that."

Balam shook his head irritably. "*Chicleros* tread like mist, not clumsy oxen. Perhaps it's a looter, separated from his party. Stop fidgeting. Be still and be ready. Even a dazed bandit is a dangerous one."

Pacal raised his pistol, steadying it with both hands. He glimpsed movement through the underbrush.

A woman stumbled into view.

Pacal recognized the American, streaked with filth and blood, and near exhaustion. Her hair was tangled and matted, and her mouth hung open.

Pacal lowered his pistol and stepped from behind the tree. "*Hola.*"

The woman froze. She was carrying a heavy stick and raised it like a baseball bat. "Stay the fuck away," she hissed.

Pacal holstered his weapon and raised both palms above his head. "We wish you no harm. You remember me. I'm Pacal, Riga's brother."

The woman made no move. "Why are you in the woods?"

"We are looking for your party."

The woman nodded toward Balam. "Who's that?"

"Balam. My friend. He knows these woods better than any man alive."

"I remember you." She lowered her weapon a bit. "My name is Linda Stein."

"Linda Stein," Balam said. "Come and eat. You do not look well."

"Touch me and I'll kill you."

"I believe you."

The woman approached cautiously. Balam offered her fruit. She snatched it, studied it, took a small bite, then wolfed it down, the juice running down her chin.

"Where is your party?" Pacal asked. "Where is Riga?"

She tensed and her eyes revealed a sudden fear. "The attack. An attack. They are all gone."

"Looters? Banditos?"

Linda shook her head. "Lunatics." Her voice began to crack. "Wild men."

"Wild men?" Pacal asked. "There are no wild men. Only evil men."

The day keeper placed a hand on Pacal's shoulder. "The woman speaks true. There are wild men in the forest."

"The attack!" she cried. "In the night. We were attacked and we were helpless and Riga is dead! All my friends are dead!" Linda trembled and tears filled her eyes. Her body shook with violent sobs. She sank to her knees. "All dead," she murmured. "All of them."

Pacal's heart raced and his throat tightened like a fist. Riga, dead? He swallowed. He knelt and put his arm around the woman. She flinched, eased, and buried her face against his chest and cried, shaking.

* * *

"I'm through. I can't face any more." Linda glared at Pacal and pushed him away. "Can't you get that into your thick skull?"

She had just retold the story for the third time. She could add nothing more and the horror made her sick.

"I do understand," Pacal said gently. "But you must tell it

again. I don't believe you have seen all clearly. Remember, and tell."

"You don't hear a damned thing!" Anguish squeezed her voice. "Nothing changes, no matter how many times I tell it."

"Again. Tell it again."

She sighed, and repeated the story, shaking. He interrupted every few seconds with another gentle question, his calmness only aggravating her. Who did he think he was? Some tribal cop, uneducated, untrained. And uncaring, questioning her with clear eyes, though he'd just been told his sister had probably been sliced apart.

He forced her to think about the little details of the attack, separating things she saw from things she assumed. She found her tension slipping away, her terror subsiding.

Some tribal cop. She had dismissed him so readily. The man had a mind like a whip.

After the fourth retelling, Pacal relented, and stared up at the canopy for a moment. "Some of your party escaped."

"I don't believe that."

"You saw the deaths of two of your party. You did not *see* Riga die, nor the others. You heard shouts urging you into the pool, to seek the safety of the caves. You saw your companions retreating toward the pool. When you came to, you were dazed. Many bodies lay about, but only two of your companions. You saw enraged wild men pacing the *cenote*. Men who have accomplished their mission are not enraged."

Linda considered this. Wishful thinking, yet the logic was sound. "The moment I escaped, I had a slim hope—even a belief—that they'd gotten away. The hours since, and the nightmares, killed that hope. But you have a point."

"I have a *sister*. I will find her or die trying."

Linda pointed to his holstered weapon. "Will you use that?"

"Yes."

"It's not enough. Bullets don't stop these monsters."

Chapter 30

Grant collected driftwood for a dozen torches, enough to allow them to conserve precious flares and flashlights.

He had reconnoitered the *cenote* a second time, only to find the berserkers still pacing. "We can't sit here forever," he told Elisa. "Let's see where this cave takes us. The air is fresh, and this driftwood comes from the surface. Somewhere ahead is a way out. The tanks are heavy, so we'll leave them here. If the cave becomes impassable, we come back here and fight our way out."

"Or get lost and starve to death in the dark."

"There's a better than even chance of that. But sitting here doing nothing gives us a hundred percent chance of starvation."

Elisa leaned close. "If we don't get Gene to a warm place soon..."

Tennyson shivered, his face ashen. His eyes fluttered slightly open. "I won't be a damned anchor. Let's walk."

"That settles it then. We go upstream."

The far end of the room constricted into a throat, the water rushing through at their feet. Grant waded ahead, waving his torch, stooping through the next fifty yards, and the passage opened to a larger cavern. The walls receded and shadows played on hollows and knobs of limestone. The river flattened, splitting into braided streams only inches deep.

Grant checked his compass. "Still headed northwest. Fan out, and don't lose sight of the walls. Limestone caves split into any number of rooms and passages. Elisa, you take the right, I'll take the left. Call out whenever you find a side cave. We investigate all of them." He turned to Riga. "Stay with Gene and carry the torch," he said in K'iché. "Keep him warm."

Elisa found a gap angling up the right wall like a scar. Grant shined his flashlight into it. It curved upward, its interior lost to view. "Wait here," he said, and pulled his way into the crack and shimmied upward until the cave narrowed to a slit only inches wide. He backed his way down to his companions. "Dead end. There are bound to be lots of them and we need to mark each one."

Riga stepped forward and took one of Grant's driftwood sticks. She held it in the flame of her own torch until the wood smoldered and caught fire. She blew out the new flame and scratched the wall with the burnt tip, drawing a single vertical stroke by the entrance.

"It's a 'one,'" Elisa said.

"Riga," Grant said. "You understand English!"

She nodded.

"And Spanish?"

She again nodded.

"I'm such a jerk, speaking English like you didn't exist. Please forgive me. You are now the official marker of caves."

The slightest of smiles crossed her face. Grant had never seen her smile.

* * *

The cavern wound along, honeycombed with vents, holes, and tubes. Progress was constantly halted to inspect side caverns, most impassable after short distances, but several winding deep into the rock. Grant meticulously examined and marked each.

The mouth of cave twenty-three was barely large enough to crawl through. Grant scrabbled in, switching on his flashlight every few feet, pulling himself along on his chest. He edged around a sharp incline, banged his head against the ceiling, and swore loudly. Enough of twenty-three. He eased back, feet first. His left hand, searching the rock behind him, rattled into a loose pile of small, hard objects. He shined his light.

Human bones.

He lay in a smear of debris and dust, the remnants of ages old decomposition. He knew human vertebrae by touch, had handled them many times. In this dark, oppressive slot in the earth, with thousands of tons of stone restricting him, a shiver ran through him. He gasped for breath and his pulse pounded in his temples. He closed his eyes and counted ten. *Breathe slow, breathe slow*, drowning his claustrophobia in the timed mantra. He could handle this.

He opened his eyes. The skeleton lay incomplete and jumbled, as was always the case in anything outside Hollywood. Bones were bones, and once connective tissue disintegrated, bones scattered.

He knew the remains should not be disturbed. But the site might go undiscovered for another hundred years and his blundering had scrambled them anyway.

Screw it. He peeled off his shirt and scooped the bones into it and wriggled his body backward down the twisting shaft. He emerged and rolled onto the floor, panting heavily.

Elisa shined a light in his face. "You look like you've seen a ghost."

"Close," Grant replied. He opened the bundled shirt, revealing the bones and artifacts.

Elisa sucked in her breath.

Grant spread the items on the rock and pulled his shirt back on. "I've loused up a site. Sue me."

She touched the remains and picked up a femur. "Large individual. One of our friends, no doubt. Well-preserved, but very old."

She selected a blackened, corroded piece of metal, eleven inches long, three wide, and riddled with rusty holes. "This is what's left of a broadsword. See the twisting of iron strands in it? Vikings didn't cast a single poured strip of iron into a sword, like in movies. Cast-iron like that would shatter upon impact. They wound multiple, super-heated strands of iron together and beat them into one sword, giving it strength." She picked up a vertebra and turned it over. "Did you leave any behind?"

"After pissing my pants, I gathered every scrap. This guy was deposited in a high cave during high water. These caverns get gully-washers every few days in the rainy season. Bad news is, it's the rainy season. We get a gully-washer, we're dead. That's not all.

Remember, we found remains downstream. We assumed they were victims of sacrifice or ritual funeral. And now this. It's no longer a fluke, it's a pattern. There are lunatics that pretend they're tenth-century Norse berserkers. Their dead wash downstream from the direction we're heading. We're walking right into them."

* * *

They stopped to rest on a broad shelf above a surging set of rapids. Grant propped a dying torch by Tennyson's side and did what he could to make him comfortable. Gene's tremors diminished and he seemed to be improving.

Elisa watched as Grant checked and rinsed Tennyson's wound. He tenderly dried it and pulled off his own shirt and spread it across Tennyson's chest. That was no small gesture. One grew cold quickly down here when one got wet. Grant seemed to know Tennyson well, knew what to say and when to say it, and when to toss in an insult that would coax a pained smile. Elisa felt a touch of envy; her entire adult life, she could not recall a friendship that approached theirs. Her only true friendships ended with childhood.

Grant glanced at her. She looked away, a flush of warmth coming into her cheeks.

Tennyson's head lolled and he slipped into sleep. Grant chuckled softly. "I guess we make camp here."

Elisa's stomach clenched. She tried to remember the last time she'd eaten, and cupped some water from the stream and drank. "I'm so hungry I could eat a cow," she grumbled.

"'Horse,'" Grant said. "The expression is 'eat a horse.' We eat cows all the time."

"Any large mammal would do right now."

"We can go for days without food. Gene can't, and needs food to get his strength back. He'll fade if he doesn't eat soon."

The light of the torch was dying. "Got to conserve these," Grant said. "We'll douse this flame and sleep in the dark. It'll be absolute, and that can be overwhelming."

"I'll be alright."

He turned to Riga. "How about you?"

Riga nodded slightly. She slid across the rock shelf to Tennyson's side and lay down behind him, encircling him with an arm and a leg for warmth.

Grant ground the torch out on the rock.

Elisa felt about and found a smooth section of floor and lay down. The hard floor pushed uncomfortably against her, and she curled into a position in which she could rest her head against her forearm.

Tennyson's breathing came long and regular, less labored than before. Soon, too, she could hear Riga slipping into sleep.

Grant squirmed uncomfortably. He had given his shirt to Gene. A noble thing, but he would soon succumb to chills.

She sat upright. She could no longer see him, and that made her suddenly and surprisingly miss him. She could hear him move, and she imagined him turning his back toward her. "Grant," she whispered. "Carson."

"What?"

"Carson, you'll freeze. Come over. We should be close for the warmth." She meant it as much for herself as for him.

A moment's silence, and then she could hear him slide across the floor toward her. "Thanks. Not exactly the Ritz Carlton, is it?"

"Norwegians don't stay at the Ritz."

She lay down again and rolled her back toward him. Grant relaxed with a sigh. Were there multiple meanings in that sigh?

The stream sluiced past, burbling, and occasional droplets fell from the cavern ceiling to splash into the stream. After a moment, she drew a deep breath, and eased her body closer until they touched. He hesitated, and then his hand moved lightly onto her shoulder. She snuggled against him.

His hand moved onto her neck and drew back her hair and massaged the tense muscles there, then slid down, lightly upon her shoulder, and crept over her side, lingered, and touched her breast. She rolled to face him, her hips pressing against his. He began unbuttoning her blouse, and she slid her hands behind his head, her fingers lacing through his hair, and pulled him close and kissed him. His hand slid down her stomach, curled around her waist, and pulled her tight against him.

* * *

Riga listened. They had thought her to be asleep, but they did not know how restless and disturbed sleep was for her every day of her life.

The sounds continued, desperate lovemaking, sighs and caresses, quickening breaths and movements, gasps, and finally stillness. There was no roughness, nor brutality in the sounds, only tenderness. It was lovemaking unknown to her.

She drew her arms closer about Tennyson, leaned close, and kissed his neck. She breathed in his scent and lightly stroked his hair.

He stirred, but slept on.

Chapter 31

Zotz glided through his chambers, silent as shadow, lingering a moment at each.

The news troubled him.

It had been a year since the outsider had been imprisoned. Before that, it had been three years since the previous one, a peasant. The disappearances rekindled fear in the outsiders, but that had not been enough.

A grave robber had been slain at the Temple of the Fox, ending that desecration, but these new outsiders were northerners, Americans, not superstitious peasants. Armed with the knowledge and science of the world.

They would destroy his world.

Ah Puuc reported their deaths, claiming they'd drowned in the Well's caves, but he could produce only two bodies.

Zotz went to a brazier of glowing coals, fanned it hotter, and sprinkled a handful of gray powder on it. The coals hissed, sparks flashed, and fragrant smoke drifted up. He inhaled deeply, and seated himself on a stone bench. He glanced around the room, his favorite among all his chambers. His prizes, the treasures of the outside world, filled the room. Books were stacked high, some in languages he understood, some he did not. Maps were spread out on the tables, and lined the walls. An assortment of tools lay scattered about.

He selected a book and thumbed through it. Pictures of aircraft abounded, and he caressed them, dreaming of the wonders of the great, wide world.

That world could never be his. He had a sacred duty that did not allow such indulgences. He replaced the book, selected another, one filled with accounts of adventures and explorations in the darkness beyond the sky. A man of darkness and close spaces, he thrilled at the idea of a great unbounded darkness beyond the earth, stretching to infinity, unconfined.

One of the women had escaped. Ah Puuc had at least admitted to that, but insisted that her wounds were mortal. He could do no less; she had slipped into the forest, from beneath their noses. An outsider, a woman, hurt and bleeding, had eluded berserkers in the night forest! Outsiders were all but blind in the dark, and blundered about like drunken pigs.

Ah Puuc assured him that the berserkers would find her body soon, even before the worms and ants and scavengers could consume her. She would become one of many who simply vanished in the forest, never to be seen again. But one could not place faith in Ah Puuc's claims.

Zotz had been patient with Ah Puuc, and had been rewarded with incompetence and sedition. The owl god must think him deaf, blind, and foolish.

There would be a new moon tonight, and excellent darkness. He would go abroad. The Americans' friends would come looking for them soon. Attention must be diverted away, but events would only be delayed by such limited measures. Outsiders swarmed inexorably closer, in ever greater numbers. The forest withered and shrank, their fires consuming it, closer each season, dirtying the distant sky with billowing gray smoke.

The outsiders tore at the old ways with science, examining the nature of the universe from the infinitesimally small to the incomprehensibly large. But they had not discovered all the mysteries of the universe. Some things they could not begin to imagine.

His world was slipping away. A cleansing of the forest was in order.

Zotz selected another volume, his favorite, and read aloud: "There are more things in heaven and earth than are dreamt in your philosophy."

Outsiders gathered on the horizon, like a storm. They would be stopped. They would be swept away.

The ancient one would be awakened.

Chapter 32

Colonel Santiago stalked about, simmering, dangerous, and José Cabrillo kept a watchful eye on him. Garcia, heavy-lidded and puffing disinterestedly on a cigarette, sat nearby on a fallen tree trunk.

The *cenote* shimmered like a diamond in the filtered light of the forest. Cabrillo longed for a swim in its crystalline waters to wash the sweat and grime of the trek from his body. But there would be no swimming.

Santiago had been examining the site for an hour, stooping to feel the earth, peering at bits of foliage. Finally, he shook his head. "Many have been here within the last few days. The place has been scoured, cleaned by people adept at going unnoticed."

"The Americans?"

"Of course it was the Americans," Santiago snapped. "They gave away their location over the radio. They camped here."

"Why would they disguise it?"

"Because, idiot, they found things of enormous value, here and elsewhere. That they have moved on confirms that the other site is richer by far than this, but the two are linked in some way."

Cabrillo nodded, trying to keep his expression neutral. Let Santiago go on thinking him a fool. That would be remedied in the end.

"The evidence is nearly erased," Santiago continued. "Another day of growth, another thunderstorm, and even I could not detect it. There are just enough broken grasses and faint impressions to give it away."

"You are a great tracker."

Santiago shot him a contemptuous glance.

There were stories about Santiago, many embellished, many too horrific to be anything but true. The bastard was a cipher, however, never revealing more than the faintest glimpses into his past, revelations calculated to inspire respect and fear.

Garcia stubbed out his cigarette, and leaned in. "The Americans are armed, Colonel. I am not eager to die."

Santiago ignored him, and moved to the edge of the *cenote*, stooped, casually tossed a pebble into it, and studied its depths. He had turned his back on Cabrillo.

Cabrillo stepped closer. How easy it would be to slip up behind him, shove him in, and keep him there until he drowned.

The Americans had indeed been here. Cabrillo could see the faintest signs of disturbance. He was not so blind and stupid as Santiago believed. He'd hoped to find the Americans and take revenge for the death of Manuel, his beloved brother, the hardest worker he'd ever known. A true craftsman, and not a mere looter like himself.

He had assumed the Americans killed Manuel. Now, looking at this place, he had doubts. The site had been cleaned, just as Santiago said. Erased.

Cabrillo had seen American archaeological sites before, had even worked for an American team one summer. They taught him about ruins, what to look for, and after they left he returned and removed enough to feed his family for a year. Americans were careless about securing or even obscuring sites they'd left, despite dreading beyond measure exposing their secrets to men like him.

The Americans *had* been here. But so had someone else, and the Americans had disappeared.

The Well of Spirits. Strange things were known to happen here. Now he could see for himself. It would not do to challenge Santiago just yet. It would be best to confront the spirits that haunted the forest with as many men as possible.

Santiago turned and looked him in the eye, his face a mask. "We will go where the Americans found their vanished pyramid. Northwest. The gringo idiots broadcast the coordinates over the radio. You shall lead and I shall keep an eye on the both of you.

From behind."

Garcia looked hurt. "Señor does not trust us?"

"Trust is for fools, and fools die in the jungle." He spat on the ground and withdrew a cigarette from his shirt pocket. "I will not die."

Chapter 33

Juan Santos switched off the police radio in the Santa Elena station, unable to suppress a smile. That ridiculous Maya policeman, Pacal Itzep, had radioed for help, just as expected. Santos had jotted down the message, and read it twice more.

Pacal had found an American, a woman, wandering alone in the forest. She had survived an attack by wild men and had fled her camp. At least two of her party had been slaughtered like pigs. The story gripped Santos; it had been but a year since a *Norteamericano* had run afoul of El Petén, and such an untimely event would spark fire among both the provincials and the *federales* in Ciudad de Guatemala, as well as in Washington. It would set off an earthquake and he, Juan Santos, would be near the epicenter. What glory!

He shook his head, struck a match, and set the note afire. A great story, but it could not be told. Not yet, anyway.

There was no way to keep missing or murdered Americans from becoming international news. Americans thought the world revolved around them. Perhaps they were right. No matter. This story would break soon enough.

He unlocked his desk drawer and pushed aside a stack of papers, exposing a rumpled envelope near the bottom. The envelope contained three thousand *quetzales*, half the fee from Santiago.

Pacal had radioed for help, just as Santiago predicted. His calls would go unheeded for at least seven more days. After that, the news could break. By then, Santiago would have time enough to do whatever he had to do.

Santos riffled through the bills, withdrew a few, and stuffed them into his pocket. This would be a fine day for eating and drinking. Business with Santiago was good and getting better.

There was really no alternative. One could do as Santiago asked and be richly rewarded or one could refuse.

Refusing was the same as putting a pistol in one's mouth.

* * *

Linda trudged along after Pacal and Balam, her dread growing with each weary step. They headed toward the Well of Spirits. They had to go; there was no other choice. But accepting it didn't make it easier.

They'd rejuvenated her with food and rest, treated the insect bites that covered her arms and legs, and cleaned the million cuts and scratches that drove bugs into frenzy.

Balam, the old man, amazed her, gliding through the forest like a ghost, whereas Linda stumbled along like a drunk. Even Pacal had trouble keeping pace, blundering ahead in comparison to his friend.

Pacal expressed little confidence in his call to Santa Elena. The dispatcher, or whatever he was, professed great concern and promised a veritable dragnet to bring the wrongdoers to justice, his tone gilded with mockery.

Linda wondered what the hell she'd signed on for with this pair, defenseless, in the remotest corner of an out-of-the-way country where people disappeared all the time. Her throat might be slit and her body never found.

Yet they treated her well. If they'd wished her harm, they'd have done it by now. And it sure felt better than being out here alone.

They made camp as the sun's rays fell across the jungle in a long slant. Pacal built a small fire and Balam prepared a tin of rice for boiling.

Linda studied the old man at length. "You are a *chiclero*, Balam?"

"The best," the old man said, chuckling. "Though chicle does not pay as well as it once did."

"Balam is also day keeper," Pacal said.

"What's that?"

"A human calendar. Americans have digital organizers to memorize birthdays, weddings, deaths; we have day keepers. It is a respected, traditional position. Balam knows the days of a hundred people."

"A thousand," Balam corrected.

"Old man, I could replace you with a smart phone."

"One that can also gather chicle and minister your wedding ceremony?"

"Point taken. A day keeper is an advisor, a shaman, a healer. He performs work that your nation divides amongst accountants, lawyers, priests, and therapists.

"And at a fraction of the cost," Balam added.

"I thought he was your father."

"He is my oldest friend. Riga and I have known him most of our lives." He paused. "Our parents died when I was a boy. Balam took us in and cared for us."

"Tell me about your parents."

Pacal stiffened. "You are American."

It was not a question, and Linda was not sure how to respond. "So?"

"You are ignorant of the hemisphere."

Linda waited.

Pacal stabbed the fire with a stick, scattering sparks, and took a seat on the ground. "Guatemala is an old country. Before it was the country of the Spanish, it was the country of the Maya, for thousands of years. Five centuries ago, the Spanish defeated my people, but the past is never truly past, is it? It shapes every moment of the present. In the eyes of many Spanish, we are a subjugated people, unwelcome in our own land. They periodically experiment with integrating us, but always come back to merely grinding us down.

"When you grind people, they rebel. We rebelled in 1954, 1962, and 1982. The government branded us Marxists, so Americans sent money and arms to fight us. In 1982, I was nine and Riga was eight when the horror returned.

"My family's village lay in Alta Verapaz. The army came in the night and encircled the town. Gunfire woke me, and Mother gathered Riga and me together, crying. I asked where Father was, but she did not know. He had gone into the street to see what was happening.

"Bullets tore through the walls of our house. Riga began crying, and mother held us on the floor. Screams and cries for help came from the street.

"The door burst open, kicked in by a soldier. He shouted and shoved us outside, and more soldiers herded the people into the center of the village. I did not see Father. The young men had been taken away, toward the fields. We heard much gunfire from that direction. All around me, children cried, women screamed.

"The captain of the soldiers strode over from the direction of the gunfire. He stood tall, and had steel and hatred in his eyes. I thought he was Satan. He studied us as though we were rats, and yanked an old man from the group. 'Where are the communists?' he demanded.

"Old Perez shook his head. 'I do not know any communists,' he replied. 'I am a farmer.' The captain drew his revolver and shot him in the face. Perez's wife screamed and threw herself upon his body, and the captain shot her in the back.

"'Who else harbors communists?' asked the captain. No one answered. He yanked a young woman, our neighbor, from the group and put his gun to her head. She shrieked and collapsed, clutching his leg; his gun roared and half her head disappeared. He pulled another woman from the group. 'Who here are communists?' She cried and said there were no communists here, but perhaps there were some in the next village. He pointed his gun at her, then lowered it, and told his men to take her. They beat her senseless and raped her as the captain watched.

"'You Indians are all the same,' the captain said. 'You hate Guatemala. You are given the chance to fight communists and you refuse. What do I have to do to convince you to be patriots?'

"The captain approached my sister. He touched her hair. Riga pulled away, sobbing, and he grabbed her by the hair and yanked her back. He said to Mother, 'Perhaps your children can persuade you.'

"Mother threw herself upon him, striking him wildly. He struck her in the face and staggered her, and his men pummeled her with the butts of their rifles. I ran to help her, but one of the

167

soldiers slammed me in the face with his rifle, breaking my nose, and aimed his rifle at me. He told me to take one more step. I couldn't move, paralyzed with fear.

"Mother's face was destroyed, her teeth knocked out. Barely conscious, still she crawled toward them. The captain laughed and kicked her, and asked if she knew any communists. She couldn't answer, and he shot her. He seized Riga and threw her to the ground and tore her dress off. She shrieked and the captain told her to shut up, and cuffed the side of her head, splitting her scalp and spraying blood. He held his hand over her mouth to silence her. She kicked and fought but she was helpless.

"He forced himself into her and grunted like a pig as he bore down. Riga's eyes were wide with terror and pain and she stopped struggling and simply gave up. The captain finished and rolled away from her, motioned to two of his men, and they too raped her. Riga had stopped screaming with her voice, but her eyes screamed and screamed.

"And in my terror I did nothing.

"Finally, they threw her onto Mother. I crawled to them, sobbing, and huddled close together with them. They lay still and quiet. I could feel Riga shaking, her body convulsing with pain and sobs. I buried my face against Mother's shoulder and cried uncontrollably, knowing she would hug us and make us better, but she lay still.

"The soldiers left the village. We never saw them again. They went west and north from village to village, looking for more communists.

"My father had disappeared. The bones of forty-seven men were found in a mass grave in the jungle.

"Since that night, Riga has not spoken. I wish that she could speak. Then perhaps she could forgive me.

"Our village shattered, no one could care for us, and we went to Guatemala City. We lived in the street, stealing food. Once, when we had been two days without eating, Riga went with a man into an alleyway and came back with thirty *quetzales* in her hand. I knew what she had done, but I did not say anything because we bought food and ate well. The next night, she went with more men, and again the following night.

"We lived in the street for a year, until one night Riga

beckoned a passing man to come to her, just as she did every night. I watched from the shadows with a large stick in my hand to make sure no one hurt her. The man held her by the shoulders and looked into her eyes. He did not run his hands over her, but simply held her in a strong grip and looked at her. *Into* her. He spoke, but I could not hear. I ran to them, shouting, swinging the stick. The man turned to me and looked into my eyes, a great sadness in his face. Recognition seemed to come to him. I thought that perhaps he knew me. He said, 'Do not be angry. I will not harm your sister.'

"I swung and hit him. He flinched, but did not move away. I took Riga's hand and pulled her away, but something told me he was not one of the pigs of the night.

"He asked if we had a home. We shook our heads and he told us to follow him. He led us to a battered house in an Indian quarter. He was Maya, like us. Alone, like us. He fed us fish and beans and bread, and we slept in a bed for the first time in a year.'

"The man took us off the street. He brought us to Chultun in El Petén. He taught me to fish and to read. Riga never went to the street again. She grew to adulthood and took many lovers, but never again took money. She conceived and bore a child out of wedlock, a boy, Chiam. The father, who was married, would have nothing to do with them.

"Balam is the man who saved us from hell."

The old man had been listening silently with half-closed eyes.

Linda swallowed hard against the lump in her throat, and blinked back tears. Despite a life of privilege, she had spent a life feeling overlooked. She had no idea how lucky she'd been. No idea. She had regarded Riga with amusement. Riga, the sweet, simple country girl trying to fit in with the sophisticated Americans. Pacal, the provincial tribal policeman. The horror of their lives unveiled itself like a nightmare.

Pacal poked a stick at the fire. "The massacre of our village was but one of hundreds. Americans think the world is a chessboard. Perhaps you are right, but pawns are sacrificed in chess. My mother and father were slaughtered and my sister reduced to a shell for a fucking chess game."

Linda searched for words. "Pacal—"

He looked at her. "No. Do not pity me. I could not save my

mother and sister. I cowered like a babe in my fear."

"But you were just a child."

"There can be no excuse. I did nothing and have lived each day with that shame."

"You are guilty of nothing," Balam said. "You are ignorant of what you have inside, and do not allow yourself to see it."

"What I have inside is emptiness. Nothing changes the past, Balam."

"You became a policeman," Linda said, "to help your people."

Pacal snorted. "Police work is not the most respectable profession here." He paused. "I will find my sister. I failed her once and destroyed her life. I will not fail her again."

"We'll find Riga," Linda said, not at all believing it.

Balam rolled a cigarette and lit it. He seemed far away as the smoke curled about his face and drifted up into the trees.

In the distance, a group of howler monkeys raised a chorus of whoops into the night.

Chapter 34

Mayor Ernesto Hidalgo looked out at the downpour from his veranda, dismayed. What an abysmal night to be out, especially in his pale gray suit. He'd wrangled fifteen years of good use from the suit, but not by abusing it in the elements. He thought about changing into dungarees and a work shirt. But no, the suit would survive. Tonight, it would be smart to present his best side.

Tonight marked a new moon.

He dared not miss his rendezvous on such nights. He'd done that once, and once only. He'd showed up faithfully ever since, even though the Ghost appeared on only one of every four or five new moons.

He held a tightly wrapped bundle close against his chest, stepped off the veranda into the rain, and hurried across his yard to the warehouse. He unlocked the dented roll door, rattled it upward, and slipped inside. He glanced at his watch. It was after midnight. He'd started early, but prudence demanded it. He'd learned that the hard way eleven years ago.

Lightning flashed, illuminating the yard just outside the warehouse. Hidalgo took a seat in a battered old chair, set the bundle on his lap, and leaned back to wait.

Time passed. Hidalgo yawned, and roused himself. He opened a thermos, poured a cup of coffee, and took a sip. It wouldn't do to sleep. He could sleep later, deeply, with a bottle of tequila to assist him.

The Americans had been silent for quite some time, and dark rumors of trouble slithered like snakes about town. Hidalgo could ask a few questions later. Not now. In the morning perhaps.

Lightning flashed again, the thunder booming simultaneously, causing him to jump.

The Ghost stood silhouetted just outside the warehouse, still as a statue, watching him.

Hidalgo crossed himself, shocked with fear, as always. He would never grow accustomed to seeing this giant phantom lurking in the darkness.

The Ghost spoke in a low, guttural voice. Hidalgo knew a smattering of K'iché and Yucatec, and though the Ghost spoke a tongue similar to those, it remained elusive. He had a feeling that the Ghost knew Spanish also, but refused to speak it.

Hidalgo steeled his nerves, advanced, and set his bundle down on the dirt floor.

The Ghost remained, unblinking, staring at him in shadow. It scooped up the bundle, unwrapped it and peered inside, then tossed its own bundle to Hidalgo.

Lightning crashed, bathing the warehouse in a flicker of brilliant white, outlining the Ghost. Hidalgo averted his eyes; the Ghost preferred anonymity.

Another flash and boom. Hidalgo glanced up. The Ghost had vanished.

The mayor exhaled heavily, realizing he'd been holding his breath. He sank back into his chair and felt his fear drain from him. After seventeen years, these late-night transactions still terrified him.

He stood and pulled down the roll door, shutting out the storm and the thing out there in it. He lit a small kerosene lamp that bathed the warehouse in warm, yellow light.

He picked up the bundle and set it on the work bench in the back of the building. He untied the leather strip that bound it and the bundle fell open.

A handful of Mayan figurines lay within, along with a second, smaller bundle. This, he reminded himself, made these nightmares worthwhile, and the ancient, exquisite figurines fetched top prices from the Dutch buyer who visited Flores twice a year. Hidalgo would make more from that sale than he would make in a year otherwise. A shame that good citizens had to supplement their incomes with disapproved vocations.

In exchange, he provided the Ghost with rubbish. Books mostly, purchased second-hand in Ciudad de Guatemala. The Ghost preferred books on mathematics, art, and science.

Hidalgo opened the second bundle, excited and curious. He had never been given more than a single bundle.

Odds and ends of *modern* make made up the second bundle. A wristwatch, notebooks, a pair of glasses, a baseball cap…

The cap. Recognition dawned on him. It belonged to Tennyson. These items all belonged to the Americans. He quickly wrapped them back up and retied the bundle.

A cold sweat beaded on his forehead.

The Ghost had killed the Americans. Hidalgo stared at the bundle. He had to get rid of it as soon as possible. If caught with this, he would be hanged for their deaths.

He stopped. The Ghost clearly brought these items for other than trade, to serve a different purpose. Hidalgo could not simply dispose of them.

The Ghost *meant* for Hidalgo to disperse them in the looters' market. They would then be uncovered and looters blamed for the disappearance of the Americans. Some poor bastard would hang for it.

Hidalgo had no choice in the matter. The Ghost would know if his wishes were ignored, and would likely tear him to pieces as punishment. The Ghost would know.

He hid the two bundles in a locker. Time must pass and the evidence grow cold. Hidalgo would wait, and plant the Americans' belongings in the Flores home of a corrupt old banker that had unwelcome, amorous designs on his sister. The *federales* would receive an anonymous tip, the thief's house would be raided, the thief apprehended.

Tennyson and Grant were his friends, but what else could he do? He couldn't be faulted for their disappearance, and he didn't relish the thought of hanging for it.

He eased the roll door up and hurried through the rain to his warm, dry home.

Chapter 35

One Day to Solstice

Wakefulness came reluctantly, deceptively. Grant rubbed his eyes, unsure in the total darkness if his eyes were even open. He stretched his arms and lightly touched Elisa's back, the memory of her warm embrace returning.

He found his clothes and slid into them, then eased back to her, his stomach and chest against her back. He found himself stirring once again.

She twisted around and kissed him, her tongue tickling his. She abruptly stopped and turned away. The passion they'd shared in the night felt suddenly wrong.

Grant touched her shoulder, and felt her stiffen under his touch. He withdrew his hand. It had been a release, an escape, from the horror. Nothing more. "Do you have regrets?"

She took his hand and pulled it around her waist, and drew herself against him. "I needed you last night," she whispered. "I still need you today."

"It was for both of us," he said. "Our friends are gone, and it's my fault. Please forgive me."

She leaned close and kissed him. "There's nothing to forgive. We all chose this."

Grant struck a match and lit a small bundle of sticks. Riga cradled Gene in her arms, rocking him gently.

Grant took a quick inventory of their assets. "We've got seven flares and one candle left. Matches, we've got plenty." He switched on a flashlight. The beam had grown weaker and the other flashlight was dead. "We need to stick to driftwood torches, but wood's getting scarcer the farther we go upstream." He gave Elisa a meaningful glance. "And we're hungry," he whispered.

"We have to get out," she said.

The flickering firelight played in her pale blue eyes and highlighted in shadow the contours of her face. Something greater, deeper, shone in her skin and her eyes, visible only through the lens of intimacy.

She seemed to read his thoughts, and her eyes glowed with warmth.

Grant eased alongside Tennyson and examined him. His arms and hands were clammy and fever heated his skin. "Time to hit the road, buddy," Grant said. He helped him to his feet. Tennyson stumbled and Grant hooked his arm around him for support.

Tennyson coughed suddenly and violently, and sucked in a clipped breath.

Grant felt the shiver run through Tennyson's body. If they didn't find the surface soon, he'd be burying his friend in this cave. And the rest of them would not be far behind.

* * *

Robert Lindsay lingered on the edge of sleep, considering the stump of his finger. It had swollen and the pain had snaked into the rest of his hand. Infected. He had no doubt about that. The consideration now was whether he could fight it off or die, rotting of gangrene. The irony struck him; godhood didn't stop the flesh from rotting.

He thought back to the girl, the first time they brought her to him, the first of many times. How sweet his moments with her were! He guessed it had been many months since her last visit. He closed his eyes and let the memory wash over him...

He sat up, leaned against the wall, and listened. Footfalls, approaching. His pulse quickened.

They were bringing the drink!

Anticipation consumed him. His skin tingled.

The footfalls drew closer. He still marveled at his uncanny hearing, so many times more acute than before.

No, he had that all wrong. His eardrums felt pressure with no more sensitivity than they ever had. His alertness had blossomed.

He could now discern numbers and individuals by sound, and he picked out three. Wonderful! Whenever there had been more than one, they had brought the drink.

He recognized the approach of two of them, his usual jailers. Sneer and Shimmy, he had dubbed them. The third sounded different, and he didn't recognize the gait.

The bolt rattled in the door. He could smell the drink, and shivered. His jailers entered and thrust a vessel forward. Lindsay clutched it and gulped it down, fighting the urge to gag.

He finished, wiped his mouth. Sneer regarded him with contempt. Shimmy seemed to take his cues from Sneer, lacking much independent thought of his own.

Lindsay didn't give a crap what the goons thought. Soon he would be as powerful as them. Then he'd kill them.

He could feel his blood rushing, his pulse thudding in his body. Good. The elixir tightened its grip. He felt power growing, unlimited, unbound, and clenched his fists hard, his nails biting into the flesh of his palms, drawing blood. The blood smell filled his nostrils.

Sneer and Shimmy turned and left, leaving a lantern bowl glowing on the floor, the first time they'd left him with light.

A young woman stepped through the doorway. The first woman he'd seen since entering the underworld.

Like the goons, she stood over six feet tall. Striking good looks, with the features of the Maya, the broad, oval face and aquiline nose, but with paper-white skin. A gauzy red robe hung loosely on her supple body.

A delicate, pungent scent tickled his nose. She was fertile, ready to conceive. He felt himself becoming aroused.

She appraised him, head to toe. Her eyes warmed, and a faint smile crossed her face.

The girl slowly pulled the drawstring on her robe and the garment fell to the floor. She stood before him naked, and raised her arms for him.

Life surged through him. He tore off his clothes and embraced her, holding her tight. He ran his hands over her. She yielded into him, gripping and squeezing him. His desire became exquisite, overpowering. He pulled her to the floor.

Her legs encircled and squeezed him. She grabbed his hair and pulled his face toward hers and kissed him and bit his lip. Lindsay forced his tongue into her mouth and squeezed her breast. Nails raked his back, breaking his skin. Blood trickled down. His excitement welled with animal abandon to a height he'd never imagined possible. He pushed into her, her flesh soft and yielding, and she bit and scratched, her strong legs squeezing him like a vise.

He drove deeply into her, faster and faster.

He exploded in a convulsion of pleasure unlike any he'd experienced, his senses singing with his new power and drive. The girl convulsed, and cried out. Time stretched and ceased to exist, becoming only the sweetness of the moment.

Afterward, Lindsay lay panting like a wolf, staring at the ceiling. The girl lay quiet, her breathing and heartbeat drumming. Her breasts rose and fell.

He felt himself stirring again, not surprised that it should be so soon, scarcely a minute after they'd finished. He felt limitless. He pulled her close, and they made love again, as passionately as the first time.

Three times more. The exquisite pain of raking nails spiked his senses and excited him. Each time the girl writhed and arched, a savage thing.

At last, the girl pushed Lindsay off, rolled away, and quickly dressed. Lindsay had never felt so alive. He eyed her with renewing vigor, and reached again for her. She kicked his hand away and darted to the door. His face flushed with anger and he sprang to his feet, but the girl slipped away and slammed the door behind her. Her delicate footsteps receded.

He kicked the door, and paced like a caged jaguar.

The girl had come and gone, escorted by her goons.

She had not been brought for his amusement. She was not his concubine.

He'd serviced her like a damned beast of burden, a stud animal. Served a purpose, nothing more.

And if he had fulfilled his purpose, what further reason was there to keep him alive?

* * *

Grant stopped and checked his dive compass, twisting it in several directions. The needle twitched and jumped and spun. He took a couple of steps and retraced them, holding the compass steady. "We got hitches in the magnetic bearing."

"Hitches?" Elisa asked.

"Nervous needle. The earth's got magnetic field anomalies all over the globe, but I wouldn't expect one here in a limestone formation where there's no iron. It's screwing with my readings, but I think we're still tending northwest."

He turned to Riga. "How are you holding up?"

Riga nodded without expression, pale in the dim light. Her forehead glistened with sweat, and she trembled.

Grant shook his head. "May I?" he asked, extending his hand.

She stiffened and edged away, eyeing him with sudden suspicion. Grant withdrew his hand.

"It's all right, Riga," Elisa said. She gently took Riga's arm and felt her wrist. "Pulse is a bit fast." She placed a palm on Riga's forehead. "No fever. She's cold, but sweating."

"Riga?" Grant asked gently.

Riga shook her head and looked upstream.

"She's afraid," he said. "Of where we're headed."

"Do we continue?"

"No choice. We'll be blind in the dark soon." He looked Riga in the eyes. "Can you continue?"

She hesitated, and shook her head.

"Are you afraid of the dark?"

She pointed upstream and touched her head.

"You fear something ahead?"

She nodded, almost imperceptibly, puzzlement on her face.

"But you'll continue? It's the only way."

Elisa held a hand out to her. "Riga, Gene will die if we stay."

Riga again looked upstream, nodded bleakly, and took Elisa's hand without conviction.

* * *

Grant scrambled over a sill of rock, stooped underneath a long low ceiling, and slid a few feet in thin, slick mud. The cave opened higher, and angled slightly upward. He swept the room with torchlight. He wiped sweat from his eyes and realized how tired he was. They'd been at it a long time since the last break, maybe four hours. Hunger gnawed at his stomach.

Riga came up behind, sliding as he had. Tennyson had to crawl over the sill unaided, as two could not fit through together. Elisa brought up the rear.

"Let's catch a breath here," Grant said.

Everyone sat to rest, except Riga. She moved to the cavern wall, and ran her hands along it, and proceeded to the other side, examined it in the same manner, and gestured to Elisa.

Elisa touched the wall, and peered closely at it. "The stone's been worked here."

Grant switched off the flashlight and lit a torch. He ran his finger over scratches in the surface. "See what you mean. Tool marks." He stooped and felt the floor. "This has been chiseled and ground too."

Riga glanced about, frowning. She put her ear against the stone wall. Her eyes grew wide and she beckoned to them.

They pressed their ears to the wall.

Grant heard a faint sound, barely audible above the trickling and dripping of the caves. A slow, steady rasp, heavy and rough. "Elisa, do you hear it?"

"Grinding?"

"Now it's stopped."

"Caves play tricks on the senses."

"But we both heard it."

Riga moved next to them, wide-eyed. She seized Grant's arm and pulled him, motioning him to retreat.

Grant shook his head. "Riga, this is the main channel. There's no way out back the way we came."

Riga gripped his arm, her nails digging into his flesh. She turned to face Elisa, her eyes pleading.

"Carson, she's terrified."

Grant peered ahead.

Riga released him, took hold of Tennyson, and urged him to stand.

"I'm a little concerned now myself," Grant said. He took Tennyson gently from her.

"Listen!" Elisa cried.

Another faint sound drifted to them, a muffled rush. A strand of Elisa's hair fluttered. She brushed it aside, curious. "A breeze. An opening to the surface?"

Grant suddenly understood. He'd heard the sound before, in a deep Kentucky cave, the sound of hurrying death. "Flash flood! The air is being pushed towards us. Run!" He motioned them in the direction they'd come.

Riga grabbed his arm again and pulled, shaking her head frantically.

"Riga, we've got to get to higher ground."

The sound grew louder, the breeze rising as if a squall approached.

"Carson," Elisa said, "We haven't passed a high shelf or a side vent in the last half hour."

He nodded. The water would sweep in in seconds. He glanced about, waving his torch, searching for elevated ledges or slabs. The roar of the approaching torrent promised a wall of water that would inundate the room. A few tiny nooks were scattered about, offering no refuge. A narrow low slit lay to the left, in the corner of a shallow basin.

There was no safe haven from the flood.

"Make a run for it," Grant said, turning from the sound.

Riga snatched the torch from his grasp, ran toward the slit, stooped and scrambled into it, beckoning them to follow.

"Riga, no!" Grant shouted. "That's the low point in the room!"

"She knows something," Elisa said, and started after her.

Grant shook his head, shrugged his body tightly against Tennyson, and followed.

The slit bent under the overhanging rock and opened into a cavern thirty feet wide. Riga glanced about and darted to the left, stopping before a slab of tilted limestone. She dropped the torch and pulled against the slab, struggling against its massive weight. It moved a fraction of an inch, shedding grit.

The wind rose around them, rippling their clothes. The rush of sound grew into a roar.

"Help her!" Elisa cried, and ran to her.

Grant eased Tennyson to the floor, and heaved with them against the slab.

The slab grated sideward, grit flaking from it, slipped, fractured, and broke into pieces, exposing a narrow opening. Crumbling stone steps angled upward into darkness. Riga stepped inside, turned, frantically waving them after her.

Grant handed Elisa the torch, and pushed her into the opening, and shouldered Tennyson inside just as the flood burst into the cavern. Water swirled about his legs, enveloped him to his waist, and dashed him against the wall of the corridor. He lunged free, turning to see a wall of water foaming, fluorescent in the dim light, rushing past the opening and pouring onto the bottom steps.

"Climb!" he shouted. Water blasted into the slot.

The staircase angled up, tight and low-ceiled. Cold water lapped at Grant's heels, engulfed his knees, his waist, his chest, swirling in the stairwell, threatening to drag him under. He slipped, slid under the surface, swallowed water, regained his footing. He staggered another few steps higher, pushing Tennyson ahead of him.

The corridor leveled into a long tube. Grant turned to check the progress of the water in the staircase. It had stopped rising. "Rest here," he gasped.

He eased Tennyson into a sitting position and slid down to take a seat next to him.

"Goddamn close," Tennyson muttered.

"There must have been a hard rain on the surface to cause a flash flood," Elisa said.

"It rains hard every day this time of year," Grant said. "That flood was artificial."

"That grinding sound—?"

"A flood gate opening." His gaze fell upon Riga. She sat holding her legs tight against her chest, her chin resting on her knees, shivering. His heart thudded in his chest, and he slapped the stone wall, hard, trying to rein in sudden anger. "You *knew*."

Elisa moved closer and put her hand on her shoulder. "You knew what was coming."

Riga nodded slowly.

"How?"

Riga shook her head, confused.

"Have you been here before?"

Again Riga shook her head.

"Then how the hell did you know?" Grant shouted.

Riga shook her head frantically.

"Shut up, Carson!" Elisa snapped. "Can't you see she's as confused as we are?"

"That was no lucky guess. She knows this damned cave."

"We'd be dead if she did not, but she's never been here."

"You want me to believe she's some kind of psychic?"

"I didn't say that. But she *knows* things she's unaware of."

"I'm not buying it."

Tennyson coughed and raised his head. His eyes burned. "Carson, shut the hell up."

"Oh, now you perk up, when your little girlfriend catches some heat."

Tennyson swung his leg and kicked him. "Enough! I've had it with you, Grant. Sometimes things just get screwed up. You don't blame the nearest, easiest target. You don't blame Riga. You don't blame Billy Osprey. Sometimes things just get screwed up."

Heat rushed through Grant's face. "Don't tell me about Osprey, you little prick. You weren't there. You wouldn't come within a hundred miles of me." He sank to the floor, breathing hard, trembling. Silence hung in the air, bloated with heat and cold.

Grant's pulse slowed and his anger abated. Finally, he turned to Riga. "We *would* be dead. I'm an asshole. Please forgive me."

Riga nodded, her eyes unreadable.

No one spoke for a time. Grant stared into the dying torchlight, too ashamed to look at any of his companions. He could feel their eyes on him, especially Elisa's. He felt like an idiot, letting love slip away.

The thought alarmed him. Had his feelings for her gotten to that point? She was beautiful; even the grime of the caves couldn't mask that. But it was her presence, her keen intelligence, that attracted him. He'd been thrown with her into extreme danger, and extreme situations forged powerful emotions. But love? Couldn't pick a worse time.

He nodded toward the ebbing flame. "May I?"

She glared at him, and handed him the torch.

He fanned and blew it back to life. "This is our last torch. Twenty minutes left in it at best. Keep your eyes open for driftwood."

"We haven't found any in ages," Elisa said.

Grant advanced up the staircase. The corridor narrowed, forcing them single-file. He checked his compass. The needle fluttered and spun worthlessly.

The corridor constricted and ended in a rough stone slab, four feet high, chiseled to fit snugly in the opening. Grant pushed against the stone. It resisted, and he leaned against it and shoved. The stone grated against the wall, flaking bits loose, tipped and gave way, sliding to the floor with a dull thud.

A squared tunnel lay beyond, low and narrow. Grant stooped and peered in. It curled to the right a dozen feet ahead, and appeared to open wider. He stepped aside and let Riga and Elisa crawl ahead, and guided Tennyson on hands and knees ahead of him.

Ahead of him, Elisa gasped. "Carson! It's... it's not real."

He ducked through and stopped. He stared ahead, swallowed his breath.

The tunnel opened onto a shelf of rock on the edge of a vast cavern, the largest he'd ever seen. The domed ceiling soared overhead, four hundred feet high in the center, curving down into walls a thousand feet away on either side of them. Fifty feet below them, a black lake shimmered like silver in the dim light, stretching away before them.

In the center of the lake stood an island the length of two football fields, a magnificent city of white stone covering its entire width and breadth. Fires dotted the city, giving the gargantuan cavern a dim glow, and dappling the lake with shimmering gold.

Grant sank to his knees, overwhelmed, unable to breathe, unable to speak. He had explored the greatest sites of the ancient Maya, explored their ritual, sacred caves, but all paled in comparison to what lay before him. He knew in an instant what they had stumbled upon, though he could scarcely believe his own eyes. It was impossible, it was myth, yet here it was, a vision torn from the books, from the legends and religion of the Maya. He had to speak the name, to convince himself that he was actually looking upon it.

"Xibalbá," he whispered.

The underworld of the Maya.

The Place of Fear.

Xibalbá.

Chapter 36

Pacal lay on his belly in the mud, ignoring the multitude of scratches and welts on his arms and legs, resisting the temptation to swat at the insects buzzing about his face. Any sudden movement could give them away. He could endure a few thousand mosquitoes.

Linda lay at his side, trembling.

Her "wild men" were undoubtedly looters, scruffy and disgusting, too long in the forest. Pacal had encountered the type many times, and they could be merciless and terrifying indeed, and he understood the depth of her fear. Yet she refused to remain behind. Pacal took her hand and squeezed it reassuringly. She glanced at him, wide-eyed, and yanked her hand away.

Balam lay just ahead, motionless, peering through a fallen tree. Something—someone—moved in the clearing beyond him. He glanced back and motioned them forward.

Pacal hated inaction, but wondered at the wisdom of moving closer to the danger. He crept forward, and eased a clump of ferns aside, straining to see.

He caught his breath.

There was no camp, not a trace, but Linda's story was confirmed. Three pale giants paced the rim of the *cenote* erratically with furtive, darting eyes.

The wild men.

He turned to Linda. She stared ahead, shaking, her breathing rapid and clipped.

"Balam," Pacal whispered, "we must go."

The old man scowled, put a finger to his lips, and led them away from the *cenote*. Twenty minutes later, he halted. "We could not speak back there," he whispered. "The spirits of the forest have senses far keener than our own. They would have heard us and butchered us."

"Who are those men?" Pacal asked.

Balam hesitated. "They are unlike any other. They are Maya, in part. Ferocious fighters. You cannot fight a single one and expect to live."

Linda regarded the old man closely. "You know them."

Balam nodded.

"Who are they?"

"You already know the answer."

Linda shook her head. "How—what do you mean?"

"They are what you sought."

Surprise and comprehension crept into her face. "Norsemen? Impossible. They're Maya."

"They are both. They are the descendants of Norse berserkers. The last of their kind."

"Impossible."

"You saw their size, their weaponry. Have you ever seen Maya like that?"

She shook her head.

Pacal looked at her. "You expected *Vikings* in Guatemala?"

"We knew the Norse reached this area a thousand years ago. We didn't expect living relics."

"Your camp is gone."

"So is our proof."

"Why would they attack you?"

"Both Maya and Spanish believe this area to be haunted," Balam said. "It is indeed haunted, but not by dead spirits. These spirits are flesh and blood, and do not wish to be found. They will go to great lengths to remain hidden."

"How do you know this, Balam?"

"Because," Balam said, "I am one of them."

Chapter 37

Pacal struggled for words. Balam never lied; lies fell beyond his nature. Or did they? Pacal wondered if he knew Balam at all. "You do not resemble those men in the least!"

"No. This is why I live in society outside the forest."

Linda stabbed a finger at him. "You are *not* one of them. They're murderers."

"They are warriors. They kill only when assigned the task of killing."

"If you are one of them," Pacal said, "why do you not approach them?"

"Did you not observe? The berserker spell is upon them. It would be suicide."

"It is a temporary state?"

"The trance could last hours or days."

"I've never seen you in such a trance."

"You did not recognize it as such and I have the capacity to suppress it. It is a dangerous addiction."

"But you have lived with Riga and me our entire lives!"

"I was already an old man when I found you, Pacal."

"What now? The wild men are here. Riga is not!"

Pacal turned toward Linda. "If Riga and your friends still live, they are where the berserkers dwell. Come."

* * *

Twilight settled over the forest. Linda paused in the march, and wiped her face. Her body ached, protesting every step, and

186

exhaustion threatened to overwhelm her. Where was the damned second wind the fitness Nazis always babbled about? Emptiness ground at her. "Stop, please. I have to stop," she gasped, surprised how worn her own voice sounded. "Please."

Pacal hesitated, but Balam moved swiftly ahead. "We cannot stop," the old man said, glancing back.

"Damn it, stop! I can barely see where I'm going."

Balam turned and motioned Pacal to stop. "Do not raise your voice. Follow closely, step where I step. Your eyes must adjust." He started off again.

"Pacal," Linda said, a note of pleading in her voice.

"I am sorry. We follow or we abandon your friends and my sister and return to Santa Elena for help. That will take days. Unacceptable to me, but you are free to do as you choose."

"I'm afraid, Pacal."

He came to her side and lifted her arm, pulling it around his shoulder. "You have no strength left."

Linda shrugged out of his arm and stared at him. Like most Maya, Pacal was not a big man, but his shoulders moved with strong muscles. His strength felt good, reassuring. She relaxed and let him support her.

Balam finally stopped beside an outcropping of weathered limestone, all but invisible in the darkness. "Silent now, you blunderers. Become a ghost. A thousand paces ahead a great pyramid once stood. The entrance to the underworld lies there, but we will enter another way."

"The underworld? A cave?"

"There are giants in the earth, the white bible says. The berserkers live there."

"Damn you, Balam, you have told me nothing my whole life."

"I told you more than you realize. The time has never been right to reveal all. Until now."

Balam ran his hands over the face of the stone. He paused and probed a tiny fissure with his fingers. He pulled against it, grunting, and a slab of rock crusted and slipped, shedding dirt and humus. He leaned on the rock and it gave way, revealing a tunnel descending into the earth. He scowled at Pacal, breathing hard. "No, that wasn't at all heavy. Many thanks."

Cool air issued like a sigh from the tunnel. Balam disappeared into the darkness.

Pacal turned to Linda. "Are you able?"

Linda pushed past him and followed Balam into the darkness.

Chapter 38

Grant shook his head in disbelief.

"Carson," Tennyson murmured. "Is it...?"

"There's no other explanation. Xibalbá. The Place of Fear."

Elisa looked at them, shook her head.

"The Mayan underworld. A place of death, demons, and gods. Turns out it's more than myth." Grant remembered the torch and quickly doused it.

They sat still and quiet, drinking in the scene. Three magnificent, terraced pyramids dominated the center of the city. Great torches lit each corner of the pyramids, throwing a yellow glow over the white stone of the structures. Shadows danced in the torchlight, giving the city the eerie quality of a living creature.

The central pyramid towered high above the others, three hundred feet in height, nearly brushing the ceiling of the vast dome. A broad stone staircase mounted its steep façade from base to summit, bounded on either side by carvings of gigantic feathered serpents, their gaping, fanged mouths yawning at the base of the structure. Grotesque carvings of warriors, priests, kings, and gods adorned the tower. Atop it stood an elaborately carved temple, unlighted, in ruins.

"There's our missing pyramid," Tennyson said.

The two smaller pyramids stood a mere third of the central pyramid's height, one adorned with stylized skulls and demons, the other with scribes and jungle beasts.

At the foot of the central pyramid's staircase, a paved plaza, fifty yards wide, stretched out. A dirt-floored space fronted the plaza, bounded by gently sloped grandstands on either side.

"Ceremonial ball court," Grant whispered, pointing to it. "Teams played for sport but also for ritual and to settle grievances. Losers frequently were beheaded."

Hundreds of smaller stone buildings of varying sizes jammed the city. Near the ball court and central plaza, they were arrayed in a grid that disintegrated into a maze of twisting, narrow streets just beyond, hidden in shadow. The colossal structures about the center gave way to smaller houses on the outskirts.

Darkness and decay hung over most of the buildings, their walls crumbling, the thatched roofs sagging or gone. Yet from a handful, warm yellow light spilled from open windows. Even those suffered a degree of neglect, as if the occupants had simply lost interest.

Huge, pale men moved about like spirits.

As they watched, two giants passed in the street. One suddenly flew at the other, flailing away, and they grappled and rolled on the ground. He gained the upper hand, beat the other savagely, then suddenly stopped and stalked away. The other lay still for a moment, rose and shook himself, and sauntered off as if nothing had happened.

"Berserkers," Elisa whispered. "Rage without inhibition, injury without pain."

"Look at this place," Grant said. "A city this size would have housed thirty-thousand people. I see only a handful."

"Last vestiges of a dying race. That's the inevitability of it. How could anyone live in this pit for long?"

Grant stared, trying to fathom the enormity of it all. A cult of hybrids, a living, lost city of ancient Norse and Maya, thriving in the 21st century? Flat-out impossible, yet here it was. They had discovered the archaeological wonder of the ages, one that would rewrite the history of the Americas. His heart raced, but anger at the slaughter of his friends welled within him. He wanted to descend upon this city and kill everyone he saw.

Yet that would not happen. A living miracle for science lay before him. At all costs, they must escape Xibalbá and bring its discovery to the world.

Grant shook the thought. Screw discovery. Survival came first. "These people come and go to the surface. We have to find out how."

"We can't just follow them out."

"No, so we watch and we wait."

"How long? We're starving."

The vast, domed cavern seemed to glow, a trick of the firelight playing upon white and gray limestone. Great stalactites, fifty feet long and as thick as redwoods, hung from the ceiling, dripping water with regular ticking. Stalagmites rose from the lake to point at companion stalactites above, and five stalagmites and stalactites had grown together into complete columns four hundred feet tall.

Far to their right, a shelf projected from the wall into the lake. Clearly artificial, its masonry had a utilitarian look, like old stone docks and wharves of Europe. A black canoe floated low in the water next to it, gently rocking.

Beyond the dock, on the far side of the cavern, Grant could make out another dock, surmounted by an ornate, framed opening carved in the cavern wall. A dugout canoe was moored there also. Torches illuminated both docks.

Grant pointed to the farther, ornate dock. "I'll bet the mortgage that's the way in and out, maybe the only way. That's where we need to be."

Movement caught his eye at the nearer dock on the outer edge of the cavern. Five figures emerged from the shadows onto the dock and boarded the canoe.

Elisa nodded. "That's where we would have emerged if we were still on our original route."

"Then those are the bastards that opened a floodgate to drown us."

"Maybe not. Could have been routine maintenance. The river is constantly flowing, but maybe they flush out the lake once in a while."

"Wishful thinking, Elisa. They tried to drown us."

"Either way, they think we're dead already."

The dugout eased away from the dock. Oars sprouted from the gunwales and dipped into the water, rippling the surface with the reflected gold of the torches. The figures leaned into the oars in unison and propelled the craft across the lake toward the island. The boat sliced the water, reaching the city dock in little more than a minute. The figures disembarked and busied themselves tying ropes and unloading bundles.

Grant peeled off his shirt and tossed it aside. He shifted his legs over the shelf and slid down into the water. He felt for the bottom without success.

"Where are you going?" Elisa asked.

"To the main entrance. We've got to scout it."

"Now?"

"No point waiting for a nightfall that won't come, and each minute delayed is a minute hungrier and weaker. I'm going to check the depth first."

He pushed away from the ledge and dove under, kicking toward the bottom. The cold water chilled him. He knew that it was likely crystal clear, but in the dim cavern may as well have been ink. After thirty feet, he gave up and returned to the surface.

"Can't find the bottom. This is one deep pond." He looked at Riga and Tennyson, and pulled close to Elisa. "I'll check out the floodgate first, then the far dock. The way out has to be at one of them."

"We'll never get Gene that far."

"Not without a boat. There's one canoe left, and I plan on a little burglary." He turned to go.

"Carson..."

He paused. Elisa pulled him close and kissed him. "Be careful," she whispered.

Grant reached up and caressed her cheek. "Keep my friend alive," he whispered, easing away, "and stay out of sight."

He hugged the wall of the cavern, barely rippling the water. He paused occasionally to feel for the bottom, on the chance that a talus slope may have accumulated and built a ledge. He could find none.

His awe of the sheer scale of this gigantic cavern grew. He'd dived miles of labyrinthine caves of the Yucatán, and knew of hundreds of miles of caves in Belize and Guatemala. This dwarfed any cave he'd seen, including Mammoth in Kentucky and Carlsbad in New Mexico.

He could see that the island had formed from an ancient collapse of stone from the ceiling, evidenced by jagged fractures in the ceiling. The great mass of stone must have crashed into the lake long before human eyes ever beheld it, creating an island thirty feet high. Ultimately, time and water would finish the job. A great fall of stone would crush Xibalbá and all that would mark its location would be a vast sinkhole.

Distances proved difficult to judge. The vast, arching dome, the sheer volume of space, distorted perspective, but Grant tried to memorize in some way everything he saw.

At last, the stone dock loomed ahead, projecting at a right angle from a niche in the wall, several feet above the water. Two torches, set atop pylons, lighted it with dim, flickering fire. Grant entered the shifting pool of light, clinging to the shadowed wall. He paused and studied the dark recess, listening intently. Hearing nothing, he eased to the dock, pulled himself up, and peered in. The niche receded some twenty feet into the wall, and a staircase disappeared into the floor.

A burble of moving water came from somewhere within the structure. Grant felt all about for openings or gates; internal mechanisms lay hidden within, and their workings might yield vital information.

The structure's surface lay in plain view, frustratingly exposed. He peered down into the water. In the light of the torches, he could see to a good depth. He slipped beneath the surface and swam along the dock wall, feeling his way.

He discovered a series of wooden discs, each a yard in diameter, recessed in the walls. The floodgates.

He continued around the dock, surfacing periodically for air. On the opposite side, as he dove under the surface, a sudden powerful tug of water caught him and pulled him forward in a rush. A black opening loomed before him and he was propelled toward it. He realized his mistake: the underground river beyond this cavern had a constant surge, and a single floodgate remained open to maintain that flow.

The water pulled like a great, unrelenting hand. He twisted his body, thrusting his feet out, and slammed into the wall, his right leg stiff against the opposite side of the opening. The current threatened to suck him in, the surge pinning him against the wall. His lungs ached for air. He worked his arms and legs into position against the wall and kicked away. Digging his fingers into the stone joints and kicking again, he gained a few inches, his progress in the current agonizingly slow. Starved of oxygen, his muscles burned with pain.

Losing strength, in a few more seconds he'd be sucked into the flood gate. Grant mustered his waning strength and kicked with all his might away from the wall. He gained a bit, and was pulled back. He adjusted his angle and shoved away again, this time breaking the current's hold on him as he burst toward the surface.

His head struck a massive object. Pain ricocheted through his skull and black specks gathered in his mind. He moved laterally and felt above with his hands. Something blocked his path to the surface. He threw his hands against the object and pushed. It yielded, shifting to one side, and Grant breached the surface, gasping a long, desperate breath. He grabbed the top of the dock and clung to it, inhaled deeply, his cheek pressed against the cold stone. Panting heavily, he rested, trying to collect his thoughts. He turned to see what he had collided into.

A heavy wooden canoe bumped gently against the dock.

He felt warm sticky blood. Nausea swept through him, and he vomited. Blackness swirled in his vision and the world went dark.

Feeling himself slipping again under the water, he snapped back to consciousness. His thoughts grew fuzzy and out of focus, and his eyelids heavy. He shook his head, trying to rally his thoughts.

The exertion of the swim, the struggle against the floodgates, and the blow to his head had dazed him. He could not return to his companions, not without rest, and would drown before he got a third of the way back.

The city remained quiet. No sign that he'd been spotted. No movement at all, just the warm, flickering light of a hundred fires. The flames tantalized and beckoned with a hypnotic glow, urging him to sleep.

He studied the open niche, in plain view. What about the staircase? He gripped the edge of the dock and raised himself out of the water, swung his leg onto the dock, crawled on his belly to the stairwell opening and slipped down it. Just below the dock, a heavy wooden door barred the way.

He pulled against the door, but it held fast, the strain bringing dizziness back with a vengeance. He stumbled and slipped back into the water, causing the dugout to clatter against the dock.

The dugout.

A big one, a war canoe, hewn from an enormous tree trunk. The gunwales rose high enough that a person might lay in the bottom, hidden in shadow. If no one approached, he could rest and pilot the craft back to the ledge.

Grant again clambered onto the dock, steadied the boat, and eased over the gunwale into the canoe. He lay still, breathing hard, listening, his head crashing like a cymbal. He needed rest, but sleep was suicide. Just a bit of rest, his fogged mind argued.

No! Stay awake, damn you.

Against his will, his eyelids drooped.

Chapter 39

Elisa Anderssen bit her fingernail as she watched the city. The berserkers from the floodgates had disappeared into the maze of streets and alleys. She turned her attention back to the faraway dock.

Something had gone wrong.

Carson had pulled himself onto the dock in broad view of the city and been lucky enough to escape detection, then simply disappeared.

Seconds morphed into minutes.

Cold fear gripped her. Carson was not overly cautious; he'd lower his head and run through a brick wall—or try—on an impulse. Therefore, he'd gotten trapped or hurt.

Or worse.

She shook her head. She had to assume he lived and needed help. Any other assumption led to inertia.

She eased over to Tennyson, who had drifted into sleep, shivering.

Riga looked up, fear lining her face.

"Riga," Elisa said, "something's happened to Carson, and I'm going after him. Stay with Gene. I'll be right back."

Riga glanced at the dock, and shook her head fearfully.

"I have to help him." Elisa squeezed Riga's hand gently, and slipped quietly into the water.

The futility of it struck her as she eased along the cavern wall. She likely had two injured men to somehow express across this dark, flooded underworld to an exit undoubtedly guarded by the homicidally insane. Why on earth did she think she could succeed?

Concentrate on the task at hand, she told herself. *Self-doubt poisons you.*

The floodgate dock seemed impossibly far, and she fought the urge to hurry, trying to be invisible. Ripples in the water reflected light, and light would give her away.

She kept an eye on the city. What could she do if discovered? There would be no escape. Surrender—immediate surrender— would be the only way to distract them from either Grant or Riga and Gene, and afford them any possibility of escape.

She reached the halfway point and paused. The city dock remained quiet. The chill of the water seeped into her and she felt herself shivering.

She reached the dock. Deserted, as far as she could tell. She could make out an opening in the floor, tucked into the niche. Could there be berserkers in the structure below? She put her ear to the stone and heard the soft rush of water, and pulled herself around the perimeter, hand over hand, to the opposite side.

As she rounded the dock, a sudden tug of current strained against her. Tightening her grip on the edge of the dock, she pulled her body higher out of the water. The black hulk of a canoe loomed ahead.

Grant lay motionless in the bottom. Holding her breath, she touched his face, and felt his neck for a pulse, stifling a sob of relief.

She scanned the city again, swung a leg onto the dock, pulled herself up, and edged into the canoe and lay beside him. "Carson." No answer. She shook him gently, ran her hands over him, searching for injury. She felt a stickiness in his scalp, and her hand came away warm with blood.

* * *

Linda descended into the gloom, feeling her way along the coarse stone, cautiously testing each step, pointing this way and that with a weak flashlight. The air moved gently, moist and cool, a welcome relief from the thick, wet atmosphere of the rainforest, and boosted her spirits. Maybe there was hope after all.

The tunnel corkscrewed and wound, attesting that it had once been a natural cave. She had never counted herself claustrophobic, but she had never found herself in such an extreme environment, either. Countless tons of earth and stone perched inches above her head. She caught herself holding her breath.

Despite the gloom, Balam plunged ahead, sure-footed as a mountain goat. He would periodically stop, wait impatiently for Linda and Pacal, and resume his way with an exasperated sigh and a curse.

Pacal picked his way along, measuring his steps, at one point stumbling into her when she'd paused to feel her way. She stiffened at the contact and shrank from him. "Forgive, *por favor*," he said softly, dropping back several paces.

She paused, silent for a moment, and resumed her way.

Did he hate her? His attitude had been politely aloof at best. Maybe it was cultural. Maybe he hated Americans in general. Whatever, these two men were all she had in the world at this moment. They might hate her but she felt safe with them.

Balam stopped suddenly and Linda bumped into him. He squeezed her hand gently and released it. "Slow now. And silently, for once in your life. Look ahead."

She pointed the flashlight. A few feet ahead, the tunnel narrowed into an angled fissure, blocked by rubble.

"The cave collapsed," Linda said.

"Ah, so you are a geologist," Balam said. "Wrong. I blocked it. Many years ago."

"You, Balam?" Pacal asked.

"I am the only man alive that knows this passage."

He lit a candle and melted a pool of wax onto the floor and anchored the candle in it. He pried a large rock from the fissure and set it aside with a grunt. He turned and scowled. "Must a feeble old man move all these rocks by himself?"

Linda suppressed a smile and began pulling rocks loose.

They labored for an hour until the narrow crack cleared. Without a word, Balam twisted his body and squeezed inside.

Linda entered the slit, her back pressed against one wall, her breasts scraped by the opposite. She envied Balam's wiry frame and wondered how the stockier Pacal would manage. After a short distance, the opening constricted, its ceiling lower, barely two feet high. She flattened and pulled herself along on her stomach.

She emerged from the low slot, scuffed and sweating, onto a broader, higher tunnel. Balam waited, silhouetted against dim light ahead, a hint of a smile for her. "Turn off your flashlight," he whispered.

Pacal squirmed through and stumbled out with a last struggle. Glowering, he opened his mouth to speak.

Balam put a finger to his lips and turned down the tunnel.

A faint glow. The tunnel opened ahead into a larger space.

Linda stepped out into a vast cavern. She gasped and staggered, the sudden, overwhelming change of scale giving her a touch of vertigo.

"Impossible," she whispered. "Impossible."

* * *

Elisa felt about in the canoe and found a short paddle. She unhitched the line and pushed the boat gently away from the dock and slipped again into the water alongside it, the canoe shielding her from view of the city. If spotted, she hoped the canoe would appear adrift, and wouldn't stir undue suspicion and haste. She swam slowly along the cavern wall, easing the canoe with her.

Hope began to grow. She had covered some fifty meters, undiscovered. Quiet hung over the city, its inhabitants going about their business.

At the halfway point, a chorus of shouts echoed through the chamber, the alarm raised. She peeked over the gunwale. A dozen warriors scrambled about the island dock, unhitching lines and tossing them into a large craft obscured in shadow on the far side of the main dock.

To hell with caution. Elisa slung her leg over the gunwale and lunged into the dugout, sat bolt upright and stabbed the water with her paddle, leaning into it with all her strength. The canoe darted forward, the dark lake glittering with the sudden disturbance.

The berserkers heaved their craft away from the dock. Oars

sprouted in rows above the gunwales on both sides and dipped the water and pulled in perfect unison. The craft shot from the island with astonishing speed, rounding the shadowy far side of the island dock.

Elisa instantly recognized the sleek, elegant lines of the boat, its graceful curves of overlapped planking. A tall mast, unrigged and useless on this windless underground lake, rose from the center, draped with ragged banners in lieu of sails. Rising from the bow stood a ghastly, reptilian carving, its eyes glaring, its jaws agape, baring saber fangs.

A *drakkar*. Dragonship.

She stared, dumbfounded, suddenly aware that she knew nothing. She had excavated a rotted dragonship from a peat bog in Norway, and supervised construction of a replica for television. That boat held historically accurate, right down to the wooden pegs that held it together and the pitch that waterproofed it. She had taken it to sea off Oslo with her students and sailed hundreds of kilometers along the Norwegian coast.

She had underestimated not the skill of the boat builders, but of the boatmen themselves.

These berserkers, possessed of tremendous power and a single-mindedness she had never imagined, fairly flew across the water. The oars flashed in swift precision, dipping and stroking the water.

Redoubling her efforts, she strained into her paddle with a vengeance, but the heavy canoe seemed to crawl. She gauged the distance remaining. In another minute she would reach the tunnel. As she glanced back, her heart sank.

The dragonship knifed toward her, throwing bow waves high and white. She would not reach the shelf. Even if she did, what would it matter? They would be slaughtered there or tracked into the tunnel and killed.

Their options had run out. Yet hope, however slim, remained for Riga and Gene.

"Riga," she shouted in English, watching the approaching dragonship. "Stay hidden, stay low, but run!" She struck the water with her paddle, ruddered the canoe about, and headed in the opposite direction.

The dragonship veered with her and narrowed the gap swiftly.

She glanced at the shelf, hoping not to give away Riga's position.

Riga remained crouched and hidden in the rocks.

Three dark figures crept from the tunnel behind her.

A chill struck Elisa. "Riga! Behind you!"

The rush of water nearby grabbed her attention. The prow of the dragonship loomed over her, mere feet away, the dragon's head grimacing, as if preparing to strike and kill.

She pulled Grant to her and rolled overboard an instant before the collision. The ship slammed broadside into the canoe, shattering it with a crack like a gunshot. She plunged beneath the chill water.

Blackness enveloped her and the surge from the passing ship pushed her down, deeper and deeper.

Chapter 40

Linda tried to make sense of the surreal. A vast dome, a shimmering black lake, a sprawling city. A swirl of commotion on the lake before her. A cry of alarm—she could have sworn she heard Elisa!

A sharp crack of sound, a reverberating echo. A ship, swarming with the wild men.

A dragonship!

A movement in the shadows to her right. She wheeled to face it.

The figure hesitated and darted toward them.

"Riga!" Pacal cried. "You're alive!"

Riga embraced him, sobbing.

* * *

Terror gripped Elisa as the rolling water shoved her deeper. The dark hull above rushed past, seeming to go on forever. Her lungs ached for air.

The rush of water tore Grant from her grasp. Unconscious and bleeding, he would drown in seconds, merely an arm length or two away. She felt and kicked about, desperate to make contact.

She struck her head and shoulder hard against the hull, feeling rough wood lash her skin. Kicking against the hull, she pushed away, broke the surface and gasped for air.

A powerful hand closed like a vise upon her wrist and yanked her from the water, wrenching her shoulder, and slinging her over the gunwale and hard to the deck. She coughed water and lifted herself. A body slammed into her, driving her back down. She shoved the dripping body away in reflexive terror.

Carson!

Elisa touched his neck, found a strong pulse. She wrestled him over, face down, and opened his mouth. Water trickled out and she turned him again, tilted his head, pinched his nostrils closed, and blew into his mouth. After a few breaths, he sputtered and lurched over, vomiting water.

His spasms subsided, and he turned blearily to her, tried to speak, and coughed up more water.

"Easy," she whispered. "You're three-quarters dead."

Lining the sides of the ship, massive warriors leaned into oars and pulled in unison. A breeze tossed a few strands of her hair as the boat sped across the water.

The largest of their captors stood glaring over them, fists clenching and unclenching. Grant raised himself above the gunwale and returned his gaze evenly. "The fuck are you looking at, Olaf?"

The guard kicked him, driving him to the deck.

Grant winced, and smiled weakly at Elisa. "That wasn't too bright, huh?"

The guard turned and spoke to his companions. The language was Mayan, punctuated with a smattering of Old Norse. He appeared to be in command of the boat.

Grant turned to Elisa. "Gene? Riga?"

"Hiding on the shelf. You were hurt so I came after you."

"They're taking us to the shelf."

"You and I are likely dead, Carson, but we can give our friends a chance. I yelled to Riga to run when I was discovered."

The captain barked a command and the starboard warriors dipped oars in unison and stroked once in the opposite direction. The ship came about and the port oars stroked, braking the boat, its hull grating against the rocky shelf. Every third warrior on port reeled in his oar and seized shield, sword, and battle axe, and sprang over the gunwale. An eerie cry burst from them, like the baying of wolves and the whooping of howler monkeys.

The landing distracted the captain. Elisa glanced at Grant. He drew himself up unsteadily, careened over, caught himself, took a step toward the warrior.

Elisa shook her head. "Don't even think about it."

"It's all about angles," he whispered. "Just friggin' math." He steadied, and threw himself at the captain, buckling him at the knees, wrapping the man's legs together and heaving. The giant stumbled.

Elisa stood and shouted, "Riga, get Gene into the tunnel and run!"

The giant twisted around. Grant held on, pinning the man's legs together. The giant flailed, unable to reach him.

Another sprang forward and cuffed Elisa across the mouth, sending her to the deck. She rolled, dazed, and spat blood. A third seized Grant around the midsection and yanked him free of the captain and slung him into the wall of the boat.

The captain's eyes burned, and he snatched up a battle axe and advanced on Grant.

A commanding voice boomed. The captain looked toward the shelf, confusion in his eyes. The voice boomed again, an unknown word, and a murmur ran through the warriors.

Elisa scrambled to the gunwale. Cornered by berserkers, Riga and Tennyson stood alongside Linda and two others. Elisa recognized the Maya policeman. Riga's brother, Pacal. He leveled a pistol in the face of the nearest warrior.

The other, a lean, gray Mayan, stood with outstretched hands. The old man's voice boomed once more. The captain lowered his axe. The old man spoke to Pacal, who shook his head angrily. The old man placed his hand on Pacal's pistol. Pacal swatted the man's hand away, pointed it again. After a moment, he lowered the weapon.

The giant reached for it cautiously.

Pacal turned and threw the weapon far out into the lake. The berserker's fist slammed into his face, sending him sprawling to the ground.

Chapter 41

Santiago felt renewed appreciation for the old training. He had grown lazy and soft pushing pencils and tourists in Belize City, had forgotten how grueling and satisfying life in the forests and hills could be. The demands on willpower and strength were great, the rewards greater still.

He'd lain in wait, watchful, hidden in underbrush for nearly two days, leaving the worthless Cabrillo and Garcia hidden in the forest a kilometer back to wait for his return. He had eaten only a bit of salted pork, plus the occasional bug that wandered past. Hunger gnawed at his stomach. His left arm itched with the crawling parasites that had eaten their way underneath the skin, yet he remained still.

He had found the site of the vanished pyramid.

Even the most astute observer might have blundered right past it. Despite years as a finder of profitable ruins, he'd have missed it himself had he not known exactly where to look. This was not a forgotten ruin. It had been subtly and skillfully removed.

What were the damned gringos up to? They had erased their encampment at the Well of Spirits and searched this place. But where were they? They had not returned to Tikal or Flores; he would know. No, they were still abroad in the forest.

The Americans had maintained radio silence since his last intercept. They'd obscured this site and moved on, probably north and east, sneaking back into Belize in the remote north, away from controlled border crossings, laden with treasures stolen from Guatemala.

Yet he had scoured the forest floor in every direction, looking for sign of their passing, finding none. Perhaps they knew of his presence. Perhaps they had come upon Cabrillo and Garcia and slit their sorry throats.

Even Santiago's patience knew limits. Perhaps he'd erred in judgment. He shook his head, trying to banish the thought. Doubt cursed weaker men. Not him.

Sweat trickled down his brow and onto his nose. He tilted his head and a drop fell to the ground. He daydreamed of his noisy air-conditioner in Belize City. He endured yet another mosquito bite without flinching. The forest grew abysmally quiet, and his doubts mushroomed.

The Americans had taken their plunder and headed for the border.

He cursed himself, swatted the next mosquito, and sat up.

There could yet be hope if he acted swiftly. Miller, the English bastard in Belize customs, could arrange difficulties in passage for the Americans, slowing them enough that Santiago could catch them and slit their throats. Miller would expect a hefty bite out of his profits, but any profit surpassed none.

He brushed the filth from his clothing.

Then came the crack of a twig to his right. Santiago snapped his revolver in that direction, listening, unmoving.

The sound of footfalls in soft leaf litter. Movement. Several figures eased through the jungle, obscured by foliage and the lingering mist. The gringos, returning. Their course would bring them within thirty paces. Excellent. At that angle and range, the gringos would be dead before they hit the ground.

But something alerted him, something amiss. They moved as phantoms, not spoiled American academics.

Three massive men strode into view, dressed in bizarre clothing and bearing antique weapons. Each carried a brace of dead howler monkeys, iguanas, and birds slung over their shoulders. Their flesh glistened with sweat, ghostly pale, whiter even than that of the gringos.

Even in the shade of the forest, they squinted against the morning twilight. They moved silent and swift, like spirits of ancient warriors, the sound that had alerted him an aberration, out of character with the silence of their passage.

The leader paused, signaled his companions to a stop, and shot a searching glance in Santiago's direction. They stood motionless as statues. After a moment, the man resumed his march and stopped twenty paces away. He stooped and strained against something in the ground.

The men descended into the earth. The rough, low sound of stone against stone came to him and then silence reigned.

Santiago hesitated, looking about for more giants, and sprang forward and raced to the spot where they had disappeared. Nothing, not a doorway, not a tunnel, not even a crack. Only muck and weeds. He fell to his knees, disbelieving, and searched the ground. The vision of pale giants gliding through the forest had been like a dream. Perhaps he had dozed and dreamed the whole thing.

A blade of grass caught his eye. It had been bent and was slowly returning to form. He touched it and traced a finger about an area that outlined a faint footprint. He then found another and another.

He plunged his fingers into the loose, moist soil, his hand sinking to his wrist before striking a hard surface. He probed until he felt a metal ring. He pulled it, gently at first, and then with all his strength.

A stone door lay there, expertly hidden, massively heavy. He could not budge it. He released the ring and rocked back, panting.

None of this made sense. It defied logic. The Americans had vanished, and the forest was prowled by strange men who did not like to be seen, strange men with strange weapons, weapons from ancient history.

Ancient *European* history.

The Americans entered El Petén on a crazy mission seeking traces of explorers a thousand years past. The gringos were likely dead, erased as expertly as the tracks these men had left. Santiago's face flushed with excitement. The Americans were fools, but with fools' luck they had found far more than they sought.

They had found Vikings.

Chapter 42

Elisa lay face down in the fore of the ship, her hands bound painfully behind her back, her face pressed against the rough planking, gagged by a heavy leather cord. Rancid bilge water slid across the deck with the rolling of the boat, splashing against her face and entering her gagged mouth, causing her to sputter and choke.

A warrior stood over her, his bare foot resting upon her back. She felt his eyes roam her body, sending a shudder through her. She twisted her head about to see; he stared at her with eyes black and dilated, with a flat, lifeless quality. Dead Eyes. She wondered if Dead Eyes was devoid of a soul or merely insane.

Dead Eyes spoke in clipped commands to a brute with a smashed nose like a cauliflower. Broken Nose, Elisa decided, was the ship's first mate.

Grant lay nearby, also bound and gagged, watching her. He forced a smile.

Beyond him lay their companions, similarly bound, except for the old man, who gazed, unbound, at the city. The old man had seemed important to Pacal, yet Pacal was as surely a captive as she was. Had he been betrayed by a friend?

The ramparts of the city loomed over the boat. Dead Eyes turned aft and growled instructions. The tongue was strange, but rang with vague familiarity. A word grabbed her attention: *styrboord*. The Old Norse word was unmistakable. Starboard. The steering board, the rudder, always mounted on the right hand aft side of Viking vessels, a root of nautical lexicon for centuries. As she expected, the ship swung about and the left side of the boat bumped gently into the dock. Vikings always approached "port" on the left to protect the steering board on the right.

The giants tossed and secured lines, and Dead Eyes hoisted Elisa with one hand from the boat and swung her over the gunwale onto the stone dock. Her companions soon stood beside her.

The old man approached. Dead Eyes blocked his path. The old man ignored him, pushed his hand away brusquely, and drew his knife. Elisa readied herself to kick out at him.

"I have spoken to the captain," he said in English. "Be quiet and still, all of you. They will kill you without hesitation." He cut her bonds and gag, and proceeded to free the others.

Pacal said, "Balam, how do you know this place and these men?"

"I have told you already. I am one of them. Quiet now, Pacal. You are among berserkers."

The berserkers shoved the captives together into a knot and herded them into the city. Grant looped Tennyson's arm over his shoulder and supported his weight. Tennyson's ashen face sagged, and his head bobbed against his chest. Grant spoke softly to him, worry in his eyes.

A jumble of decaying buildings crowded onto narrow streets. The dock fronted a broad boulevard, some thirty meters in width by a hundred long, lined with torches atop stone pillars. The boulevard opened onto the ceremonial ball court, its sand floor bounded by sloped terraces.

Stone buildings of all sizes lined the boulevard. One structure, large and forbidding, dwarfed the adjacent temples, its high walls topped by ramparts, lacking ornamentation.

Grant nodded toward it. "Doesn't look Mayan," he murmured.

"It's a fortress," Elisa said. "A castle keep, if you will. The Norse have transplanted a few European ideas of architecture here."

Centered at the far end of the ball court, a stone platform stood upon a raised dais of stone a half-meter in height. Brown and black stains streaked the entire structure.

"The sacrificial altar," Grant said. "Still in use, it seems."

Beyond the altar stood another low terrace, in the center of which stood a honey-colored crystalline stone, five meters high and two wide. It had the look of sculpture, its sinuous form and smoothly rippled surface twisted and drawn like an enormous piece of blown glass. Its transparent interior caught the firelight and played with the light in a kaleidoscope of color and shape.

"It's beautiful," Elisa whispered. "A sacred stone?"

"It must be," Grant said. "I've never seen anything like it. Anywhere."

Pacal paused and touched the crystal. Dead Eyes slapped his hand away and shoved him along.

"You break it, you buy it," Linda said.

Pacal continued to study the crystal, frowning.

Thirty meters beyond the crystal stood the gigantic central pyramid.

At the end of the ball court, the giants prodded them left onto a narrower boulevard. It ran arrow straight fifty meters to the base of the second pyramid.

Gloom cloaked the avenue. Small stone houses lined the street, most in disrepair, and others little more than rubble. Rotting and sagging thatched roofs clung to some of the structures. Dim light glowed from a few, but most were dark. Debris piled the edges of the avenue and spilled into the street. Rank odors of decay emanated from every corner.

"Housekeeping's a little lax," Linda said.

The denizens of Xibalbá moved about the darkened streets in small numbers, stopping to watch with sullen eyes. Most were men but women moved furtively about, keeping their distance.

"They're afraid of coming into the open," Linda said. "Afraid of us."

Children scampered in the darkness, clambering over the debris, keeping pace with the party. A small girl, filthy and ragged, no more than ten, stepped into the light, her eyes curious and wild. Elisa smiled and a look of awe came into the girl's face. She took a step closer.

Elisa held out her hand.

The girl darted forward and touched her. The guard closest growled and chased her away, again into the shadows. The other children scattered.

They passed into shadow, and something rattled and sagged beneath Elisa's foot. She had stepped on the rib cage of an ancient corpse. Her foot sank into the mass and she felt the scurrying of a small creature across her ankle. She shuddered and kicked free. The rat squealed in protest and skittered away.

The party stopped in a small courtyard at the foot of the smaller pyramid. Its sides climbed in three terraces to a flattened peak, upon which stood a low, rectangular temple. Light glowed from within the temple.

Dead Eyes called out. The light in the temple flickered, and a massive form darkened the entry. A huge man moved with deliberate power and grace, like a great cat, from the temple to the edge of the pyramid. He paused, looked down upon them, and descended the steps.

The figure reached the courtyard and approached Dead Eyes.

Dead Eyes trembled.

* * *

Grant stared at the man, who loomed seven feet in height, easily, a giant even among these giants, with a chest like a redwood, and long arms knotted and thick with muscle. He wore a black leather robe and loincloth, with a gold and black leather headdress, crested in black feathers that gave him the appearance of even greater height, over eight feet. Narrow black eyes glared malevolently in the firelight, from a coarse, raw-boned face of indeterminate age. Grant had the uneasy feeling that his age was far greater than one could imagine.

Dead Eyes stammered through his report. The giant listened silently, appraising the captives one by one.

Grant eased closer. Dead Eyes spoke a Yucatec dialect rife with peculiar phrasings and unknown words, but Grant picked up his meaning as he described the heroic capture, spiced with references to his own bravery and cunning.

When Dead Eyes finished, the giant waved him aside, with some annoyance. Dead Eyes looked relieved.

The dark giant addressed the old man. "Balam," he growled. "I thought you dead."

"I do not die well, Lord Zotz."

Zotz gestured toward the captives. "You have brought outsiders amongst us."

Balam remained still.

"That is forbidden."

"Many things are forbidden, but things change."

Grant, still supporting Tennyson, eased his friend to the ground. He turned to Zotz. "This man needs care," he said in Yucatec.

Zotz looked at him. "You speak our tongue."

"The tongue lives on," Balam said.

"I'm a scholar of your people," Grant said. "Will you help my friend?"

Zotz moved close. He studied Tennyson for a moment, looking him up and down. In a flash, he grabbed Tennyson by the arm and jerked him from the ground with a single hand, closed his other arm about his neck and twisted viciously. There was a sharp crack as Tennyson's neck snapped, his eyes frozen in horror. Zotz tossed his body aside like a rag doll.

The whole episode happened in the blink of an eye.

Grant stared for a split-second, in shock. Blinding fury suddenly gripped him. He threw himself at Zotz.

Zotz seized him by the shoulder with a grip like the talons of an eagle, and struck him in the face, the blow of a sledgehammer. Grant sprawled to the pavement. Darkness swam in his eyes. He tried to rise, and stumbled to his knees.

Elisa dashed to his side and steadied him.

Riga lunged at Zotz. He seized her by the throat and hurled her into a pile of debris. She struggled to her feet. He seized a battle axe from one of the warriors and advanced upon her.

Grant's head throbbed and the wound in his scalp reopened and dripped blood. He held onto Elisa's shoulder, pulled himself to his feet, stumbled forward. Pacal and Linda struggled in the grip of their captors. Pacal twisted and dropped and slipped free, and wrenched the warrior's arm about and brought it down across his own shoulder. The arm dislocated at the elbow and the warrior recoiled in pain. Pacal darted to Riga's side.

Zotz raised the axe above his head.

Balam stepped into Zotz's path. "You will not harm these outsiders."

"But I shall, Balam. And you are next."

"It is forbidden."

"The slaying of gods is forbidden. The slaying of outsiders is commanded."

From the shadows in the street came hurrying footsteps. "Lord Zotz, hear Balam out. The law demands as much."

Zotz whirled. He gripped his axe, his eyes ablaze. "Ah Puuc. How timely. I thought you cowered with your friends in Mitnal."

"Balam is again among us, bringing outsiders to Xibalbá. *Skraelings*. A high crime, true, but a crime which may have reason." Ah Puuc let his gaze move among the warriors. "We must at least hear him out."

Zotz lowered his axe. "Very well. Speak, Balam. Why should these invaders live even another moment?"

"I've been gone many years, as commanded," Balam said. "As you say, the killing of gods is forbidden, and therefore you cannot kill these outsiders." He pointed to Riga and Pacal. "Behold your gods, citizens of Xibalbá. I have returned with Ixchel, goddess of flood. And with the mightiest of gods, the lost ruler, come to reclaim his throne."

All eyes were upon Pacal. Pacal looked from Balam to Riga, confused.

Shock flashed across Zotz's face, and vanished, replaced with malevolence.

Balam's eyes flashed and his voice rang through the cavern. "Our master has returned. Behold Feathered Serpent, great Kukulcán!"

Chapter 43

Grant steadied himself through his pain, looked quickly from the old man to Pacal, to Zotz.

Zotz shook with barely contained rage. "Impostors! Look at them! Look at this little man! Would Kukulcán be such a weakling?"

"True," Ah Puuc said. "This man is not the equal of the weakest among us. However, the law is clear; one revealed by the jaguar must be considered."

Zotz held his silence, still trembling. At last, he visibly regained his composure. "Very well. We will consider them. Now get them out of my sight." He stalked away, and scaled the pyramid from which he'd descended, vaulting up three or four steps at a time.

"Balam," Pacal said. "Are you insane?"

Balam turned away without a glance.

Twelve warriors, their axes extended, ringed the outsiders and prodded them along, shepherding them back to the ball court and into the fortress.

The structure was a true rampart, fortified on all sides, riddled with niches and portals, studded with defensive abutments. The entrance loomed atop a steep staircase, rendering successful assault upon the gate a near impossibility. High crosswalks spanned the interior, organized around a broad tower. Warriors could be dispatched in seconds to the four walls of the square structure. A wide platform traversed the length of the main outer walls, a formation repeated at three levels.

The prisoners were led through a trap door in the deck of the upper level, and down a stone staircase into a gloomy maze of tunnels, stairs, and rooms at crazy angles. After many turns, their captors herded them into a small cell devoid of furnishings. An oil lamp guttered weakly, throwing nervous shadows onto streaked, filthy walls. The door thundered shut behind them, and the echo hung in the air.

Grant's scalp had stopped bleeding, but his head still throbbed. Nausea caused his gorge to rise, and he broke into a cold sweat.

Gene was gone. He'd failed yet another close friend. Was this what he'd signed on for? Was this how he was expected to lead?

Snap out of it. Dwelling on it wouldn't save anyone.

Elisa shivered, her eyes wide, seeming on the verge of collapse. Linda appeared near exhaustion. Pacal spoke softly to Riga and held her. She drew her knees close in and wrapped her arms tight around them, and stared at the floor.

"Get some rest," Grant said matter-of-factly. "For our escape. Start thinking of ways out of this mess."

Glances passed between his companions.

He turned to Pacal. *"Yo habla español."*

Pacal studied him, expressionless. "English, too."

"You didn't reveal that little fact when we first met."

Pacal shrugged.

"Hidalgo said you're a policeman."

"Hidalgo was being generous."

Linda said, "Pacal and Balam found me in the forest. I'd be lost or dead if not for them."

"You came back for us, Linda."

"No choice."

"You had a choice. Thanks."

"Where in hell are we?"

Grant gave a sweep of his hands. "We're actually *in* hell. Welcome to Xibalbá."

"Xibalbá! That can't really be real, can it?"

"Here it is," Grant said. "Realm of gods beneath the earth. *Cenotes* were believed to be entrances to Xibalbá, and so they are. We've stumbled into the discovery of the millennium, a living lost city beneath the earth, peopled by a hybrid race of Maya and

Norse. A race of giants. Did you get the names? Zotz? Ah Puuc?"

"Who are they?" Elisa asked.

"Mayan gods. Zotz is the bat demon, god of darkness and caves. Ah Puuc is the owl, the death god, ruler of Mitnal, ninth level of the underworld. The Land of the Dead."

"He rules nothing, as far as I can tell," Linda said. "Zotz is clearly the boss here,"

Grant thought for a moment. "In Mayan religion, Ah Puuc rates above Zotz in the pecking order, but this Zotz dude is one scary son of a bitch. He rules by sheer size and intimidation."

"Ah Puuc seemed a bit elusive out there, resisting Zotz subtly," Elisa said. "There's a power struggle."

"What do you make of that giant crystal?" Linda asked.

Elisa shook her head. "It's a bit like cordierite, the Norse sunstone. Sunstone was used for direction finding at sea, by polarizing sunlight. This would be the largest ever found if it is."

"Nah, it's not cordierite," Grant said. "It's a tektite. Glass fused from sand by a blast of intense heat. Lightning makes a few now and then."

"Must have been one hell of a lightning bolt," Linda said.

"It's way too big for a lightning tektite. It's from a meteorite impact."

"You can't be serious."

"Impact tektites are tiny, a few centimeters across. This one's a giant freak. It'd take a cataclysm to forge a tektite like this one. A world beater."

"Like Chicxulub." Pacal said.

Grant looked at him, surprised. "Hell, I think you're right. The rock that killed the dinosaurs. It smacked down near here, on the edge of Yucatán. The Chicxulub crater's visible in deep sensing radar offshore, and the onshore rim is defined by an arc of *cenotes* in the fractured limestone. The sacrificial *cenote* at Chichén Itzá is one of them."

"I don't care about the geology," Elisa said. "Pacal, who is this Balam character?"

"He is like a father to Riga and me. He raised us."

"Does he speak of his past?"

"When I was a boy, he would tell stories of the Maya and the deep woods. He's a *chiclero* and a day keeper. I thought that was all."

"Are you sure he's on our side?" Elisa asked. "He led you and Linda into this trap."

Pacal glared. "Balam has given his life to my sister and me."

"That fits," Grant said. "A balam is a jaguar spirit sent by the gods to the realm of men, to teach and aid them." He hesitated. "And the jaguar labeled Riga, Ixchel, and you, Kukulcán".

"Obviously, we're not gods," Pacal said, his face darkening. "We were within seconds of dying. Balam was just buying us time."

"Who is Ixchel?" Elisa asked.

"Goddess of flood," Grant said. "A destructive little lass that punishes with storms and flowing waters unless appeased by human sacrifice."

"A bit of a stretch for our sweet Riga," Elisa said. "But she *knew*. In the cave, she knew a flood was coming. She knew how to escape it, knew where the hidden tunnel was. We'd be dead if she hadn't. So for all intents, Riga *is* Ixchel, goddess of flood."

Riga stared at the floor, and shook her head.

"Well, it's an angle we can play," Grant said.

"Think about it," Linda said. "Zotz, Ah Puuc, Balam. The Xibalbáns have kept their gods alive. Riga has been *taught* to be a goddess." She looked at Pacal. "Tell them of your childhood."

Pacal hesitated, and slowly recounted his family's destruction, and subsequent salvation by Balam. After he finished, he fell silent, then added, "Her whole life, Balam told her things he did not tell me. He would speak softly to her long into the night. Teaching her. She did not understand, but she was learning the secrets of Xibalbá."

Grant leaned toward him. "If Balam taught Riga to become Ixchel, he was training you to be Kukulcán."

"Balam told me nothing of Kukulcán, nor of Xibalbá."

"You grew up with the stories of this place."

"Ghost stories and fairy tales! Nothing of the reality of Xibalbá."

"Maybe Balam prepared you for the real thing. Kukulcán ruled as the greatest of gods, but he was also flesh and blood. Balam wanted you accepted as Kukulcán, in the flesh. Elisa, when did the Norse first cross the Atlantic?"

217

"They discovered Iceland in 860 AD, and Eric the Red discovered Greenland in 981. Leif Ericsson sailed west around 1002 and reached Nova Scotia. Did you hear them use the word *skraeling*? The Vikings that reached America had to battle Indians in Nova Scotia. Called them *skraelings*. It means savages, or sometimes the Ugly People."

"Kukulcán was an imported god," Grant said. "He was Quetzalcoatl, the Feathered Serpent, to the Toltecs. He was also a real man, a historical figure, that became king and pissed off the priests, so they exiled him in the year 987. The official angle was that Quetzalcoatl was driven out by Texcatlipoca, the Smoking Mirror, a god of evil.

"He fled south in boats and arrived in Yucatán upon 'a raft of serpents.' He became 'Kukulcán, the Feathered Serpent,' to the Maya."

"The Feathered Serpent," Elisa said. "You saw the *drakkar*, the dragonship, adorned with the head of a great serpent."

"The Maya had ocean-going canoes, but no sail technology. Imagine seeing for the first time a great ship enter your waters, adorned with the menacing head of a serpent, topped by a billowing sail and colorful banners like the plumage of a jungle bird. The Feathered Serpent, manned by towering, pale men, with hair and beards like gold and fire. Gods from the sea."

"How did he end up in Guatemala?"

"Maybe the new gods fell into disfavor. Kukulcán was beloved, but maybe he was driven from Chichén by followers of the old order. Or maybe he and his followers went willingly to live as gods in Xibalbá, leaving a power vacuum in Chichén.

"Five centuries later, light-skinned, bearded men appeared from the sea, again in great sailing ships. Montezuma figured Feathered Serpent had returned, and laid his kingdom at the feet of the visitors. Cortez graciously accepted his role as living god.

"What little remained of Maya civilization collapsed. The Petén Maya were the last holdouts. European diseases pretty much decimated the American civilizations. Remember Tayasal, near Flores? So how were El Petén Maya able to resist for so long? I've got a theory about that.

"Suppose you had a small class of superhuman warriors, with the DNA of disease-resistant northern Europeans. They wouldn't succumb to smallpox, tuberculosis, influenza, and the rest of the disease cocktail the invaders introduced. So they held off the Spaniards for decades before finally retreating to their stronghold of Xibalbá.

"We're playing a shitty hand here, but we *do* hold two cards. One, there's a rift between the rulers. Two, we've got our own goddamn gods. If we're going to have a chance, Riga *must* become Ixchel, and you *must* become Kukulcán."

"Look at me," Pacal said. "I'm a dwarf next to these monsters. They won't buy it."

Linda touched his arm. "Don't be so sure. Balam, the jaguar spirit, *selected* you. He raised you for this." She paused and leaned close. "He scripted your destiny."

Chapter 44

Ah Puuc inhaled acrid, smoky air, his heart quickening. The aroma of berserker Communion hung in the Temple of Zotz, the lair of the bat god. A dangerous, unpredictable lunatic awaited him. He readied himself and pushed aside the curtain of rotting skins that covered the entrance to Zotz's chamber.

Zotz sat slumped on his bench, deep in trance, his eyes glazed and darting, his lips trembling, his breathing quick and hard.

Ah Puuc watched silently, his anger seething.

Zotz had not stolen rule of Xibalbá merely by virtue of his enormous strength. The thief also possessed that rarest of gifts, the gift of dream sight. Under the spell of Communion, Zotz saw things seen by neither man nor god.

Zotz saw the future before it happened. He had seen the arrival of the outsiders many days before they'd entered the forest.

The gift came with flaws, however. Zotz often misinterpreted visions, though no one dared challenge him. The visions had increasingly become his surrogate law.

After a time, Zotz shook himself, blinked, and looked up at Ah Puuc. He rose and stalked to and fro about the chamber, his pace accelerating.

Ah Puuc waited. It was best to say nothing until addressed.

Suddenly, Zotz stopped and faced Ah Puuc. His face grew dark. "You are bold to oppose me, Ah Puuc."

"Oppose you? Only as the earth opposes the river that shapes it, Lord Zotz."

"You challenged me before the people."

"I merely quoted law. I do not wish you at odds with the law in the eyes of our people."

"You think them capable of distinguishing lawful from unlawful?"

"Yes."

"You are wrong."

"You killed a prisoner."

"He was an outsider and he was dying. Xibalbá cannot be exposed and it cannot support the invalid."

"Balam has returned. Word spread like floodwater."

"And he'll be put to death for treason."

"He must receive trial, just as the others must. Law, you know."

"Ah yes, the others. Balam lays claim to Ixchel and Kukulcán." Zotz snorted. "He's a clever little thief, I'll grant him that. He bought them time. That's all that saved them. And him."

"But why would he bother?"

"Balam has been corrupted by the outside world. He's fallen to its material lusts, and has brought these thieves here to help cart away the riches of the ancients. Balam's Kukulcán is a craven schemer, and his Ixchel is mute, and simple of mind." Zotz regarded him levelly. "And yet you cannot mask your excitement."

"It captures one's interest, to be sure. Balam made a pronouncement, rightly or wrongly. He's performing his duty as a jaguar spirit, though, and must be heard."

Zotz drew himself up to his full height and loomed over Ah Puuc. "I do not believe you carry final word in the affairs of Xibalbá."

Ah Puuc bowed slightly. "I, of course, defer to the will of the people."

"And to your Lord Zotz."

"Of course, my lord." Rage gathered in Zotz's eyes. Ah Puuc decided it would be best to divert the topic. "You wisely did not incarcerate Balam with the outsiders. Where is he held?"

"It is none of your concern."

No matter. Ah Puuc knew where they were holding Balam. His spies let nothing go unreported in Xibalbá. "Perhaps the newcomers might be spared, to become one with us."

"Their blood is weak."

"And the women?"

Zotz paused. "The mute whore is a false goddess and must die. The small one is of no concern. But the golden-haired one, ah, she is of the race of the northern gods. She speaks the tongue of the north. Recall, Ah Puuc, that I have seen with the dreaming eye that a woman threatens Xibalbá. *She* is the one."

"But if she is of the god race, she has value to the blood of Xibalbá."

"You disgust me. You shall not have her. She must be destroyed before she destroys us." Zotz fell silent for a moment. "We hold trial tomorrow. At noon."

"At solstice."

"If Kukulcán has returned, is it not fitting that he ascend on a holy day?"

"And our other prisoner?"

"He dies with them, immediately upon conviction."

"You believe the newcomers are connected to the prisoner?"

Zotz grunted. "You cannot be so foolish as to believe their arrival was an accident. Surely they came searching for him."

"It crossed my thoughts."

"A great coincidence. As if a Xibalbán let word slip that a man given up for dead still lives, here in a land that they do not even believe exists."

"It is indeed remarkable."

"But our citizens are incapable of such intrigues. It has the handprint of one of our best. One of our gods. Perhaps *you*."

"I assure you that no word of the man escaped this realm."

Zotz watched him through near-shut eyes. "These are but a vanguard, owl. Many more will follow. Their numbers grow and the forest shrinks. Solstice offers our people a great salvation."

A sudden thought, one Ah Puuc had never considered, came into his mind. "You intend to invoke Smoking Mirror."

"I will protect my land and people."

"It is against the law!"

Zotz shrugged. "Not for Kukulcán, who has apparently returned. The people yearn for Feathered Serpent to be enthroned once again. If this man is he, I shall not interfere."

"Smoking Mirror has not been invoked in five centuries."

"True, when last the land was threatened. And the land is threatened once more. Kukulcán may invoke it if he so chooses. It's his duty to protect the people, just as it is mine."

"If he is Kukulcán, he will be angry that you have imprisoned him."

Zotz gave a look of mock horror. "Oh my. That is true."

Ah Puuc bowed. "Very well. The ceremony of Smoking Mirror shall be at your disposal at the moment of solstice." He turned to leave.

"And, Ah Puuc…"

"Yes, Lord Zotz?"

"Treason will be dealt with severely."

Ah Puuc slipped out and descended the steps of the pyramid.

He crossed the boulevard and paused at the base of the central pyramid, the Temple of Kukulcán. The great crystal stood before him, twinkling and shimmering with firelight, the light playing in its honey-colored depths. He placed a hand upon the beautiful stone and caressed it.

Smoking Mirror. The preposterous idea could not possibly succeed. But that Zotz intended to try meant just one thing: he was afraid.

And therefore more dangerous than ever.

Ah Puuc turned and left, his pace quickening.

Zotz was afraid.

Chapter 45

SOLSTICE

Time ceased to be real. Grant and his companions could not measure its passage. They could only wait in the dark.

Twice they were given water and small portions of nuts, fruit, and tough stringy meat, which they consumed ravenously.

Grant examined every inch of the cell, searching for flaws. They hashed out idea after idea. All possibilities pointed only toward the moment they would be fetched from the cell. They would rot here until they were either taken out or they died.

At last the cell door rattled open. Five warriors entered, brandishing torches. One yanked Grant to his feet and shoved him through the door, and he and his companions were hustled from the keep to the ball court.

A crowd there milled about, maybe two hundred individuals. Mostly men, but a smaller number of women, perhaps several dozen, mingled amongst them. Children scurried about in the shadows of nearby alleys.

"Looks like we're a big draw," Linda said.

Grant nodded. "The main event."

The crowd parted and the warriors led them toward the sacrificial altar and the gigantic tektite. The last place he'd hoped for, but the one he'd expected.

Scarcely a hand was laid upon Pacal and Riga, probably out of respect or fear. Most likely both. Good. That card was still in play. It wasn't much but it was something.

Near the altar, a great iron vat of liquid boiled and smoked over a bed of embers, a pungent smell hanging in the air. Two women brought baskets full of bright, red-capped mushrooms and dumped them into the vat and stirred.

Elisa nodded at the mushrooms. "Fly agaric. Highly poisonous uncooked, highly hallucinogenic cooked. Long suspected to be a berserker drug."

Grant sniffed the air. "That's not the only ingredient. Peyote's cooking in that stew."

"How is it you know the smell of peyote?"

"You learn a thing or two here and there."

A murmur rippled through the crowd, and all eyes turned to the right-hand pyramid. Ah Puuc descended. To the left, Zotz emerged from the temple atop his pyramid, gazed over the assembly, and began descending.

"Pacal," Grant said. "Those guys get the small pyramids. The grandest is vacant and waiting for Kukulcán to reclaim it."

Pacal studied the pyramid.

"You're our only hope, Pacal. Play it well."

Another contingent arrived and threw Balam to the ground. Riga ran to his side and eased him to his feet. Pacal followed.

"Ah, my children," the old man said. "Welcome home." One eye had swollen shut. Dried blood caked his shirt. A spasm of coughs wracked him, and Riga held him close.

"Be still, Balam," Pacal said.

A commotion arose in the direction of the keep. Two giants dragged a writhing, struggling man, his face covered with a hood, his hands bound behind his back, into the ball court and slung him to the ground. A giant yanked the hood off.

Robert Lindsay lay in the dust, panting. He coughed and slowly raised himself up on his arms. His gray hair and beard had grown long, matted, and filthy, his eyes sunken and dark. His clothes hung in tatters from loose-skinned, emaciated limbs and torso.

The giant kicked him down again.

"Robert!" Grant cried. He stepped forward but was shoved

225

back.

Lindsay raised himself and looked about, squinting and shielding his eyes. Confusion shaded his face. "Grant? Grant! What are you *doing* here?"

"Mounting a heroic rescue, clearly."

"You came for me?" Tears welled in his eyes.

"The trick will be getting you out."

Several warriors began to rap the end of their axe handles against the pavement. More joined in and accelerated the rhythm, and a rumble filled the space. All turned.

"The bat's coming," Lindsay wailed. "The goddamn *bat!*"

Ah Puuc and Zotz arrived simultaneously, too precisely to be coincidental, Grant thought.

Ah Puuc was draped in a robe of brown feathers, topped by a hood in the likeness of an owl's head. His limbs were painted ochre and red, in intricate geometric patterns.

A quilt of black furs enshrouded Zotz like shadow, its hood a likeness of a gigantic, slavering bat.

Grant *hoped* it was just a likeness.

A massive iron axe hung over Zotz's back, its thick, curving blade a full twenty-four inches broad and thirty deep, and two inches thick at its center, its hilt ornamented with inlays of gold, opal, and jade. It would be difficult for most men to even lift, yet Zotz carried it with ease. Though nicked and scarred, the edge of its honed blade glinted with the light of the fires.

Zotz strode toward them, looking from face to face. Many averted their eyes.

He stepped in front of the tektite. "We come now to trial, my people," he said, in the hybrid language of Xibalbá. "We have guests, outsiders—in fact, burglars—who would plunder Xibalbá. I would kill them all, but for one reason; they come in the company of Balam, the jaguar spirit, deserted from Xibalbá these many years."

"Such is the role of the jaguar spirit," Ah Puuc said. "To walk among men and to help them."

Zotz fixed his gaze upon Ah Puuc. "Balam claims he has returned with Ixchel and great Kukulcán. I govern Xibalbá only until Kukulcán—the rightful, true Kukulcán—returns. If that has happened, I humbly and lovingly submit to his rule." Zotz

226

gestured toward Pacal. "Behold Kukulcán, in the flesh!

"Sadly, godhood cannot be presumed," he continued. "The law demands proof through Communion. Kukulcán, the greatest of berserkers, cannot be overwhelmed by Communion."

Zotz shoved Grant aside, seized Lindsay by the wrist, and hoisted him off the ground with a single hand. Lindsay writhed in his grip, helpless, whimpering. "This one, of all these intruders, most typified the blood of the berserkers. He was tall and strong and fair-haired when he came among us. I allowed him to live and to be initiated, indeed even to reinvigorate the line of our people with his own blood. He came to fancy himself a god. Ha! He is not even a man. Communion reduced him to a cowering rat." He slung Lindsay aside like a rag doll.

"It's a setup," Elisa said.

Grant turned to Pacal. "You understand? You won't be allowed to pass. You'll fail and you'll be killed. We all will."

"Many thanks for your encouragement."

"We have to make a break for it."

"We'd not last a minute."

"Got anything better?"

Pacal nodded glumly. "I have to pass the test. Wish me luck." He took a deep breath and stepped forward, hands raised. "I am Kukulcán," he shouted. "When I left the world, I left order in Xibalbá. I ordained Ah Puuc as ruler of the underworld, yet I return to find my work undone. The bat has stolen rule over Xibalbá, but his rule ends now."

The warriors about them were transfixed.

"Well, that got their attention," Grant whispered.

The amusement in Zotz's eyes turned acid. "This man is small and weak like all outsiders. He is well-schooled by Balam to mouth claims of divinity, and damns me as a usurper. I have no claim to the throne of Feathered Serpent. Do I not reside in the temple of the bat god?"

Murmurs and unsure glances swept through the crowd. The warriors looked from Zotz to Balam to Pacal.

Ah Puuc stepped forward, his eyes fixed upon Pacal. "I am charged by law with the unenviable task of divining gods, and I have performed that task. Listen to me: this is no man. This is indeed Kukulcán. God has returned to us!"

Linda squeezed Grant's arm. "Wow. Ah Puuc's cast his lot. There's no turning back."

"He doesn't believe it himself, but at least we've got an ally now."

Balam looked at him. "Ah Puuc's declaration formalizes it. Pacal now has the law on his side."

"Hey, I'll take it, Jaguar Man, but he has this goddamn test to pass."

"He will pass it."

"The bat," Lindsay muttered. "Don't let the bat get you."

Zotz motioned to the vat of black liquid. "Communion!" He took a bowl and scooped the liquid and drank it down, then handed the bowl to Ah Puuc, who also drank. The berserkers came forth and drank, one by one, followed by the women. Only the children kept away.

The drinkers began to fidget and pace. A tremor passed through them like a ripple on a pond, spreading, and they glanced about, nervousness mutating into something intense and dark. Their eyes burned with a familiar deadly look.

Zotz and Ah Puuc stood motionless, like nightmare statues. Changes crept into their faces, a flushing of the cheeks, a dilation of the eyes. Zotz's fist clenched until his nails bit into the flesh, and blood trickled from between his fingers.

One by one, the men and women paced, ever faster, talking to themselves. Many began to strike themselves. A handful fell into frenzy and lashed out at anyone within reach. Zotz growled, waded into them, and cuffed them left and right, sputtering curses, restoring a semblance of order.

After the last had taken Communion, Zotz glared at Balam. The *chiclero* ignored him and drank. The old man shuddered and steadied himself.

Zotz approached Pacal, tense, like a tethered bull, his breath rapid and clipped, his eyes flashing. He motioned toward the vat. "Please accept Communion, Lord Kukulcán."

"Don't do it," Linda said.

Pacal glanced at her. He scooped a bowl of the drink and gulped it down. "That's some shit," he sputtered in English, his eyes watering.

"More," Zotz said. "Kukulcán's judgment ration, by law, is

triple. As you surely know."

Ah Puuc nodded. A look of fear came into his eyes.

Pacal scooped and drank twice more.

The crowd fell silent.

Grant watched Pacal closely, and didn't like the changes he saw. Pacal made a clipped moan, clutched his abdomen, grimaced and doubled over, shuddering. Sweat slicked his face. He gritted his teeth, and seemed to be choking back the urge to cry out.

"What's this?" Zotz said. "This man reacts as any outsider would."

Pacal swayed, his eyes clenched shut, and sank to his knees and slowly heaved over.

"Judgment is passed," Zotz said. He unslung his great axe. "The deceit is exposed. It is time to end it."

Chapter 46

Cabrillo probed the darkness, testing each step, his fingers gliding along the damp, moldy wall. For all he knew, his next step might send him hurtling into the pits of Hell.

He should be working in the sun on his family's *milpa*, harvesting the corn, or in a snake-infested jungle, anywhere but here. This was a prison. No, worse. He'd experienced prison, but he'd never experienced anything like this.

He led, followed too closely by Garcia. Santiago brought up the rear. Guns were drawn; Santiago's, no doubt, leveled at their backs. Garcia, shaking like an old woman, would have his .38 too near Cabrillo's spine, his finger too tight on the trigger. Cabrillo thanked the saints that Garcia never cleaned his weapon; with any luck, it was frozen with rust.

Cabrillo hefted his own weapon, his grandfather's old carbine, a reassuring warhorse that had seen action in the 1950s against Indian revolutionaries. Cabrillo had spent many happy hours in the forest hunting with the rifle. Many monkeys and pigs had fallen to it, even a jaguar.

He'd never killed a man, but a disturbing certainty plagued him that he would before the day ended.

Santiago had promised great riches. They had yet to see any, but Cabrillo had never encountered such a place.

And Santiago had jabbered on about giants in the earth.

They descended cautiously through the tunnel. Garcia switched on a penlight to illuminate the uneven stone steps. Santiago cursed and snatched the penlight from him, and they proceeded in absolute darkness.

"This is a crazy errand," Garcia whispered. "You say there are giants. If so, we should leave. We should bring more weapons and men."

"Shut up," Santiago said. "We are to become rich. All of us."

"You perhaps," Cabrillo muttered, "but not us."

"These men will kill us," Garcia said.

"They are ill-equipped, armed with axes and knives," Santiago said. "It is some kind of cult. There are probably more than the three I saw. How many more, who can say? Ten? Twenty? That does not worry me. We can kill every one of them before they lay a finger upon us."

Cabrillo shook his head. "And if there are thirty? Or fifty?"

"Fifty giants hiding in the forest? Don't be a fool. I've worked El Petén for thirty years."

"These are the ghosts of El Petén," Garcia said with resignation. "That is why you have not encountered them."

"They are hiding something," Santiago said. "Perhaps a tomb. There are few great tombs yet undiscovered. This one will be the richest of them all."

Cabrillo considered the possible wealth that lay ahead and the odds of living to enjoy it. If Santiago allowed them to live at all, he'd claim the lion's share. Cabrillo had no illusions on that score. His own portion would be a pittance, most of which would go to his family in Ciudad de Guatemala, with little left for him. Santiago would retreat to Belize and live like a king in a villa by the sea.

The tunnel corkscrewed downward, the silence broken only by the dripping of water and their own footsteps.

Cabrillo stopped suddenly. "Voices. Far ahead." He clicked his rifle safety off and crept ahead. His heart thudded and he cursed himself for an old woman. Ahead, the tunnel turned sharply left, illuminated by a faint glow. A gentle breeze fanned his face. He eased into the turn, peered around. It opened onto a larger space with a ledge against a stone wall, glowing with a dim light. He paused to listen, and stepped out upon the ledge.

In the center of a vast, domed cavern stood a great city of stone, upon an island in a shimmering black lake.

"We are the richest men in Guatemala," Santiago murmured.

After a moment Cabrillo said, "I see no one, but I hear them."

"Most of the city is dark," Santiago said. "It is inhabited by a handful. Ours for the taking."

The ledge was a masonry dock of sorts. Two dugout canoes bumped against it. Cabrillo steadied one while his companions climbed in. He settled into the bow. Santiago took the stern, again positioning himself with an eye towards his own security.

They took up the broad oars and dipped them quietly into the water and eased the craft toward the city.

A stone wall, twice the height of a man, encircled the city. Sections had collapsed, the rubble spilled down into the lake. Cabrillo lifted his paddle and let the craft drift into the shadows alongside the island. "You are wrong about the number we face."

"This is no time for cowardice." Santiago motioned to a ruined breach in the shadowy wall to their right. "We land there," he said, and ruddered the craft toward it.

The canoe scratched to a stop on a pebbled beach. They dragged the canoe onto it, and paused to listen. Santiago moved ahead, exposing his back. Cabrillo considered this, and poked Garcia with the barrel of his carbine, prompting the reluctant little thief along, and followed quietly.

"Remove your boots," Santiago whispered. "Tread as shadows."

They crept barefoot through the breach. A few paces inside stood a small building with a collapsed wall, its black interior exposed. Santiago motioned them within, snapped on his flashlight, and played it about.

A human skeleton lay in a jumble against the far wall, amid withered pieces of leather armor. A necklace of emeralds and gold lay draped on the bones.

Garcia started toward it. Santiago grabbed him by the shoulder. "Leave it. We secure the city before we weigh ourselves down with baubles."

"We should collect what we can and get out."

"Shut up. You will be a king if you see this through."

"A dead king."

"Listen. We have not seen men, but we hear them. They are gathered in one place. We will see what we are dealing with. See this through, Garcia, or I will cut your heart out myself."

Garcia began to mouth a reply, and nodded glumly.

Cabrillo nodded toward the skeleton. "The dead rot where they fall. This is not what sane men allow."

Santiago scowled. "Is there anything you are not afraid of?"

The street was a littered corridor, snaking through crumbling houses. They approached one from which a faint glow emanated. Santiago motioned Cabrillo forward. Cabrillo crossed himself and slipped closer. He edged alongside the doorway, raised his rifle, and craned his neck to see in.

A small flame guttered atop a clay lamp, its flickering light causing the room to dance. A wooden bench and table. Animal skins. Jars and pots.

Weapons.

Axes, broadswords, bows, daggers, and shields leaned against the wall, displayed reverentially, each polished and hewn, the edges of blades gleaming in the dim light.

Santiago had said something foolish about Vikings. Cabrillo now believed it. These weapons were for carnage. He stepped back. "We must leave at once."

Santiago shouldered past him and peered within, then backed away. He seemed unsure, and shook his head. "These are worthless against firearms. We shall see it through." He turned and slipped into the street.

The voices grew louder and the glow of firelight brightened just ahead. Another ruined building, larger than the houses, loomed. The street opened onto a larger space. Santiago slipped into the interior of the building, and Garcia followed.

Cabrillo glanced back the way they had come. He could be back in the canoe before they could catch him. He took a step, cursed silently, and slipped into the temple. The far wall lay ruined, one corner reduced to waist-high rubble. They crept to the collapsed section and peered out.

Cabrillo caught his breath.

Hell was real, and it was peopled.

Chapter 47

Phantasms flitted through Pacal's vision, and the world spun drunkenly. His head throbbed and his gut burned with fire. Something dark and turbulent ran through him, shivering him. He shook his head, trying to clear it. The spinning waned and images crept back into focus.

Zotz loomed over him, his axe raised, the killing blow ready. Waiting. *Anticipating.*

He had seconds—if that much—to beat the drug, or at least to show *something.* He struggled into a wobbling crouch, slipped back to one knee

Ah Puuc spoke, small and faraway. "You cannot strike yet, bat. The tested one struggles but is not yet overcome."

A murmur of voices, a sound of consent.

Zotz growled something unknowable, but lowered his weapon.

Pacal knew he must stand, but his body resisted. He swayed, unsurely, upon his knees.

He heard his name called, and turned to the sound.

Riga.

Pacal coughed, and looked into her eyes. "Riga, you *spoke.*"

Fear creased her face. She shook her head.

"I *heard* you."

Again she shook her head, more forcefully.

"She said nothing, Pacal," Linda said, her eyes shining.

Pacal wanted suddenly to take Linda in his arms and kiss her, ached to do so. Yet he could not. He shook his head, dismayed.

The American was beyond his grasp.

Then realization struck: the thought—the desire—had come from *her.*

Whispers crept into his mind.

They were not his.

They swarmed and grew into emotions and thoughts not his own. They belonged to those around him, growing into a cacophony, all within his mind. He could hear shouts and laughs and curses, rising in crescendo. Hate and fear and anger and love raced through his mind.

He covered his ears and shut his eyes, hoping to make the invasion of noise cease. The voices merged into a din, like the shouting of a mob.

An image: he saw himself swept along upon a swift black river. An abyss yawned before him, its black depths stretching into infinity, and the river pulled him relentlessly toward it. The chasm beckoned, its darkness promising shelter, its walls promising silence and escape from the roar of voices.

He would enter the abyss and never leave. It would embrace him with quiet.

It would imprison him.

Forever.

No one could escape from the abyss. The current within would be too strong to fight. The abyss offered isolation.

The abyss promised insanity.

In his thoughts, he battled the black river, and began to withdraw from the abyss. It fell away, its dark void closing, its chill grip loosening.

The voices and emotions that had invaded his mind still swirled within him, growing distinct. But now they distilled into patterns.

They became ordered.

The black river evaporated, and Pacal crouched again in the sand of the ball court, his eyes shut tight.

He could make out individual voices. He could *understand* them.

Body and mind merged, his senses aware for the first time in his life. He heard the plinking of water droplets from a distant stalactite, and his nostrils filled with a tapestry of scents.

235

Electricity coursed through him.

The world, shrouded in fog, and now the fog lifted, revealing dazzling light, color, sound, and smell.

He focused on the warrior standing over him, a bull of knotted muscle, the one called "Dead Eyes." He would probably slice Pacal open without hesitation.

Pacal looked deep into the warrior's eyes. *I am Kukulcán*, he thought. *Your master.*

The warrior took a step backward.

I have returned to lead you.

Dead Eyes. No. That was not his name. *Chac. Your lord has returned, Chac. Lay down your weapons.*

The warrior hesitated, his eyes locked on Pacal's, knelt, and lay his axe upon the ground.

Zotz scowled. "Still he struggles. This man is less a god than anyone here; he shall be the first to die."

I am Kukulcán.

Pacal felt a sudden shock and wariness in Zotz. A sharp new thought, freighted with fury and hate, pushed the shock aside.

So. You have the gift. We shall see if that makes you god.

"Balam has fetched us false gods," Zotz bellowed. "One a thief, and one a whore." He stepped close to Riga and slapped her to the ground.

Heat surged through Pacal, a pure white-hot rage. He drew into a crouch and launched himself at Zotz, bowling him over, and unleashed a flurry of blows. Zotz threw up his arms, shielding himself, and seized Pacal and hurled him aside.

Pacal regained his knees but a kick to the side of his head flattened him. Zotz leapt in and placed his sandaled foot against Pacal's neck.

"I can crush your neck in an instant, false god," Zotz said. He leaned forward slowly, applying weight.

Pacal felt the crushing pressure but no pain, and tensed his muscles.

Grant moved closer. Two warriors seized him and pulled him back.

Ah Puuc advanced. "Remove your foot. Now."

Zotz smirked. "Ah Puuc? Again?"

"Remove your foot, bat. The judgment must be made by the

people."

Zotz ground his foot once more and stepped away. "I release him to the people."

Ah Puuc backed away.

"Good," Zotz said. He faced the crowd. "You have witnessed the lie. Does any man doubt this? Speak up."

The warriors looked from Zotz to Ah Puuc. Some fingered their weapons nervously; all cast sideward glances at each other.

Grant looked at Elisa and Linda. "This is about to get bad. Be ready to run."

Zotz motioned toward the prisoners. "No? Then fetch them to the altar. The blasphemer dies first."

Chapter 48

Two warriors dragged Pacal to the altar and forced him face down across it. He twisted and turned to Zotz. "Let me face my executioner."

Zotz ignored him. "It is solstice. A sacred day of Kukulcán. The shadow serpent descends the Temple of Kukulcán today. We were asked to believe that Kukulcán has returned to lead us to salvation. It was worse than a naive hope; it was a veiled attempt to plunder Xibalbá." Zotz motioned toward the ceiling of the great cavern. "The light of Kukulcán will shine upon us and free Smoking Mirror."

"Heresy," Balam said. "Smoking Mirror is the enemy of Kukulcán."

"You've been too long in the world of men, Balam. Smoking Mirror is the great protector. We *must* summon him." He gestured toward the prisoners. "My axe can deal with these few, but that will not fetch us salvation. Many more come, more than even the berserkers can repel. Five centuries ago, Smoking Mirror drove the outsiders from Xibalbá. They learned of the Place of Fear, but have forgotten and returned. Smoking Mirror must again drive the outsiders from the forest."

"Perhaps it is unwise to war against them," Ah Puuc said. "Their vengeance may be terrible."

"Enough from you, appeaser! It is solstice." Zotz raised his face upward, cupped his mouth, and let out a plaintive howl.

A low rasp answered from far overhead. Great masses of earth and vegetation fell and splashed into the lake. A black crease in the ceiling of the cavern appeared and slowly widened. A shaft of sunlight suddenly split the gloom, angling down, bathing the pyramid of Kukulcán in gold.

The sunlight painted a ribbon of shadow upon the grand staircase of the pyramid. A hush fell over the underworld. Minutes passed. As the sun climbed, the ribbon crept down the ramparts, the terraces of the pyramid giving the shadow a humped shape, slowly undulating like a gigantic serpent.

Like the shadow of Kukulcán, the Feathered Serpent.

Grant's arms were pinned behind his back until his elbows met, and his shoulders felt as though they would tear from his body. He forced the pain back, and glanced about. All eyes were on the shadow serpent.

He looked at Balam. The old man might be crazy and unpredictable, but there was no time to waste. "What's happening?" he asked in Spanish.

"Something terrible. The shadow must not reach the bottom."

"This place is on the verge of revolt. Can we push it?"

"Good and evil are in collision. Salvation lies in Pacal."

Mystical nonsense, Grant thought. He sized up the warriors nearest him, singling out the most vulnerable. He could, with luck, wrest a weapon from the warrior, instigate a fight, and let the chips fall.

"Pacal, my beloved son," Balam said in Spanish, "you have something within, something wonderful. Use it, and quickly, or we shall be dead within minutes."

Pacal blinked through the dust and blood that smeared his face, his eyes glazed and his flesh pale. Grant doubted he understood a word of it.

Pacal glanced at him and nodded weakly.

Grant stared in astonishment. Had Pacal just read his mind? No, ridiculous. Delirium guided Pacal's actions at the moment, and his seeming response merely coincided with Grant's thoughts.

Pacal looked at him again. *No, Grant. I hear your thoughts.*

"Use it, Pacal!" Balam urged. "Now! Turn it upon your enemies."

Craziness. The old coot actually believed Pacal was some kind of mind-freak god.

239

"Use it!"

Grant turned to Elisa and Linda. Their eyes gave him the answer, but he asked anyway. "Did you…" He paused. "Did you *hear* Pacal?"

They nodded.

"I thought I was nuts." He turned again to Pacal. *You hear me?*

Pacal nodded.

How?

The Communion drug altered me, opened doors…

We're about to be executed. Fight the son of a bitch.

He resists, too strong, cannot defeat him.

Fight him!

Pacal suddenly turned away. He looked past them all, into the shadows of Xibalbá.

Grant concentrated: *What's out there?*

Pacal ignored him, and stared into the shadows.

Pacal, you must become Kukulcán!

Zotz turned away from the shadow serpent. "It is time." The bat god raised his axe, his eyes burning. The axe reached its zenith and Zotz's great muscles gathered in his arms and shoulders for the blow.

"No!" Linda cried.

Riga struggled, helpless against her captors.

Become Kukulcán.

* * *

Santiago watched in silence, his face solemn. "I have underestimated," he whispered. "We need an army. And we will get one."

"I'll have nothing to do with it," Cabrillo said.

Santiago faced him. The wickedness in his eyes sent a chill down Cabrillo's spine.

Garcia pointed. "The gringos!"

Cabrillo could see the Americans, bound, helpless.

The crowd encircled a stone platform at one end of the courtyard. One warrior stood atop the platform, addressing them in a booming, angry voice.

"Mother of God," Garcia whispered.

The warrior towered over the rest, the largest man Cabrillo had ever seen, and cloaked in a hideous black robe crowned with the head of a gigantic bat. The giant suddenly fell silent, and raised his axe.

At his feet, bound and bleeding, lay an Indian, different from the ghost giants. The Indian twisted his neck and looked directly at them.

The bat giant hesitated and glanced in the direction of the prisoner's gaze.

"They see us," Garcia whispered.

"No," Santiago replied. "They are in the light; we are in darkness."

Cabrillo shot him a glance. The bound Indian *knew* they were there. "They are the creatures of the night. Not us. The gringos are to be slaughtered."

"Good. It will occupy these brutes and allow us to escape."

"They do not deserve to die."

"They came to your country to steal its wealth. Should thieves not die?"

"Not like this."

Cabrillo felt a sudden confusion, a jumbling of thoughts, noise, in his mind. A buzzing, like an insect. He shook his head.

Help us.

Cabrillo looked at Santiago. "What did you say?"

"I said thieves should die."

Cabrillo looked at Garcia.

"I did not speak," Garcia said.

Help us, Cabrillo.

That voice! It hummed in his brain. He put his fist against his temple and tried to press the voice away. He looked at the bound Indian. The man stared back.

Help us now you must help, Santiago will lead you to your death.

The monstrous executioner held the axe high, prolonging the torture, a cruel tormenter and a helpless victim. In another moment the axe would fall.

Help us now!

Cabrillo raised his rifle and fired, and the blast echoed through the cavern.

Chapter 49

The gunshot caused Linda to flinch. *What the hell happened?*

The bat god reeled, his left arm flying backward, the forearm shattered amid a spray of blood. The axe clanged off the altar to the pavement, narrowly missing Pacal.

Zotz clamped a hand over his wound, and blood welled from between his fingers. He stared at the wound, a look of bewilderment on his face.

The gunshot echoed, pulsing through the dome. The warriors, stunned, cast about in confusion. Linda's captor loosened his grip.

The shot had come from the ruined temple Pacal had singled out. Though the facing wall was dilapidated, Linda could see nothing within its black interior.

A second shot thundered. Zotz dropped into a crouch behind the altar. "Outsiders! Find them and kill them!"

Linda's captor threw her aside, unsheathed his broadsword, a look of confusion on his face. Could it be he'd never heard a gunshot before? It must have seemed an impossible thunderclap to him.

Zotz retrieved his axe, shouting, pointing at the shadows bordering the plaza. Another gunshot. A bullet pinged off the opposite grandstand.

Linda grabbed an obsidian dagger from the belt of her distracted captor. He swatted at her, and returned his attention to Zotz. She reached Pacal and began sawing his bonds. "Are you hurt?"

He shook his head. Linda at last freed him, and he struggled to rise, slumped down again.

Grant jammed an elbow into the stomach of his captor, twisted, and raked the man's eyes. The giant grunted and swung a fist. The blow glanced off Grant's shoulder and flattened him. Grant rolled away, and scrambled to Linda and Pacal.

In the chaos, warriors swarmed about, helter-skelter, confused.

Zotz darted from the altar and shoved a handful of warriors toward the prisoners. "If they move, kill them." He directed a contingent leftward and the other rightward. The two columns fanned out with precision and speed. Zotz dispatched three warriors the length of the plaza toward the main dock. The shooter, whoever it might be, would soon be surrounded.

Zotz approached the tektite. A contingent of seven, each with a red slash painted across the face, followed and arrayed themselves about him. Zotz peered up at the Pyramid of Kukulcán.

Linda followed his gaze.

The shaft of sunlight, brilliantly spotlighting the pyramid in gold, angled slowly as the sun moved across the earth above.

The shadow serpent inched down the great staircase.

* * *

Santiago whirled upon Cabrillo and slapped the rifle aside. "Goddamned fool!"

Cabrillo looked him in the eye. "The Indian was to be butchered."

The man's stupidity knew no limit. "That Indian is a tribal policeman! He *cannot* leave here alive."

"I did not come here to kill Indians."

"*Jesu!*" Garcia whispered, pointing. "They are surrounding us."

Two columns of wild men splintered from the main body and fanned out. One column reached a position to their left, eliminating that escape route.

"We must return to the boat," pleaded Garcia. "Now!"

"They have no guns," Santiago said. He raised his revolver, drew careful aim on the foremost warrior of the left-hand column, and fired.

The warrior's shoulder twitched, and blood welled from the bullet hole. He glanced at the wound, and quickened his advance.

Santiago fired again, this time striking the man in the abdomen.

The warrior shuddered and fell. Blood poured from the wound.

"See?" Santiago said. "They indeed can be killed."

The warrior smeared the blood onto his forehead, arose, and resumed his advance. Santiago fired again. The warrior barely flinched.

"You cannot kill ghosts!" Garcia shrieked.

Santiago stared at the bloodied, advancing warrior.

He raised his weapon and drew aim again, and realized that his hand trembled.

* * *

Grant helped Riga raise Balam to his feet. "I've got him. Help your brother."

"Leave me be," Balam snapped. He shrugged free of Grant's grasp, waded among the milling warriors, and seized Ah Puuc by the arm.

The owl god pulled free and faced him, his axe raised.

"Lower your weapon, Ah Puuc. Your time has come."

"You presume too much, traitor. I am a loyal Xibalbán."

"Don't be stupid, and don't confuse loyalty to Xibalbá with loyalty to Zotz."

"Your band of thieves has attacked us!"

Balam pushed the owl god's axe aside. "The shooters are not ours. They followed us here to loot the city. Now is your only chance. Do your duty, owl god. Save Xibalbá."

Ah Puuc glanced at Zotz. "Do not ask me to seize the city. I do not know that I can."

"If you can't, Ah Puuc, you and I will be dead in a moment. Kukulcán has returned. You know it in your heart. It is your sacred duty to restore him."

Ah Puuc looked at the fallen, bleeding Pacal.

Balam shoved him. "*You* sent me into the world to search for him. I completed my task. Look on him and know."

"All I see is a man," Ah Puuc growled.

"Look closely! Many berserkers are loyal to you. Summon them to him!"

Grant watched them, fighting the urge to intervene. He had little idea what the hell kind of intrigues were going on, but he realized the moment in which Xibalbá's rule would be decided had come. And, with it, their only chance of escape.

Chapter 50

Cabrillo slid another bullet into his rifle, slapped the bolt shut, fired, repeated the process. Though coldly efficient, he cursed himself for lack of a modern automatic weapon. No degree of efficiency with an antique bolt-action would turn back this horde.

The wild men tightened their vise on them. Cabrillo shot a glance at his companions. Santiago trained his revolver on the one he'd shot twice already, fired, missed.

"The ghosts are upon us!" Garcia wailed.

"Shut up. Ghosts do not bleed." Santiago said.

"You are trembling," Cabrillo said.

"Shut up!" Santiago gripped the gun with both hands to steady his aim. The muzzle flashed and the jaw of the lead warrior blew apart and hung from his face. The man sank to his knees, clutching his destroyed face with one hand.

"They die like all men," Santiago said.

Then the impossible happened.

The fallen giant staggered to his feet. A not-quite-human cry emanated from the remains of his mouth, and he staggered forward, raising his broadsword above his head.

Cabrillo froze.

"Shoot, damn you!" Santiago shouted. "Kill them!" He fired into the bloodied warrior until the hammer clicked on empty chambers. At last, the giant stumbled and fell into the dust and lay motionless.

"These monsters don't know how to die," Cabrillo said. His grandfather had once killed a man with this carbine at five hundred paces with a single shot, yet Cabrillo shot one warrior three times before the man collapsed.

Garcia thrust his pistol at the wild men, stabbing it like a knife, firing wildly.

"Calm down!" Cabrillo snapped.

No use. Garcia whimpered like a dog. Cabrillo grabbed him by the shoulder and slung him aside, glancing at Santiago. "We *must* fall back. In another minute we will be surrounded."

Santiago fumbled his reloading, spilling bullets. He snatched them up. "Fall back," he said. He fired once more, turned, and slipped through the ruined rear wall of the temple.

Cabrillo shoved Garcia into the alleyway after him.

Santiago stopped suddenly.

Three hulking figures emerged from the blackness of the alleyway, silent as shadow.

Cabrillo fired twice, hoping to hit something. A giant grunted.

"Shoot our way through," Santiago said. He started forward, drawing a second gun from a shoulder holster, and blazed with both guns.

A warrior reeled and crashed to the pavement. The other two pressed on.

Cabrillo glanced behind. Warriors poured into the ruined temple and through the collapsed rear wall into the alleyway. Santiago whirled and fired. Garcia shrieked, bolted toward the grandstand, and bounded up.

Santiago followed. The closest warrior rushed in, his axe poised.

Cabrillo fired a hurried shot, heard the sharp snap of bone splintering, saw the warrior's leg bend where it should not, and leapt onto the lowest grandstand tier. A rush of air fanned him and he felt a sudden tug at his pants leg. Metal rang against stone. An axe had been hurled. Another warrior closed in, bleeding from a shoulder wound.

The looters climbed to the summit of the grandstand and dashed along its length. The canoe was lost to them, the wild men surging into the streets, blocking all escape.

"We are dead," Garcia sobbed.

"Not yet," Cabrillo said. He gauged the situation. Any turn would end in swift, brutal death. Straight ahead, the great pyramid towered above them.

Garcia halted and spun about. "Nowhere to run!"

Cabrillo shoved him toward the pyramid, pointing upward. "Then climb!"

* * *

Pacal held Riga close, not wanting to let go. He would keep her safe this time if it cost him his life.

She suddenly wrenched free and stared into the distance, her eyes wide, horror written on her face.

Pacal followed her gaze. Three armed Spanish men raced along the top terrace of the grandstand. The shooters.

"The tall one," Grant said. "That's Santiago, the son of a bitch who outfitted us. He followed us!"

Pacal's memory stirred. He'd seen two of them in Santa Elena, drinking and throwing money about. He didn't recognize the tall, gaunt one, the one Grant called Santiago, yet he felt a vague revulsion, a prickling of his skin. He must have known him also from Santa Elena.

Riga fell to her knees. She folded her arms about herself and rocked back and forth. Her eyes glistened and sobs racked her body.

Pacal looked again at the fleeing Spanish, then again at Riga.

She stared up at them, transfixed, terror-stricken.

He delicately entered her mind, searching. Emotion struck him in a flash of white-hot intensity, a whirlpool of fear, hate, pain, and revulsion, directed at the Spanish. *At the tall one.* Blunt force stabbed his abdomen, an invasion of his body. He winced and staggered. He felt his gut, expecting to find himself bloodied with a gunshot wound.

Nothing, not a mark on him.

It was Riga's horror and pain he felt.

A malignancy had eaten at her across the years, and now roared to life and crashed down upon her, consuming her, greater than the fear of this awful place, the horror of remembered torture and rape.

Recollection burst upon him, a cellar door thrown open to reveal a dark pit below. The horror of childhood, the gaunt soldier with the cruel black eyes, the soldier that destroyed their lives; the monster that killed his father and mother and raped Riga in the street. His own inaction and shame.

The monster had returned.

Blood drained from Pacal's face. His stomach lurched. He'd driven the pain of that night into a small manageable place, but it had burst free to make him that terrified little boy once again.

His blood surged, acid and fire.

He focused his thoughts into a bolt of rage and willed it at the gaunt man.

Monster! I will destroy you!

The Spaniard stopped suddenly and looked about. His companion crashed into him and shoved him aside.

Pacal twisted his mind with fury.

The Spaniard clutched his head, shrieked in pain, and stumbled onward.

* * *

Garcia raced after Cabrillo and Santiago. At the end of the terrace, a gap separated the grandstand from the base of the pyramid. The wild men closed in, but Garcia and his companions would gain the pyramid first.

And then what? They could climb the pyramid, the most defensible ground in this pit, and pray that none of these monsters lay in wait at its summit, and spend their last days besieged, dying slowly and painfully by starvation or quickly and painfully by violence.

An arrow whistled past Garcia's head. It struck stone and sent sparks flashing.

Another arrow, glimpsed from the corner of his eye. Pain lanced his calf. He screamed and collapsed. The arrow protruded all the way through his leg, blood trickling from both the entry and the exit wounds. He clamped his hands onto the wounds. He glanced up; Cabrillo and Santiago reached the pyramid and bounded onto the lowest steps.

They had no chance of reaching the summit; the archers would bring them down like game birds, just as they'd brought him down.

Six giants rushed toward him.

He lurched toward the pyramid, and stopped. He hated the thought of waiting for death, but saw no point in trying to outrun his murderers. He sank to his knees to pray.

Chapter 51

Ah Puuc took a step toward Zotz, and stopped. Though severely wounded, the bat god seemed oblivious, the berserker Communion keeping his pain at bay.

If he confronted Zotz now, he would be cut down without hesitation.

Balam seized him by the shoulders. "Make your move, damn you!"

"Zotz controls the berserkers. It is suicide."

"You are dead already. Zotz will abide you no longer."

Ah Puuc.

He turned.

Pacal stared into his eyes, measuring him.

Ah Puuc.

Yes, Kukulcán.

Summon the berserkers to me.

They will abandon Zotz?

Only if you do. The people are angry and confused; many will fight for us, many against us.

"Do it!" Balam hissed.

Ah Puuc's heart hammered. He stepped between the guards and the captives, shoved the guards back, and spoke in a hushed voice. "Balam speaks true; Zotz has betrayed Xibalbá." He helped Pacal to his feet. "This man is your god. His power exceeds my own, and even that of Zotz. Reveal yourself, Kukulcán."

Pacal steadied himself and stared into the faces of the guards.

One dropped to one knee and averted his eyes. The others followed.

"No," Ah Puuc said. "Stand and reclaim Xibalbá for Feathered Serpent."

The warriors rose to their feet.

"Quickly, Ah Puuc!" Balam hissed. "The sunbeam cannot reach the vessel of Smoking Mirror."

"I did not think he could succeed with the invocation."

"He can and will. Lead your warriors."

Ah Puuc hesitated, then raised his face and let out a low ululation that rose in pitch until it filled the air with a shriek.

Warriors all about turned to him.

Ah Puuc ceased his call and motioned to Pacal. "Kukulcán has returned. He has consumed and survived more of the Communion than any warrior could manage. He has passed his test." He looked accusingly at Zotz. "You rule Xibalbá no more!"

Zotz gestured to his contingent of seven. They sprang forward as one, weapons raised, wailing like banshees.

"His Temple Guard," Balam said. "The greatest warriors, loyal to him to the death."

"Defend Kukulcán," Ah Puuc cried. His own contingent of five leapt forward and clashed with the rushing Temple Guard. Within seconds, fifty more warriors had thrown themselves into the fray, evenly divided.

* * *

The shrill, lilting cry jolted Garcia from prayer.

Half a dozen men stopped ten paces away, frozen in their tracks. They turned to the sound, listening, and bolted toward Garcia.

He clinched his eyes shut and sucked in his breath. Perhaps the blow would be swift and merciful.

The wild men ran past, and he felt their passing in the breeze upon his face.

He opened his eyes. The six reached the end of the grandstand and leapt down, crossed to the pyramid, and began to ascend. Similarly, the wild men pursuing his companions stopped and began descending. The two groups met and clashed.

Thunder arose from the courtyard. The warriors that had been dispatched in pursuit returned to engage in combat.

The murderers fell upon each other.

Garcia could not believe his luck. He felt his throat to assure himself it was intact. A miracle! A sob of relief and joy escaped him and tears welled in his eyes.

He gripped the arrow point protruding from his leg, and tugged. Pain shot through, lightning and fire, and his vision darkened, his mind threatening to shut down. He released the arrow and gasped for breath, and willed the darkness back.

The courtyard churned with violence. Ferocious blows were thrown and countered with equal ferocity, and men and women alike fell with horrific wounds. The gringos, surrounded by the melee, withdrew toward the opposite grandstand.

Garcia turned again to the pyramid, took a step, and collapsed. He could never climb the tower.

Santiago and Cabrillo scrambled upward. "Do not abandon me," Garcia wailed.

Cabrillo turned and motioned him away. "We cannot help you, Garcia. Get out while you have a chance!"

Garcia cursed him. He peered over the rear wall of the grandstand. The alleyway, six meters below, stretched away into blackness.

He swung his legs out, each movement driving pain through his leg. He lowered himself, dropped and tumbled to the ground, the arrow twisting in his leg, and bit his lip to keep from crying out.

Blood squeezed from his thigh with each awkward step, marking his path, and hysteria whispered at the edges his mind.

Chapter 52

Elisa gasped at the violence. All she had known of berserkers—their logistics, weaponry, training, and tactics—was wiped away by the ferocious reality unfolding before her.

These berserkers hurled themselves into battle, swinging axes and broadswords in great arcs with blinding speed, abandon, and precision, the lightning movement never slowing. Blows fell, and blows were parried on shields of leather and wood.

She could see no battle lines, no discernible divisions, yet the warriors fell upon each other as if each knew this moment had been coming for years or centuries, and knew where their loyalties lay.

The din of battle filled the air—shouts, clashes of metal upon metal, metal upon wood, and the wet thud and crunch of metal upon flesh and bone. Moments earlier, the berserkers had been dispatched with speed and precision in pursuit of the intruders, like murderous phantoms, a dagger thrust. Summoned now to battle, they unleashed a fury unseen in a thousand years.

Women darted in and out, to slice and stab and cut, inflicting precise and frightening damage, favoring the hamstrings and Achilles tendons as targets. One of them stumbled, and an axe cut her down without mercy.

The fighting spilled from the ball court onto the plaza surrounding the altar. The pavement grew slick with blood and warriors slipped in the wetness, yet the fallen fought on, stabbing and slashing from pools of their own blood.

* * *

Grant retrieved a shield and weapons. He thrust the shield into Elisa's hands and found another for himself. He ushered Elisa, Linda, Pacal, and Riga to the edge of the courtyard and onto the lowest terrace of the grandstand.

Ah Puuc hurled himself into battle, a man possessed, and hacked and sliced like a demon. Though smaller than most, he drove first one, then another opponent relentlessly until he coolly delivered the fatal blow.

Yet numbers turned against him.

Grant grabbed Pacal. "Ah Puuc is losing. You've become Kukulcán in spirit; now prove it."

Pacal nodded, and Grant pushed a sword into his hand.

Pacal cast the sword aside. "Not that way. I wouldn't last a second." He drew a deep breath, and waded into the battle, unarmed, hands raised.

A berserker lunged with a hoarse yell, his axe raised.

"Pacal!" Linda cried.

Pacal spread his arms wide, inviting the blow.

The warrior stopped, shook his head, took a step back. He lowered his weapon, raised it again, and tossed it aside. "Lord Kukulcán," he said.

Another berserker rushed the unarmed one. Pacal turned to him, and he too suddenly halted and lowered his weapon. Pacal turned to another combatant and that one ceased fighting, and then another and another. "Spare your brothers' lives. Fight only for me."

Pacal had turned the battle with the look of his eyes and the penetrating lance of his mind.

As if he truly were a god.

The dead and dying lay strewn about the plaza, but scores of warriors and women fought on, a growing number defecting, one by one, to Ah Puuc's contingent, turning upon their comrades. Numbers tilted in his favor.

Defeat loomed for Zotz.

The sunbeam reached the tektite, scattering light, and a glow suffused the ball court. The great crystal shimmered iridescently—yellow, orange, red, blue—a thousand hues in the light. A cackle of laughter rang like a dead bell. Zotz stood before the crystal, bathed in the light.

Balam said, "We are too late."

Grant shook his head. "Too late? We've got the son of a bitch beat!"

"Too late to stop the rebirth of Smoking Mirror. Zotz is most assuredly not beaten if the ancient one awakens."

* * *

Robert Lindsay slipped into the shadows and watched in horror, transfixed by the carnage.

The cauldron beckoned, its aroma tantalizing. His mind raced, images and ideas materializing and vanishing in a flash.

Hyde is winning the war, Dr. Jekyll.

He shook his head, trying to clear the nonsense. He had to stay rational or he'd be dead within minutes.

Hyde always wins.

Elisa and the other woman retreated to the high ground of the grandstand. Where did they think they could go? They had no chance of leaving Xibalbá, dead or alive.

Grant shouted orders, no surprise there, and glanced his way. Lindsay shrank into the shadows and froze.

Too late. Grant called to him, his voice small and distant.

If Grant wanted to get himself killed, fine. Getting killed wouldn't solve anything. But, damn it, they'd come to *rescue him.* He should do something.

Mr. Hyde…

He craved another drink from the cauldron.

Zotz's warriors were collapsing, many defecting to the other side, but the goon seemed unaware or unconcerned, and caressed the giant crystal, staring into it, trembling.

Another thought bubbled up. *Rally to me, fight with me.*

He shook his head frantically. Block it, he told himself. He needed another taste of the berserker drug. The cauldron was unguarded, the whole damned vat, the crazies preoccupied with their stupid little war. He could steal a drink and be back in the shadows in no time. He studied the melee, and evaluated the pitfalls of rushing the cauldron.

That Maya man stared into Lindsay's hiding place. Grant had given away his position, damn him.

Fight with me, Robert Lindsay.

The man shot brain waves at him, *into* him.

He squeezed his eyes shut and covered his ears. The alien thoughts evaporated.

The cauldron stood unguarded.

Jekyll, won't you join Hyde for a little drink?

Yeah, a little drink would bring his own powers up to where he might actually compete with these monsters. They sure had paybacks coming. He raked his fingernails across his scalp and broke the skin, allowing blood to cascade down his face. Dr. Jekyll, the gentleman berserker.

Mr. Hyde...

And like Jekyll, he could use a little drink.

Blood trickled onto his lips. The taste and smell made his heart race.

He dashed to the cauldron, cupped the liquid into his mouth and drank greedily, and fled back into the shadows.

Chapter 53

Zotz watched his warriors desert and collapse, rule slipping from him. Yet all was not lost. He dashed to the cauldron, raised a goblet and drank it down, and another, and another, as prescribed in the ancient ceremony of Smoking Mirror. His blood tingled with each swallow.

Legend spoke of one who had consumed as much, four centuries past, in an attempt to summon Smoking Mirror, and had immediately fallen into madness. None since had tried. Yet there had never been a warrior so powerful and intelligent as he, and he would succeed where no other could.

Communion coursed through him, liquid fire, and he felt his heart quickening and his mind expanding.

He'd held sway in Xibalbá for five decades, years in which the outsiders had been kept at bay. For five decades, Zotz had protected an ungrateful people.

The shaft of sunlight enveloped him and Smoking Mirror, warming them together. As the crystal heated, vapor curled and hissed from fissures in its surface. He studied his reflection in the crystal's folds. A monstrous caricature stared back.

He inhaled the gases deeply, thrilling to their aroma.

Smoking Mirror had slumbered five centuries. The time was now right and just for his return.

The crystal's deep honey color glowed. Zotz caressed the warm, smooth surface, now hot to his touch. Legend held that Smoking Mirror had been forged by the hammer of Thor, long before the race of men. Zotz believed it; Smoking Mirror was otherworldly in both beauty and menace, and he had a notion, gleaned from the books of the outsiders, of its mysterious, cataclysmic origin.

Ah Puuc shouted commands, rallying more traitors against him. Time grew short. He scooped and filled a fourth goblet, gulped it down, and tossed it aside. He removed a small clay jar from his cloak and poured a fine gray powder into his palm, and rubbed it between two fingers. He ran his fingers over Smoking Mirror, searching. He located a deep fissure and poured the powder into it.

The bat god lifted his axe above his head and swung with all his might, striking the crystal at the fissure.

A brilliant white light flashed like lightning. The crystal fractured cleanly and a slab the size of a man sheared and fell to the pavement, shattering into a thousand shards.

The powder flashed again and again, white, dazzling, hissing, crackling. Acrid white smoke poured from it, engulfing him.

Whiteness blinded him. He coughed and stumbled back toward the Smoking Mirror, his mind racing, thoughts yielding to sheer awareness, Communion burning in him as never before.

The whiteness faded, and shapes took form. Vision returned. Color and light swirled through the Smoking Mirror. He felt drawn into the light, slowly at first, then faster and faster, until he fell into a cavern of light, a cavern without end, beyond time and comprehension.

Zotz ceased to exist.

He was reborn.

He became Néen Tz'u'utz'ik, the Smoking Mirror, slayer of gods and men.

He trembled, and convulsed violently, yet felt only clarity and power and rage. The spell of the berserker was as nothing compared to this.

The world snapped into focus. Light, sounds, and smells, all but nonexistent before, revealed themselves in undreamed of detail. He saw the swiftest motions in the world in incremental moments. He lived for the first time.

A great task awaited him.

Néen Tz'u'utz'ik would slaughter the outsiders, just as he had done five centuries before, and he would thwart Kukulcán, as he had done a thousand years before. But this time he would not merely drive him away.

This time, he would kill Kukulcán.

* * *

Ah Puuc thrust and parried, sensing victory at long last in his grasp. The last warriors loyal to Zotz had fallen back into a small cordon surrounding the bat god. Zotz himself stood trembling, his face a mask of stone. In another moment his contingent would be completely destroyed. Could victory truly be so swift?

Balam grabbed Ah Puuc's arm. "Stop the advance. You send your men to their deaths."

Ah Puuc swatted Balam's arm aside. "Zotz has but a handful of berserkers left. The outcome is no longer in doubt."

"Zotz no longer exists! He has become Smoking Mirror, and will not be taken so easily."

"He is still a mortal man. Do you think he cannot be killed?"

"He will kill you first if you insist upon a close-quarters fight."

"Berserkers fight no other way. Be silent, old man. We end this now."

* * *

Pacal focused his mind on Zotz, his face hard with concentration. Cold sweat broke upon his body. He felt his mind would explode.

Zotz stared back, his face twisted in hate.

Pacal could feel the transformation in Zotz. He could feel the fury and power, like a freight train out of control, an alien rage, irrational, subhuman, superhuman.

Pacal's heart thudded and he gasped for breath. Nausea welled in his gut and throat, and pain ballooned in his skull, pushing against the backs of his eyes.

The commotion around him diminished. The sounds of battle, the clang of metal upon metal, the shouts, grew small and faraway. He heard Balam's voice, barely audible. Balam grabbed him, shook him, but his entanglement with the mind of the bat god held him fast.

Balam struck him across the face.

Pacal blinked and staggered, jolted free. He collapsed, and

clutched his head in his hands.

"Balam," he rasped. "My mind. The pain…"

"You've glimpsed the mind of the devil."

"I can't defeat him."

"Perhaps not. Smoking Mirror defeated Kukulcán a thousand years ago. But you must try."

Zotz remained by the tektite, shaking. His last warriors fell back, driven nearly to his feet, still defending, ten against forty. A minute later, they too lay dead. Only Zotz remained, his face blank, staring, dazed.

"Hold, warriors!" Ah Puuc cried. "Do not approach singly. Encircle him and await my signal."

A circle spread around the bat god, the warriors wary, their weapons raised and ready.

The slightest smile curled Zotz's mouth. He sprang forward suddenly. His axe flashed. The blade swept through the necks of two berserkers with a spray of blood. Their heads fell, thumped dully, and rolled away. The blade reversed in an instant, cleaving a third warrior through the chest, separating bone and muscle and splitting the heart before emerging from the other side of the body. Three berserkers were dead before they hit the ground.

Zotz bore on, lashing out with impossible speed and precision. Two more fell. The remainder leapt aside and retreated, stunned.

Zotz became still.

"Fool!" Balam hissed. "Withdraw your men before he kills them all."

"They know but one way to fight."

One warrior drifted to the side in an attempt to outflank the bat god.

Zotz hurled himself at him in a breathtaking burst.

The warrior threw up his shield. Zotz's axe struck the wooden shield with a crack like lightning, splitting it in two, scattering shards. The shield clattered onto the pavement, the warrior's severed arm still slung in its straps.

The warrior fought on, blood gushing from the stump of his arm. Two more blows cut him down. The engagement lasted a mere instant.

Again, Zotz ceased his onslaught, and leaned on his great

dripping axe like a crutch, watching, with a grim smile.

"Gods, deliver us," Ah Puuc said. He waved his men again into place around Zotz, surrounding him in a wider circle, a dozen paces wide.

Zotz slowly turned and faced Pacal, the vacancy in his eyes replaced by unrestrained hate. He took a step closer.

"It's me he's after," Pacal said.

"He shall not have you," Ah Puuc said.

"I am not sure you have any say in it."

Zotz took another step. The surrounding circle of warriors moved with him, keeping him at the center. He stopped suddenly and twisted his head, looking into the distance.

Pacal followed Zotz's gaze but saw nothing. "Something distracts the monster." Pacal focused again upon him. Hard.

What do you see?

Malignancy slapped him, and his stomach knotted. He steadied himself and bore into the morass of rage.

What do you see?

Outsider, invader, infidel!

Pacal cast his mind in the direction Zotz looked, and found a mind filled with terror.

One of the looters was fleeing alone, in the dark and hurt.

Zotz bellowed and lunged toward the circle of warriors, opposite Pacal, clearing his path with a single sweep of his axe. A warrior fell, his abdomen laid open. Zotz burst through the circle before the others could react. He raced to the edge of the plaza and disappeared into the shadows.

* * *

Ah Puuc stared at the bloody wrecks of men and women all about. His remaining warriors watched the shadows, weapons poised, and cast quick glances at him.

He'd gained their trust and failed them completely. Zotz had slaughtered seven berserkers in the blink of an eye, a feat the bat would have been incapable of just moments before. Ah Puuc had been powerless to stop it.

The stories of Smoking Mirror, told and retold across centuries, had accumulated a patina of myth. He had doubted the stories held much truth, but Balam had understood, and now he, too, understood.

Smoking Mirror had returned. He had overwhelmed and erased Zotz, magnified his powers many times over, and transformed him into a terrible, uncontrolled inverse of himself.

As man and god, Zotz was deceitful, egomaniacal, powerful, and vicious. As Smoking Mirror, he would be unstoppable.

Chapter 54

Garcia stumbled through the maze of streets, swearing and sobbing. He had an idea that he headed the right way. He'd navigated the rank slums of Guatemala City by night, and had always emerged without a scratch, though many would have gleefully slit his throat for a few *quetzales*. He could certainly navigate these dark streets.

Somehow, the thought did not cheer him.

He stopped frequently to listen. The sounds of the underworld were brittle, indecipherable, and hung in the air, directionless. Ghosts of sound came from near and far, trapped and echoing in a world of stone and water.

His leg seeped blood and threatened to buckle with each step, and scraped across the pavement, infernally loud. Fond of loud parties and loud women, he now prayed only for silence.

He could still hear the commotion of the ball court. Good; as long as the sound of fighting diminished, he moved in the right direction.

Away.

He rounded a turn and stopped. This street looked just like the last, littered with debris, crowded with crumbling houses. Had he been going in circles?

Closing his eyes, he listened again to the battle in the distance, and took a deep breath and hurried onward.

A few paces farther, he stopped abruptly.

The sounds of fighting had ceased.

Warriors without wars had time to punish others. One side

had emerged victorious. Now it would come looking for him.

Garcia quickened his pace, wincing with each step, rounded another dilapidated structure, and found himself at the broken rampart of the city wall. A moment of hope.

He scrambled through the breach. Ahead, untouched, lay the dugout. The black water of the lake lapped against the stones, wetting and glistening them in the dim light.

A muffled noise came from somewhere behind him. He swallowed, biting off his breath, and cupped his hand to his ear. Something lurked back there, in the shadows.

Something searching.

Garcia hurried to the boat, slipping on the rocks and banging his knee painfully, wrenching the arrow in his thigh.

He leaned into the canoe and pushed, managing to slide it a few centimeters. It was enormously heavy, hewn from a massive tree trunk. Hiding it when they had arrived had seemed a good idea at the time, and three men could lug it back onto the lake. One small, hurt man was a different story.

He heaved, and the canoe crunched over the gravel a bit more, damningly loud. He heaved again, harder this time, and gained a half-meter.

More heaves, and the prow of the boat dipped into the lake. Almost there.

A sound, a guttural *whuff*, came to him from the darkened streets behind.

He redoubled his efforts against the stubborn canoe. The prow bobbed on the water.

Behind him came the rapid pad of footfalls. He spun about, saw nothing, and with a last shove, freed the boat from the shore. It shot from his grasp and he grabbed the stern. Its momentum pulled him into the lake but he held on, finding himself in waist deep water. Another step farther, he probed with his foot and could find no bottom at all. He dove over the gunwale into the canoe, and was propelled out onto the lake.

He turned to see a hulking figure racing toward him.

Crying out, he seized the oar, splashed it into the lake and pulled frantically. The canoe responded to his frenzied strokes and slid swiftly away from the shore.

Gasping, he looked back. He'd pulled well out of reach, and

the canoe could outdistance even the best swimmer, and certainly one of these heavily laden giants. He would reach the outer tunnel in moments. Freedom and life awaited outside.

His pursuer covered the distance in a heartbeat and leapt from the gravel bank out into the lake. The leap was not humanly possible, yet the figure caught the stern with both hands, and its great weight drove the stern under and the bow shot off the surface. Garcia screamed and slid down the rough floor of the boat, catching a glimpse of his attacker.

The face! A mask of hate, intent upon destruction. Terror gripped him; he lost control of his bladder, and slid, paralyzed, toward this reaching horror, the arrow in his leg digging into the wood, tearing wider the puncture wound, until panic and instinct took over. He kicked the grasping hand and lurched sideward, clawing the gunwale, and tumbled overboard with a splash.

He sank, feeling no bottom, and kicked away from the canoe, terrified to return to the surface to face the devil. He could not go far underwater, but could not force himself up just yet, and swam until his lungs ached and his mind dulled. Still he kicked. At last, his lungs in agony, he angled upward and broke the surface, and gulped air.

The monster was two arms' lengths away. Garcia had swum back to the canoe.

A claw-like hand seized the arrow protruding from his leg and drew him back, pulling him closer to that evil face. A hand clamped about his throat.

His mind darkened, filling with void. It was the void that whispered from the shadows as he'd crept along the streets of this place. He'd kept it at bay until now. The void terrified him more than the monster.

The monster spoke in guttural Spanish, its hot breath beating in Garcia's face: "The undiscovered country, from whose bourn no traveler returns…"

* * *

Cabrillo tumbled onto the topmost platform of the great pyramid, exhausted and panting. He rolled onto his back and lay still, staring at the high, arching ceiling of the cavern. At last, he looked about.

Santiago hunched over on hands and knees, gasping. After a moment, he eased toward the precipice, his revolver drawn and ready. Cabrillo wiped the sweat from his eyes, and looked over the edge, ready to fire.

The wild men had broken off pursuit, just when they were nearly upon them. Cabrillo crossed himself and whispered a prayer of thanks. Good fortune, however inexplicable or unearned, should never be questioned.

The square below had grown quiet. Corpses littered the pavement.

"They fight our battle for us," Santiago said. "With each one that falls, our chances go up."

"What a marvelous strategy," Cabrillo growled, breathing hard. "Under such leadership, we have captured the greatest building in this evil city. Damn you."

Santiago turned away from the edge.

"Garcia escaped," Cabrillo said, still studying the ball court below. "The monsters are distracted. We should descend while we have the chance." He turned back to Santiago.

Santiago stared, transfixed, into the ruined temple that crowned the pyramid.

The wooden roof beams had rotted and collapsed long ago, the thatching disintegrated into dust. Black grime and mold blanketed everything.

Cabrillo swallowed. Beneath the rubble and filth lay unimaginable wealth.

Gold gleamed in the dim light. Golden rings, goblets, batons, and chains lay about the ruined interior. And silver, black with tarnish, and exquisite carvings of jade, and emeralds as green as the deepest forest, and iridescent opals, white as milk. And magnificent swords, axes, spears, clubs, daggers, and shields, adorned with inlays of pearl and emerald.

At the center of it all, upon a platform of gold, bedecked in jewels and weapons, lay a blackened, broken skeleton. A stone motif above it depicted a great winged dragon.

Cabrillo caught his breath, mesmerized, forgetful of the imminent danger. He'd grown suddenly, unimaginably rich.

Santiago fell upon the treasure like a child, running his hands

267

over it, tossing it, scattering it, laughing giddily. Cabrillo selected a jade dagger, its hilt carved with elaborate glyphs, and touched the blade reverently. He wanted to dive into the hoard, but doubt crept into his thoughts.

All this wealth, this undreamed of wealth, lay untouched atop the highest pyramid in the hemisphere. None had dared touch this place in ages. Why?

The murderous giants had preserved it for their master's return.

And now Cabrillo and Santiago had defiled the master's treasure and final resting place. He backed away and turned to look out over the courtyard again. Dozens lay on the bloody pavement, and others tended to wounds, some horrific and mortal.

The Indian cop gestured and directed the rest with certainty. He had assumed leadership. The cop turned suddenly. His eyes fixed upon Cabrillo.

Abandon the murderer!

Cabrillo shook the thought from his mind.

Warriors gathered fallen weapons and moved onto the terraced grandstands, facing outward, securing the high ground about the courtyard.

The giant, the one Cabrillo had shot, the one that truly terrified him, had disappeared.

From the distance, at the edge of the city, came a terror-stricken cry. From the point at which they'd first landed.

Garcia.

Cabrillo shivered, picking out a path through the dark streets below, trying to find a way to the canoe. Perhaps, if he could trace a short enough route, they might reach it in a dash.

He spotted it in shadow and could make out the breach in the city wall.

The water rippled and glittered. A dark figure emerged from it.

The canoe drifted on the lake, capsized.

Chapter 55

Pacal massaged his forehead, trying to banish the ache. The confidence he'd felt minutes before slipped back to reality.

Godhood? What a bunch of bullshit. He could imagine what would befall his sister when the truth became known.

The survivors had entered the keep, the women and children shepherded by a phalanx of warriors. Pacal counted his warriors. "Only three dozen left," he murmured.

Ah Puuc waved his hand about. "Zotz has brought ruin. Yet most of the women and children have survived. We know that one woman and her children fled into the city."

"They will likely die there," Balam said, looking at Pacal closely. "What is Lord Kukulcán's wish?"

Pacal held his gaze. He knew what was expected of him.

Balam nodded.

Pacal turned to Ah Puuc. "What is the minimum number needed to defend the keep?"

"Two dozen, My Lord."

"Dispatch twelve warriors to her house to fetch them back. Archers shall provide cover from the keep as long as they are within sight."

"Excellent, My Lord." Ah Puuc hurried away.

"Did I do that right?" Pacal whispered.

Balam's eyes twinkled. "As if born to it."

"I cannot lead these warriors. They are efficient killers, and their weapons and skills are alien to me. I'm a phony policeman and a bad fisherman. I can teach them nothing, yet you ask me to

269

masquerade as a living god."

"Kukulcán leads from compassion. The berserkers haven't seen that in a thousand years. It is the stuff of legend, and they hold you in awe for it."

"Am I sending them out to die?"

"They'll gladly die for you."

"That's not what I asked." Pacal studied the streets, picking out the tiniest of details, hearing sounds he should be unable to hear. The berserker drug had somehow rewired him and did not seem to be wearing off. But a god?

He had long sensed that something different—something *wrong*—cursed him. As a boy, he'd seen things other children seemed oblivious to. He'd *anticipated* things, sensed things transpiring beyond his sight. Balam had always shown an uncanny ability to see things that lay ahead. Pacal had once dismissed it as luck; now he understood.

Perhaps this vast, domed cavern, far beneath the earth, its countless tons of stone enclosing a pure, still lake, provided the quiet spot that blocked the noise of the cosmos to the degree necessary to reach this new plateau. Xibalbá itself formed the crucible for the gift, and the berserker narcotic sparked it and set it ablaze.

Zotz had become Smoking Mirror, the ancient horror of the Toltec, a ghost story to keep children huddled in their beds at night. Now he walked and hunted in the city. Pacal focused his mind toward Zotz, searching.

He sensed a presence, creeping through the shadowy alleys. He concentrated, and sparks exploded behind his eyes, fury and malice, unhinged from reality, driven by single-minded purpose. The mind human and predatory, incoherent and venomous, the ultimate end of the berserker.

The predatory mind drew him in.

A voice, distant and urgent, warned him away. With great effort, he wrenched his mind free.

Balam stood beside him, his hand upon his shoulder, looking into his eyes. "You withstood him. You are no longer overwhelmed by Zotz."

"I'm not so sure about that. At least I know my enemy now."

"You only think you do. You or he will be dead by the end of the day."

"As always, speaking with you is such a joy."

Pacal considered Linda for a moment, and felt her presence safe within the keep.

It dawned on him that he'd thought first of Linda and not Riga. *Selfish prick!* What was wrong with him? He'd given his life to family, not to strangers. He pushed the thought—and Linda— aside, and focused his mind toward his sister.

He felt her fear and loneliness. Riga struggled to communicate with the Americans, but her well-being was now intertwined with theirs. To protect her, he must protect them.

His thoughts drifted back to Linda.

For Riga's sake, he assured himself.

* * *

Linda followed Elisa and Grant, escorted by three warriors, through the dim, twisting tunnels of the great keep of Xibalbá. She held her scavenged axe awkwardly, adjusting her grip on the heavy leather and wood shield. She had tried a broadsword and was shocked at the weight. It would have been worse than useless, it would have been a dead weight to drag around, exhausting her.

The axe was smaller than the great battle axes of the warriors. Linda could swing it with some force and accuracy, yet she harbored no illusions that she could defend herself with it. The best she could hope for was to buy a few seconds for herself and her companions.

Elisa carried a pike and dagger, Grant a shield and broadsword. Riga carried only an obsidian knife, adamantly shaking her head when urged by Grant to take more.

Linda stopped. A peculiar sensation struck her. Her thoughts grew unclear, noisy, like radio through the crackle of an electrical storm. A voice, a presence, emerged from the static, seeking them out. Searching.

Stalking.

The skin prickled on the back of her neck. "Feel anything?" she whispered.

Elisa and Grant shook their heads. "Do you?" asked Elisa.

Linda looked into Riga's eyes. "You feel it, don't you?"

The look in Riga's eyes was answer enough.

"It's coming for us, isn't it?" Elisa asked.

Linda nodded. "And it won't stop until we're dead."

Grant slapped the wall. "Don't sweat it. This place is impregnable."

Linda looked at him. "You'd make a lousy salesman."

Chapter 56

Santiago rifled through the glittering treasure hoard, mesmerized, a child in a candy store.

"We cannot stay," Cabrillo said.

Santiago ignored him.

"Santiago! The crazies have retreated into the fortress. If we are to leave here alive, it must be *now*. You can come back for your treasure."

Santiago thought for a moment, crossed to the edge of the pyramid, and peered over. "They will spot us coming down this staircase."

Cabrillo gazed at the city below. Little could not be seen from atop the pyramid. Perhaps that had been the intent; the master of this temple commanded a view of the entire city. He studied the maze of streets and alleys. Many ended in blind walls, with many more hopelessly dark and disorienting. A few would take them swiftly to the exit, but risked exposure.

Santiago cracked open the barrel of his revolver, reloaded, slapped it shut again. "Five shots left. How much ammunition have you?"

Cabrillo popped the bolt of his carbine, slid in a bullet. He reached into his pocket and withdrew three more. "Not enough."

Santiago followed the precipice around. Cabrillo kept a few steps behind him, resisting the urge to shove the bastard over the edge, letting him do what he did best. Santiago might be crazy, but he was a genius of martial planning.

The pyramid rose in a series of seven high terraces, each

marked by a narrow ledge. Santiago paused at the side directly opposite the courtyard, cloaked in dim light. He stooped and tested the stonework. Cabrillo watched, and did the same. The masonry seemed well-fitted, yet the tight joints afforded numerous handholds.

"We descend the wall," Santiago said. "*Aqui*."

Cabrillo peered over the edge, and glanced at him.

Santiago smirked. "You do not think I'm going first, do you?" He leveled his gun at Cabrillo's chest, and replaced it in his holster. "Don't worry. I need your eyes and trigger finger."

Cabrillo slung his rifle over his shoulder. He sat on the edge, swung his legs out, rolled onto his stomach, and felt with his foot until he found a deep joint in the masonry. He took a deep breath. "*Muy loco*," he muttered, and lowered himself over.

He edged down, wedged his fingers into cracks, and let his weight press against the steep wall. Coarse limestone scraped his torso. He anchored a foot and probed with the other, found another joint, and lowered. He glanced down and the world began to tilt. He closed his eyes to let the spin of the earth pass, his head resting against stone.

His foot slipped and he slid an arm's length before catching himself.

He'd made more progress by accident than by design.

Sweat beaded and trickled down his face. Though still a young man, tough and strong from years of toil, the exertion of descent sapped his strength.

Speed was the key. He gritted his teeth and let his body slip down the wall, frantically grasping and releasing masonry joints. The blocks raked at his shirt and trousers and made a grating sound as he slid. At any moment he'd lose his grip and plummet to the street below.

His feet touched upon the narrow ledge.

He stood trembling. Sweat stung his eyes. He crossed himself and whispered a prayer.

"Excellent," Santiago called. "You have survived a fraction of your trip in grand style. I am proud to follow your courageous example." He lowered himself over the edge.

"May you fall to your death."

"Pray for me, Cabrillo; if I should fall, I shall aim for you and we'll greet the floor of the underworld together."

Cabrillo steadied himself, lowered over the edge of the terrace, and resumed his descent. He breathed hard, fatigue creeping upon him. He crossed three more terraces and paused to catch his breath and look up.

Santiago still descended, a terrace above.

Cabrillo's mind clouded, and the edges of vision darkened, a shade being drawn, the same sensation he'd felt when he'd watched the ceremony in the courtyard.

That Mayan cop invaded his mind again. He squeezed his eyes shut. Distraction would kill him.

The thoughts searched for him, stronger. Cabrillo had understood them before, like spoken words, but these thoughts tore at him, incoherent and laced with acid.

These thoughts were not those of the cop.

Shuddering, he forced the venom from his mind. "Santiago," he whispered. "Clear your mind and block out thought. We are hunted by a monster."

He studied the area below. Seeing no movement, he drew a slow breath and proceeded down the slope more recklessly than before. He reached another terrace. The muscles in his arms ached and his shoulders cramped. His fingers dripped blood and shook with fatigue.

Three terraces to go.

Santiago lagged, taking far too long. The bastard shot him a contemptuous look, but the look faded as he saw past Cabrillo into the shadows below. Cabrillo followed his gaze.

A beast of a man emerged from an alley, sinuous and graceful like a jungle cat. One arm hung limp at his side. His head swiveled side to side, listening and sniffing the air. The demon Cabrillo had dreaded, the giant he had shot, hunted them.

Cabrillo remained motionless and swallowed his breath. The giant had not spotted them.

Alien thoughts assaulted Cabrillo's mind. He tried to blank his mind, build a wall around it, but still he sensed the giant probing, its hatred invading him. He wanted to shout at the thing and distract it, anything to expel it from his mind.

The giant looked up, and its bright, burning eyes locked onto his own. A growl. It gathered itself and leapt upon the pyramid and scuttled up the face like a creature born to the mountains.

Cabrillo clung to the slope between terraces, unable to bring his rifle into play. He had two choices; slide quickly to the lower terrace or climb to the next highest. He heard a scuffling sound, and he glanced above.

Santiago clawed his way upward.

Cabrillo had been abandoned without a word. His face flushed hot and he slapped the stone face. He hated Santiago, but desperation had bound them together in their best hope for survival. The bastard had severed that bond.

The thing below closed rapidly. Cabrillo climbed, his muscles burning, sweat stinging his eyes. The growl came again, terrifyingly close.

His right hand gripped a heavy block. It wobbled, loose in rotting mortar. He glanced down, squeezed his fingers far into the joint around the loose stone, tearing flesh from his hand, and heaved. The stone rocked in its cavity and grated outward. Cabrillo looked down, gauging his target, a scant three meters away, and yanked the stone free. It bounced downward and struck the giant's wounded arm with a sharp crack.

The giant bellowed and slid downward. His eyes flashed with surprise and rage.

Cabrillo's heart jumped. The monster could be defeated!

The giant struck the lower terrace, and teetered, struggling to right himself. The block clattered down the pyramid and shattered against the pavement below.

The giant regained balance. His wound bled and he clutched it with his good hand. He looked up and resumed his climb, faster even than before.

Cabrillo clawed at the wall and scrambled upward, reached the next terrace, swung his leg onto it, and pulled himself up.

The beast regained and was upon him, its massive hand shooting upward, grasping.

Cabrillo unslung his rifle and aimed. The monster swiped it aside. The rifle discharged and sailed out into space. Cabrillo kicked at the bloody wound of the wild man, drew his hunting knife, stabbed the wound, slipped free, and struggled up.

A wetness splashed against his face, his severed finger bleeding again, and his hatred for Santiago flooded back over him, burying his fear. He remembered his promise to himself, made in a dimly lit hotel room.

Kill Santiago.

He could not prevent his own death but he could fulfill his promise.

The monster swiped at him, nearly catching him. Its footing slipped, and it adjusted and righted itself.

Cabrillo lunged upward, and gripped the tip of his hunting knife between his thumb and index finger. Santiago scrambled onto the terrace directly above. Cabrillo aimed and hurled the knife upward. The blade nicked Santiago's thigh, clattered off the stones, and fell away. Santiago winced, and continued his climb.

Cabrillo had failed.

* * *

Pacal turned at the sound of the gunshot. It sounded like it came from the far side of the central pyramid. Sound reverberated through the vast dome, becoming more directionless with each echo.

He concentrated his thoughts and sent them searching, exhilaratingly, as though part of him flashed through space, unbound by flesh, pure energy.

He found them. There were three, all together. He probed the first.

He suddenly reeled, poison searing his mind. The monster! Shaking, he strained to push the venom from his mind. He gasped for breath, dreading to continue, but it had to be done.

The second mind. The thief—Cabrillo—that had fired upon Zotz and given Pacal new life. Perhaps a potential ally.

The third mind. His abdomen knotted once more, and his skin prickled. His heart thudded and a rush of hot blood filled his face. He had found the gaunt man, his childhood nightmare.

Shaking, he cupped his head between his palms and focused his anger at the man. "Monster! Destroyer of children!" A missile of unbridled fury sprang from Pacal's mind and hurtled through space.

* * *

Santiago screamed and clawed at his head. He teetered and grasped at the stones. A trickle of blood ran from his nostril.

Cabrillo felt the monster's hand close upon his ankle like a vise. He clung tightly to the pyramid.

Santiago shook his head furiously, crying out once more, blood spraying from his nose, his eyes squeezed shut. He slipped, struggled for balance, toppled backward, clawing the air, and plummeted downward.

Cabrillo ducked. Santiago glanced off his shoulder, flailed wildly, and struck the giant in the chest, dislodging him. The giant's crushing grip upon Cabrillo remained, and dragged him free of the wall.

The three caromed down the pyramid, spinning in long, violent cartwheels, and slammed into the pavement below.

Chapter 57

Pacal studied the streets and alleys, second-guessing everything, chewing a fingernail. He glanced at Ah Puuc and dropped his hand to his side. It wouldn't do to be a nervous god.

Zotz had disappeared. The gaunt man had disappeared. They had simultaneously blinked out, as if a switch had been thrown. Perhaps Zotz killed the bastard and died himself. Pacal concentrated, trying to find them, but sensed only a vague malignancy out there.

The people of Xibalbá had gathered in the keep, yet a woman and her children had fled into the city amid the chaos of battle. Isolated and alone, they made easy prey for the bat god, if it indeed still lived. The rescue party he'd dispatched would likely be destroyed as well.

Balam advised that it would be foolish to assume Zotz's death, and that they should draw him into the open and kill him from the safety of the keep. It made sense, but Zotz had thus far shunned the killing zones of the keep's archers. He had become shadow.

Pacal studied the central pyramid. It was impossibly steep, its steps in full view. He turned to Balam. "Does the Pyramid of Kukulcán have another staircase?"

Balam shook his head. "Only the one."

He examined the terraced walls. Plaster had once encased the stonework and still remained in places, yielding a smooth, unscalable wall. Yet the structure suffered from centuries of neglect, and great slabs of plaster had peeled off here and there, and lay in rubble at the base, the exposed masonry coarse and deeply jointed.

"Damn it. They've descended the opposite side of the pyramid," Pacal said. He concentrated. A fuzziness, a stunned, disoriented echo of consciousness, entered his mind. "The monster is there, down and hurt. We have our opportunity. Balam, come. Ah Puuc, stay and protect our people."

* * *

Santiago opened his eyes and let the fog dissipate. He touched the back of his head and his hand came away bloodied.

He coughed and spat blood. With each breath, his torso rebelled, sharp and vicious, a tidal wave of nausea rolling through him. He felt at least one broken rib. He forced the pain back, refusing to succumb.

The blood he coughed concerned him more than the pain.

He rolled onto his knees, and stared dumbly at his ankle, his foot at a right angle, the ankle shattered.

A spasm wracked him, and he gritted his teeth. He spat more blood onto the pavement and sat back, trying to calm his breathing.

The monster lay upon its back, its chest rising and falling, its eyelids fluttering.

Cabrillo lay face down nearby. The traitor stirred and pushed himself up, winced, and clutched his shoulder.

"Cabrillo," Santiago rasped. "You are alive. That is good."

Cabrillo struggled to his feet. "I think I've separated my shoulder."

The giant stirred.

"The monster is coming to. Quick, Cabrillo, kill him while you have the chance."

"Kill him yourself." He pointed at the shattered rifle of his grandfather, its barrel separated from the stock. "I have no weapon."

"I lost my revolver in the fall."

"That is a shame."

"Use a stone. Bash his head in."

"I'm not going near him. The thing is not even human."

"Then carry me out of here, quickly. I'll make you wealthy beyond imagining."

"Wealth is temporary. Death, a bit more permanent." Cabrillo held up his hand. The stump of his missing finger bled, staining the bandages red. "On the pyramid, you turned and fled. You left me."

"I sought higher ground for our defense against this monster."

"That night in the hotel, you wished to teach me discipline. For that, I swore I would kill you."

Santiago's face darkened. "Ah, so that's it?"

"I could kill you right now."

"Go ahead then."

Cabrillo shook his head. "Working for you I became something I'm ashamed of, but I refuse to become *you*." He kicked Santiago in the face, spinning him about and landing him face down on the pavement.

Santiago wiped blood from his mouth. *Manage the pain*, he demanded of himself. Give no satisfaction to the traitor.

Cabrillo walked a few paces away, stooped, and picked up the fallen knife. He returned, rolled Santiago over, seized his wrist and pinned it against the pavement. "You have built a life on pain and torture. Have you any curiosity about the effectiveness of your methods?" He pressed the knife blade against Santiago's index finger and leaned heavily into it.

The knife bit and blinding pain shot through his finger. A snap, as the bone was cleaved through. This time, he could not stifle his cry.

Cabrillo shoved him away. Santiago cradled his hand, swearing. Blood poured from the stump of his finger.

Cabrillo tossed the finger to him. "A memento."

Darkness gathered. Santiago squeezed shut his eyes and willed himself stronger. Revenge became his purpose for survival. He opened his eyes.

The beast shivered and stirred nearby.

"I would kill that thing if it was a man," Cabrillo said, "but it is not and I am certain it would kill me first. You have a choice. Crawl to that thing and throttle it with your own wicked hands, or crawl into the shadows and pray to God it doesn't scent your blood."

The giant grunted and its great body shuddered.

"You have perhaps a minute, perhaps less. I must leave now. I pray that the thing does indeed catch your scent."

Cabrillo turned and limped into the shadows.

Santiago spat and wiped his mouth on his sleeve. The ghastly thing stirred. It is a man, he told himself. *Kill it.*

He pulled himself closer.

The giant's eyes blinked open, unfocused.

Santiago's skin prickled and he scrambled away.

The sudden exertion wracked him with bloody coughs. Fear overcame the fire within his broken frame and torn organs. He wanted only to get away.

A ruined building stood nearby, its doorway beckoning. Blackness inside, promising invisibility. He could reach it, hide, escape the monster. He dragged himself toward it.

The thing grunted, but Santiago dared not look back. The doorway was all that mattered now. In a moment he had covered half the distance.

A smear of blood marked his passage.

He glanced back.

The giant raised and sniffed the air, turned, and spotted him.

Santiago shrieked. Warm wetness spread in his pants as his bladder let go. He scrambled toward the doorway. He reached it and pulled himself into the darkness.

A grip like a steel trap seized his shattered ankle. He clutched the frame of the door, but the grip pulled him free and dragged him backward. His nails clawed the dirt.

The monster lifted him from the ground by a single hand, and he was drawn closer, hanging upside down. Foul breath blew into his face. The eyes, burning with hate, froze his blood.

The thing regarded him for a moment, then drew him back and swung him like a rag doll at the wall of the house.

The last thing Santiago saw was the stonework of the ruined house rushing toward him.

Chapter 58

Under cover of a dozen archers, the platoon filed out through the gate of the keep, rushed to the base of the pyramid, and rounded the far corner. Away from the torch-lit plaza, gloom draped the structure. They entered the shadows and slowed, weapons raised. Alongside the pyramid lay a narrow plaza, and the dilapidated structures nearby afforded ideal places for ambush.

"Too late," Pacal whispered. A smear of blood marked a path from the pyramid to a broken house. A dark shape lay in the doorway. Pacal approached warily, and Balam arrayed the warriors about to protect against sudden attack.

The body of a looter lay crumpled there, his legs twisted and broken, a bone protruding through the skin of his thigh. But it was the head and face—or what was left—that shocked Pacal. The features had been smashed and the skull crushed, but the gaunt, cruel nature of the face resonated deep within Pacal's memory. He swallowed hard, and his eyes glistened. A weight lifted from his soul.

Balam muttered a curse. "Smoking Mirror's power and fury exceeds even that of legend. He thrashed this thief against this house as if he were slaying a rat."

"Don't weep. This is the devil that destroyed Riga." Bloody tracks led past the pyramid into the alleys to the right. "Zotz is hurt. Now is our chance."

Balam placed a hand upon Pacal's shoulder. "He's immune to pain, and he will be the one tracking and killing. Return us to the keep. If we are caught in the open, we are dead."

* * *

Robert Lindsay hurried through the streets, glancing behind.

He'd witnessed the looters fall from the pyramid. Didn't matter; the bat would somehow survive. "Work it out, Jekyll," he muttered. "No time for Hyde."

Two options; get to the keep or get out of Xibalbá. Either way, avoid the central pyramid, stick to the alleys. Zotz likely would lurk near the pyramids.

He slipped down an alley to his left, and paused to listen. The city had fallen silent, its citizens dead or in hiding. He moved on, grateful for lucid thoughts, tormenting though they were. Maybe the drug was wearing off, but he doubted that. Berserker rage lasted hours, even days.

Somewhere deep inside, Hyde laughed.

Lindsay came to an intersection of alleys and looked back to examine his passage.

He froze.

Not forty feet away, Zotz stood before a dark house, his back towards Lindsay. The bat's head swiveled, as if listening.

A faint rustle reached him from inside the house.

Tattered cloth covered the windows of the house. From behind the curtain came the faintest glint of light. Someone hid inside.

Zotz smashed the door with one blow, and stepped through the doorway.

A cry of alarm, a scurrying within.

Lindsay had his chance. Zotz had not noticed him. He turned to run, but something stopped him. The girl's voice. He crept closer.

A copper brazier of smoldering coals dimly lighted the interior. He saw the girl, the sex slave that had been sent to his cell. She cowered in the corner, shielding three filthy children, and clutched a baby to her breast.

A baby.

Lindsay stared. How long had it been since he'd been with the girl? The infant couldn't be his. Could it? Jesus. He'd spent his whole life without children. Was it possible he'd found one, on the very day of his execution?

A flush of hotness crept through his body, and fog through his mind. The dementia of the bat god seeped into his brain. Zotz's thoughts were devoid of conscience; he regarded the girl and her children as neither friend nor foe, but simply traitorous, unworthy of life. Something else, something vile, also raged within Zotz, a blind hatred for the infant.

As if he *knew* this was the offspring of an outsider, and could not abide something so unclean. New blood was no longer desired; the child's existence affronted him.

The bat advanced toward them. The girl cried out.

Lindsay stepped closer.

She saw him, and her eyes widened, in a desperate, unspoken plea. What the hell did she expect of him? He could no more stop this monster than she could. But her dark eyes pleaded, begged for help. The children covered their faces and shrieked.

Zotz seized her by the wrist and pried the baby boy from her grasp. He raised the child aloft. The woman screamed and struggled to pull the boy free.

Do something, Jekyll.

"My children," she rasped. Her face was without hope. "My children. My baby!"

Your son.

When she had first come to him, she had been a lightning bolt of unrestrained, unrepentant, unworried sex, brazen; her purpose, to satisfy him and produce offspring. But in spite of her wanton appetite, she served as little more than livestock, and in his drugged euphoria, he had used her in that way. Now he saw the desperate, loving mother beneath the emptiness. She crawled back to Zotz's feet and stood up shakily, grasping for her crying baby.

Your son!

Lindsay swallowed. His body coiled, the Communion drug's residual power boiling again to the surface.

Zotz toyed with the screaming infant, dangling him by a leg above the girl, a cat with a mouse. How long would the game keep him amused?

Lindsay's hand gripped a masonry stone. It wobbled in its

mortar bed, and he pried it free. He steeled himself, lunged, and struck Zotz in the side of the head. The bat hood flew off, and blood spilled from the wound. The giant stumbled forward, knocking the girl over, and sank to his knees. The baby was slipping from his grasp.

Lindsay caught the baby. He glanced down into the child's face. It looked into his eyes, and stopped crying.

Warmth flooded Lindsay. His son! Tears welled in his eyes. He wiped them and gasped at a moment of joy he'd never imagined possible. He hugged the little boy to his face.

But the monster regained his feet.

Lindsay rushed to the girl, helped her up, and pressed the baby to her. "Get out," he cried.

She staggered toward the door.

Lindsay threw himself upon Zotz's back and locked an arm about the giant's neck, and pummeled him. "Get out!" he bellowed. "Get to the keep!"

She hesitated.

"Run!"

She spoke sharply to the children and herded them past. She stopped and turned back. "Your son's name is Coyopa," she said. She fled from the house.

"Coyopa," Lindsay said. "God of thunder."

Zotz steadied himself. He paid no attention to the woman and children, and grasped awkwardly for the man clinging to his back.

Lindsay held fast. "Coyopa!" He struck again with the stone, and Zotz managed to knock it from his grip. He pummeled Zotz's face with his fist, pulled closer, steadying himself, tightening his choke hold. He bit down on his ear, pulled violently back, and tore the ear off.

"Coyopa! Remember the name, you ugly bastard!"

Zotz seized his wrist and heaved. Lindsay held, slipped, and flew across the room.

The giant turned in the direction the girl and her children had fled. He hesitated, then took two steps after her.

The girl would be nearing the ball court now, but could still be caught. She needed more time. Lindsay scratched a handful of gravel and threw it at Zotz. "Over here, goon!" He crawled toward him.

Zotz sprang upon him, lifted him with one arm, and wrapped his other around Lindsay's face.

Buy them time, Dr. Jekyll. He flailed and kicked and clawed.

His head and neck were wrenched violently. A sharp crack, a white flash of pain. His body suddenly failed to respond, and fell limp.

Darkness filled his eyes.

Jekyll had defeated Hyde.

And Coyopa lived!

Chapter 59

Pacal surveyed the keep's defenders; twenty-four berserkers manned the ramparts, a handful wounded. Zotz would not take on this many in such a fortification. It would be suicide. He turned to Ah Puuc. "You're certain this fortress is sound?"

"There are no open approaches; the killing zone surrounds us. Our granary and larder can feed an army for a year. Two dozen can fight off two hundred from this rampart as long as they wish. But we still have a dozen warriors out searching. They are in danger, not us."

"Balam?"

Balam hesitated. "The keep is impregnable."

An anguished cry came from the far corner of the ball court. Three children scurried from the shadows and ran toward the keep, urged along by a young woman clutching a baby. She snatched a broken spear from the battlefield and stole a glance behind her.

"Open the gate," Pacal cried.

Zotz burst from the alley and raced after them.

"The keep's soundness will now be demonstrated," Ah Puuc said.

"We shall see," Balam replied.

The woman and children would not make the gate without help. "Archers!" Pacal cried.

Five warriors raised bows and loosed a fusillade of arrows. Zotz darted sideward and the arrows whistled past harmlessly. The archers restrung a second round of arrows, and Zotz charged again, closing the gap.

"They won't make it," Ah Puuc said.

Pacal clasped his hands to his head, and focused hard on Zotz. *Cease!*

Zotz skidded to a stop, his head whipping from side to side, searching.

Pacal turned his mind to the five archers. *Let fly on my signal. Middle archer, aim straight for him. Outer four, space your arrows each a pace apart. Steady… now!*

The second fusillade of arrows flew. Zotz again dodged sideward, and the outermost arrow sank into his thigh, the iron point piercing through to the opposite side. Zotz ripped at it, snapping the shaft off and leaving the broken arrow in him. He stumbled forward, righted himself and raced after the woman.

"Unbelievable," Pacal muttered.

The family reached the steps of the keep and staggered up. The warriors pulled them in and the gates were thrown shut behind them. Zotz crashed into the gates an instant later, shaking them violently. The archers scrambled to gain a suitable firing position. Zotz was now directly below. They slung arrows and drew the powerful bows. At such close range, they couldn't miss.

Zotz had vanished.

Pacal blinked in disbelief. In an instant, Zotz had slipped below their vision and melted into the shadows like a ghost.

"See?" Ah Puuc said. "Smoking Mirror cannot enter."

Pacal continued to search the alleys. "I saw more than I would have believed. Keep watch. Balam, take me to Riga and her companions. We return within five minutes. Defend us well, Ah Puuc."

* * *

"What happened out there?" Linda asked.

Pacal recounted Zotz's pursuit of the woman and her children, and his disappearance at the gates of the keep. "I've never seen anything like it. He is superhuman. Ah Puuc believes we are safe; I'm not so sure."

"No one is safe while Smoking Mirror lives," Balam said.

"This is nuts," Grant said. "But, Pacal, you can read minds?"

289

Pacal shrugged. "I'm not sure how to describe it. But I've always had an inkling of it. I could sense *something*—emotion, movement—when I couldn't see it. Now I hear whole words, sentences, in my mind. The berserker drug unleashed it. I believe this gigantic cavern amplifies it."

"So what happened to Zotz? I'm guessing he's taken the berserker drug many times before now."

"He has," Balam said. "But now he's released Smoking Mirror. That can only occur at summer solstice, when sunlight embraces the crystal."

Grant nodded. "Tektites trap water and gases. Nitrogen. Too much nitrogen in the bloodstream, you go nuts. You saw Zotz pouring gray powder in the tektite's fissures? Dollars to dimes, that was magnesium. Stable until you heat it, then you run like hell. The tektite was steaming hot from the sunlight, and the axe blow ignited the magnesium."

"Narcotic drug, narcotic gas, and a light-and-sound induced seizure," Linda said. "So he's stuck in an adrenaline hyper-drive. How did Zotz come by magnesium?"

"The ore is mined in Guatemala," Pacal said.

"Zotz has access to a great many things," Balam said. "The powder is indeed the key to Smoking Mirror, Zotz's improvement upon the ancient traditions. Smoking Mirror has again been loosed upon the world, just as Communion set Pacal free. Pacal has been unwilling to harness this ability, but it is real, and it is why I went out into the world and found him, and it is why he is Kukulcán in the flesh. And it is why he is the only man alive that has a chance of defeating the monster."

* * *

Smoking Mirror thrilled to his newfound powers. As Zotz, he'd been the most powerful of men, yet now possessed strength and agility never imagined. He moved like a phantom, swiftly and silently, with a quickness alien to mortals. His senses detected everything the world offered, and he could bend the thoughts of men.

The outsiders, the usurpers, the traitors would be destroyed, one by one.

Yet memory troubled him. He had seen something of the future, something dire for Xibalbá. What was it? It lurked at the boundaries of his new consciousness.

He had foreseen the arrival of the outsiders. But there was more. An outsider had been revealed as the destroyer of Xibalbá.

Smoking Mirror drove Kukulcán into the sea ten centuries ago. This time, Kukulcán would be slain, and the forever struggle between Feathered Serpent and Smoking Mirror would be ended.

But another one troubled him more than Kukulcán.

A woman.

A woman had been revealed to him under the spell of the berserker drug. The Norse woman, of the northern race of Kukulcán. A witch, versed in the secrets of the North. She alone understood the mystery of the berserkers. Feathered Serpent lusted after her and had hidden her in the keep.

Smoking Mirror grunted. Kukulcán couldn't save her. No one could. Smoking Mirror was a phantom, and no wall could keep him out forever.

Gliding through dark, empty alleys, he returned to the Temple of Zotz, scaling its opposite, shadowy face like a spider. He stripped naked and examined his wounds. Yanking the iron point from his thigh, he cleaned the wound, and bandaged it tightly, then selected a strap of iron and splinted it against his shattered wrist, bound it with leather cord, and tested its strength. He swung the arm like a club. It made a formidable weapon in itself.

Satisfied, he entered his armory and selected a centuries-old, rusting coat of chain mail and pulled it on, cinching it tight about his waist with a heavy leather belt. The hooded coat reached below his knees, a coat made for a god of war. It weighed as much as a man and would turn away the strongest axe and sword blows. He was now invincible to all but the needle-like iron arrow points, but he would not again present himself to the archers. There would be no need.

In a dark recess, he tore away a ragged curtain of skins, revealing a small dust-choked antechamber, a hidden room that had not been entered in many years. He cleared away a rotted grass mat from the floor, revealing a deeply grooved stone slab. He wedged his fingers into the grooves and heaved the slab aside. A staircase descended into blackness, but blackness was as

291

daylight to him. The way would take him down through the heart of his pyramid, into an escape tunnel known only to him, into the heart of the keep.

Into the very place Kukulcán had secreted away his Norse witch.

Chapter 60

Linda slumped against the wall, exhausted. Grant and Elisa went about the room examining everything, kids in a toy store. Riga paced, her expression lined with worry.

Pacal had returned to the outer keep rampart, leaving Broken Nose as their protector, the last line of defense within a barricaded room. Broken Nose watched the outsiders with curiosity, but swiveled his head at each little sound, gripping axe and shield tightly, steadfastly refusing any effort to engage him in conversation.

The square room served as an armory and storeroom. Oil lamps guttered and flickered all about, set on wall sconces, and cast a dim, shifting light. Weapons of both Mayan and Norse make—and some a hybrid of both—were arrayed all about. Each wall had a single doorway barred with a heavy timber on the inside, through which warriors could dispatch quickly to the four sides of the keep. Centered in the floor, a round shaft plunged into darkness. The sound of running water emanated from far below.

"Europeans designed keeps like this against long sieges," Elisa said, peering into the shaft. "Defenders might be stuck inside for months, even years, so everything was provided. This shaft taps an aqueduct for drinking water. Waste removal too. Ingenious! Linda, come take a look."

Linda shook her head, numb to academic curiosity. She'd not slept in ages, and had fled enough rainstorms and slogged enough swamps, struggling to live to the next minute, to quell any interest in indoor plumbing. She wanted only to survive. And rest. Boston was a world away, shining like a fond memory, and she doubted she'd ever see it again.

All the gear and belongings of their expedition had been cached in a corner of the room. Ah Puuc explained that Zotz would claim the lot for himself, but Xibalbán law demanded that spoils of war become communal property for one year before appropriation by the gods.

Linda found a bundle drawn up in a modern shirt, the khaki torn and stained with dried blood.

"Frank's," Grant said softly.

The bundle contained Stansfield's glasses, watch, pocket knife, journal, college ring, a cigarette lighter. Grant handed Linda the lighter.

Grant searched for their guns without success.

A small pouch spilled open and seven short cylinders clattered to the pavement. "Last of the flares," Grant said, pocketing one and handing two each to the women. "Use wisely."

"We had more stuff than this," Elisa said.

Grant nodded. "Looks like Zotz helped himself to a few things, law or no law."

They went back to exploring the room. Each weapon represented a spectacular example of something all but vanished from the world. Swords and chain mail, war clubs edged with obsidian blades and shark teeth, leather armor—a trove of unparalleled significance lay all about. Whole treatises could be written about any single artifact in this moldy room.

Linda could not muster their enthusiasm. Maybe she lacked the curiosity gene that separated scholars from hacks. Whatever. At the moment, she didn't give a damn.

As they studied a leather shield, Grant traced its stamped ornamentation. His hand brushed Elisa's, intentionally. Elisa kept her hand in contact with his, and smiled at him with shining, soft-lidded eyes.

Elisa glanced her way, and Linda pretended to be asleep. So they had shed their hostilities since the attack on the camp. Okay, she thought, a bit ashamed at the split-second of jealousy that stung her. They'd been good to her even though she felt like a fifth wheel, a socialite chasing a romantic fantasy. Unlike her smirking ex-husband, they understood her. Maybe she fit with them after all.

Riga paced, returning again and again to the well, her face creased with puzzlement, like someone piecing together a memory that lingered out of reach.

Good people, Linda thought, comforted. In her exhaustion, numbness rose like a tide. She stretched, trying to loosen her joints and aching muscles. Her eyelids grew heavy and she drifted into sleep.

* * *

Pacal fingered his axe, adjusting his grip. The berserkers could see that he held it awkwardly. Yet they had deferred to him without hesitation, accepting him as king and god. *Misplaced trust,* he thought. These men would die for him, yet he lacked any justifiable right to lead. He could tell them nothing of tactics and strategy. He could barely even lift the damned axe he lugged around.

Ah Puuc, too, could see that Pacal lacked real authority. If not for Kukulcán, Ah Puuc could reclaim leadership once Zotz was out of the way, and had seemed hesitant in his commitment to this fight.

Ah Puuc would bear watching.

Balam remained at his side, whispering the necessary knowledge of the city, the keep, and the people of Xibalbá.

They moved from battlement to battlement, checking positions. With the safe return of the woman and her children, the search party had been recalled, bringing the keep's defenders again to thirty-six. Still too few to satisfy Pacal, but every bit of the kill zone could be observed every second with at least nine men to a wall.

Pacal tried to focus his thoughts and search for Zotz, without success. Zotz had obscured his own mind from Pacal's probing. Pacal drummed his fingers on the wall. "Do you think Zotz has abandoned the fight?"

"He will never stop," Balam said.

"We have the keep well defended," Ah Puuc said. "Zotz attacked once and was beaten back, and was wounded in the doing. He will try and lure us out. We will not be drawn out."

"I hate waiting," Pacal said. "We should be on the hunt."

Balam shook his head. "If we are drawn out, our numbers are divided. Zotz will seek the weakest point, devastate it, and disappear again. We must wait. Our strength is not in our number, but in these mighty walls. He grows weaker by the minute, though he feels nothing. Time is on our side. He'll try again, soon."

"Riga and her companions are safe?"

"As safe as anyone could be, considering."

Pacal turned again to trace the streets and alleys below, searching for blind spots. "A frontal attack will fail." He thought for a moment. "Zotz is insane but not stupid. He will find another way in."

"There is no other way in," Ah Puuc said.

"Balam, you alone knew a forgotten passage into Xibalbá. Perhaps Zotz knows a secret, too."

Ah Puuc turned to look at the pyramids. His face suddenly clouded.

"There is a way in, isn't there?"

"None of which I'm aware," Ah Puuc replied. "But the temples…"

Pacal looked at him closely. "What of the temples?"

"Kukulcán's Temple is forbidden to all but Kukulcán. The Temple of Ah Puuc is forbidden to all but Ah Puuc and those invited, as is the Temple of Zotz."

Pacal gripped Ah Puuc's arm. "Then Zotz knows things about his temple no one else knows."

Ah Puuc nodded.

Pacal shoved past him and raced toward the inner keep entrance.

Chapter 61

Linda awoke with a start, jolted by the sound of a heavy crash. Elisa, Grant, and Riga stared in the direction of the guard post. Another crash came, and the high clear ring of metal striking metal.

Broken Nose positioned himself between the door and the archaeologists, weapons ready.

Grant took up an axe, shield, and pike and motioned the others to the opposite doorway.

A loud thud. The door groaned and sagged. Another blow, and it fell inward, splintering into planks.

Zotz appeared, covered in a great suit of chain mail. He kicked aside the remains of the door, and stepped into the room. He looked from face to face, his lips moving silently.

Broken Nose howled and sprang forward, slashing with his sword.

Zotz met the attack with his shield. Splinters flew as he parried the blow. He unleashed his axe. Broken Nose deflected it with his own shield, but subsequent blows drove him back. He stumbled, recovered, and drove forward again.

Grant grabbed Linda and pushed her toward the opposite door. "Get the door open and get out! All of you. We'll delay him and then follow."

Linda leaned into the heavy beam that secured the door. It held fast. Elisa and Riga took hold and pulled. The beam slipped a fraction of an inch, and slid roughly out of its cradle and fell to the floor.

Linda gathered up a shield and short sword, and moved toward the door after Elisa and Riga, keeping her weapons raised against Zotz.

Zotz parried Broken Nose's attack, and countered. The blow caused Broken Nose to stumble again, and he lost his defensive stance. The instant gave Zotz all the opening he needed, and with another lightning-quick slash, he split open the berserker's abdomen. Broken Nose's intestines spilled out upon the floor with a wet slap, splashed with blood and bile from a gaping cavity. His eyes glared wildly, but he made no sound and continued to swing away, even as he sank to the floor.

Linda fought back a violent urge to vomit.

Zotz turned to her and stared into her eyes. Something grim and alien pushed into her thoughts.

Terror paralyzed her. Her mind screamed to her to move, but she stood rooted to the floor. Grant shouted, barely audible, a thousand miles away. The room hushed. She tumbled into the dark mind of Zotz.

Someone seizing her arm, pulling her away. Turning, slowly, her world one of mist. Elisa, shouting.

The edges of the room grew harder, coming back into focus, the invasion of her mind repelled. She grew dimly aware of Grant shouting, the monster approaching, Elisa pulling her out of the room. And blood, red flowing blood, everywhere.

* * *

Grant stared in amazement at the fallen berserker. Broken Nose somehow clung desperately to life, and waved his sword weakly, blocking Zotz's way. A feeble attack by the warrior had been just enough to break Zotz's concentration and apparent hypnotic control over Linda, and the monster had returned his attention to the warrior, a caricature of a grin on his face. One swift blow would end it, yet he seemed to enjoy the slow kill.

Grant could do nothing for Broken Nose. The warrior would be dead within seconds and Grant's companions needed him for whatever slim chance remained. He backed through the door, keeping his pike trained upon Zotz.

Broken Nose glanced dully at Grant. His eyes asked for no

help or pity. He'd performed his task to the best of his ability, had proved loyalty to complete strangers, for nothing more than the whim of someone he imagined to be a god.

Grant saw in the dying warrior the face of his friend, Billy Osprey, loyal until that night Grant accused him of wrecking his career. A close friend had died for his loyalty. Now, in the bowels of Xibalbá, a stranger lay dying out of loyalty to him.

Grant took a step closer. "Get away from him, you ugly goon." He eased forward, jabbing with the pike, hoping to frustrate and distract Zotz.

"*Bin*," Broken Nose rasped, motioning him away. "Go."

Grant jabbed again, careful not to engage until he had an opening. He'd seen the uncanny quickness Zotz possessed; one wrong move would mean instant death.

Broken Nose clawed forward, swinging. Zotz sidestepped, and Grant lunged. The pike glanced off the chain mail. Zotz snorted and grabbed the pike, wrenching it from Grant's grasp, snapped it in two, and cast it aside.

Grant brandished his axe awkwardly. Not much of a match, he thought.

Broken Nose shuddered, his body wracked with spasms, and lunged and swung once more. Zotz parried, hooked and yanked the sword loose, and sliced off the berserker's head.

Grant struck, hoping the bat was off guard for just an instant. The blow glanced off the chain mail, ringing, and the axe was torn from his grasp. Grant threw up his shield in time to absorb the counter blow.

The blow shocked like lightning, stunning and numbing his arm, splitting his shield. He stumbled back, absorbed another blow, and stumbled into a rack of weapons against the wall, spilling them. He grasped another long pike, and slipped in the blood that pooled across the floor. He jabbed at Zotz's lower leg, below the mail, and pierced the calf muscle.

His next step connected to nothingness and he fell backward into the well, and plunged into the darkness to splash into the river below.

Chapter 62

Elisa stumbled through the pitch-black corridor, hands outstretched, focused on the sound of her companions following close behind. As long as she could hear them, they were alive and together.

The corridor snaked and slanted downward, a multitude of tunnels splitting off from it. She stuck to the main corridor, hoping it led to the outer ramparts of the keep.

They entered a section of corridor dimly lit by a small oil lamp. The corridor forked, dividing into a black tunnel and another dimly lit one. Elisa stopped. Linda and Riga emerged from the darkness behind her and she motioned them past, into the lighted tunnel, and turned to wait.

Seconds passed and Elisa got a sick feeling in her stomach.

Grant said he'd be right behind but was nowhere to be seen. She hesitated before she followed her companions.

A steep flight of stairs plunged into darkness. "This place is a friggin' rabbit warren," Linda whispered. She looked about. "Where's Carson?"

Elisa shook her head. She didn't want to say it, didn't want to think it.

"We have to go back for him," Linda said.

"No. Carson stayed behind to slow Zotz for us. If he's alive, he'll find us. If not, returning will take us right back to Zotz."

"We have to!"

"No! Use your head." A tear slid down her cheek. She wiped it away.

Riga put her arm around Elisa.

After a moment, Linda nodded. "You're right. I'm sorry."

Elisa collected herself, forced herself to examine their predicament. "These tunnels are endless, but we can't still be inside the keep. The entire structure isn't fifty meters wide."

"Think we may be going in circles? This thing seems like it was designed to confuse."

"It was. Defenders would know it well. Intruders would be lost."

"And we get to go deeper into this maze," Linda said.

They descended slowly, out of the dim light. After a moment, something made a click, and a pinpoint of light flickered, dimly lighting the stairwell. Linda had flicked on Stansfield's lighter.

"We can't let him see us, Linda!"

Linda shook her head. "Darkness favors Zotz, and it does us no damned good to kill ourselves in a fall down the steps."

Elisa considered this, glanced behind her again, and nodded, dreading the thought of facing the dark again anyway.

The steps opened into a larger passageway. Linda stopped and gasped, and Elisa collided with her and Riga. Riga wrapped her arms tightly about herself.

Rats squealed and scurried away, disappearing into the room's dim reaches.

The room stretched ahead into darkness, a vision of hell. The remains of hundreds, thousands, of people lined both walls, stacked like cordwood, some of them complete skeletons with grinning skulls, some mere piles of white and sepia bones. Ghastly, mummified corpses filled the room, the brown skin stretched over their bones like parchment, hair clinging in tufts to shriveled scalps, eye sockets sunken and black with desiccated tissue.

Many glinted with jewelry of silver, obsidian, jade, and gold. Some rested upon ancient, rotting shields, their fingers clutching knives or swords.

The upper layers of bodies had the jet black hair of the Maya. Nearer the bottom lay the most ancient layers, marked by corpses with blonde, brown, or red hair, the first generations of the Maya berserkers, the gods of the north.

Fresh corpses, not more than days old, filled the room with

the stench of death. Maggots wriggled amid loose, hanging flesh. Elisa recognized one of them from the attack on the camp.

The hall of the dead overwhelmed her. Pursued by a demon of hell, her grip on reality weakening, she bit her lip, biting off the urge to scream. She couldn't lose it, not now, not here. Tennyson and Grant were dead. *She* had to lead. "Keep going. We have to get through here."

Linda hesitated, trembling.

Elisa shoved her. "Move, Linda!"

Linda looked at her, wide-eyed, and moved ahead.

Elisa tried not to look at the remains, and forced herself to think analytically. "This room *had* to exist. To maintain the secret of Xibalbá, the dead had to remain within Xibalbá. No surface burials. Gods keep their dead unseen and uncounted. The underworld had to have an even deeper underworld."

"But there were remains scattered in the streets."

"Maybe after decomposition, some were returned to the city. Ancestor worship, perhaps."

"We've found Mitnal," Linda said. "The Land of the Dead, Ah Puuc's realm. By law, Zotz cannot enter Mitnal. Maybe we should stay here."

"Zotz no longer exists, and I doubt he gives a shit about laws. Keep moving."

Riga motioned to them and cupped a hand to her ear.

Linda nodded, put a finger to her lips. "Listen."

From far behind came a shuffling, dragging sound. Every few seconds it paused, then resumed.

Elisa held her breath. *Please be Grant. Please be alive.*

The sound drew closer.

The last twist in the tunnel was a scant ten paces back. No good. If Zotz got that close, they'd be dead. In a moment, man or monster would be revealed.

Elisa made up her mind. "Carson?"

In reply came a low, throaty growl.

"Run!" Elisa cried, pushing Riga along. They dashed through the hall of the dead.

Zotz burst into the room. Elisa turned to see him and shuddered.

Grant and Broken Nose had inflicted more damage upon the

bat god. He limped badly and blood and filth smeared much of his body. Still human, but nightmarishly so, and still in dogged pursuit despite horrific wounds. He rushed after them, narrowing the gap.

"There's no way out!" Linda cried.

Elisa looked ahead. They neared the far wall but she could see no other passages. The only way out was the way they'd entered. They would have to get past the monster to get out.

Elisa cast about, frantically searching.

Zotz barreled ahead, bellowing like an enraged bull. He would be upon them in a moment.

"There!" Linda cried, pointing.

A pile of rubble marked an indentation in the far wall. A section of wall had collapsed, revealing a narrow fissure in the natural limestone beyond, barely wide enough for a human. They raced toward it.

"Put out your lighter," Elisa said.

"What?"

"Do it!"

Linda snuffed the flame and they plunged into darkness, surrounded by ten thousand corpses.

Elisa listened to the swiftly closing footfalls behind her, counting them, timing them.

Linda reached the slot first. "Tight," she grunted.

Elisa collided with Riga in the dark. She sized up the crack and her heart sank. It would be a slow squeeze into the passageway. She could hear the footfalls drawing nearer. One of them would be still within the monster's grasp when he reached the fissure. She shoved Riga ahead. "You next!"

She turned, dug in her pocket and gripped a flare, and held her short sword in the other hand, counting footsteps. Closer, closer...

At the last instant, she averted her eyes and snapped the flare. It burst with a shower of sparks and a blinding flash of white and lavender. Zotz loomed over her, bathed in light, mouth agape, maddened eyes dilated and glaring. He howled and threw up an arm to shield his eyes, and crashed into her like a freight train. Elisa slammed into the wall, and her sword clanged to the floor. Stunned, she regained her balance, thrust the flare into his face.

He screamed and swatted, striking her arm, knocking the flare from her grasp. She snatched it up again and thrust it against him.

Riga squeezed past her and darted past the groping, swinging giant. "Riga, no!" Elisa cried. "Stay in the crevice!"

Riga shot her a glance, an infinite sadness and fear in her eyes. Blinded, Zotz lunged and pinned Riga against the tunnel wall. She bit his arm.

Elisa again thrust the flare into his chain mail, filling the tunnel with the stench of burnt flesh. He stepped sideward and Riga fell to the floor, scrambled past, and fled down the tunnel.

Zotz spun and lurched into the wall, grasping wildly.

"Over here, you son of a bitch," Elisa cried. He spun about and swiped at her, missing narrowly. "Come get me," Elisa said, backing into the crack. She could draw him from Riga for a few seconds more.

She thrust again, and squeezed into the slit and edged away. Zotz lunged, his great body striking the walls of the fissure, unable to enter. He clawed for her, his outstretched fingers raking her cheek and drawing blood. He seized her collar and drew her closer. She jammed the flare onto his hand, tore free, and squeezed deeper into the rock.

"Come on, freak! Come get me!"

He clawed frantically, screaming gibberish. He backed away and hurled himself futilely against the vent, unable to squeeze his massive bulk within. Again and again he threw his body at the crack.

Then, abruptly, he spun about and vanished down the hall.

Elisa exhaled, overcome with shivering. She would have collapsed had it been possible in the narrow confines of the slit.

Realization slapped her. *The beast now pursued Riga alone in the dark.*

Chapter 63

Cold water shocked Grant to his senses. The momentum of his fall plunged him deep under the surface, yet he felt no bottom. He swallowed water and the panic of drowning gripped him. His mind spun and he kicked wildly, heedless of direction.

He broke the surface and thrust his hands about frantically, seeking solidity. He felt a stone shelf just below the water, pulled himself onto it, and propped himself up on his hands and knees. He coughed up water in violent spasms, and collapsed, gulping in cool air in sharp, rapid breaths.

* * *

Pacal burst into the armory, nearly stumbling over the disemboweled guard on the floor. His heart sank. Zotz had found a way in, and Riga was missing.

Footprints crossed the blood-slicked floor. "Zotz passed this way," Ah Puuc said, examining the tracks. "Your friends also. I believe they are unhurt."

Pacal called Riga's name but received no answer. "What lies in that direction?"

Ah Puuc looked at him. "Mitnal. My kingdom. The Land of the Dead."

* * *

Riga stumbled blindly ahead, feeling her way in total darkness. She had but two flares and dared not waste one, despite her terror.

She moved alone through a hall of rotting corpses, feeling with outstretched hands, corpse after corpse—dry, brittle flesh, snatches of hair, protruding ribs, gaping jaws and missing teeth, empty eye sockets. She shuddered with each body she felt. When her hand sank into a cracking, sagging rib cage, revulsion overwhelmed her and she sank to her knees, sobbing.

Be strong.

She slapped her cheek, twice, marshaling her resolve, and resumed her search through the catacombs. Her foot caught upon a pile of rubble and bones and she stumbled, sending her headlong to the rough floor. Her knee smacked into a protruding block, and pain stabbed her leg. She clutched the knee and gingerly felt it. The kneecap moved and slid sideward underneath the skin, dislocated. Nausea threatened to plunge her into unconsciousness, and she bit off a cry.

Struggling to her feet, she lurched forward, dragging her ruined leg.

She felt the side tunnel open on her right. She entered, finding a tighter, narrower catacomb, also jammed with the corpses of centuries. She wasn't sure why, but she had sensed the catacomb's existence, and would trust her instincts. She somehow knew these ancient passageways.

The smaller catacomb ended in a dilapidated wooden door. She tested it, found it loose, and heaved against it. It swung free and splintered, its rotted wood held together more by habit than structure, and crashed into a broken heap. A staircase descended, just as she somehow had known it would. She exhaled in relief, the nightmarish hall of corpses now behind her.

She doubted she would reach her goal alive, but she had to try. Escape, however temporary, had been within reach at the narrow vent, but that was unimportant now. Greater things awaited her.

She knew what she must do.

But time had almost run out. Zotz would soon abandon the others and pursue her. In his world she moved tentatively, while he moved through it with surety and speed, and she would be caught and slaughtered.

Her knee throbbed, dizziness washed over her. She pinched her arm and fought to stay alert through the pain.

Absolute quiet suddenly reigned. The distant screaming of the monster had ceased.

Zotz was again on the hunt.

Riga had gained time, not much, but perhaps just enough. It would have to be; there would be no second chance. She quickened her pace.

A tickle, a nudge, entered her mind. Pacal, his mind searching, nearby, no longer on the ramparts, but somewhere within these tunnels. She stifled a sob of joy, and a tiny hope glimmered where before had been only despair.

The passageway twisted. She had been many hours under the earth, but always in the company of friends. Until now. Now she stumbled along alone and in blackness, underneath thousands of tons of stone. She gripped the flare, yearning to ignite it. Not yet. It was much too valuable to squander.

The steps ended in a low, arched tunnel. She could hear a burble of running water. After a moment, she waded into a knee-deep channel of water. The aqueduct.

The cool water seemed to wash away a bit of her desolation. She cupped water to her mouth and drank, immersed her knee in it, easing the pain, and pushed upstream.

* * *

Smoking Mirror hurried through the tunnels, cursing himself, pounding his chest.

His eyesight had recovered from the witch's fire. Yet his mind and body had been a prison. Now he'd broken free. Zotz had died and Smoking Mirror had been reborn, but the feeble mind of Zotz still clouded his marvelous new perception.

He could see and know things obscured before. What a fool he'd been.

The Norse witch would not destroy Xibalbá.

The Mayan whore would.

He could see it now. He had overlooked her. And it had dawned upon him in the Land of the Dead, when she'd escaped him.

Though ill-educated and mute, she knew things about Xibalbá that the outsiders could only guess, and she shared, however weakly, this strange new power.

Smoking Mirror shook with fury at the thought of destruction that could be wrought by a simple-minded whore.

She must die, and soon. She could not be allowed to live another hour.

He would find her and kill her, but not too swiftly. That would be too good for a whore.

Whores deserved far worse.

Chapter 64

Linda, wedged into the narrow crevice, listened to her breath and heartbeat, and the plinking of water drops falling from the ceiling. "Think it's safe?" she whispered.

"It'll never be safe," Elisa replied. "Ready?"

Linda took a deep breath, sparked her lighter on, cupped the flame with her hand. A soft orange glow illuminated the catacomb.

The hall of corpses stretched beyond the light. She had to get away from this horrifying place, with its dead of a thousand years lining the walls. The crevice had been comforting, its solid walls pressing against her, keeping the horror at bay. Now, with light, the misshapen bodies in their grotesque kingdom again surrounded her. Cold sweat beaded on her face.

"Ready," she said.

They crept through the hall. Linda brushed one of the ancient corpses and it disintegrated with a rattle of bones at her feet, the skull bumping against her leg. She kicked it away in disgust.

They found a side tunnel, broken corpses laying scattered at its floor. Linda paused, peering into it. "This was obscured when we passed the first time."

Elisa nodded. "Riga forced her way in. And Zotz followed."

"We can't abandon her."

"No. We can't." Elisa entered the tunnel.

After a short distance, they entered another catacomb, more claustrophobic and terrifying than the larger. Physical contact with the corpses was unavoidable. Linda shuddered as she brushed against body after body.

"And if we find Zotz?" Linda whispered.

"If we find him, we kill him."

"Damn, that's a good plan."

Elisa laughed softly. "It's all I've got."

Linda stopped suddenly, and put her finger to her lips to shush Elisa.

A muffled sound, a scraping, somewhere behind them. Another sound—footsteps—followed.

"He's in the outer catacomb," Elisa whispered. "He's circled back around." She looked in the direction they were headed. "Fight or flee?"

"Hide. Ambush the son of a bitch."

Elisa looked at the corpses, and nodded slowly. She moved to a narrow gap among them and squeezed in among the dead. "Heaven help us," she whispered.

Linda did the same and snuffed the lighter.

The corpses pressed against her, coarse and brittle and foul. Bones and mummified flesh scratched her, and pieces fell. Dust wafted from them and filled her nose and throat with a suffocating, stinking miasma of crumbling tissue. She fought the urge to gag, covered her mouth and nose, pulled one of the corpses across her, and gripped her sword tightly.

Bring me home from this, Linda thought. *Please bring me home.*

The footsteps sounded in the smaller catacomb. The monster was with them now. She could feel an alien mind searching.

A faint glow preceded him. Linda's heart sank. Zotz hadn't carried light before, but had returned with a torch and was hunting them. Even he had to be blind in absolute darkness. Didn't he? Ambush depended on surprise, but that possibility all but vanished now that he could see. It didn't matter; too late to change plans now.

The light and the footsteps came closer, just around the turn. Linda held her breath. Zotz crept closer, just a few feet away. She would allow him to pass and then slash below his chain mail for his Achilles tendon. Her hand trembled, and she tightened her grip on her sword.

Just a few seconds more…slash, and keep slashing until one of us is dead…

A torch appeared around the turn, held aloft by Pacal.

Linda cried out and stumbled from the tangle of bones. She rushed to him and burst into tears.

* * *

Riga left the aqueduct and descended the next flight of stairs. They lay just where she'd known they would. She was no longer surprised to find things as she expected.

She felt her way down an incline to another passage, a small corbelled archway, similar to the aqueduct above, but somehow dry. She followed it and reached a stone wall blocking the way.

She had just two flares, but now she needed light, and snapped one to hissing life. She squinted against the brilliance and surveyed the tunnel and barrier.

She *knew* this wall.

A crumbling veneer of red plaster coated it, painted with scenes of laborers and noblemen, paying homage to a goddess immersed in a river. Elaborate glyphs depicted *chac*, the rain, and the floods and cycles that sustained a great civilization. She understood now the lifeblood of the ancient Maya and the vitality of the seasons. The Maya carved an empire out of an infertile jungle by mastering the floodwaters and turning swamp into farmland.

She had found the Seal of Ixchel.

I am Ixchel, goddess of flood, she told herself.

Emotion swept over her, and she wept. *I am Ixchel. I bend the waters of heaven and earth to my will, to save my people.*

She could not believe she had such thoughts, yet they came to her freely. She *could* be Ixchel. She had never been anything, but she *could* be Ixchel. She knew it.

She knew this place. It was just as she'd known it to be.

I am Ixchel, goddess of flood.

Dim memories rushed back to her. She had been taught this since she was a little girl. Balam had taught her. As a child she delighted in his silly old stories. Now she understood. They were more than stories, they were the secrets of her people, guarded across a millennium, known to few. They were her destiny.

Balam had made her Ixchel.

311

The stone barrier formed the release valve of a great reservoir that once sustained the thousands of Xibalbá in times of drought. Beyond it resided a great weight of water that would flood this channel and sweep away everything in its path.

She heard a splash in the darkness somewhere far away, and froze.

Another splash. Zotz drew nearer.

Riga's confidence faltered. Goddess or not, she would come face to face with a demon in a matter of seconds. Fantasy would not protect her from the demon.

She caressed the seal. Centered in it was a round stone, the keystone, in which was carved a square indentation. She tried to move it, without success. She gripped it with both hands and strained against it, again without success. When the time came, she would be incapable of what needed to be done. She would be helpless before the demon.

No. That was wrong. Her companions—her *friends*—needed her. They needed Ixchel.

But she couldn't break the seal!

Balam had spoken of a key. The seal could only be broken with the key. She examined the keystone closely. Its diameter was half the length of her forearm.

She looked about. A heavy wooden beam, as long as a man, was fitted snugly into a narrow slot in the wall. She pried the beam loose and worked it free, and it fell heavily to the floor. She could barely lift it, but managed to drag it to the seal.

The end of the beam fit exactly into the keystone. She had found the key.

The truth suddenly dawned on her. The design of the Seal of Ixchel meant only one thing. It could be opened only once, and the breaker of the seal would be performing her last act on this earth.

Success would be rewarded with death, swift and merciless. If she failed, her death would be slow, and horrible beyond imagining.

Come get me, demon. I challenge you to come and take me.

She felt a terrible fury in response, and a ragged, shadowy thought.

I am coming for you, whore.

The flare sputtered and went out.

Chapter 65

Pacal raised his hand, signaling a stop.

He closed his eyes, feeling the labyrinth with his mind. He sensed his sister close by, but direction was unreadable. The tunnels confounded his new ability.

He suddenly sensed a great hatred and rage.

"Riga is near, but so is Zotz," he whispered. He motioned his companions to silence and moved swiftly ahead. He reached a staircase, paused, and descended.

Moments later, the party waded into the aqueduct.

* * *

Stunned by the fall, Grant struggled to clear his head, and his scalp wound had reopened. His body felt like he'd been trampled by buffalo, and he pinched himself. He washed his bleeding scalp in the stream and splashed his face, then settled back, concentrating. *Get moving, you stupid idiot, do something, anything, just don't fade out.*

A splash. Ahead, around the next bend.

"Something wicked this way comes," he muttered. He twisted into position to face his enemy.

The end would be quick. He'd lost his weapons in the fall and there was no place to flee except into the water. He could make his last stand, and would surely be dead in a moment, but he might inflict damage. That might buy his friends a chance.

He glanced behind him. The water! Hell, that might make a weapon. With a little luck, he might pull Zotz into the water with him and drag him under until one or both of them drowned. He backed to the edge of the reservoir, and braced himself.

An orange glow flickered just beyond the bend.

"Come on, bat."

The glow brightened and Pacal came into view. Behind him, Balam, Ah Puuc, Elisa, and Linda.

"Grant!" Elisa cried, rushing forward.

He tried to answer, but only slumped against the wall and slid to the floor.

* * *

Smoking Mirror bent to the floor and sniffed. The whore had passed this way, making no attempt to mask her path, and he tracked her with ease. He would pry open the whore's legs and take her violently. He would kill the whore and her friends, kill them and devour their bones. Xibalbá would be restored. Xibalbá would be his, he would kill all who resisted. Xibalbá now could claim a god worthy of rule, a god for eternity. Xibalbá would be safe, and traitors would no longer reveal her secrets.

The whore skulked about nearby, her breath, her *heartbeat* giving her away. He could feel her mind.

Yet something seemed wrong.

It was too easy. Could she really be that stupid? He focused upon her to get a sense of motive.

A presence shared the aqueduct with him, but not her. The others gathered near, coming for battle.

The air carried to him the tangy scent of blood. Ahead, in the darkness, in the stream, his enemies, trapped and wounded, awaited. He quickened his pace, anticipating good, quick kills.

* * *

Pacal led the group slowly ahead, brandishing a lit torch.

"A thousand years ago," Balam said, "Feathered Serpent battled Smoking Mirror and was cast out. Smoking Mirror is a powerful, evil god, a deceiver. It is said that he will be locked in combat with Kukulcán forever."

Water splashed in the darkness ahead, and Zotz appeared, dressed head to knees in a coat of chain mail, streaked with

315

blood.

"Forever is too fucking long," Pacal said. "This ends today." He advanced. Ah Puuc followed close behind.

A warning rumbled from Zotz's throat.

Pacal crouched, blocked out everything but Zotz, and focused his entire body and mind into a single thought, a laser of consciousness.

Die!

Zotz staggered, clutching his head, and howled in pain.

Pacal pressed his attack, focusing ever harder as he advanced.

Zotz took a step backwards, tore his gaze from Pacal, squeezed his eyes shut.

Pain stabbed Pacal's mind. He reeled, and his torch fell into the stream with a hiss. He writhed and covered his face, pain crashing over him. A roar filled his mind, like a great rush of water, a tsunami, the assault of Zotz's mind upon his own.

Zotz twisted his head again, and Pacal felt his body jerk involuntarily. Pain shot through his skull like a bullet. His eyes throbbed with it, as though pressure inside his skull would blow them from the sockets. His vision blurred, images dissolving into a million specks of black. He fell to one knee and clutched his head. *Fight back,* he told himself. He had to become Kukulcán, or it would end here, with the deaths of them all.

He struggled to his feet, and another bolt of pain shot through his skull, doubling him over. Overpowered, defenseless, he could barely lift his arms.

He heard a shout—*for Kukulcán!*—and a howl like that of a wild animal. Ah Puuc sprinted past, axe raised, throwing himself at Zotz, slashing with abandon, driving Zotz back.

The onslaught against Pacal's mind faltered and broke. He steadied himself, tried to imagine a shield in the air before him, protecting his mind. He focused on the shield and forced it to expand, deflecting Zotz's thought weapon.

Ah Puuc pressed, until Zotz caught the blade of Ah Puuc's axe with the hook of his own and wrenched it free. He buried his blade halfway through Ah Puuc's torso on the backswing.

Ah Puuc slumped, still clawing at Zotz. He looked at Pacal and sagged. His eyes turned to glass, and he toppled face down into the water.

Zotz kicked the body aside.

The debilitating pain in Pacal's head evaporated, yet his limbs grew numb. His vision cleared. His mind shield held.

He gathered himself and hurled another thought weapon at Zotz.

Zotz staggered, shook his head, and slouched forward.

Zotz had adapted, just as Pacal had. His power equaled or surpassed Pacal's.

"I cannot stop him," Pacal gasped.

Zotz approached slowly, hefting his axe.

From faraway, a thought coalesced in Pacal's mind, obscured by the noise of Zotz's mind.

Brother, I am here.

Riga?

I am here.

I cannot defeat Zotz.

I will lead him to the lower aqueduct. There I will kill him.

Riga, he will kill you!

It is the only way.

Balam spoke. "You must listen to her, my son."

I love you, Pacal.

"No! Zotz dies here and now!" Pacal snatched the spear from Balam's hand, spun and hurled it. The spear flew as if launched by a cannon.

Zotz lunged sideward, but the narrow confines of the aqueduct constrained him. The missile struck his calf, below the coat of chain, piercing through half its length. He staggered back, clawing at the shaft.

Grant sprang at the giant, grabbing the protruding spear, wrenching it. The sudden twist caused Zotz to spin away. Grant held fast, and continued to pivot the weapon about. Zotz gripped the shaft, snapped it free, and struck Grant, slamming him into the wall.

Pacal rushed in and swung his sword, focusing his thoughts on clouding the bat's mind, confusing him. Zotz dodged, seized Pacal's wrist before he could finish the blow, squeezed with the crushing pressure of a vise. Pacal felt the bones in his wrist crack, and his sword fell with a splash, yet he drove forward, unleashing a barrage of blows into the face of the bat god.

Pacal's momentum drove Zotz backward. Grant grabbed the broken, protruding spear once more and twisted, and hooked his legs around one of Zotz's. Zotz kicked free and swung an open hand against Pacal's head, knocking him away. The aqueduct spun crazily and Pacal collapsed, helpless, at Zotz's feet.

Linda and Elisa stepped forward, weapons raised.

Chapter 66

Riga staggered up the staircase, her ruined knee fighting every step, and emerged into the tunnel. In the flicker of light she saw her companions, just beyond the great bulk of the bat god. Zotz advanced on them as a cat stalks an injured bird, slowly, deliberately.

Riga ran to him, lunged with her obsidian blade and slashed his exposed leg. Zotz bellowed and spun about.

She jumped back and faced him, knife raised.

She opened her mouth to speak, but no words came. With great concentration, she cried out in a single, sharp yelp, and focused her thoughts.

I am the whore, I am Ixchel, and I will destroy you, demon.

Zotz glanced back at the others. In that instant, Riga darted in and slashed again, before leaping out of range.

The whore is quicker than you. She raised the blade to her scalp and drew it across her skin. Blood streamed from under her hair and ran down her face.

Whore blood.

She turned and ran through the dark, without fear, knowing where to step, where to pivot. She found the incline and plunged downward.

Heavy, rapid footfalls followed her in pursuit, gaining on her.

She reached the stone seal and snapped on the last of the flares and dropped it onto the floor. She struggled to lift the heavy beam, and managed to raise it to her side.

Zotz appeared from the connecting tunnel. He glared at her,

his shadow dancing in the white light of the flare.

Come try and kill your whore, bat.

He took a step forward, and another, then paused warily, his eyes narrowing.

Closer, she thought. He was not close enough, could escape back into the connecting tunnel. If the flare burned out, she would be helpless.

Kill your whore. Come, she thought to herself, just a bit closer...

Kukulcán has cast you out, deceiver. Treason shall not be rewarded this time. I, the whore, have defeated you and restored Feathered Serpent to the throne.

He took a step closer.

The whore will feast on your remains within the hour.

Zotz slapped his chest, crouched, gathered himself, and rushed forward.

Riga wheeled and drove the beam into the seal with all her strength. It loosened and plaster fell, but the seal did not break. Water trickled from its edges.

Riga felt an instant of failure, and struck the seal once more. A spray of water hissed from it, but still it held fast. Zotz was almost upon her. She jammed the beam against the seal and swung the other end into the onrushing giant. The beam struck him full in the chest, and the collision drove the beam through the seal, fracturing and shattering it into rubble.

A wall of water burst through the rupture, slamming Riga into Zotz. A roar filled her ears and the tunnel flooded in a rushing torrent. Zotz clutched at the joints in the wall, but the surge of water tore him loose.

It hurled Riga through the corridor. The flare burned brilliantly, strobing with an otherworldly light in the crystalline water.

Corpses were ripped from catacomb niches and swept along with them.

The rushing water dashed Riga against the walls and swept her forward. Her shoulder separated with intense pain. She fought upward against the flood and found a pocket of air a hand's width from the ceiling of the tube. She gulped in a moment's air before being sucked under again. Zotz clawed frantically against the irresistible flood, but the great weight of his coat of mail, that had rendered him invincible, now dragged him under. With soul-deep satisfaction, she saw that terror had taken the place of his fury. His wide eyes found hers.

I am Riga, I am Ixchel, she thought triumphantly, returning his glare.

I am the whore you foresaw and I have destroyed your false reign on Earth.

I am Ixchel!

Chapter 67

José Cabrillo, battered and bruised, stumbled from the tunnel into the boiling morning of the rainforest. It had never felt so good and he fell to his knees and kissed the rotting forest floor, sobbing joyfully.

He had dragged himself through the hell below, not encountering another soul. This place, he'd heard so many times, was haunted. Now he knew it to be true.

He started through the forest, paused, and turned to look again at the entrance. Even so close, it was nearly invisible.

The wonders beneath his feet, the awesome, ruined beauty of the lost city, already seemed like a dream. The hoard of treasure atop that incredible pyramid could make him a king among men for the rest of his days. He had always clung to the dream of all looters—the dream of finding that one vast, lucky treasure.

He shook his head and turned away.

He was through with looting. It had been a job, a way to feed his family in the slums of Guatemala City.

Some other fool could have that job.

Santiago was dead. That was good. But Garcia had simply been a greedy fool. He did not deserve to die.

His brother was dead. No treasure was worth that.

His family needed him. Alive.

He turned and limped into the dripping forest. He had a secret and it would remain a secret.

No one else would die because of him.

* * *

A thousand ancient corpses littered the rim of the underground lake, swept there by the flood. Zotz's body was nowhere to be found, the great coat of mail having dragged him to the bottom of the subterranean lake.

They found Riga's body floating on the lake, twisted and broken.

Pacal and Balam burst into tears, overcome with grief.

They placed her body reverentially alongside that of Ah Puuc upon the deck of a dragonship, and set it adrift on the lake. A flaming arrow arced toward the ship and set it ablaze in the manner of the Norsemen. Flame consumed the craft, climbing high, and freed the bodies of two gods from the world of men.

The crushing sense of loss overwhelmed Linda. She held on to Pacal, and wept.

Chapter 68

Carson Grant, bathed and clean-shaven, felt like a new man despite the universe of soreness throughout his body. He slipped out of his hotel room in Flores and went down to the bar and dragged a pair of tables together on the veranda. Dusk gathered, and lightning flickered in the distant sky. Grant argued with the owner about the lighting, and then handed the belligerent little man a hundred *quetzales* to bring out two additional floor lamps. The owner's outlook improved dramatically and he hurried to accommodate the request. He returned and set up the lamps and switched them on a low light setting.

Grant switched them brighter.

The owner's face drooped, crestfallen. He owned the latest adjustable dimmers and was eager to demonstrate his good taste in décor. "Señor's friends, perhaps, would prefer the lights low? A little mood lighting, for the ladies?"

Grant shook his head. "Trust me on this."

He took a long drink from his beer. His whole body ached, a confusion of bandages. The medical attention he'd gotten in Flores had patched him together pretty well, though, and he couldn't stand lingering with fussy nurses any longer.

Failure hung like a pall over everything. Robert Lindsay—the friend they'd come to rescue—was dead. Stansfield dead. Watts dead. Grant's best friend, Tennyson, dead. Riga dead.

A respected Belizean businessman, missing. The world was a better place for that.

The networks back home branded this the "lost expedition"

and rushed camera crews out to intercept them before they left the country. The ambulance chasers licked their lips. Grant's past had become an issue once more and the university swung into full damage control, trying to explain how he'd ever been added to a dig team, one that had gone off freelancing. The dean assumed the inevitability of lawsuits, and the university president wanted some goddamn heads.

At this particular moment, Grant just didn't give a shit. The school had canned him years ago anyway. What mattered was, his friends had died, and he'd been at fault. Screw the rest of it.

Failure, yes. Yet somehow, triumph emerged from the wreckage.

Elisa, Linda, and Pacal arrived and joined him.

Grant ordered a round of beers without asking. "Might as well make ourselves comfortable tonight. The *federales* will be barbecuing us for days, if not weeks. Good news is, they might keep the networks out of our hair, as long as we give Guatemalan TV a scoop or two. CNN, CBS, and NBC will be here tonight. So far, though, the Petén Department police are pretty cool with our story."

"They appreciate easy explanations," Pacal said. "They particularly like having your companions die at the hands of looters. Zotz helped in that regard. He was an exceedingly clever devil. Many of your things turned up on the black market in Santa Elena, a sure sign you'd been attacked by bandits."

"The bodies will be autopsied in Guatemala City. The story won't hold up."

"Yes it will. Days will have passed. The obvious will still be obvious; your companions died violently, their wounds the result of machete-wielding thieves."

Grant shrugged. "Hope you're right."

"You can still come with us, you know," Elisa said.

Pacal shook his head, avoiding Linda's eyes. "Not yet." Glancing nervously about the bar, he dragged his chair closer and leaned in, looking from one to another, settling upon Grant. "You will live up to your end of our agreement, yes?"

Grant nodded. "It's the only way. The world's closing in on Xibalbá. The Petén shrinks every day. Xibalbá might escape detection for another five, maybe ten years, but not forever."

"Three years is all I need," Pacal said. "I'll return to Xibalbá when the questioning ends. Balam and I will prepare the people to leave the city. They're aware of the outside world, but aren't ready to face it. They are strong, but they are like children. It will take time."

"We'll meet you exactly three years from today at the entrance to Xibalbá."

"And the last berserkers of the north and the last stronghold of Mayan civilization will emerge into the modern world."

Grant whistled. "Imagine. If we manage to stay out of jail until then, we'll have the biggest archaeological discovery of the last hundred years to present to the world. We'll be bigger than Schliemann, Carter, and Bingham combined."

"Don't let it go to your head," Elisa chided, pinching him. "The Xibalbáns come first. They've followed a warrior's code of morality a thousand years old. They're giants, they're illiterate, and they live beneath the earth in a city out of myth. It'll be everything we can do to keep them from becoming sideshow freaks."

"I'll bring the world to them slowly," Pacal said. "When they emerge, they will be ready."

"We have Kukulcán on our side," Linda said, smiling at Pacal. "Feathered Serpent, god of enlightenment. If he can't prepare them, who can?"

Pacal blushed.

Grant smirked, and decided to take the moment's pressure off Pacal. "Robert had been incarcerated and was at the end of his ability to reason. But the Xibalbán girl, Akna, she saw the man that he once was, that he still was. He threw himself on that monster for her and her children. He could have just kept running and hiding."

"We need a solid story," Linda said. "The world learns the truth in three years, but until then, an elaborate lie will do. I'm in, but after things die down in a few months, you're on your own, Carson."

Grant looked at her. "Well, that stinks."

"Tough. I'm making an early return to Guatemala. There's research in Petén to be done. If Pacal needs help, that is."

Pacal looked surprised and a bit sheepish.

"Maya women are a bit more reserved than American women," Elisa said, laughing.

"I could use some help," Pacal allowed.

Grant nodded. "An outsider to help with the transition. Hell, we'll all be unemployed soon anyway."

They fell silent, listening to the tropical night. Grant drained the rest of his beer and ordered another. "We've lost good friends down here. You lost your sister. All because we wanted to keep our mission secret."

"Riga was lost many years ago," Pacal said. Tears welled up in his eyes. "I was her brother, yet I could never save her. She'd been broken, and moved through life without hope. Balam taught her to be Ixchel even without her knowledge, but you asked her for help. No one had *ever* asked her for help. She found a purpose to her life. She realized her destiny. I could see it in her eyes—she was fulfilled, alive. For that I thank you."

Elisa asked gently, "How is Riga's son taking it?"

Pain filled Pacal's eyes. "Balam is with him, but he is inconsolable. Chiam's mother is gone. She was everything to him, and he was her whole life. That will tell you how difficult it was for her to leave him. She had never left him before." He paused and wiped his eye. "I return tonight to be with Chiam. The police will come and fetch me again, but after that he will accompany us to Xibalbá. Just as I will prepare the men and women for the outside world, Chiam will prepare the children."

No one spoke for a time. Elisa broke the silence. "Pacal, you have a gift. I don't know how it works but you have to share it with the world. So much can come from it."

Pacal shook his head. "I intend to explore whatever has come alive in my mind, but on my terms. Something may be different, but I am no god. Xibalbá needs me first. Someday I'll share my ability with the world. But not yet."

"Fair enough," Grant said. He raised his bottle in toast. "To Pacal, Kukulcán, the Feathered Serpent. Lord and Master of the Place of Fear."

"To friends and family," said Pacal.

They each raised a glass and drank, then sat back in silence, gazing out over the town and Lago Petén Itzá.

The sky had fallen dark and the lightning flashed closer. A

327

breeze picked up and rippled the surface of the lake. A soft rain began to fall, wetting the streets and buildings and making them glisten. Two Maya girls giggled as they passed a boy, and scurried past the veranda to escape the rain.

Faraway, fires ate the edges of the forest.

AUTHOR'S NOTE

Place of Fear is quite obviously a flight of fancy. It's true that Norsemen dominated Europe and the high seas of the North Atlantic and Mediterranean for hundreds of years, their exploits well documented in the fabled Norse *eddas,* as well as in the awed and fearful accounts of other countries. And while archaeological evidence proves Vikings reached North America a good five hundred years before Columbus, no credible evidence exists that they ever ventured farther south into the New World than Newfoundland, and perhaps Maine, much less the Yucatán peninsula. So think of this tale as a "what if" of alternate history.

The descriptions of berserker tactics in the novel are based on experts' best guesses. No one alive today has ever witnessed an actual berserker in action. Which is probably lucky.

The Mayan names used are real. Zotz, Balam, Ah Puuc, Ixchel, Kukulcán, Xibalbá, chac, Coyopa—all come from the pantheon of Maya religion and lore. Sadly, nearly all of the ancient texts were destroyed by invading Spanish Conquistadors intent on displacing the religion, and history suffers greatly for that crime. Modern names of ancient cities, such as Tikal, are not the original names given by the citizens of those places. No one knows what Tikal's real name was.

Though their great cities collapsed or were abandoned centuries ago, the Maya continue to thrive as a people. Some thirty Mayan dialects live on, including the prevalent Yucatec and K'iché referenced in the book.

Mexico, Belize, and Guatemala are rich in archaeological treasures, but struggle financially with the care for these sites. Visiting these countries provides much-needed capital, so do so if you can. Awe-inspiring sights await you there.

--kp

ABOUT THE AUTHOR

Ken Pelham's debut novel, **Brigands Key**, a first-place winner of the Royal Palm Literary Award, was published in hardcover in 2012. **Place of Fear**, a 2012 first-place winner of the Royal Palm, is the much-anticipated prequel to **Brigands Key**. The book is a prequel in the loosest sense, and each novel may be read as a stand-alone.

To order the **Brigands Key** Kindle ebook edition, visit Amazon.com. The Gale Cengage Five Star Mystery hardcover edition is also available online.

Fans of **Brigands Key** will find a short story about the island in **Treacherous Bastards: Stories of Suspense, Deceit, and Skullduggery**, on Amazon for Kindle readers. Three more stories about the island's sordid past make up **Tales of Old Brigands Key**.

Horror fans will find two chilling stories in **A Double Shot of Fright: Two Tales of Terror**, guaranteed to cause insomnia.

Ken grew up in the South Florida town of Immokalee, and lives with his wife, Laura, in Maitland, Florida. A member of the International Thriller Writers, the Florida Writers Association, and the Maitland Writers Group, he dabbles in cycling, fishing, and scuba diving, to varying degrees of success. Visit him at **www.kenpelham.com** for updates on his work, musings on suspense fiction, and an account of travels in Belize and Guatemala for background for this novel.

25694879R00203

Made in the USA
Charleston, SC
12 January 2014